A WAR OF WITCHES

SUZANNE SNOWDEN

A War of Witches
The Witch Wars, Book 2
Suzanne Snowden

Published by Industry Books
Copyright © 2025, Suzanne Snowden
Cover art by Danielle Fine

ISBN: 979-8991440264

DEDICATION

For my mom, who would have loved this.

CONTENT NOTES

2025 was quite a year. I expressed some feelings about it in this book. It's darker than the first one, but after 2025, so am I. Look out for some social commentary with a liberal take. If that's not your cup of tea, I understand. This book also features consensual, open-door sex scenes between mature adults. If that *is* your cup of tea, read on...

PROLOGUE

Adam

December 31st, 2025
Rockefeller Center, New York City

"You're saying you made a cancer vaccine out of magic?"

The reporter was understandably resistant to the proclamation I had just made on morning TV. We started our interview in the studio with people milling around outside on the plaza, looking through the windows at us.

Moments before, I had introduced myself as Doctor Adam Parrish, pediatric oncologist from the Children's Hospital in Washington, D.C. and explained that I was there to announce a medical breakthrough that would mean the prevention of cancer. I included introductions for my colleagues, Jake Rawlings, a big bear of a man, and Abe Goree, his small and wiry counterpart, both formerly doctors with the National Institute of Health. Next to them stood Farhad Al-Masri, the benefactor of the Cancer Research Center in Virginia that developed the vaccine.

Abe Goree had educated and guided the country through a pandemic years before and was a known entity standing there detailing the clinical trial data from the past year. Jake was there to be a witness to the miracle his daughter had received when magic cured her cancer.

I was there to explain that the missing ingredient in the development of a vaccine for cancer had been magic.

"That's correct," I said. "I'm here to explain to you that there is magic in this world, and it is something certain people are born with. Those people are witches. I am one of them. We're a small group—only .06 percent of the population or about five million people. There have always been witches, but we have kept the secret of our world to protect ourselves from persecution. We are announcing it now in order to make the vaccine to prevent cancer available to everyone on the planet."

The reporter followed up with, "You said vaccine before—is there also a cure for cancer?"

"No, but we hope there will be one day soon. The miracle Doctor Rawley's daughter experienced was the work of just one person. We isolated that magic to create this vaccine."

The reporter was welcoming to all the A.M. guests on their news program, but his skeptical expression told me I was not getting a pass on the bombshell I just dropped. He would need some proof.

I said, "I'm happy to show some of the magic I have that allows me to heal minor injuries."

"Alright," he said, but with hesitation. He wore the expression of a man bracing for disaster, like he was already mentally composing his apology tweet. 'Here we go,' he was thinking, 'another Al Capone's vault. Another over-hyped prime-time embarrassment, people will call me Geraldo.'

Farhad brought out a sharp knife and ran it across the back of his hand, slicing fairly deep and surprising himself with how much that stung. The reporter stepped back, not expecting blood to be drawn right next to him.

I reached out to put pressure on the wound to stop the blood from flowing.

Under my breath I said with some humor, "Went a little deep there, didn't you?"

He cursed softly, and his dark eyes narrowed from the pain of my pushing down on his hand.

"Just fix it, Adam."

Farhad was a witch too, and a billionaire, not used to suffering of any kind, much less public suffering on national TV. He was taking one for the team there, to help me demonstrate witchcraft, so we could distribute the vaccine we had worked so hard to make.

I told him, "Don't worry, I got you."

While a cameraman zoomed in for a close-up shot of Farhad's hand, I lifted the towel off the top and saw the bleeding had stopped. I cleaned the area and swabbed the cut with some antiseptic, then explained the healing magic I was going to use.

"Now I'm going to close the two sides of skin together, so he won't bleed more or get an infection."

I focused my mind on the slice and willed my wife Vivienne's healing magic to do as I asked and mend the rift in his skin. Slowly, the two sides drew together. The crew in the studio grew silent.

When the wound was nearly gone, I looked up and saw fear on some faces around me.

I said calmly, "Magic can do amazing things, and this is just one of them. Healing is a rare gift. But it's important to know that witches never use magic on people who are not witches. It's the primary rule of witchcraft."

The reporter seemed to remember his place then and said, "That was incredible to see, but I think people will probably assume that was some sort of magic trick." Realizing his wording, he laughed and said, "You know what I mean. They won't think that it was real."

I nodded. "I do know what you mean. That's why I have one more demonstration for you on the plaza."

He threw to a commercial and made a promise of more magic to come.

Out on the plaza, I braced myself, trying to work up to what I had planned.

"Can you get the ice skaters out of the rink?" I asked the producer, a woman gripping a legal pad who had been hovering since I arrived.

She looked alarmed but then ran from the area, I assumed, to make that happen.

It was cold. I worried about whether what I was about to do would convince people that magic was a real thing in the universe. We had practically no time to put the announcement together, and frankly, I was just winging it. My boss at the International Council of Witches told me there were witch factions protesting the decision to reveal witchcraft, and they thought taking me out might stop the whole thing.

And so there I was, being proactive and telling the world about witchcraft before they could off me.

Then the reporter was talking again, and I was out of time to think about it anymore.

"Welcome back to our live coverage of the announcement about a new vaccine for cancer. Dr. Adam Parrish has revealed that the secret ingredient for the vaccine is magic, and he is here to show us another example of real magic in our world that we never knew was here." He winked at me. "Take it away, Dr. Parrish."

Glancing at the ice, I saw people lined the whole rink, but there were no more skaters. I studied the middle of the rink and decided that was where I would put it.

Gasps and exclamations around me let me know I was on the right track, but I kept staring at that center spot in the rink. After a minute, I saw the base of the tree come into view, and I relaxed my hold on it slightly so that I could lower the Rockefeller Christmas tree slowly down into the center of the ice skating rink. Once it was solidly in place, I released the stress in my shoulders and looked around me to see faces staring at the tree and faces staring at me.

I said, "That's called telekinesis."

CHAPTER ONE

Adam

December 31st, 2025
Washington, D.C.

"So you're a fucking witch."

Samuel Marsh, my best friend of over forty years, stood on my doorstep and looked as though he was about to deck me. There was fury there, just below the surface, and I steeled myself just in case he was about to let it out. I wanted to let him, I just didn't know if I had it in me to stand still with a fist coming at my face.

"Yep. I'm a witch."

His eye twitched.

Oh, fuck. Here it comes.

After a few seconds he said, "And you didn't think to mention that even once in the past forty years?"

"Couldn't."

"But now you can."

"Yep."

His mouth tightened. We faced each other, our breath visible in the cold December air, and for some reason, I thought about our first day of med school, and how he had asked out every pretty girl we ran into until he had a week's worth of dates lined up. I'd opened my front door thousands of times to find Marsh standing there.

Suddenly, I found myself scared to death that I might lose my best friend.

Then he said, "Why the fuck aren't you a warlock?"

That made me smile. Maybe this was going to be alright. I said, "Why don't you come in and I'll explain the world of witches, and we can drink some whiskey?"

He muttered, "Witch motherfucker," and shoved past me into the hallway.

I followed him a few steps into my study.

"Vivienne!" He smiled when he saw my wife sitting on the couch. She had been gone for a year, back in time to 1502 to bring her granddaughter Alice with her to the present day. Of course, Marsh didn't know any of that, and I realized the day was going to be even rougher than I had anticipated.

I clapped him on the shoulder. "Marsh, this is Alice." I motioned to the pretty fourteen-year-old sitting beside her grandmother on the couch. But he was looking at Vivienne and putting things together.

"I suppose you're a fucking witch too, Vivienne."

She frowned. When he went on to say, "And you too, young lady. Everybody here is a goddamn witch…" Alice frowned, and Vivienne stood. I felt her power rise and tried to calm everyone down.

"It's just Marsh. He's being an ass. Let's give him this day to adjust. Marsh, say you're sorry to Alice."

"Yes, Samuel and to me as well." Vivienne leveled a glare at Marsh that made me glad I wasn't him. "This is a nice way to greet me after I've been gone for a year. I thought we were friends."

"I thought we were, too!" He threw his hands in the air in frustration.

Vivienne took pity on him and said gently, "Samuel, this is my granddaughter, Alice. Alice, this is my good friend Samuel. He's having a bad day."

Alice said, "I'm pleased to meet you, Samuel. Grandmother says I have bad days, too." I watched Marsh take in her not quite right British accent, similar to Vivienne's but just a touch stilted.

Marsh sighed and rubbed a hand over his eyes. He gathered his words together and said, "I'm sorry. It's not you I'm mad at, it's him. I'm sorry, Alice." Then he looked at my wife. "Sorry, Vivienne." Without even turning my way, he said, "Let's do this out back." He made his way through the kitchen and down the steps to the backyard.

Grabbing a bottle of whiskey, I put some ice in two glasses, and I followed him to the rocking chairs in front of the fire pit. I set the glasses down and poured us both a tall drink. When he took the drink I offered him, I picked my own up and toasted, "To forty years."

He lifted his glass and glared at me as he said, "Forty fucking years."

I set my drink down. "I take it you saw the news this morning?"

He yelled at me. "Yes, asshole, I saw the fucking news this morning because you called to tell me to watch the fucking news this morning! You want to tell me why I had to hear this shit on the fucking news instead of face to face?"

I held my hand up. "I'm sorry. It should have happened that way. But I just found out last night that there are some groups in our world who are not happy with my revealing the secret. It had to be done now, before they could get to me and stop it. Overnight, I had to prepare a way to introduce the fact of witchcraft to the world and explain about the vaccine. It was a lot."

His brows drew together. "Well, that sounds great."

Then after a moment, "Are you in danger? Are they in danger?" He jerked his head toward the house.

"Most likely, yes, for me. I don't know for sure about them." Our eyes met. "Or you, or mother, or Connie, or Grant, or Maria. I'll have security for everyone. You won't have to talk to them. They'll just be around."

We both took a big drink and rocked in our chairs for a minute. He held a hand up to the side of his head. I stood and went up the back porch steps to get him some Tylenol. Vivienne was at the kitchen sink, watching him with sympathy.

"Does he have a headache? Should I help him?"

"Definitely not. But thank you." I kissed her temple and headed back down with the medicine and water for him. He swallowed the pills. We both rocked in our chairs again in silence, Marsh with his eyes closed.

"I'm sorry," I said at last. "You're my best friend in the world, and I have wanted to tell you for forty years. But it's something we could never say to a mortal." His eyebrows raised slightly at my description of him as a mortal. "It takes a toll on a witch. To never be completely honest with those you love. I'm actually grateful for this chance to tell the world about us." I could see he was not yet swayed, so I said, "Nothing will be different for you and me."

He scoffed at that. "How can nothing be different? You're a lying motherfucker, that's a change. And you didn't trust me enough to tell me this very important thing about you."

I stopped my chair. "It meant death to tell the secret. If anyone found out I told you, I'd be killed, and my mother and father would have had to go into hiding. I could not tell you."

"But why?" he said. He set down his drink. "Why all the secrecy? And for so long? It's just some extra abilities, right? Like super heroes. For Christ's sake, everybody loves those guys."

I shook my head. "In movies, they love those guys. But not that long ago in real life, they were burning those guys. Also, there was this little thing called the Inquisition. You may have heard of it. Witches are not universally loved."

He made a face like that was bullshit. "You just need a good branding campaign. Get some celebrities or TikTokers to say you're cool, and that's that."

I laughed. "Marsh, I appreciate that you're not judging. I really do. But I think you may be underestimating the fear people will have when they find out their neighbor can tell if they're lying. Or that their neighbor can move cars with their mind. Or can hide from them by cloaking themselves." He perked up at that. I added, "Like they become invisible."

He whipped his head my way. "Are you serious?"

I nodded.

"Can you do that?"

I shrugged my agreement.

"Fucking show me right now!" he demanded.

I laughed again and thought to myself, *that's more like it*.

"Not a good place or time." I pointed to the houses on either side of us and behind us.

"Whatever." Marsh picked his drink back up and stood. Holding his glass by the rim, down at his side, he wandered around the yard for a minute. The cold wasn't bothering him because he still had on his winter coat. I was wearing only a button-down shirt and a suit jacket, and the cold was definitely hitting harder for me. I placed my hands under my arms to warm them up.

Walking the perimeter of the yard, Marsh said from the back left corner, "I always knew you were into something." Then, a couple of minutes later from the back right corner of the yard, "I thought you might be a Freemason. You know, off doing Illuminati shit." He came back to the fire pit and sat down heavily in the rocking chair. "Or maybe you were like the Equalizer, taking care of shit nobody else wanted to take care of." He looked for my reaction to that, but I didn't give him one.

That was a damn good guess, though.

The ice in my drink clinked together as I tipped the glass and finished it.

Then he said, "How many witches are there in the world?"

I had included that information in my television spiel, but I knew he just needed to have all the details from me in person in order to process them. "Five million or so. That we know of."

He watched a cardinal land on my bird feeder. "You still getting bird pictures?"

"Tons," I said. I hadn't texted him a bird portrait from the feeder in a while.

"And how do you know?" He was still looking at the bird feeder, but I knew he meant witch numbers, not bird pictures.

"Blood tests from babies at birth. There are markers."

Marsh shook his head in disbelief. "Is that what Connie does?" He scrubbed a hand over his face. I knew my friend, and I could see he was putting it all together. My son Grant's mother, Connie, was a geneticist, and she was a witch, and Grant was a witch. It was all hitting him.

"It's a big part of her practice and her research. Yes."

After a while, he asked, "Is it true about the vaccine?"

I gave a small nod. "Yes."

"Congratulations." He stopped his rocking and lifted his glass to me.

Then he set the glass down. "Now tell me everything I need to know."

CHAPTER TWO

Vivienne

T
he media discovered Adam's house. He had discussed with us it would likely happen, but Alice and I were not prepared for all that entailed. Police cars cut his street off at each end with flashing lights. News trucks lined the street behind, and drones flew overhead.

He had to bring his talk with Samuel in from the yard when they saw that.

"I think I fried their signal, but I don't know for sure. I guess we'll find out if Marsh and me sitting in the backyard makes the news tonight." Adam stood at the front window, peering out from the side of a curtain, studying the fiasco outside. He tried to make light of things, but I knew he was worried.

"That's not even legal in D.C. airspace," he said, dropping the curtain.

"Could be the feds." Samuel held a glass full of ice and soda water up to his forehead. "What do you mean, you fried their signal?"

Explaining his magic to Samuel was not something Adam had prepared for very well. He took a second to think about it, then said, "It's a type of magic I have. To manipulate fields of electricity."

Samuel's mouth formed a straight line. "I didn't see you do it."

Adam sat down heavily in one of his leather chairs across from Samuel on the couch. "You wouldn't see it. A lot of magic is like that."

Samuel rolled his eyes. "Fantastic."

Adam said glumly, "I tried to tell you that."

Outside, a man's voice boomed at someone not to go beyond a barrier.

We were under siege.

I said, "Samuel, you are welcome to stay with us tonight. I would not like you to go back out into that crowd."

Adam said, "She's right. Stay here. We can watch TV and drink ourselves stupid."

"I can't." Samuel said. "I'll be on duty later." He checked his watch and stood. "I should probably get home in case I need to get to the hospital in a hurry. It might take a while to get out of here."

"Wait," Adam said. He looked to me for an opinion. "There's one more piece to the story that I think you should know." I nodded my head at him that, yes, Samuel should know about how I came to be here.

Samuel sat back down on the couch. "Wonderful," he said.

I laughed at him. "Don't be so gloomy. You'll be the only mortal in the world to hear this story. Ever." I sat on the couch next to him and leaned in to confide. "Only a handful of witches know it. It's a secret you can tell no one. Do you want to know?"

He looked worried. "I don't know. Do I?"

Alice piped up, "Yes!"

Samuel raised his eyebrows at her energy. He shrugged and said, "Alright then, Alice. Go ahead and tell me."

My girl liked to stir things up and loved a good reaction. She sat up in her chair, tossed her long red hair over her shoulders and began the tale. Widening her blue eyes and leaning toward him, she said, "Grandmother and I are from London in the year 1503."

Samuel frowned.

That frown delighted Alice, and a wide smile broke out on her own face. This would be perfectly normal for a teenage girl, but not so welcome in a young witch. We did not call attention to ourselves. I would have to work more on her awareness of the current volatile situation in the world. Then I checked myself—no, we did not have to live in the shadows anymore. That reality would take some time to soak in, but it would be good for Alice. She had not been happy to leave her friends, and all she knew in England, but I told her women had more freedom in America and that would suit someone with her spark.

Alice leaned toward Samuel. "Last year, when she touched a manuscript in the monastery in London, she got sucked through time here to Washington, D.C!" She waited for his reaction to that, and Samuel's face did not disappoint. With dramatic flair, she continued, "It brought her to the manuscript at the Library of Congress where Adam found her! She was gone for almost a year. I thought she was dead." Her eyes widened in agreement at the disbelief on Samuel's face. "Then she came back just in time to help me when I gained my powers." Alice touched his hand to emphasize her next point. "This is a perilous time for witches. We need guidance not to hurt people or show our magic."

Samuel gave her a small smile at that.

"Then she taught me about your time, and we both used the manuscript again to travel back here to Adam. I can travel through time because I have her blood and her DNA." She leaned in to him again. "No one else can do it but us."

Samuel sat there in silence for a moment and then said, "So you just touched the manuscript and got here? How does that work?"

"Good question," Adam said, his eyes closed and head resting on the chair.

"We do not know," I said.

Samuel sat back on the couch, closed his eyes, and ran his fingers through his white hair. I felt for him.

I said, "My father illustrated the manuscript. He may have infused it with magic. Or it might just be my magic. We're not sure."

Samuel gave a curt nod, sat up, and said, "My best friend is a witch. His wife and granddaughter are witches, too. They're also time travelers, here from 1503." He looked around at us to see if that was about right. Alice and I nodded, and Adam opened his eyes and gave Samuel a thumbs up.

"Got it," he said, standing. "Best to go home now, I think."

Adam stood too and clapped him on the back. "Are you okay? I know this is a lot. Witches are real...time travel is real..." Walking Samuel to the front door, he said, "I just didn't want any more secrets from you. Come back over when it all sinks in and you have more questions."

Samuel looked at the chaos outside, shook Adam's hand, and said, "Yeah. There might be a few."

Vivienne

It was not just Samuel that Adam had to debrief about his life as a witch. He also had to talk to his co-workers and neighbors. Herb Tolley had been Adam's friend and next-door neighbor since childhood and had left him several phone messages, each one more terse than the last. After Samuel left, Adam could finally answer Herb's FaceTime call.

I did not want to intrude but heard the discussion as it unfolded while we were both in the kitchen. I prepared lunch while they spoke. Adam sat at the table on his phone.

"That's quite a lot of police cars out there today, Parrish."

"I know. I'm sorry." Adam rubbed his eyes. I saw Herb on the screen with his wife Sally next to him.

Herb said, "Have you lost your mind? What the fuck is going on?"

"What I said on TV is real. I'm a witch, and so is Mom, and so was Dad. Witches are real."

Herb was silent.

Adam said, "Tell you what... why don't we postpone this discussion until a few days from now, when other stories will no doubt surface on the news? I hope," he laughed and looked at me. "That's something I didn't even consider. What if no other witch in the world comes forward? That would be funny."

Hearing the exhaustion in his voice, I came up beside Adam and leaned into view. "It's true, Herb. All of it. We are the same people you know. Just also witches. Adam has been through so much that I think he needs to rest now. Can you meet later?"

Adam pulled me to him and put his arm around my waist. "It might be good to do a Zoom call later with all the street like we did during the pandemic. Can you set that up, Sally? Maybe get the Justice in on that too? This is going to affect everybody."

"Yes, I'll do it," she said. "After dinner tonight. Is that good with you?"

"Good," Adam said. "Thank you, Sally."

She gave him a sympathetic look. "You both hang in there. We'll see you later."

Herb was still silent. Watching Adam.

Adam gave him a nod and clicked the call off.

He pulled me closer, with his face against my stomach. Lifting my shirt, he kissed me there and then rested his cheek against my skin. I played with his hair, running my fingers through it. It was longer now than when I had left him a year ago and streaked with white strands. Adam sighed against my waist. "God. I needed this."

After a moment, he said, "I still need to call the hospital."

"I know," I said. "Let's just be still for a moment. Then when you're ready, you can do that too. I'll be right here." He squeezed tighter, his face still pressed against me.

"Thank God," he said.

I leaned down and kissed his head. Adam was taking care of the entire world. I vowed to take care of him.

CHAPTER THREE

Sitting down in my study to check my email and the million text messages I had amassed, I wondered if the day would ever end. It was only a few hours ago that I had announced on national TV that witchcraft was real, and I was trying not to show it, but I was actually terrified about the potential consequences. Professionally, I was probably cooked. And personally... I honestly didn't know, but I thought there was a good chance we'd have to move and maybe even go into hiding. But by the end of the day, I would have talked to all the people in my life who mattered, and it would be done. I told myself I would get through the day. I just had to talk to the neighbors at night and the hospital before that.

Eleanor Rodgers was first. She was the head nurse in the oncology unit at Children's Hospital and had been my good friend for many years. After the newscast in the morning, she had sent me a quick text. "Jesus. Parrish. This is weird even for you." And I appreciated it because it told me all I needed to know. She trusted me and would roll with this. It helped that we had been through so many life and death situations together at work. When you witness children dealing with cancer daily, your tolerance for bullshit gets real low, and your ability to prioritize becomes supreme. She was probably thinking, 'Good for you- you're a witch. Now, can you get over here and help me with this kid?'

She answered as soon as I called. "Good God, Parrish. What a day."

"Yeah, it's been something. What's happening there?"

I heard her walking, and she said, "Hold on." Then she said, "I'm in room C." She took a breath. "Honestly? There's a bit of hysteria. A couple of staff. Some parents."

"Hmmm..." that was not good. "What parents?" I asked.

"Millie Carter's, Jason Starr's."

"Fuck." Then I said, "They'll be fine with Price. Can you ask him to take them on for me?"

"Yes." She paused. "But have you talked to admin? You may have bigger fish to fry."

"Why? Have they talked to you?"

"No, but a couple of them were down here. Wandering around with their flies open."

Eleanor had never been a fan of admin.

"Okay, thanks. I texted Price to cover my rounds for me, maybe even for a week. Things are pretty hairy right now."

"I bet." We let a moment of silence sit between us.

"Is it true?" she asked. "Is there a vaccine?"

"Yes, Ellie, there's even going to be a cure. That's why I did all this. Everybody should get it. I want the whole world to get it. No more dying kids."

I heard her sniff a little. "Was it you who gave Emily her miracle?" She was referring to the toddler Vivienne had cured of her cancer over a year ago.

"It wasn't me, but it was magic. And it's what we're trying to make a reality for the world."

Then she said, "Then let me know what I can do. Admin can fuck off. These parents won't care *who* you are if you can help their babies."

Adam

Grant and his girlfriend, Maria, came over in the afternoon to stay with us. I had been worried about them and about Mother all day and was relieved when they decided to just stick it out with us at home. I asked Marsh to check in on Mother when he got off duty, and he agreed. Her security detail said she had gotten some visitors that she refused to see, and I assumed they were reporters. Mom was eighty-six but could still outsmart a reporter, and I decided I probably should worry more about the reporters.

We all sat in the study and remembered that it was New Year's Eve.

"How did we forget this?" Maria laughed. "It's a major holiday!"

Vivienne said, "In our time we exchanged gifts on the eve of the new year."

Alice looked at me and said, "It's fun." Her less than thrilled expression pointed out that the reason she was not getting a present this New Year's Eve was because I had woken up and promptly outed witchcraft to the world. I pulled the wallet out of my pocket and got out my credit card. Holding it up, I said, "How about this year you pick your own present?"

"What is that?" She did not look impressed with my piece of plastic.

I said, "You know how stores are on the computer? You use this like money to buy things."

She plucked the card from my hand while Vivienne tried to stop her by holding her arm out and telling her no, that was unnecessary, she would be fine without a present this one time. But seeing Alice finally showing an interest in something in our world, Vivienne gave in and said, "You can get a book. I'll find you a website, and you get my permission before you purchase."

After Vivienne got Alice got situated at the desk in front of the computer, Maria clasped her hands together and swooned. "I love you as a girl dad."

I shook my head. "You want one too? You can have the card after her."

Sitting close to Maria, Grant said, "Somewhere, I think in Ireland or Scotland, they have a tradition called 'First Foot' where the first person who enters the house after the stroke of midnight really matters. Like, that person can make or break the year. I think they prefer brunettes, but I prefer blondes." He played with a lock of Maria's long, golden hair. "You should step outside at 11:59 and then back in at 12:00 and make our year."

"Not this year," I said. "Nobody leaves the house this year."

Adam

After I had killed the mood in the study, I went back to the bedroom to tackle the last hurdle for the day: the neighbors. Not just neighbors. Best friends for my entire lifetime. Herb and I had grown up next door to each other and were more like brothers than neighbors. The way he had looked at me earlier on our call was eating at me. It was like he didn't know me. I wanted to reassure him that he did know me, probably better than anybody else.

Vivienne got comfortable on the bed with a few books surrounding her. As she reached under her reading lamp to turn it on, she caught me watching her and smiled. When she and Alice came home on Christmas Day, I spent the entire afternoon showing Alice how to order things online and ended up buying them both a whole new wardrobe. I knew that under the lavender silk robe she wore, Vivienne had on a short pink satin nightgown. I leaned back in my chair and gazed at my wife.

That woman is mine. I looked at her with satisfaction, and no small amount of wonder.

When Herb and Sally joined the call, I thought at least Sally appeared to have some sympathy. The others, I couldn't predict. Well, Greg would probably take it okay. Facing the street from our houses, Herb's house was on my right. Next to him were Greg and John.

Greg had been our friend since high school. When we were growing up, it wasn't cool to be gay, but Herb and I had a powwow about it and decided: fuck those assholes at school, we were going to be friends with Greg because he had a car and was also really good at the guitar. These seemed like the best attributes a teen could have, and we wanted them. Herb was black, Greg was gay, and little did they know I was a witch. Our parents called us the Three Musketeers, and we really were for those teen years. Neither Herb nor I ever did pick up an instrument, but Greg learned them all and now played for the National Symphony, along with his husband, John.

Greg leaned into the screen and said to me, "I always thought you were a little witchy bitch."

I nodded. "Thanks, Greg. Hi, John." John waved at me. They both looked fancy, and I wondered if they had plans to go out.

"How are you?" John said. I shrugged, like 'as good as I can be right about now.'

Greg's blue eyes never left mine. "How the hell did you keep this a secret?"

I shrugged. "I had no choice. But it wasn't easy."

He took in my ragged state and pursed his lips. "You look like shit."

"And you look great, as usual."

He wasn't smiling.

And then he said it. "You should have told us. You could have."

So. Not ready to forgive all this yet. Got it.

"I'm sorry," I said, and looked over at Herb too.

Greg said, "Whatever. Maybe take an Ambien after this and get some sleep."

Linda and Phil popped onto the screen next. She had inherited the house to the left of mine from her mother. Linda's long black hair was piled high on her head in a braid sprinkled with gray. She was a couple of years older than us but seemed not to age; her light brown skin was as smooth as it had been when we played together as kids and later teenagers. All of us had crushed on her hard in our youth. I knew that was her grandbaby sitting in her lap and wondered if it had been hard for her son to get to the house to let her babysit. Her husband Phil was an ex-football player for the Saints and looked fairly ridiculous, waving a toy at the baby to keep him amused.

"Hey Linda, who do you have there?"

"This is Spencer, Terrence's baby boy. They're here with us tonight for New Year's." She waved the baby's hand.

Carol and Sam from the north end of the street joined the call just then, and the Justice and his wife from the south end of the street joined the call next. I couldn't give a rat's ass what these people thought, all of them newcomers to the street and not very nice to boot. But the situation we were in as a group was my doing, and I had to own it right now in front of them all.

"Thanks for joining the call, everybody. I know it's New Year's, and you might want to do things, so I'll make it short."

"We couldn't do anything even if we wanted to. Can't get our car out."

That was Sam from the north end.

"I know, Sam, and I'm really sorry about that."

Linda said, "You could get a Lyft."

Yes. Linda was on my side.

"I mean, if you want to get out that bad on New Year's," she said. Phil grinned and waved the toy at the screen as if trying to calm down Sam as well.

We were all quiet for a moment.

"I just wanted to touch base with everybody to say I'm sorry that what I said on the news today has affected our street so much and looks like it will continue to do so. The police are there as a safety measure. They are aware of who we all are and will let us come and go. Unfortunately, they won't be letting other cars onto the street. I don't know for how long. And I have no idea when the media insanity will die down."

"I usually walk the kids to school." That was Carol from the north end, Sam's wife. She was dressed up too, in a red sparkly thing with her blond hair all styled and ready to be seen. Despite her bitchy vibe, I actually really did regret that they were going to be impacted by the press.

"I'm really sorry about that, Carol. I would advise taking them in the car. Or even keeping them home for a bit." It was looking more and more like the knowledge I just dropped on the world was not going down smooth. Carol should look out for her kids.

She made an impatient sound. "Why are we having to deal with this? What even is a witch? Are you in some Satan worshiping group?"

I did not know what to say to that.

The floor creaked as Vivienne stood up to come stand beside me. She leaned down to show her face to the group. "We are most certainly not a Satan worshiping group. We worship our Father in Heaven, who made us all. He made me a witch. I am just as he intended me to be, as is Adam, as are his mother and his son. We differ from you only in our abilities. Everything else is the same. If you feel you need a little extra help with the children, please feel free to ask me. I will happily walk with you to school. My granddaughter Alice would be happy to babysit if you ever need a responsible helper." She paused. "We are your neighbors. That's all that matters." She squeezed my shoulder and walked back to her books on the bed.

Linda and Phil, Greg and John, and Sally all nodded their agreement with Vivienne.

"That's right," I said. "We're neighbors, and I just wanted to make sure you all have my cell phone number, so you could call me or text me if you ever need anything." I gave my number out and then said, "And if the media asks you what your opinion is of me or us, obviously I want you to say whatever you want. If there are any updates on the street, I'll let you know. And I guess, Happy New Year."

Everyone said Happy New Year and left the call. The Justice and his wife had not said a word, but that was the norm for him. I texted Herb, "Marsh came over today and we talked. Do you want to meet in the middle?" This was what we called meeting at the fence separating our houses in the backyard. There was a missing plank we met up at sometimes to see what was up.

I saw he read it, and I waited for his reply. The dots in his text flashed, but it was taking too long. Then he typed, "Let's do it tomorrow. Lots going on tonight."

"Tomorrow," I texted back. I set the phone down and looked at Vivienne. "That could have gone worse, right?" She made a face like, oh yeah, that could have gone *way* worse.

She closed her textbook. "Your friends will come around."

"Herb's having trouble." I stood and unbuttoned the cuffs of my shirt. God, I was fucking exhausted. I dropped my pants and shrugged out of my shirt when I saw Vivienne watching me. I raised my eyebrows. "Is that a look of interest I see?"

She tilted her head slightly to the side. "Yes, of course. But you've had a long day, Adam. You need to fall into bed and rest."

At that, I dove onto the bed and pulled her to me, sweeping the books away in the process. She shrieked and then covered her mouth with both hands. "Adam, we have guests," she whispered loudly at me. Then, with some irritation, "You really need to stop dropping my books on the floor."

"I'll pick them up." I held her tight and thanked God for this one thing that made everything else okay. Then I fell asleep and did not wake until midnight when someone bombed our house.

Chapter Four

Vivienne

The heavens exploded over us as we slept. I awoke from a nightmare to find it was real and the room was collapsing in on us as we lay on our bed. There was a loud crack overhead, and Adam rolled over me, taking the weight of an enormous chunk of the ceiling as it fell. Then there was an eerie quiet broken only by pieces of smaller debris pattering down. Adam moaned next to me in the dark, and I willed myself to move.

"What do you need?" My voice sounded muffled and not like my own.

Streetlight filtered in through dust near the window, and I saw a twisted mass of building materials many feet across lift off of him and hover inches over his back as he lay still underneath. It was untethered, and I realized he was using magic to free himself. He groaned as he threw the mess to the side, where it fell with a frightening crash.

"My back," his voice was weak. Pushing myself up to kneel beside him, I ignored lacerations on my arms to place both my hands over Adam's back. There was terrible disarray, and I knew he must have been in excruciating pain. My hands, filled with healing power, flowed over him, repairing everything that needed fixing or replacing. I had never expended so much energy so quickly, and I fell down onto the bed with him, cutting my face on chunks of the wall or ceiling. It had only been moments when he pushed himself up and broke our connection. "I'm fine now. Let's get the kids."

"Alice!" I slipped off my side of the bed and lunged for the doorway. Large chunks of plaster and other types of debris blocked it, but I pulled with all my strength. "No!" I screamed in frustration.

I continued to yell for Alice and worked feverishly to move things out of my way, praying to God that the turret had not been hit. Adam used his telekinesis to move the debris away from the door when we heard voices on the other side of it.

"Grant!" he yelled. "Push in on the door now!"

Adam moved me out of the way as the door burst open toward us. I scrambled over the pieces of broken wood and wall, cutting my feet on sharp things as I did. I looked to the entrance of the turret and saw instead an enormous pile of stone and the night sky above it.

The turret was gone.

I brought Alice to this place. I brought her to this house to kill her. Alice is dead.

"No." I reached back for Adam, and he caught me in his arms before I collapsed to the ground.

"She's here! She's here!" Maria pulled Alice around from behind her and pushed her toward me.

"Oh my God, thank you, God." I pulled her to me and held her tight, sobbing my thanks. Putting my hands on either side of her face, I said, "Where were you?"

"In the study with Grant and Maria. We watched a ball drop." She was in shock.

When I saw everyone was unhurt, I headed to the front hall as best I could and stepped into some boots I had at the front. I was yanking open the front door when something stopped my motion.

"Hold up there, soldier. I'm coming too." Adam also stepped into shoes and handed me a coat to put over my nightgown. He peeked outside through the window on the side of the door. "I see three. There may be more." He looked back at me. And Maria. "They're here for me, not you. I can handle this."

I slapped his hand away from the door and stepped out onto the porch. He gave a short laugh and said, "Alright then. I guess you can come too, Maria. Grant, guard Alice."

"Dad!" Grant was beside himself.

"We'll be fine, I promise. I need you to guard Alice."

Grant said, "I will, but... Maria."

Adam said, "Put Alice behind you. You can look through the window. I have a shield on Maria."

Adam followed me out onto the porch, and we both braced ourselves against the ice-cold wind. I had already hit the three coming for us with pain. Dressed in dark clothes and wearing black masks, they were slightly bent but kept coming, so I knew they must have loaded up on painkillers before. I thought of them bombing my granddaughter and hit them with the highest dose of pain I could muster after having healed Adam moments before. But I wasn't worried. My magic was replenishing, and I could feel it growing again, giving me what I asked from it, as it always had. One man dropped to his knees, and I headed toward him.

Adam took the other man walking across our street from the Supreme Court. The man shot at Adam with a weapon, firing so many bullets at a time that I cried out. But the bullets hit Adam's shield and littered the street in front of him. Adam lifted his hand and used his magic to rip the gun from the man and toss it down the street. Then he threw something else at Adam. It was not physical or visible, but I could feel that it was heavy in its intent to damage. When Adam caught it and absorbed it, the man halted.

Maria went to the right. A man there said something to her in a voice filled with persuasion. She stood still, but not before raising her arm toward him. He stopped as well. Maria hurled a stream of fire at his head, and he tossed her into the air. As the fire engulfed him, the man released his hold on Maria, and she fell to the ground.

Adam and I stopped before our targets, and we decided at the same moment to end the threat they posed to our family. Adam threw all his power out at the man in front of him, who then crumbled onto the street. The man's magic flowed like a torrent out of him and into Adam. My magic squeezed the heart of the man in front of me until he fell over onto his side, dead. It was a quick but not painless death, and I couldn't feel sorry about it.

I went to Maria then. The man she had hit with her fire was still burning on the ground in front of Herb's house. Maria was bleeding profusely from the back of her head.

"Dad!" I heard Grant's anguished cry as he raced down the steps. "Get Alice." He leaned over Maria, and I had to nudge him back so I could work.

"I'm healing her. Let me, Grant." He sat back but kept one hand on her cheek while I worked.

It was not life-threatening. She had a head wound, but no internal bleeding. Her wrist and elbow were both fractured, but I was able to repair those quickly, and when I saw that the color was returning to her face, I said, "She'll be fine. Take her into the house now and apply pressure to the wound on the back of her head." I moved away from the burning man and wrinkled my nose at the odor of his flesh on fire. I stayed there, unwilling to go inside until we were sure there were no more assassins on our street.

Herb stood on his porch, as did all the other neighbors on their own porches, even the Justice. Herb said, "Bring her here. We've got a bed."

Grant picked Maria up gently and walked with her in his arms up Herb's steps. Adam went back to his study and came out with the blanket he had given Alice for Christmas. Wrapping it around her, he walked Alice to Herb's porch while she inspected the bodies on her way past them. When they were safely inside, Herb walked back down with Adam to look at the men dead on the street. Adam pulled a mask off of one, and Herb pulled off the other one.

Herb said, "Who do you think sent these dummies?"

Adam looked at the men. He shrugged his shoulders. "Well, these are witches. So, probably witches who want me dead because I told their secret. Or, there's a crazy guy named Father Andrew Barry who tried to kill us both in London last year."

He looked up at me to see if I agreed with those possibilities. I gave a brief nod.

He added, "But Barry wants to keep you alive. Me, not so much."

Grant came back down Herb's steps then with some words for his father about taking Maria with him into the street.

"What the fuck were you thinking? If that guy had been just a second quicker, Maria could have fallen from thirty feet instead of ten. She could have broken her neck!" Grant gestured a little wildly at the dead men in front of him.

"She shouldn't have been out here at all. You could have handled it, and so could I. Neither of them should have gone out there. Why the hell did I have to stay and guard Alice? Do you not know I could handle that situation?"

Adam held his hands out to calm Grant. "I know," he said. "I didn't want them to come out either. But they're grown-ass women who could also handle it. And Grant," he paused and waited for his son to meet his eyes. "I needed you on Alice." Grant was a veteran with combat experience and formidable magic to draw from. I knew this was why Adam had asked him to stay with her.

They stopped fighting then because police officers with guns trained on us walked slowly forward from both ends of the street.

Herb raised his voice to them. "Oh, for Christ's sake! These people are the victims here! Their house just got bombed, and these dead guys tried to kill them all. With a child in the house!" This last fact appeared to be the final straw for Herb, and it endeared him to me greatly.

The police officer in charge said, "Drop your weapons if you have them and put your hands on your head."

Herb shook his head. "Son, they do not have weapons. They do not need weapons. They protected themselves from assassins just now. Where are the rest of you guys who are supposed to be helping guard this street?"

"Dead!" the police officer yelled. "Now put your hands on your head!"

We did as we were told.

Adam and I kept watch on the street to make sure no one else approached. After a while, they let Herb go home and let us sit on our porch, covered by a thick comforter Sally brought over. The neighbors went back into their houses while Adam and I sat on the steps of his childhood home with the remains of the turret partially on the street and partially on Herb's porch. Under the blanket, we held hands.

Six people had died. Nine if you counted the people who tried to kill us. Adam was torturing himself over the deaths of the four police officers and two guards. I listened to him call Farhad to tell him that our night shift guards had died. Farhad Al Masri was a billionaire from Oman who had financed Adam's development of the cancer vaccine after I healed his wife of cancer. He also insisted on offering security guards for us all, and I was sure that number was to be increased after the night we just had.

When he finished his call, I said, "I'm sorry about the guards. Did you know them?"

He shook his head no.

"And I'm sorry about your house."

He laughed. "Seriously?"

"Yes. I loved that turret. I love this place." Leaning my head on his arm, I whispered, "I love you."

"This is all because of me."

"No," I raised my head to him. "It's not. You made something the world needed. Some refuse to see that."

"It put you all in danger. I should have expected that."

"A bomb? You should have expected a bomb?"

"Yes!" he retorted. "A bomb is the only thing that could get past our shield. I should have had a plan."

I studied his face. He was not going to let that go. And maybe he was right. Maybe we shouldn't have stayed there after his announcement.

"We'll find a safe place to live until the house is rebuilt. And we'll make sure it's hidden. And bombproof."

He sighed and shook his head.

More news trucks gathered at both ends of the street. The police presence grew as well, and Adam and I watched their crews take pictures and gather evidence and, eventually, the bodies of the men we killed.

We huddled together in silence for a while longer until the police in charge finished asking us questions and said they were done for the night. When Adam and I were sure there were no more threats to the street, we went to Herb's house, checked on our family, and fell asleep in each other's arms in Herb's upstairs guest room.

CHAPTER FIVE

Adam

January 1st, 2026

I woke up in Herb's upstairs guest room, prepared to kill anyone and everyone who had threatened my family. That energy was not lost on Vivienne as she sat next to me during breakfast. She placed her hand on my jiggling leg. I looked at her profile and thought again how close we had come to losing each other the night before. If that ceiling had fallen on her side instead of mine...

Grant was also stressing about the events of the night before and was smothering Maria even though, thanks to Vivienne, she had fully recovered from her injuries. She finally put a stop to it and said to him, "Look at me- I'm fine. I'm a badass, and you're just going to have to live with it."

Grant allowed a hint of a smile to show and said, "I know." He pulled her chair closer to him. "Sorry. You are a badass. I wish I could shoot fire."

Vivienne scooped some eggs onto my plate and said, "Well, you have Maria for that."

He replied, "And you have Dad to block bullets for you."

"That was fucking cool, I have to say." Herb shook his head. "I saw that automatic and thought you were a goner, Adam... And then the bullets just fell down in front of you." He motioned in front of himself as if bullets were falling. "I was like, that's some superhero shit."

I knew I was not a superhero, so I looked down. It was time to figure things out, and I needed more coffee to get my brain in gear. Luckily, Herb started the conversation.

"The news coverage about last night is *intense*. Four D.C. police officers down is..." he shook his head. "You're going to want to avoid all that press and, obviously, assassins..." his eyes met mine, and that time we both shook our heads at the situation. My gaze turned to Alice, who was sitting between Herb and Maria, pushing food around on her plate.

He said, "You need to hide out for a bit. I have a place you can start, and that'll give you time to figure out the next place. I'd recommend shaking things up." Herb had been in the foreign service, and I was grateful for this friend of mine and his exact set of skills we found ourselves needing right then.

"Gerald," Vivienne said suddenly.

"Shit," I said. "I don't have security on him. I don't know how I forgot that."

"You have a lot of things going on. It's okay. I keep up with him." Grant surprised us all with that. He put some more bacon on his plate. "I don't think he'd even agree to security, though. They'd make him visible, and he avoids that like the plague. He's been hanging out with Grandma. I bet you can find him there."

That was news to me. Gerald had said he was staying in America for a while. I guessed it was so he could catch up with mother. That she had an extra layer of help if she needed anything was a relief, but I'd still want to offer extra security for them both. I had the money, and Farhad had practically an army of highly trained security guards with valuable magic. It was clear we needed guards and more guards.

Herb asked, "How secure are your communications with this Gerald?"

"Very," Grant said. "Gerald insists." He took a bite of his bacon biscuit.

"Good. Well, maybe you can let him know about your safe house when you get there."

"Thanks, Herb. Good plan." It was a brilliant plan, really the best I could hope for right now. Because Vivienne and I were going to have to separate soon and I wanted her to be safe and with family when we did.

Vivienne

"Can you be killed?" Adam reached for my hand and tucked it up against his chest as we sat on Herb's porch swing, bundled up because of the cold. The house was getting crowded and rather loud, and we both craved some time to talk, just the two of us.

I laughed. "Are you looking for the best way to do so? We've only been married a year. Are you ready to move on so soon?"

"I've really only had you with me as my wife for a week. So, no, I'll never be done with you." He rubbed his thumb over the back of my hand. "Never."

We watched Grant try to get the police officer at our house to let him in. He wanted to get something from the study but was getting nowhere. He looked over at Adam in frustration. With a nod, Adam gave his permission.

Grant spoke to the police officer again, and the man stepped aside instantly to let him through.

Adam said, "I'm just wondering how your magic works. I saw you heal yourself in London for hours, and you seemed unconscious. Last night... if you had been hit with that ceiling instead of me... could you have healed yourself?"

Grant came out of the house, thanked the police officer profusely, and headed back our way.

I said, "In London, I was awake when I set my magic in motion. I don't know how it would work if I were injured and not conscious enough to do that."

He turned to me, exasperated. "Why couldn't you just say, 'Yes, my magic would fix me no matter what?' Why couldn't you just give me that?"

I laughed again and pulled his hand to my lips for a kiss. A reporter at the end of the street was arguing loudly with a police officer, trying to get past their roadblock. Adam watched the altercation closely.

Grant made his way back to Herb's porch, got to the top of the stairs and said to Adam, "It was important."

"I'm sure," his father responded.

It must have been extremely important for Grant to use persuasion.

After he went back into Herb's house, I thought it might be a suitable moment to address another aspect of my magic that I had not yet had time to discuss with my husband. I said casually, "It's possible my magic could have taken over and healed me. So much of it is done without my knowledge."

He narrowed his eyes at me, picking up something in my tone. Yes, I was going somewhere with that, and he knew it.

"I'm always discovering new things about my magic. Just in the last twenty years or so, I figured out that my cells need me to tell them to age. That's something we may want to explore with your magic now. Because we have exchanged our magic."

I raised my eyes to gauge his reaction.

His mouth slightly ajar, he looked at me in disbelief.

I said, "There hasn't been much time to talk about it. I was going to tell you."

"Are you saying I may have to tell my cells to age, and if I don't tell them, I won't *age*?" His voice got louder as he went. He stared at me, his eyes wide. "When exactly were you going to tell me this?"

"Adam," I said calmly, "this is not such a terrible thing." He placed my hand back in my lap, and the chains holding up the porch swing clanged when he stood up abruptly. He paced along the porch and then turned back to me.

"Vivienne, you went back in time five hundred years and left me here like some fucking Benjamin Button character aging backwards, and I wouldn't have known why! How would that look? *Grant* ages, and I *don't*?"

I wrinkled my brow and said, "What is a Benjamin Button?"

Frustrated that he had to stop and explain, he waved his hand and said, "Some book or movie character. Ages backwards."

I maintained my nice calm voice and said, "Adam, you're not aging *backwards*. You're just not aging. I was going to tell you. But then we got married, and I didn't want to ruin that night. I'm sorry."

"You should have told me!" He turned away from me again and walked to the far end of the porch.

"Goddamn it!" Adam shouted at the empty street in front of us and put some power in his voice when he did. I imagined his words making their way over top of the Supreme Court and sailing all the way to the Capitol Building. Apparently, my husband had a limit to how much stress he could handle in a twenty-four-hour period, and he had clearly reached that limit.

After a moment I said softly, "You know I don't like that expression."

Adam gave a heavy sigh and scrubbed his hands over his face. When he brought them down, he said, "Sorry." He looked at me. "Gosh darn it."

Leaning against the porch railing, he added, "Fudge."

I held my palm out, upraised. "What?"

We both started when from the other side of the porch screen, Alice said, "He means fuck. 'Fudge' stands for fuck." She stood there like an apparition, silent and still.

I gave her a disapproving look. Pointing my finger at her, I gestured for her to leave us to our adult conversation. She rolled her eyes and turned to go.

Adam shook his head and laughed under his breath.

"Your granddaughter's timing is impeccable."

"Your granddaughter as well," I reminded him. I pushed off the porch with my toe and started a slight movement back and forth with a squeak on the backward swing. "She's developed an eerie way of showing up when you least expect it. And a host of other delightful traits I look forward to sharing with you."

One side of his mouth quirked up at that, and he said, "We call that a teenager here."

Adam's eyes never left me. After a minute he said, "Okay. I understand. You were going off into the night to travel by yourself hundreds of years back in time. You had a lot going on."

"I did. But you have had a lot to deal with as well. We have time to figure it out together now. I want you to know you can control this."

"Oh, for fuck's sake!" Obviously, Adam's anxiety was still running the conversation.

He threw up his hands. "Control it? How do I control it? I didn't even know 'not aging' was a thing until this moment!" He covered his forehead with a hand. "And now I'm yelling! In public! About *magic!*" He shook his head in disbelief.

I stood up from the swing, making the chains clang again, and I matched his behavior by yelling back at him. "Well, it's complicated! That's why I didn't get into it. I don't really know how *I* control it. I just willed it to be one day, and I figured it out. You'll do the same."

"What if I don't? What if I had been here by myself and didn't even know this was something I needed to do?"

"You would have figured it out, Adam." I lowered my voice. "I'm sorry it worked out this way. You're right. I should have told you right after we exchanged powers."

We stood apart then, on opposite ends of the porch. He faced the debris of his house, and I stared at his back, wishing I could take some of the burden of his last two days from him. Inside the house, I heard Sally calling for Herb.

After a few moments I said, "And what about me?

"What about you?"

"You got some of my powers. Isn't it possible I got some of your powers in that exchange?"

He shrugged. "I'm used to the taking of powers, not the giving." Turning his head to look at me, he said, "Maybe. I don't know."

"Well, we need to discuss our magic thoroughly. I agree with you. We need to know what I might have and what you might have. We could get Marshall to divine me."

"Fuck no. Not him again." He turned back to me and said reluctantly, "I can divine."

He must have forgotten, but he had already confessed that to me on our very first day together.

"I just would never do that without your permission. It can be invasive magic. It's the reason nobody likes Marshall." He scrubbed his hands over his face again. "Fuck…" he started his pacing again and said, "But he's better at it than me."

I could tell that admission hurt, and it made me smile.

"Don't smile at me!" He pointed at me but couldn't hide his own smile. "I am actually very mad."

"I can tell," I said. "And you have a right to be. I'm sorry."

Adam reached out and pulled me to him. "No. I'm sorry I reacted like this." He held me close and rested his chin on the top of my head. "It's just after you were gone and I had your powers… they hit me all at once, and it was a lot. I could read everybody's physical state, and I knew when they were feeling sick and, oh my God, I *hated* it. It took so long to get used to it."

I knew exactly what he meant. I'd had to learn to live with it when I gained my powers, and Alice had just been through it herself.

"And now I have to get used to remembering to age myself too? So I haven't aged this whole year? I feel like I aged fifty years while you were gone."

"You don't look like you have aged," I said. "Except for the white streaks in this hair." I reached up to run a hand through his longer locks, and he closed his eyes as I did. "I'll coach you on how to age," I said. "It's just a daily check-in with your cells. We'll do it together. I'll be able to tell if you made it work."

"Thank you," he said. "I can't believe I was just yelling about magic."

Leaning back to meet Adam's eyes, I asked him, "What does it matter?"

He stilled at that.

Reaching down to grasp both of his hands, I said, "We could have had this conversation in front of every tourist currently in the Library of Congress and it would not matter. The existence of witchcraft is public knowledge now." I wrapped his arms around the back of my waist. "And I am not about to hide who I am anymore."

Adam smiled at that. He leaned down to brush his lips over mine. "You're perfect. I wouldn't hide if I were you either."

"But…" He shook his head. "Keeping the secret is going to be a hard habit to break." His eyes searched mine. "Because they don't know about dark magic, Vivienne. They don't know about persuasion. And they sure as hell don't know about possible immortality. None of that is going to go over well."

I paused before responding, then said, "I think we should keep the immortality option a secret between us, don't you?"

Standing on my tiptoes, I kissed his lips as he laughed and murmured against my mouth, "Definitely."

Adam

After our porch fight, as it would forever after be known, I lifted Vivienne onto the porch railing and kissed her until she was beautifully flushed and had no more words for me. I was internally cursing my lack of a closing space when Greg came out onto his porch next door.

"Ew, newlyweds," he groaned.

I said, "You're just jealous."

"Absolutely." He jogged up Herb's porch steps. "Hi, Vivienne."

"Hello, Greg." Vivienne led me back to sit on the swing as Greg leaned against a porch column. He was tall and lean, balding slightly now, but, as he reminded me, still a much better dresser than I ever was or ever would be. Greg kept his hair short now because he said he hated pretenders. He held a rolled-up piece of paper that he tapped on his hand.

"Have you seen the news?"

I shook my head. "Not at all. I had to turn it off." But it was time to deal with reality again, so I reached into my pocket and turned it back on.

He said, "Well, I've been watching the news pretty much since this happened last night. And it looks like you're going to have more problems than just some fanatics blowing up your house."

"Great," I said.

Greg said, "I wanted to give you this key." He held it up. "There's a room at the Kennedy Center that nobody knows about. It's upstairs; only the caretaker knew about it, and he passed this year. Here's a map I drew that shows how to get there. John goes there to read sometimes. I just thought if you ever needed a place to hide out ... you could use this."

I stood and took the map and key, even though I didn't need a key. "Thanks, Greg. I appreciate it." I shook his hand. He pulled me in for a hug, and I hugged him back.

"And you just need to let me know if there's anybody you need me to fuck up. I'm there."

"Who we fuckin' up?" Herb opened his screen door and shook Greg's hand. "Just like the old days. Let's go!"

Vivienne looked from Herb to Greg to me and said, "Maybe not."

I sat back down beside her. "We used to get into it. Greg was always the reason. He's a bad influence."

Herb agreed. "True, true."

Greg said to Vivienne, "I was protesting the patriarchy. Nobody understood that."

Herb looked at Greg, waved his hand in our direction, and said, "They're about to get out of here."

Greg said, "They should. Things are getting crazy out there."

I thought maybe it was time to watch the news when I got a text from my friend and private investigator, Tom Reeger saying just that. "CNN- NOW."

I stood quickly and grabbed Vivienne to come with me.

"Hurry," I said as I ran to Herb's den just off the front hallway, and the others followed. I fumbled with the remote until I got CNN on the screen. Father Andrew Barry was smiling at a young woman in Times Square who was allowing him to place hands on her head.

I heard Vivienne's intake of breath.

"What?" I asked.

"He could harm her." We all watched with dismay as Barry bent his head as if curing the girl of what ailed her was extremely taxing.

Vivienne said in a low voice, "The human body is fragile. I practiced on animals at first. I didn't use magic on people until I understood it. And now that I know the inner workings of the human body, I can direct it. I can determine what should happen first, what does not need to happen at all..." She shook her head at the television screen. "Andrew Barry doesn't know any of that."

The girl wrinkled her brow, then she gave a small, uncertain smile. Barry had removed his hands and was asking her if she felt better. She said yes, and the crowd surrounding them burst into applause. Barry went on about how witchcraft was not to be feared and that witches were happy to be out of the shadows now and just wanted to help the world in any way they could.

Vivienne and I shared a skeptical look.

"That sounds like some bullshit," Herb commented.

Then Barry went for the throat and said it all again, using persuasion. I whipped my head around to see Herb's reaction, and it sickened me to see my friend believing Barry that time. Grant saw it, too. Everyone in that room, and all over the world watching CNN, had just made a new witch friend in Father Andrew Barry.

CHAPTER SIX

Vivienne

We spent the first day of the new year at Herb's. I sat with Adam, Grant and Herb in the den, and we discussed our next options. When Herb learned that he and the entire CNN viewing audience had been hit with a dose of magic called persuasion, he became quiet for a few seconds and then pulled Adam aside to grill him about it. At one point, the exchange became heated.

Herb's eyes were trained on Adam, and he asked loudly, "Are you telling me someone with persuasion could enter the Oval Office and convince the President to use the military to take out his political rival? To go to war with a friendly nation?"

Adam's expression was grim, but he looked his friend in the eye and said simply, "Yes."

I felt his internal struggle to be speaking openly about his magic to his friend. Adam had such an immense store of magical ability. Herb might be dealing with the most disturbing one at the moment, but Adam was imagining his reaction to the rest of them as well. He didn't do himself any favors when he said next, "It's not like that couldn't happen with the current asshole anyway, with just some compliments or cash and a promise of airtime."

Herb yelled, "It's fucking different, and you know it!" The friends stared at each other. Herb exhaled a deep breath. "Jesus Christ." He pulled his hands down over his face. "Un-fucking believable." He stood and walked a path back and forth in his front hallway for a minute. Then he pulled out his phone and typed a quick text. From the hallway, he said to Adam, "How many witches can do this, and who else knows about it?"

Adam said, "It's rare. I don't know exactly how many. But Herb, remember, this has been around for all of our history. Witches have existed all this time without interfering with mortal society."

"Because you had to keep it secret." Herb challenged him. "But now it's out there, and what's keeping a bad witch from taking what he wants now? I assume there are bad witches? What the fuck is going to stop a dangerous witch from walking into the White House today to run things the way he wants them to be run?" Herb shouted the last part. "What's going to stop him?"

"I am." Adam stood and faced his friend. They looked at each other in silence for a moment. Adam said, "I've been taking out dangerous witches for over a decade now. Any witch who wanted to abuse the power of magic met with me. Before me, there were others who did it. Witches have policed themselves well. Witness the fact that we were invisible to you until a few days ago."

Herb said, "No offense, chief, but you're just one guy." He shook the hand holding his phone at Adam. "You've upset the entire world order. What the hell were you thinking?"

"What would you have done, Herb? Kept the secret of a vaccine for *cancer*? Just kept it for your people, fuck the rest of the world?" Adam waited for his reply.

Herb's head fell back as if he were exhausted. "How the fuck do I know?"

"Exactly." Adam nodded at his friend. "I did the best I could. And now witches are all at risk because of me. You wait- it's only a matter of time before they become the scapegoat whenever the world needs one."

Herb contested that. "Or, they become social media stars making a fortune. People are already lining up at some witch restaurant in Atlanta. Looking for witches to help them pick their stocks. Looking to date them and make witch kids..."

Herb's phone rang, and he swiped the screen to answer it. He held the phone up to his ear and said, "Hey. Can you come over?" He paused. "No, now. We need to talk. Call your brother, too." He hung up and resumed his pacing of the hallway. Herb shook his head at Adam and said, "Do you not see the security issues here? And what do you think is going to happen when people find out about persuasion and how the entire human race is susceptible to it? It ain't gonna to be pretty!" He was getting loud again.

Adam said, "Maybe they don't need to know."

Herb stopped. "What? We just leave people ignorant about it and hope they never cross a motherfucker with persuasion? Come on, Parrish!"

His blood pressure was getting dangerously high, as was Adam's, so I stood and took Herb by the hand and sent a wave of cool healing energy over his person. He took in a surprised breath and then jerked his hand away.

"I just helped your blood pressure, Herb," I called to him as he opened the front door and stepped out onto his porch. I took Adam's hand and did the same for him. "Sorry," I said.

He pulled me to him. "It's okay. He just needs a few minutes."

Grant shook his head glumly from his seat on the couch. "Herb's right, though. Persuasion is going to be the one thing people can't accept." He pointed toward the porch, where Herb was cooling off. "And if that's how family takes the news..."

It was looking more and more like the specifics of witchcraft specialties were not likely to be celebrated by modern society. At that moment, I think all three of us felt the specter of witch hunts in the air.

Vivienne

I went to the kitchen to check on Alice and Maria, who were helping Sally. Alice seemed to be adjusting well after the explosion, but I monitored her vitals, and Maria was encouraging her to talk about what she saw and felt. I thought this was good advice for anyone, so I prompted Maria to share as well.

Standing beside her at the counter, I took a spoon from the drawer and dipped it in her bowl for a taste of the cookie dough. "Delicious," I said.

"Thank you!"

Setting the spoon in the sink, I followed up with, "How are you feeling today?"

Maria stopped her stirring. She knew what I was asking about.

"That was my first time," she said. "Killing."

I said, "It was not my first."

Alice whipped her head toward me, shocked.

Sally threw some flour onto the dough that was rolled out on the table and said, "Why does that not surprise me?"

I thought that might have been a compliment from her.

Maria shook her head slightly, as if trying to dislodge something. "I can't get his screams out of my head."

Alice said, "You saved us, Maria. I was proud."

Sally stopped rolling the dough and put her hand on her hip. "That's right! You didn't go looking for him. He came at us all. You stepped up."

"Maria." I got her attention. "Sometimes we're called to act in defense of ourselves or others. I couldn't leave those men alive to come and hurt my family again." It was a quick decision for me to kill the man who had helped bomb our house. He would have killed Adam or any of us without a thought. And I knew Adam did not feel any guilt about the man he had killed.

Sally also spoke to Maria. "Herb and I are both retired military. Our son Carter is still active duty, and we've all had to respond to bad actors in our careers, especially Herb. He was stationed in some of the worst hot zones in the world when he was active. I hate to think about what he's seen." She blew at her hair that was falling in her face and then couldn't help it and moved it with her hand. She left a flour smudge on her light brown cheek. "But none of us regret our service or what we did. It was necessary." She pointed her finger at Maria to emphasize her point. "What you did was necessary."

I patted Alice on the shoulder on my way to sit at Sally's table. "We've spoken about this before. Magic is both miraculous and dangerous. I'm sorry you had to witness it so early."

"Me too." Maria went back to her stirring.

Alice put her arms around Maria, leaned her cheek against her back, and said, "Thank you for protecting me." I saw Maria swallow and try to hold back tears.

Alice said, "I'll go with you next time. Grant can't stop me."

I couldn't help my smile at that. My beautiful girl, delicate and angelic to look at, but also so fiercely protective of those she loved.

Her mother and father would be proud.

Vivienne

Standing at the back entrance of Saint Joseph's Roman Catholic Church, I felt a sense of dread that I was about to lose what had given me the most consolation and comfort of my life- my church family. My official reason for the visit was to arrange for other volunteers to take my place in the kitchen during the dinner offering. But really, I wanted to know what would happen when a witch walked into a Catholic church in 2026, after the secret of witchcraft had been revealed. Reaching for the door, I saw that my hand was shaking.

When he saw me, Father Alves stopped his trek up the stairs to his office and stood there with his hand on the railing. He was a short man, not much taller than me, and somewhere in his forties, with dark eyes and closely cropped brown hair. What he lacked in stature, he made up for in charisma. He had a rich, sonorous voice and a penchant for performance that the other priests didn't have. I had grown fond of him.

Looking at me, he wore the schooled expression of a priest dealing with a troubled parishioner, minus the compassion. He came back down the stairs and motioned for me to meet him near the entrance to the sanctuary.

He said in a low voice, "Would you like me to take your confession?"

Because I'm a witch?

"No thank you, Father. I came to let you know I won't be able to make my dinner shift for a while. My family has been through a difficult time, and we may need to live somewhere else."

He crossed his arms. "Again?"

Where was the concern for my family? There was an attitude in his tone that was unusual for us. Maybe suspicion? Or judgement? His eyes suggested it was judgement.

"That's probably for the best," he said.

I raised my eyebrows. "Why is that for the best?"

He gave me a hard look. "You know why. Follow me."

We took the stairs to his office, and once there, he closed the door. He picked up a paperweight in the shape of a cross on his desk.

Was this for real? I shook my head. "You can't possibly think that you'll need a cross to protect yourself from me. I do not need an exorcism."

"Then tell me what to think, Vivienne. You're a witch, right? Adam Parrish brought you here. What is it you can do and why are you here at Saint Joseph's?"

I stood before him, completely unsure for once in my life what to say. Should I tell him specifics about my magic? Should I tell him what happened to Adam's house, how strangers had targeted us and how Alice and I now had to leave Washington to be safe?

Taking a seat on the leather couch, I waited for him to sit behind his desk.

I said, "I am a witch."

I watched him to see how that landed. His expression darkened, but he stayed put.

"My powers are primarily to heal. Adam and I are married, and we are raising my granddaughter, Alice." I hoped that would remind him that until that morning, I had been a normal congregant. A person with friends in this very church and a family to take care of.

He said, "Primarily?" Of course, that was the word he'd focus on. It was clear to me then that discussions about witchcraft with those just learning about its existence must always be forthright and truthful. I would not lie to him.

"I can also harm. But I have only ever used that magic to protect myself or others. It's rare. Most witches have minor magics that don't add up to much in their daily lives." I paused. "Or yours."

We sat in silence as he processed my words.

Then he said, "The Catechism of the Catholic Church states that practices involving witchcraft and the occult are sinful. Sacrilegious. These practices attempt to access supernatural powers through means other than God."

"God granted me these powers." My tone was sharp, but I couldn't help it. About this one thing in my life, I was entirely certain. "Everything I can do was determined by our Heavenly Father. A witch's magic is with them at birth. It's in their very DNA. Tell me, Father Alves, who do you suggest designed a human's DNA if it was not our God?"

His jaw clenched, and I saw that his struggle with the official doctrine against witches was not something he could abandon lightly. It was not only disappointing, it was infuriating.

I was no longer shaking. I was on a mission.

"The Church is very clear on this," he said as I opened his office door.

I stood to go and said, "Yes. They were very clear during the Inquisition, as well."

CHAPTER SEVEN

Vivienne

We were going somewhere, but Adam wouldn't give me details. Since we couldn't get into our house, Sally loaned me some clothes. I dressed in a long black skirt and a black cashmere sweater that made Adam whistle when he saw me. He wore a blue button-down shirt under a dark suit borrowed from Herb. Adam took my hand, and we waited on the porch for a Lyft. We had to meet it off of our street since police and reporters still barricaded both ends. We walked across the street and between the Supreme Court building and the Thomas Jefferson Building of the Library of Congress to meet up with our Lyft driver on First Street. When it arrived, Adam opened the door for me, and I slid into the back of a large white vehicle. Inside it was warm and cozy. Our driver, a middle-aged black woman with a colorful scarf over her long hair, turned to welcome us and ask where we were going. Adam told her, "2125 E Street Northwest. CVS store."

She said, "Might not be open today."

"I called. It's open." He sat back as she started driving. I had never seen him so tense. Placing my hand on his face, I leaned over to kiss him softly on the lips. Tiny kisses to soothe and distract.

He pulled me closer and kissed me harder, deeper. Then he pulled away, looking me in the eye. "I need time with you." I snuggled into him, and there it was—that scent of pine that clung to his clothes, his skin. It settled over me like a familiar blanket, quieting everything else. With my head on his chest, I could feel that his heart was beating too hard. I willed some calm into him. He took a deep breath and kissed the top of my head. His lips still on my hair, he murmured, "Thank you," and I felt his heart beating normally again. He kissed me four or five more times there, like I was the one who needed comfort.

The car stopped in front of a store, and Adam said to the driver, "I'll be right back out. Then we're going to the Kennedy Center." He kissed my head again and hurried into the store. I wondered if the clerk would be a woman and how she might admire Adam when he gave her his money. It wasn't jealousy; I was just very aware of that man and his presence. His broad shoulders were the first thing a woman noticed. Then his chiseled jaw, covered in stubble that rasped under your fingers when you caressed his cheek. His brown eyes that darkened when he wanted more from you.

I saw how others looked at him. Like I did.

Like we couldn't get enough.

He came out of the store carrying a plastic bag. "I got us some drinks and some snacks."

"Kind of you," I said, amused.

"That's me. The kindest."

He held my hand for the rest of the ride and our magic tingled where we touched, waiting patiently for us to lay together again and let our true natures collide. The sweet tension of that feeling, that anticipation of what was to come was what I now lived for and I sometimes wondered how we had ever survived without it.

Our driver slowed down when she reached the destination, which was an impressive white rectangular building with slender gold columns all around it.

"Thank you," Adam said to the driver as he opened his door. Then, to me, in a low voice, "Follow me and keep a hold of my hand. When we get out, I need you to duck."

As soon as my feet hit the ground, Adam ducked, and I did the same. The door slammed shut, but I didn't see how because Adam had cloaked us both. We were invisible.

"You can stand now. Don't worry. The key is to look ahead as you walk. And do not let go of my hand."

I heard his bag rustling as he got a grip on it in his other hand and appeared to be tightening it up. A family of four walked toward us and I had a moment of panic, but Adam steered us off the sidewalk and said, "Shhhh..." I looked down at the grass tamped down by our feet and I wondered about the times this skill might not work. On a dirt road, in snow, and what happened with water?

After they passed, he pulled me along next to him, back onto the sidewalk. He said softly, "When you're cloaked, you need to watch out for other people. They won't move." We walked past a fountain with dozens of water plumes dancing in the air, and I heard Adam laugh when I yanked his hand, so I could stop and admire it.

We entered the front of the building and stepped into an immense lobby with red carpeting and long chandeliers composed of blocks of light. There was a giant, craggy bust of a man to my right, which I stumbled past trying to get a better look. Adam righted me as the worker at the welcome desk frowned and got up to inspect the door. We stood off to the side, only four feet away from him as he opened it again, ran his hand along the lining and then stood back, perplexed. It was thrilling and terrifying all at once. Adam squeezed my hand and moved away as the man walked back to his desk. We proceeded slowly as the man picked up his phone and called someone to fix the door.

Around a corner, there was a wide hallway with shiny marble walls. Dozens of colorful flags hung high above us. There were four sets of elevators, but Adam pulled me toward another doorway that led to stairs. As he closed the door quietly, he let go of the invisible cloak around us, and we were visible to each other again. He was searching my face, trying to read what I thought about his magic that could make someone invisible to others.

"Is it taxing?"

He seemed surprised by this question.

"No. But it's rare. As far as I can tell, only a small percentage of witches have this magic."

"That's probably a good thing."

He nodded his agreement. "My father taught me never to use it for myself." He started up the stairs. "But today I think I will."

Vivienne

Because it was New Year's Day, Adam thought the National Symphony would be off. But when we entered the Kennedy Center auditorium, they were there and getting ready to practice. He watched my face as I took in the enormous hall that seated over two thousand people. It was magnificent- all red velvet seats and chandeliers and a stage full of musicians.

Seeing my enchantment with the place, he made a frustrated sound and said, "Fine. We can listen to some music. But then I'm having my way with you, just know that."

I was fine with that.

We climbed a couple of staircases and entered one of the mid-level boxes to sit down. The seats weren't close enough for Adam, so he pulled me up and out of mine and onto his lap. I put my arms around his neck and leaned against him with a sigh. The symphony began to tune their instruments, and I heard a guitarist pluck out four beautiful notes. When he did it again, Adam whispered in my ear, "Look, there's Greg. On the guitar. And there's John." He pointed Greg out and then pointed to John on the drums. "This is a Beatles song."

I kept my eyes on the stage. "Tell me more."

"British rock band from the nineteen sixties who took the world by storm. Modern musicians all say the Beatles influenced them. They were John, Paul, George and Ringo. And it's crucial that you say the names in that order. It's a rule."

I nodded thoughtfully. "And what would happen if I said Ringo, John, George and Paul?"

He shook his head in disapproval. "Well, it's never happened because it's so weird, so I'm not sure about the exact consequence. But I know it wouldn't be good."

I tipped my head back and laughed softly at him.

The hall became quiet as the conductor raised his hands. Then Greg played the first four notes of a song and the orchestra followed. After the introduction, Adam leaned down and sang along to the lyrics about a lover who gives her everything, tenderly. He kissed my temple and then the shell of my ear. My hand on his chest found its way to undo the top button of his shirt, then the next. I caressed what skin I could, the side of his neck, his collarbone, his shoulder. He stopped singing and leaned his head back against the seat, closing his eyes. My magic was as free as the music flowing over us, but his cloak was hiding its light, and I didn't care if the musicians below felt the power of it. *Adam* was feeling the power of it, and that was all that mattered.

His hand cupped my cheek and brought my head up for him to lean down and touch his lips gently to mine. One deep, sensual kiss led to another, and I undid more buttons on his shirt. While Adam's warm hand skated up under the front of my sweater, my hands roamed all over his chest and stomach. I slowly made my way down trailing the line of hair that disappeared into his pants and he sucked in a breath when I unbuttoned them and slid the zipper down.

When my hand took out the perfect weight of his cock, Adam groaned and remembered his own hands. He lifted my skirt with one hand and ran it up over my calf to my inner thigh. Then he hooked a finger under the lace of my panties and yanked them to the side, making me gasp and leaving my clit exposed. He turned me around so that my back was to his front and our roles were suddenly reversed. He was in charge and it was my turn to try to breathe.

"Spread your legs for me." I let both my legs touch the ground on the other side of his and gasped again when I felt his thumb on my clit, circling and pressing exactly where I needed it.

The music surged as he inserted one finger in me, and then two, and kept stroking while my hands gripped the arm rests of our seat.

His voice deep and rough, he said, "Look at the stage. If I dropped my cloak now, Vivienne, everyone would see you. I hope I can keep up my concentration."

The idea of that terrified and excited me and the sound that escaped me was new. I pushed up against his hand.

"Pull your sweater up. Undo your bra."

I obeyed. Then I was fully exposed, and Adam groaned his approval at the sight.

"Touch yourself."

His hand moved urgently between my legs and he watched my own hands glide up my torso and over my breasts. As I pulled at my nipples, he said, "Pinch." The catch in his breath when I did almost sent me over the edge. I breathed a direction to him then, "Harder," and I whimpered as his hand became more forceful.

Then his tongue tasted the skin behind my ear where I was the most sensitive. My head fell back against him as he sucked and nipped there, his mouth warm and insistent, and I gave a strangled cry as my climax rolled through me. He pressed firmly on my clit as I shook, curling his fingers inside me to extend it. When my orgasm finally subsided and I lay limp in front of him, Adam pulled me around against his chest again but kept his fingers inside me and on me.

He caressed my mound softly. "Mine," he said.

With my eyes still closed, I laughed and snuggled closer to him.

"Yes," I said.

He growled, "I'm not done with you."

I wiggled against his impressive erection and said, "I know."

We spent the next hour like that. Kissing, touching and listening to what seemed like a thousand Beatles songs. As each one began, Adam told me the title and which Beatle wrote it. The National Symphony played those songs with skill and passion. I knew my magic may have had something to do with that emotion, and I wondered what the members on the stage below us were feeling during their rehearsal. When it was over, the conductor praised his musicians and told them that their artistry on that day had been nothing short of magnificent. I agreed.

"I like the Beatles," I whispered as the musicians were dispersing and we fixed our clothes.

"Me too," Adam said. "But now it's time for you to pay up, kitten."

❦

Adam

My dick was tired of the Beatles. Still rock hard after an hour of Vivienne coming all over me and bouncing on my lap, I just needed her to sit on me again in a nice chair, preferably somewhere private.

I pulled her along behind me as I looked for Greg's secret room, which was apparently in the rafters. He wasn't kidding, it really was hard to find. But once there, I opened the door with my magic and saw that it was the perfect setting for my afternoon plans. It was a corner room with a low, slanted ceiling I could almost touch. Windows faced both the National Mall and northwest toward the Watergate building. I looked out the front window and saw the very top of the Capitol, half of the Washington Monument and, to the right, the Lincoln Memorial. They were tiny from there. In comparison, it looked like I could throw a rock over to the Watergate and land it on somebody's deck. Closing the curtains, I remembered Marsh had once owned a condo there, and I wondered if he still rented it out.

I turned back to the room and saw Vivienne drawing her finger along the spines of paperbacks on a bookshelf. Dust motes danced along rays of light filtering in from the sides of the curtains. There was a rust-colored couch from the seventies that I thought might suit my needs, so I dropped my bag of goodies on the low table next to it and inspected it for cooties.

"Son of a bitch. I think it's a pullout." There was a loop hanging down below the center cushion and, sure enough, when I pulled it, a bed rose up out of it.

Vivienne's eyebrows flew up as she watched me unfold the mattress and lay it out in full.

"It's a pullout couch. Makes into a bed. Let's see if it's decent." I pushed down on the mattress, and no dust came out. I lifted it and saw no bugs. There was no blanket, but there was a mattress sheet and a cover sheet, and I became fully sold on that couch bed as the place where my salvation would take place.

I gestured toward the bed, palms up. "What do you think?"

Vivienne said, "I think you're desperate."

"Very." I took off my jacket and tossed it over the back of the couch. Undoing the rest of my shirt buttons, I jerked my head towards her. "Get on it, please."

She laughed and undressed as well. I beat her to the state of naked and sat in the middle of the bed, my back against the cushions, watching her as the clothes came off. Vivienne's skin was one of my favorite things about her. Creamy, smooth, white skin that I loved to caress from her neck to her toes. No, her hair was my favorite. Her long, silky, silver hair that fell almost to her waist and smelled like fucking heaven. And...those breasts. Heavy and pink-tipped... I decided that today would be the day I would fuck those breasts.

I wanted it all with Vivienne, and we had not been given enough time.

Finally naked, she crawled up the bed and lay down on top of me. I smoothed her hair and then wrapped it around my fist and pulled it to one side. Tugging on it softly, I said, "I want to pull your hair." She sucked on my earlobe and then nipped me there.

"Then pull it," she whispered in my ear. I tugged her head away and aimed her toward my dick, which had been hard for her for over an hour and needed to be inside her. In her anywhere, just in her. I couldn't help the moan that escaped me when she took me in her mouth and moved her head up and down over me. Her tongue worked me up one side, then the other, then she put pressure underneath. God, she was an artist. I knew I was too big for comfort, but she took me in all the way. I resisted the urge to sit back and close my eyes, choosing instead to watch her mouth as her head moved up and down over my dick and one hand played with my balls.

"Fuck, Vivienne," I groaned. "Don't stop. Yes..." Her warmth and her heat surrounding me was more than I could take, and I bucked up into her, holding her head in place. In that moment all I could think was that she was mine, and I wanted her to know. She was fucking *mine*.

"That feels fucking incredible," I said. It had only been minutes, but I couldn't take it and said, "I'm coming," and with three more hard thrusts, I exploded in her mouth and fell back on the bed, shaking with my release. Vivienne moaned around me as she swallowed me down. I stroked a hand up under her as she kneeled beside me and ran my finger over her clit as a promise of what was to come. Then I smacked her ass, and she smiled around me and lifted her head.

"You are very needy today, my love." She turned and cuddled herself next to me with her arm around my waist and her head on my chest. My heart was beating frantically, and I grasped her hand on my chest and flattened it there.

Still not able to breathe, I said, "You're killing me."

She lifted her head and said, "So you lied when you told me sex is good cardio and that it helps to extend life?" In the half-light of the room, her eyes were enormous and dark, her lips swollen and begging to be kissed.

I sat up to kiss her, and she opened those lips for me. My tongue swept in, and I thought again that I was the luckiest man on earth to have that privilege.

Pulling the sheet up over us, I said, "I'm sorry we're here instead of the Hay- Adams."

"What is that?"

"A fancy hotel with luxurious bed linens and great views."

Kissing my chest, she said, "This view is good."

Gathering her hair around my fist again, I pulled until she looked at me.

"I mean it. You deserved to be spoiled. I want you to have everything this world has to offer. But here we are in a dusty attic on the run from who knows what."

"Adam, a week ago, Alice and I lived in a nunnery, where we had no modern plumbing. I think I saw a bathroom on this floor, just yards from this room. A little perspective might be in order."

I released her hair and stroked her head gently as she laid it back down on my chest.

"And I think anybody would agree that a red diamond engagement ring is the definition of spoiling me."

I smiled. That was a good purchase. I was very satisfied with that one.

With my index finger, I traced the outline of her fingers spread out on my chest. Then, I ran my finger lightly up and down each of hers, stopping to pick up her ring finger and twist the wedding rings there.

Then I said what I had been holding back all day.

"We need to separate." It hurt as much as I thought it would. And Vivienne was not having it, which made things worse.

"No." She sat up.

"Yes."

Her eyes were angry, and I didn't blame her.

After a moment she said, "Why?"

"I have to show the world witches can be good, and the world can survive with both mortals and witches. You and Alice need to go somewhere safe where no one can find you." And by no one, I meant Andrew Barry and whoever had bombed our house. Maybe they were the same. I didn't know yet, but I would. "It may be for a few months. Maybe less."

Her eyes narrowed at that as she read my face and recognized I was trying to make things look better than they were.

"Adam," Vivienne said my name again in a very reasonable tone, "we don't have to stay in Washington, D.C. In fact, I was thinking we should go to Rome." I raised my eyebrows at that. She said, "But I think Alice and I are safest with you. You wouldn't let anything happen to either of us."

"I almost let a bomb kill you both."

We sat with that for a minute. There was no denying that one.

"I'm a target right now. Maybe the biggest fucking target on the planet. And I will be for a while." Her mouth tightened. "I still have to convince the entire world that witches can work with mortals and I still have to convince witches that mortals are worth the sacrifice of our revelation. And I need to explain that the vaccine for cancer is safe. Safe for everyone."

She yanked my shirt off the back of the couch and put her arms through the sleeves. Swiping her hair out from inside the shirt, she said, "You'll need us to help you."

I sighed. "This would be easier if you'd agree sooner."

She stopped and looked over her shoulder at me. We stared at each other for a moment.

Finally she said, "Do I not get a say in this?"

"You do."

"Then I say no. We take on the world together."

Vivienne swung her legs over the side of the bed and walked back over to the bookcase. She bent over to read the titles, making it clear she was done with me and that conversation. Pulling a thick paperback off the shelf, she said, "Lonesome Dove?"

"Good."

She set it down next to her purse.

"The Thorn Birds?"

"Good. About a priest and a family. In Australia."

She set that one aside, too.

"The Catcher in the Rye?"

"A snotty teenager has a breakdown all over New York City."

She put that one back.

I patted the bed again.

"Come back."

But Vivienne was not ready to concede. She stayed there by the bookshelf in my blue dress shirt that swallowed her. It was unbuttoned, and the sight of her like that, only partially visible... it was the sexiest thing I had ever seen in my life.

She saw the desire in my eyes and gave me a small smile.

"What snacks did you bring?"

I reached over to lift the bag on the table and deposit it on the bed. "The best snacks ever. But you have to come over here to get them."

She moseyed over and sat down on the bed in front of me, settling with her legs crossed like a kid, her belly and pussy and half of her breasts laid out right there for me to see.

When I clearly became distracted by the sight of that, she clucked her tongue and took the bag from me. She squealed when she saw the chocolate cupcakes and ripped into them first thing. Finishing the first one in record time, with her mouth full of chocolate icing and cream and cake, she said, "So all these plans today we made with Herb were just for me? You weren't going to come with us? What makes you think you can do all this alone? Normally, I would bet on Adam Parrish accomplishing anything he wants. But these are assassins after you."

I had to laugh at the last part.

That pissed her off. "You know what I mean! *Organized* assassins." She opened her water bottle and took a long drink.

"I like to think I was pretty organized."

She rolled her eyes and twisted the cap back on her bottle. "There are a bunch of them. And just one of you. You have to sleep. Who will watch you sleep?" She went from irritated to anxious just like that.

"You?" I asked. "So we'll just take shifts? I'm awake while you sleep, and you're awake while I sleep?"

She nodded.

"Okay, okay. And while you're looking after me, who will look after Alice?"

She frowned at me.

"I left Grant and Maria with explicit instructions on how to watch Alice today. To make sure not to go anywhere. To stay in Herb's basement until you all leave tomorrow. I cannot have anything happen to you or to our granddaughter. Or to Grant and Maria."

A single tear ran down her cheek. But I could tell this was an angry tear, and that she was still fighting it.

"You are all stronger together and... away from me. Please. I can't do everything I have to do while also worrying about my family being kidnapped or bombed again."

Tears filled Vivienne's eyes, but I could tell she was more mad than anything else.

"I came back five hundred years to be with you."

"And you saved my life when you did."

Her magic was raging. Dying to be released, I could feel it there, pushing to get out. I reached for her hand, but she snatched it away and tried to leave the bed.

"Stay." I tugged her back and swiped her body under my own. I held her there while she struggled against me, furious at the choice we had to make and fighting it all the way. I grunted when she sent a sharp pain first to one side of my body, then the other, and tried to kick me in the groin. At that point, I had to raise my shield against my wife's attack, and I remembered it was a bad idea to make her mad.

"Alright, alright!" I started laughing as the pullout bed squeaked in protest. "I'm sorry!" Her ferocity was truly impressive. As I let her go, she elbowed my ribs as hard as any professional rugby player.

"Ow!"

"This is not funny!" she yelled. But then she walked away from the bed. She sent a pain to my side, and I clutched it in pain and laughed again.

She said, "You deserve it! You're infuriating!"

I smiled at her. "I know." She let go of the pain within me. I rolled off my side of the bed and walked over to where she stood at the window. She peered around the curtain at the miniature monuments.

"Behind you," I said. She shook her head, sending another pain through my side. This was just a tiny one, though. Putting my arms around her waist, I snuggled my face into her shoulder and breathed deep. "I don't know when I can have you again. I want you all night tonight."

I played with the hair on her pussy, and she drew in her breath. I pulled the lips apart, and she breathed in again.

"Is that a yes?"

She nodded and turned to me.

"It will always be yes for you." Her arms went around my waist, and we stood like that for minutes. Softly touching, dropping gentle kisses on exposed skin. I pushed my shirt off her shoulder and tasted her there. She licked my nipples and nipped me there. Then she caught my hand and pulled me to the bed.

Pushing me down, she said, "But I want you to remember this." And then her magic filled the space. The gold and the silver light that smelled like desire and overpowered my brain and then the pink that tingled all over our skin. I pulled her down and over me and then rolled and pinned her on the bed again under me.

I reached for the bag and got out the lube I bought at the convenience store. Squeezing a liberal amount in my hand, I said, "I want you to remember this, too." I covered my dick and her pussy, and then she spread her legs wide for me and I entered her. I pushed all the way in, and we both stilled when we were finally together.

Holding myself over her, my eyes searched her face, flushed with desire. Her eyes met mine, and she squirmed under me. "Hold still," I said. "I want this to last."

Vivienne responded by flooding the room with a hundredfold more of her irresistible magic, and I saw the triumph in her eyes as I lost control and fucked her senseless for the next five minutes. I knew dimly that my thrusts were moving the couch and that the springs were protesting the pounding. I just lost myself in the sensation of the friction between us and the heat inside her. The scent of her hair when I kissed her neck and the taste of her tongue. She was the only thing I knew at that moment. Every breath, every sound she made was what I lived for. Her cries were getting louder. She was almost there.

"Yes, baby, just like that," I said roughly. "Let me hear you. Give me just a little more."

"Adam..." Her moaning my name in pleasure was the end of me.

I bit, and I sucked her skin, and I fucked her until I came with a shout, and she shivered along with me. Then we both heard the moan of the energy around us giving up and slowing to a stop.

The lights went out, of course. We shook our heads at each other when we realized we had done it again. Holding myself above her, still inside her, I said, "Shit. I was going to try not to do that this time."

She raised her arms above her head and stretched luxuriously against me and said, "I was hoping we would." Smiling up at me when I looked surprised, she reached up to run her hand over my jaw, and her thumb along my lips. "Together we make the world stop. They can wait for us."

Lowering my forehead to hers, I kissed her cheekbones, the tip of her nose and then brushed my lips against hers. I agreed with her. "They can wait for us."

When my breathing settled, I reluctantly pulled out, waved my hand through the cloud of blue sparkles hovering over the bed, and went to check on the light situation outside.

"It's not all the way dark yet, but it looks like the Watergate is out. There are people on the balconies." I picked up my phone and called Grant.

"Hey. The lights are out here. Are they out there? Everything okay?" He said they were out there too, but Herb and Sally were prepared for all eventualities. Their generator had kicked in, and everybody was currently watching TV.

Reassured, I hung up and went back to Vivienne.

"Husband," she said. "We do need to figure this out."

I ran a hand through my hair and laughed at the absurdity of two witches blacking out a city when they both climaxed at the same time. Maybe we needed to verbally remind each other before any activities of the sexual kind.

"Fuck it. Let's check out the rest of this place. I'll bend you over the side of another balcony box, and you can be as loud as you want."

She laughed up at me, slightly alarmed. "Do you not need a break? That was quite a lot."

I got serious. "Do you need a break? We can take a break."

She stood, cleaned herself off with napkins and threw them away in the trash can by the door. Slipping my shirt back on, she said, "Let's sit by the windows and look at the stars."

While Vivienne laid the sheet over two vinyl chairs, I brought the snacks over to the window facing the Watergate, and we sat mostly naked in the chairs, facing it. Propping our feet on the windowsill, we both dug into those snacks with a vengeance. A plane flew overhead, taking the path of the Potomac off to somewhere else. Wishing I could go somewhere else with Vivienne, I engaged in a brief fantasy of us at a palazzo in Venice. On this balcony, Vivienne would wear a silk robe, her back flush against my chest, her looking at the Ponte di Rialto, me nuzzling her nape.

At the Watergate, there was a man sitting on his balcony directly across from us, reclining with his feet propped up the same way we were. He was smoking and also looking up at the plane.

I gestured at him. "What do you think he's thinking about?"

"Probably where that plane is going."

"Should we flash him? I can drop the cloak."

She looked to the heavens. "You know what's wrong with you? I read about this in a chapter on sexual fetishes. You're an exhibitionist."

I smirked at her. "You didn't seem to mind it when I had you spread out in front of the National Symphony."

"Dear God. That's true." She slapped my arm. "But I won't do that anymore tonight. No flashing."

"What about fucking? Can I fuck you on the Kennedy Center Stage?"

She shook her head at me. "Is this a lifelong thing for you? Have you always done this?"

I thought about it. But the answer was no, I had never done

that.

"In the past, I haven't really dated that many witches. So, no. I have never cloaked myself and a partner during sex." I looked over. "Until today." And now I was torn between wanting the world to see this phenomenal woman I had that they would never have and wanting to kill anyone who looked at her twice.

"Why have you not dated witches?" She munched on her Doritos like they needed to be punished. I laughed at her, and she threw one at me.

I answered, "I don't know. Didn't want there to be expectations, I guess."

Vivienne nodded.

I asked her, "Why were you thinking we should go to Rome?"

She gave a small laugh. "Because I had a disappointing meeting with Father Alves today, that made me think the church is going to be a problem for witches. He knows me, knows what kind of person I am, but completely changed his mind about me when he learned I was a witch. I feel strongly that my work in the next days and weeks should be to convince the church that witches are not what they think."

So she was fine with getting out of town; she just wanted us to be together.

I said, "While I think you'd be the perfect person for that job, how are you planning to do it? Speak to every Catholic church in the world? Speak to God, maybe?" I raised his hand and added, "Which would be great, and I definitely think you could make some headway."

She said, "Prayer will be involved, of course. I also thought I might make a visit to God's representative here on Earth."

She let that sink in for a minute while I figured out that she meant the Pope.

I raised my eyebrows, stared at her for a long moment, then leaned over to kiss her on the forehead.

"Genius," I said.

It was almost twilight, and the sky was revealing a few of its gems. Looking up at the stars that were visible, she said, "Tell me what you think you will do in the next few weeks."

She was giving me a chance to make my case that we should go our separate ways. Vivienne had not decided yet, and I needed her to understand this was the only way I could do it.

So I told her. I said I'd likely be doing many more TV interviews. Traveling to different countries even, to reassure world leaders we could police ourselves. And the hardest part would be dealing with the witches, who could ruin it all.

She shook her head. "Your plan seems all wrong to me."

"Is it? What do I have wrong?"

Vivienne ticked things off on her fingers as she made her points. "First, Louise is the one who was tasked with teaching the world about magic. Not you. She will be good at it." Her look confirmed that the unspoken truth in that sentence was that I would *not* be good at it.

Painful but true. One point for Vivienne.

"Second, step back and look at all you are trying to take on."

I tried to take a mental step back and see the big picture, but I really didn't know what she was getting at. She saw my struggle.

"Adam, your relationship with the International Council of Witches is over. You don't do work for them anymore. Do you have a title there? Any authority?"

Well, fuck. Another point for team Vivienne. But what was she getting at?

She asked, "Why don't you let us handle the witches while you work on selling the vaccine to the public?"

In other words, stay in your lane, Adam.

And it wasn't a bad idea except for Andrew Barry. The group of them, Grant, Maria, and Vivienne, could be persuasive and formidable enough to get some of those witch factions in line. But the wild card, Andrew Barry, needed to be dealt with before I'd let them operate in the open.

I said, "I'd like to keep you as a secret weapon. Only to be used if absolutely necessary." Her lips pursed at that. "The Council of Witches is supposed to be organizing and keeping up with all problems witch related. I'm taking the lead on the relationship between mortals and witches. And the vaccine rollout. They're going to give me a team." Which I hoped was going to happen sooner than later.

She placed her elbow on the chair armrest and propped her chin in her hand. "I can see you're going to stay here and do what you think is right for all, but I advise you to concentrate on the area where you can make the most impact, and that is on educating about the vaccine."

I smiled at her solid take on my present situation. Having someone know me this well wasn't new. I had friends and family who definitely knew me. But having a lover, an equal like Vivienne calling me on my shit...it fulfilled a need I never knew was there.

I hadn't told Vivienne yet about what Barry had done in Times Square. It had happened a few days ago, on the same day I found out that there was a hit on me and I'd need to speed up the announcement about witchcraft to the world. A lot had happened since then, but now she would have to know.

"Promise me that if Barry ever finds you or approaches you that you won't engage without me. He's as dangerous as anybody in this world. I want you to contact me the minute you know anything about him."

Vivienne took my hand and threaded my fingers through hers. "I will. Same for you."

"It's not me he wants. It's you. He did something in Times Square that he said he got from you."

She turned her head toward me and frowned. "What did he do?"

"He stopped Times Square. Everything in Times Square stopped moving. The cars, the people, the video. It all stopped, and the place went silent."

Her mouth fell open.

"For how long?"

"Fifteen, maybe twenty seconds. Barry made sure to let me know you were in danger from other witches who are trying to get at me for telling the secret. He wanted you to be kept safe."

She took her hand back and rubbed her forehead with both hands.

"He wants what you have. I'm pretty sure he's convinced that if he takes your power again, you'll tell him how to use it and you'll become some super witch couple and take over the world."

She scoffed. "He's crazy. I don't know how to do what he did. I have never done that." But she looked down after she said it, and her forehead pinched.

"You may not have stopped time, but you travel through time. And so does Alice. And that's not something Andrew Barry ever needs to know."

We sat in silence for a minute. Adding Alice to the mix was something that could not help but move her. I could tell Vivienne was coming around to the idea of keeping Alice away from Barry, but she still didn't like the idea of our separating.

"Do you agree?"

After a moment, she nodded yes.

She said, "But I'm not hiding. Not from Andrew Barry, not from your witch factions. Not from mortals." Those gray eyes challenged me to say something more, but I didn't. She was done with hiding who she was from the world, and I got the message loud and clear. I also knew she'd be careful with Alice and that she'd never put her in danger. That had to be enough for me to let her go.

"Okay. That's settled." I stood and reached out my hand for hers. Then I picked her up, and she wrapped her legs around my waist.

She buried her face in my neck, and I felt her sniffling.

"I'm sorry." Moving her hair to one side of her neck, I kissed the other side and said, "I'm so sorry. I know."

"I just got back to you," she whispered.

Wrapping my arms tighter around her, I rocked us side to side while she cried it out.

After a few minutes, I said, "You want to take what's left of our snacks down to the main stage?"

She laughed at that, and I knew the worst was over.

"Yes," she said. "Bring the snacks. And the sheet. And some pillows."

Despite my fervent desire to stay in that moment with Vivienne, my mind started making a list of things to do to keep everyone safe. First on the list, no matter what, I'd give our shield to all of them before we parted. Knowing that Alice, Grant and Maria would have a shield that combined my magic and Vivienne's magic... that would make it that much easier for me to let them leave.

CHAPTER EIGHT

Louise

January 6th, 2026
Paris

The International Council of Witches had called a conclave to be held in Paris the next day. My boss, Richard Cole was the CEO of the North American branch of the ICW and, as his executive assistant, I received an invite to the gathering as well. Richard knew I was halfway out the door and probably thought this trip was some incentive to keep me employed with them. It wasn't, but I wouldn't say no to a trip to Paris. I'd worked there for almost ten years and still held the title of executive assistant, mostly because I was too valuable to Richard to move out of the head office. While I enjoyed working with other witches, my days of waiting around for a promotion were over. I had a job offer to run a non-profit in Alexandria, and Richard knew it.

I had been on many work trips with him, but never out of the country and never with so little notice. He called me at one in the morning to let me know we'd be leaving at 7:00 a.m. to fly out of Dulles to Paris. We would arrive at about eight or nine at night, which meant I really needed not to sleep on the way or I'd mess up my schedule for a week.

My son Connor was almost sixteen, and the house was stocked with food, but I wasn't going to leave him alone for an undetermined amount of time. I reluctantly called my ex-husband, Jeff. He answered surprisingly fast for 1:00 a.m. and after a pause, where he was no doubt thinking about how he could leverage that against me at some point in the future, he agreed to be over at noon to pick up our son. At 4:30 am, when

I told Connor about that on my way out the door, he groaned and pulled a pillow over his head. He wasn't on the best of terms with his father, and I could relate, but I still wasn't leaving him to his own devices. I lifted the pillow and kissed him goodbye.

Richard was in rare form on the flight, asking the attendant for another drink every hour on the hour. Before he was too far gone, I wanted to get from him my assignment at the gathering.

I said, "What do you need from me when we're there?"

He scrubbed a hand over his jaw. "I predict one big bitchfest about how we didn't give everybody enough time to put things in place. Once we get through that, I expect they'll want to hammer out some sort of unified way to address the fallout." He set his drink down. "Did you see what happened to that witch in Kansas City?"

I just nodded, not knowing what to say about it. A twenty-year-old who worked at a museum had confided to his friends and co-workers that he was a witch and had ended up beaten to death on the street. In Sacramento, a woman had to call police because neighbors had surrounded her house, chanting, "Die, witch." There were reports of protests around the world, but no threats or actual violence like in the United States. Yet.

Richard said, "I'm not sure addressing the fallout should be a one size fits all type of thing. I want you to come up with something specific for the U.S. and let me know when you do."

'Addressing the Fallout' was a pretty big task.

Honestly, the ICW should have prepared a lot better than they did for an announcement to the world that was that monumental. The old contingency plans of how to *hide* witchcraft weren't what we needed. The days were over of disappearing new witches who couldn't help practicing in public or sending PR teams to sweep in after someone made big claims. Those methods of containment were obsolete and did not translate to our new job of explaining witchcraft to all eight billion people on the planet.

And Richard was right- Americans were already a problem. To say the least, Adam's revelation of witchcraft to the world had not been received particularly well in the United States. Other countries had seemed to handle the news without hysterics, whereas the Americans had predictably chosen to run around like Chicken Little and declare an end-of-days scenario. There was a lot of right-wing TV talk about how in this new world any idiot who still did not own a gun would finally have to face the folly of his decision not to protect his family with a firearm.

We were also still a country completely divided into warring political camps. The presidential election of 2024 and the following year of contentious conservative rule had cleared the way for conspiracy theorists and anti-government fanatics to run wild. Entire government agencies had been eliminated or were under fire, and I'd seen several friends lose their federal jobs. Many quit outright, unwilling to go along with the new authoritarian regime.

So, on top of that dumpster fire, you're going to drop some information about a whole new group of secret people with secret powers that may or may not be your next-door neighbor or work bestie?

Big nope. That's a QAnon gold mine right there. Even with an entire year to plan, the PR department for ICWUS had dropped the ball, but good. There was no going back, though, so we just needed to do better with the messaging. I had some ideas, and I hoped others at the meeting would as well. They also needed to address the violence being perpetrated against the bearer of the news. Adam and his whole family were at risk, and that wasn't right.

The next morning, I dressed for success in a black wraparound dress I knew fit me well and a diamond necklace that disappeared into my cleavage. With my heels on, I stood about five nine, taller than Richard. But he didn't appear to mind. In fact, he never ever commented on my appearance at all, a trait I valued in a boss.

We arrived at the Hotel Salomon de Rothschild ten minutes before the meeting was to start. A mansion in the eighth arrondissement, the ICW had secured the venue for the entire day and night. Security personnel scanned us for weapons in the driveway, and once inside, we had to check in our phones.

An attendant ushered us into the Hall of Honor, an elegant room with Corinthian columns separating floor to ceiling windows that overlooked the gardens. Ten round tabletops covered by white tablecloths filled the room with forty or fifty people milling around, selecting seats. Above us, a gigantic crystal chandelier wanted to be the highlight of the space, but for me, that was the ceiling surrounding it. The cherubs that skirted the edges of the room and the soft, glowing colors of the mural classed up the event.

Witches could be, by nature of their secrecy, a group of grifters with minor to no oversight on the day-to-day intricacies of their magic use. The only rule that mattered was that they kept the secret. Holding the conclave in that eighteenth-century mansion in Paris was Europe's way of telling us, "Stay classy, witches."

I was not mad about my surroundings.

I was surprised to see Marshall Smith there. Richard hadn't mentioned he was coming. He was the executive director of the North American Council of Witches, just under Richard on the executive flowchart. Marshall was a hard worker, a little straight-laced, but overall on the right side of things. Most witches never let their guard down around him, and understandably so. His skill as a diviner of magical abilities was unparalleled. He could divine an unsuspecting witch in a matter of seconds, and everybody knew about it because of his work with the ICW. None of the witches at that Paris gathering were about to be caught with their shields at less than one hundred percent while Marshall Smith was in the same room.

He stood and pulled a chair out for me next to him at the dining table, where he sat alone. I thought, not for the first time, that it was too bad Marshall had a skill that was so objectionable to other witches. As far as I knew, he was not involved with anyone, but he was a handsome man in his fifties with a full head of black hair and equally dark eyes. His gold watch and tailored suit were always in place, along with his slight scowl.

"Smile, Marshall. Everybody here is scared of you. I know you love that."

He dipped his chin in acknowledgement then said, "Everybody except you."

I shrugged. "I figured out you were harmless years ago."

Richard sat in the chair to my left and acknowledged Marshall with a nod.

Marshall said in a low voice to Richard, "They're starting soon. I overheard Lucia Perez bitching about how Adam bungled things by not appearing more in public and how Andrew Berry would be a better spokesperson."

Richard shook his head at that while I shot a look over at Perez. Dressed to the hilt, as usual, she wore an impeccably fitted blue suit with a cream-colored silk scarf tucked in around her neck. While I admired her taste in jewelry and clothes, I really did not like her. I remembered Adam's meeting with all the heads of the ICW to reveal he had a vaccine for cancer, and I pictured again how she had hurled a glass of water his way. It sounded like she now had a vendetta against Adam because he had revealed the secret of witchcraft to the world. But he'd gotten the yes vote that day from this very group of witches. It occurred to me that he should be there.

"Where's Adam?" I asked Richard.

His face grim, he said, "Not invited."

Enzo Conti stood up and made his way to the podium next to the fireplace at the front of the room. He was a tall, barrel-chested man whose face looked like he'd boxed for a living. I kind of liked his no-nonsense vibe. He tapped on the microphone and said, "Everyone, please take your seats so we can get on with it." He waited a moment for people to adjust and, when he noticed the house staff still in the room, he motioned for them to exit. When the doors were closed behind them, Conti raised his arms and let a shimmering white seal flow around the room, covering the windows and doors. Marshall was looking down, doodling on his pad of paper, but I saw his head nod slightly in appreciation of the power Conti was exhibiting.

"No one can hear us now." Conti looked around the room. "I'm Enzo Conti, head of Europe. There's a bar," he waved over to the back right corner of the room, "use it whenever you want. Let's get started." He took a piece of paper out of the inner pocket of his suit jacket and unfolded it. "The first item we need to discuss is the use of heavy magic against other witches. There is to be none of that today at this gathering. Any use of cloaking, persuasion or any other mind fuckery will be met with deadly force." Conti looked around the room to make sure everyone knew what he meant, and while he didn't elaborate, his glance rested on Marshall before he moved on.

What "other mind fuckery?"

Obviously, some of that mind fuckery had occurred the last time we all were in a room together when Father Andrew Barry had used persuasion on us to get a vote in favor of revealing magic to mortals. It had taken Adam hours to undo that situation and get us to give a real yes vote. I did not expect Andrew Barry to get any more invites to ICW meetings ever again, and that was a good thing. But now I was curious about what other types of 'mind fuckery' there might be that I hadn't heard about. I made a mental note to grill Marshall about it the first chance I got. In our world, knowledge was power, and I liked to load up on it.

Conti said, "Here's how we'll do this. Each continent will get some time to speak about current concerns, and after that I'll summarize the main points and then we can each take a turn with offering solutions to the primary concerns. Sound good?" He looked around as if gauging the opinion of his order of things, but he didn't look ready to accept any opinions, so the room stayed quiet.

"Okay. My take is that Parrish did a great job with the initial announcement. He's likeable and has an excellent reputation in the mortal world. And he could speak knowledgeably about the vaccine and the potential cure for cancer. I think where things have gone wrong in the last few days is the fact that only a few other witches worldwide have come forward, and those that have shown their magic have done so in a heinous way by using persuasive magic on the entire world through a media appearance." His face darkened. "I am sorry to say that the witch was Andrew Barry, of Europe. His whereabouts are currently unknown, but when I find him..." Conti took a deep breath in and then ended that thought with, "Barry is not welcome in Europe."

He took a moment to think about his next words. "I think our key problem now is lack of education about witchcraft. And rogue motherfuckers like Barry." He looked at Richard. "North America next."

Richard stood and made his way to the podium as Conti took a seat near the front.

He led with, "Richard Cole, North America."

Looking around the room, he said, "We agree with Europe that Andrew Barry has become a significant problem in the rollout of our story. Today I declare that Barry no longer has free passage in the United States. Further, he is the subject of a Declaration of Protection made by me for the members and employees of the North American Council of Witches."

A buzz rippled through the room at that last part. Richard had essentially just put a hit out on Andrew Barry, and anyone, no matter how loosely associated with the North American Council of Witches, could pick up the contract.

Lucia Perez stood. In a strong Latin American accent, she said, "That is insane! Barry has become the face of witchcraft for most of the world, and you want to let loose thousands of witches to bring him down in front of mortals?"

Richard looked over at our table.

"Don't do it in public," he said.

Marshall gave a silent laugh and wrote on his paper, "Not in public." He underlined "public" twice.

Conti was also having trouble hiding his amusement and said to Perez, "South America will have its turn to speak next. Sit down."

She glared at him and turned to adjust her seat some, not giving him the satisfaction of immediately sitting down at his command. I also bristled at that "sit down" and wondered how drastically things had changed just in the past year that I would instantly side with a woman I so thoroughly disliked just because a man threw out an order. I mean, I knew he would have said it to a man or a woman. Just don't fucking push us right now, you know? Being thrown backwards fifty years in the equal rights movement was not something any woman had on her card for 2026, and yet, there we were. Maybe things were different for women in Europe. But I leveled a look at Conti to let him know he should be mindful of his attitude.

He didn't see it, of course.

Richard said, "The other issue to address is the use of violence toward Adam Parrish. His house was bombed while he was in residence there, along with his family." A murmur of surprise from some tables let me know that information had not made it to all witch councils. He continued, "Everyone is fine, but there was significant damage to his home." Richard paused. "I know you're waiting for solutions to be proposed at the end, but I want to put it out there that whatever this faction is that thinks they can go around bombing shit because they don't like our decisions... they need to be dealt with. Immediately." He nodded to Perez. "Your turn, South America."

Lucia Perez surprised me when she came out with some common sense right away. She eschewed the podium and microphone to stand at the front to address the group in her own confident voice. "It's unfortunate that more witches have not come forward to help explain witchcraft to mortals. The public is afraid of what a witch could do to them. They're scared that we might convince them to do things they don't want. And they're right; there are some witches who can coerce." She paused. "The heavy magics should remain a secret if we are ever to gain the trust of mortals. In South America, we are rich in earth and fire magic, as well as the creative arts and emotional intelligence." Her dark eyes swept the room. "We can not compel our members to divulge their abilities, but I, for one, will encourage them to share with friends, family, and their local media."

The room seemed to approve of that.

She continued, "Further, to honor the sacrifices that were made to keep our secret all these years..." Her head turned to every corner of the room and I remembered how she screamed at Adam in the meeting where he convinced witches to announce the secret. How she sobbed when she said her son had been one of those who disappeared because of his use of magic in public. She said, "We owe it to our people to do this right. I think not using the asset we have in Andrew Barry would be a mistake. Like him or not, he's a magnetic personality who makes witchcraft look sexy. Fun." Perez checked in with the women in the room. "He looks like an angel and charms the pants off people with that Irish accent. And that he's a priest is the icing on the cake. He comes across as non-threatening, and people trust him."

"Well, they shouldn't trust him," Richard stood up again. "About a year and a half ago, he tried to kill Adam Parrish and his friend. That seems pretty threatening and untrustworthy to me." More reaction from around the room, this time shocked.

Perez narrowed her eyes at our table. "North America is nothing but a cesspool of heavy magic users, so I wouldn't be talking about what is or isn't a threat if I were you. And he's navigating this new world just like the rest of us."

"Are you harboring him?" Richard was not letting up.

Conti stood. "Enough. Both of you had your say. It's time now for Africa to give us their concerns, then Asia." Richard and Perez both took their time sitting back down.

Africa's CEO was a tall, thin man with dark skin. He took Perez's lead and stood away from the podium. "Ndugu Mende, Africa." He took a moment to look around the room. "While I appreciate the sentiments expressed so far, I am less worried about one untrustworthy witch and more concerned about how governments are receiving the news. Particularly leaders. Promising to protect their people against witches would be a good way to persuade people to vote for them. Fear is a powerful motivator. Manipulate that and you can do just about anything you want." He looked at our table, and I think we all grimaced at the stark truth of that statement. "It will be in the best interests of politicians to demonize us and promise protection against us. I want to know how we fight that."

Africa made way for Asia, who made way for Australia. After they had all had their say, Conti took his place at the podium again and said, "Okay, now let's decide some things."

The second half of our session went less smoothly than the first. We all agreed on the dangers ahead, but there was no agreement on how to approach them. Should we lay it all out all at once or should we dole out information slowly? What was the most important thing and where to begin?

In my head, I was hearing, "A spoonful of sugar helps the medicine go down" from Mary Poppins, and I was wishing for one of the women to stand up and explain this concept to the men.

Oh, for fuck's sake.

Standing, I said, "Louise Carmichael, North America." I detected some disapproval from Richard on my left, but if anything, that made me more confident. I said, "First, *every time we talk*, let's be sure to remind them that witchcraft is the reason they now have a vaccine and potential cure for cancer." I checked in with the leaders of all the councils. "Every. Single. Time. We lead with that."

"They're afraid of us because they don't know us. We need to appoint one person from each continent to be the goodwill ambassador for witches. We need to decide what the most appealing magical abilities might be to mortals, then we need to demonstrate the hell out of those all over the world. This needs to happen by tomorrow morning. Nobody reveals the heavy stuff to anyone until the world knows about the good stuff, and even then, only after the CEOs have approved it."

I sat.

I felt Marshall laughing next to me. He wrote "bossy" on his pad, underlined it, and pointed to it with his pen.

I shrugged.

Put it on my tombstone. *"Did it need to be done? This woman got it done."*

The meeting concluded soon after, all continents having agreed with my assessment of our current predicament and promising to move forward with my recommendations.

On our way out, as Richard and I waited for our phones to be returned to us, Lucia congratulated me.

"Your suggestions were excellent."

"Thank you," I said. "I hope we can ease into the information with the good stuff first."

"Well, mortals will need to understand that witches are superior at some point. Your plan might be the best path to get there."

Well, that took a turn.

Her gaze moved to Richard.

"Good to see you, Director Cole. How is your wife?"

"Still dead," he said and moved on with his phone.

She raised her eyebrows.

"Why don't I ever remember that?" Widening her eyes, she said, "And what about you, Louise? How is your family? You, I believe, are divorced. With a son."

"Correct." I did not like that she knew anything about me.

"How old is he?"

"Fifteen. He's taking college courses already."

"Impressive," she said as she accepted her phone from the attendant. Turning to leave, she said over her shoulder to me, "Best of luck with your efforts in North America."

On the plane ride home, Cole named me the goodwill ambassador for those efforts in North America and now I had to get home, plan a whole PR campaign on how to make witchcraft look harmless and fun, and inform my family that they were about to be outed to the world as witches.

Nothing to it.

CHAPTER NINE

Marsh

January 8th, 2026
Washington, D.C.

Coming out of a six-hour surgery to repair a hairy tear in a thoracic artery, I was accosted by the head of the hospital compliance department and ordered to meet her in her office right away.

"Is it okay with you if I speak to this guy's wife first to let her know he made it through surgery?" She pursed her lips at my sarcasm and said she'd wait and escort me to her office after I was done.

Escort me?

And who is that with her? I think he's from human resources.

Am I being sued? Why is human resources here?

Am I being fired?

I tried to clear my head as I was talking to my patient's wife, but I couldn't and I ended up telling her on autopilot about the surgery and his prognosis. When I was done, she gave me a hug, and I turned to find the dour-faced twins still there, waiting for me to join them. We rode the elevator to the first floor in silence, my blood pressure rising with every floor we passed on the way down.

Entering the compliance director's office, a man stood who had been seated at the desk across from hers. I saw it was one of our security officers from the front desk in the lobby, who was always a good guy to me. He was in his thirties, a new dad, and he showed me a baby picture on his phone every time I asked about his family.

"Mark," I shook his hand. "What the fuck is all this about?"

He shrugged, as if sorry to have to be there at all. "I don't know, man. I just got a call to get up here." I turned to the compliance officer.

"Have a seat," she said as she motioned for me to take the chair next to Mark's. She wore a business suit, a little too much makeup and what looked to me like a lot of hair products. Unbuttoning her jacket, she sat behind the desk and said, "Dr. Marsh, I'm Millicent Calendar, head of hospital compliance. This is Thomas Mellon, head of human resources." Thomas gave me a nod and, like a good boy, went to sit when she waved him over to the couch against the wall. "We need to inform you that, as of right now, your employment with St. Andrews has been terminated. After a lengthy investigation it has been determined that," she picked up a paper from her desk to read aloud, "your refusal to perform a heart valve replacement surgery based on your personal moral beliefs was in direct opposition to our code of conduct at St. Andrews hospital and in violation of our contractual obligations to our patients." She set the paper down again and looked directly at me. "Mr. Mellon has the paperwork for you, and Mr. Parks is here to escort you to your office to retrieve your belongings."

She looked down and then cleared her throat slightly. "The hospital would like to thank you for your years of service to our patients and for the many fortunate outcomes you have facilitated."

I sat back in Millicent's chair.

"Fortunate outcomes?" I looked around the room.

The surgery I had declined to perform for my own 'personal moral beliefs' was over a year ago, on an eighty-year-old man with a badly damaged heart. He would never have made it through the operation, and he was fine with my decision. His family had complained, but I knew my patient was good with it. In fact, he was happy to spend the rest of his time reading and 'watching his movies,' as he said. So what the fuck was this, really?

"By 'fortunate outcomes' I assume you mean all the lives I've saved here?"

No response from compliance or HR, but next to me Mark said under his breath, "Mm-hmm."

"What the hell is this really about?" I leaned forward. "Is this about Adam Parrish?"

I saw in Millicent's face that, yes, this was about witches and magic and shit that had nothing in the world to do with me.

"You know I'm not a witch, right?"

Again, no words came out of her mouth. Well, D.C. medicine was a small world, and Adam and I had been friends for decades. I could understand that people might wonder if I was also a fucking witch. But how about just fucking asking me? All I could think of then was the surgery I had just completed and how that patient was going to need monitoring for quite a while. I pulled out my phone and sent a quick text to my co-worker, Shauna Langley.

"Hey- emergency request. I'm dealing with some shit with HR and won't be able to monitor the TAD I just did. There's also a bypass from this week. Can you take them for me?" Shauna was as skilled a physician as I had ever met, and I could leave patients in her care with no reservation. I watched the dots scroll as she typed a reply.

"Of course. I'll call the unit now. Tell HR to fuck off and let me know if you need anything. At ALL."

I put the phone back in my pocket.

"Millicent, you are on the hook for any heart surgeries that won't get done because of this bullshit. And the deaths."

HR stood and pushed some paperwork my way.

"Shove that up your ass, Thomas." I stood too and looked at Mark. "I don't keep much in my office. Let's go get it."

Marsh

I sat in our booth at the Red Lion and thought about how nice it was that a couple of drinks could settle a person's mood. It was really kind of a miracle. One minute you're seething and wanting to storm into an office and just fucking wail on the asshole who took your job as a heart surgeon, and the next you're wondering what other skills you have that might translate into anything worthwhile.

In my sixth decade, I was experiencing some new things.

Who knew that was even possible? I had a little laugh there in the booth by myself.

I was waiting there for Adam so I could warn him about my firing. They canned me for just being witch adjacent. Poor Adam was witch personified. His days at Children's National Hospital were over, and I hoped to cushion the blow for him. The door to the pub opened then, and against the light coming from outdoors, I recognized a silhouette that could be him with a woman at his side. As he got closer to me, I saw from his expression that I was too late. He had already gotten the chop.

As had Connie. He let her slide in first and then sat next to her. She was Adam's ex and worked at my hospital in research. She was still in her lab coat, and though she was always gorgeous and perfectly put together, I had never seen her wear a lab coat outside of the hospital. It had obviously just happened. I reached out a hand to her, and she squeezed it.

"Aw, hell, Connie. I should have figured they'd come for you, too."

"I'm fine," she said.

Adam's expression was so fixed that I knew he was processing the "too" and feeling some bullshit guilt about it.

I tried to reassure him. "Look, I'm not worried about this. I have money, and I'm sure witches also need heart surgeons, right?" Connie patted my hand, and Adam gave me an almost imperceptible nod.

"Joanie!" I called the bartender over. She had waited on us for literally decades, and we'd become friends over countless discussions about politics and family. She wore her dyed-black hair tied back in a braid, with a few strands loose on each side of her face. Deep creases in her cheeks and wrinkles at her eyes showed how often she laughed. She made her way over to us with a pad of paper and pen in hand.

I asked, "Since when do you need to write our order?"

"Well, we've got a genuine celebrity here," she dropped a hand onto Adam's shoulder. "Thought I'd get an autograph."

He closed his eyes.

Joanie and I laughed at him. I said, "He needs a drink right now, and so does she."

"Got it. Whiskey and wine?"

Connie said, "How about whiskey and whiskey?"

"Yes, ma'am."

When she left, Adam looked at me. "I'm sorry, Marsh."

I waved that away. "It's fine. We all probably should have seen it coming. Seems about right in Washington, D.C. right now that the most qualified person in a department should get fired for being friends with someone who's being canceled. That's what this is, right? You're on an enemies list and I'm standing next to you, so I'm also on an enemies list?"

Adam pressed his fingers to the bridge of his nose. "Most likely, yeah. And Connie. And..." he groaned and said to her, "Have you talked to Grant?" But Connie's fingers were already flying over the phone, texting their son. Her phone made a ding, and after she read the text, she set it down.

"He was on his way to your house," she said to Adam. "I redirected him here. He's been asked to leave his job at the library."

They both leaned back in the booth and covered their faces with their hands. The synchronicity of it was comical, and I couldn't help but laugh at them some more.

When they dropped their hands at the same time to scowl at me, I said, "Come on, this is kind of funny. You guys are the same person sometimes."

I watched Joanie set napkins down on our table and then the drinks on the napkins. I was struck by how normal the little things still were, while the big things were so very abnormal. There was some comfort in that. The little things still being normal.

I thought my next drink should be a Diet Coke.

Adam handed Connie's drink to her and took up his own. "Thanks, Joanie," he said and raised the glass to her. Connie and Adam both took deeper than normal gulps of their drinks and then sat them down.

Joanie said, "You okay? What's all this about?" She waved a finger in a circle at us and our current mopey mood.

Adam looked at me as he said, "I'm a pariah right now, and my best friend and my family are suffering because of it."

"I wouldn't say suffering." I looked at Joanie. "I mean, I'm day drinking with friends."

Connie said, "We did all just get fired, along with our son, who's on his way over. But yeah," she shrugged. "Doors closing and windows opening and all that." She drank more of her whiskey.

Adam shook his head at her succinct summary of our day. Patting Adam's shoulder, Joanie said, "Well, I'm sure your new status as a spokes-wizard could turn into something lucrative, so hang in there. This table needs some food. I'm bringing you guys some food."

Adam raised his index finger at her back as she walked away. In a weary voice, he said, "I think it would be spokes-witch."

"It's never boring with you, Parrish," I told him. "Never ever boring."

"Fuck," he rubbed a hand over his eyes. "I don't even know where to begin to complain about this. Admin didn't even meet with me. Just called and told me not to come back. I had to ask Ellie to pack up my stuff. She's going to bring it over here."

"Did Millicent get to you?" Connie asked me.

"Yeah, and Thomas. They ambushed me after surgery." Which reminded me I wanted to check in with Shauna to see how my patient was doing. I sent a quick text to her, thanking her again for taking that on.

We nursed our drinks in silence for a bit.

Connie said, "Did Mark have to walk you to your office? I felt bad for him."

"Yeah. Me too."

My phone dinged, and I read Shauna's text out loud.

"Patients are great. I'll keep you up to date. Word here is that you were canned, and the guess is that it's about Parrish. Correct?"

I raised my eyebrows at Adam. I'd let him determine how much of the blame to take.

"Who's that?" he asked.

"Shauna Langley. Took my patients for me."

He decided pretty quickly. "Yes." His face was resolute. "Absolutely. Let her know it was about me and that you found out the same way the rest of the world did."

I texted her back. "Yes. I learned about witchcraft at the same time everybody else did, on TV. But Adam is still Adam, still a good guy."

She sent me a thumbs up, and I set the phone down.

My buzz was anesthetizing some of the day, but in the back of my mind I was aware of big picture decisions that would need to be addressed in the very near future. I must have sighed because Adam tapped the table and said, "Don't worry, I have a plan."

"Oh, thank God, a Parrish Plan is about to be revealed. You're familiar with these, right, Connie?"

"Mm-hmm," she nodded her head as she finished her drink and raised her hand to Joanie for another.

Adam ignored our sarcasm and continued.

"I'll get Farhad to hire you at his medical facility, where they developed the vaccine for cancer. There's a ton of research going on there," he addressed that to Connie. And to me he said, "And, shit, he'd probably be happy to build another whole hospital. One that doesn't discriminate against witches."

I could see Adam's wheels turning and knew he wouldn't stop until he was sure we were all taken care of somehow. For once, I liked a Parrish Plan.

The light from outside hit us again, and this time it was Grant who walked in with Eleanor Rodgers right behind him. She was still wearing her blue scrubs and carried a big cardboard box that Grant took from her when he saw her.

"Hi buddy." She leaned down and gave Adam a hug. "I got your stuff. By the way, your 'just a bit of personal stuff' was way more than the box I packed of my personal stuff."

She slid in next to me, said a cheerful "Hi!" and placed her purse on the bench between us.

Adam stared at her, aghast.

"No," he said. "They did not fire you! Did they?"

She waved at Joanie to get her attention and turned back to him. "Fuck no! Those tiny pricked weasels didn't fire me. I quit."

God, she was great. I had always liked her, but never more than right then. Such a solid person, Eleanor Rodgers.

Grant set the box at the end of the bar and brought a chair over to sit at the head of our table. "I don't think you're allowed at this table, Ellie. This one's for 'fired without cause' only."

Adam shook his head slowly, trying to figure out what to do with this new piece of news.

I helped him. "She'll work at the witch hospital of the future with me."

Joanie brought over a tray of appetizers and drink refills, and we all dug into those cheese sticks and chicken nuggets with a surprising passion that suggested that we were not all about to lie down and die anytime soon just because we got fired. Our feeding frenzy encouraged me.

Grant ordered a drink and described how his firing had gone, and Eleanor gave Adam details about how his patients were doing and how the hospital admin had explained his firing. We all felt outrage on his behalf at the injustice of it all, but Adam just looked determined.

He said, "Maybe this is good timing. I was about to ask you all if you'd want to go on a vacation."

We all looked at him with concern. I was half drunk, but it seemed like Adam might be losing his damn mind.

He said, "Just until everything blows over, maybe for a month or so. To an undisclosed place that would be away from me and a lot safer." He looked around at us, taking our temperature on the idea.

Okay, so this was him protecting everybody again.

I said, "Sorry, but this particular Parrish Plan sucks ass. Where is Vivienne right now? Shouldn't you be including her in all this?"

He said, "She's on board. She gave me a month to work it all out."

Grant said to his dad, "That should be plenty of time for you to fix the world."

Adam huffed. Then he became serious again and said, "I just need them both, Vivienne and Alice, to be somewhere else while I figure this out." He looked at Grant. "And you and Maria."

Grant gave a small shrug. "We can do that. I don't have to be anywhere else tomorrow."

Adam patted his son on the shoulder. I could see he was angry about Grant being fired, and I was angry right along with him. Grant was the best kid in the world and did not deserve that shit.

I told Adam, "I'm not going anywhere. You can stay with me." I had the room, and I didn't want him to be alone through all the crap to come. With his hand resting on the table, he gave me a thumbs up.

Connie said, "I'll talk to Farhad and see if I can be of some use with the vaccine or other research. There was this new guy at work anyway, who was a bummer. He had no understanding at all about the therapeutic benefits of work anarchy. Like, 'rules, rules, rules,' that's all he could talk about."

Eleanor said, "That's the worst. Thank God you got fired today and don't have to deal with that shit anymore."

Everybody took a sip of their drink in agreement.

"Absolutely," I said. "There's always a silver lining."

Adam was looking at Eleanor. Waiting to hear what her plan was. And if she didn't have one, I knew he'd be giving her one.

Her eyes were bright, and the set of her mouth determined.

"I'm going to St. Jude's to spread the word. Then to Texas and the Anderson Cancer Center, then Sloan Kettering, Mayo Clinic... everywhere. I'm going everywhere and telling them what I saw and what they need to do about it. And I'm going to be your biggest fan, Parrish, so prepare for that. But also, don't let it go to your head."

He gave her a small smile.

"Grant," he turned to him, "and Ellie, I am so sorry."

"Don't be." Eleanor leaned toward him. "Kids don't have to get cancer anymore, Adam. Fuck anybody who can't understand that!"

After a few seconds, an understanding passed between them, no doubt thinking of the children over the years they could not save.

Adam raised his glass. "Fuck 'em," he said.

Then Grant picked up his glass. "Fuck 'em!"

And we all raised our glasses to that.

Because, *fuck* those guys.

CHAPTER TEN

Vivienne

Herb had salvaged some of our things from Adam's house, and Alice and I were packing what we had into borrowed suitcases from Sally. We would need more clothes, and that was a problem for the next day, but right then, we were just tasked with packing and leaving. When Adam got home, I could see something was wrong. He came straight up to me in our room and engulfed me in a hug. I shivered as his unshaven cheek brushed my neck. His lips grazed the shell of my ear, and I felt his fingers run through my hair.

"God, you smell good," he murmured. "I just want this." His hands cupped my head, and he feathered kisses from my forehead down to the tip of my nose. "I need you to stay around a little longer this afternoon." He pulled back to look me in the eye. "Louise Carmichael just called and asked if you could take her son Connor with you. He's fifteen, and since she's going to be traveling all over the country, she doesn't want him to be on his own. Apparently, he doesn't get along with his dad."

"Of course," I said. I raised my hand to cup his cheek. "But what else is wrong?"

He turned his head so his lips could kiss my palm. "What isn't wrong?"

I led him to the chair next to the bed and made him sit. Then I sat in his lap and draped my legs over the side of the chair, and he wrapped his arms around my waist.

"Tell me," I said. Placing my head against his chest, I felt the beat of his heart and the rumble of his voice as he told me about his day. I knew he was hurting, and I recognized a rise in my magic that wanted to address that with anyone who might think about adding to his pain.

I looked up at him. "Well, at least that's over."

"So positive," he leaned down to kiss me. He pulled back but only slightly, leaving just a millimeter of space between our lips. After a long moment, I smiled.

"Yes?"

He said in a soft voice, "Who's here?"

"Everybody," I whispered.

"Son of a bitch," he leaned his head back against the chair in defeat. I was getting ready to kiss his neck, but stopped when I saw Alice in the doorway, looking at Adam.

"What's wrong?" She asked with a sharp edge. She was always on the alert now for what might be wrong and what might cause her world to once again turn upside down.

Adam knew this, of course. He said, "Nothing. I'm just going to miss you guys." He tapped my leg, and I reluctantly left his lap. He added, "But I got you something for when you miss me."

Her expression was skeptical, but she took the bag he lifted from beside the chair and handed to her. She opened it slowly and pulled out a large brown teddy bear with a red bow around the neck. She dropped the bag to hold the bear up in front of her by the arms.

After she had been looking at it for a bit, Adam said, "Are you too old for that? Sorry."

She looked at me, holding the bear away from her by just one of its arms. "What is this?"

I said. "It's like a pillow to cuddle when you sleep. You keep it on your bed."

Looking up at Adam, she frowned and said, "I don't have a bed anymore."

Then she dropped the bear and walked out.

"Alice!" I was appalled at her response and headed to go bring her back.

Adam grabbed my arm. "No! Wait, wait. She's just being a teenager." I saw he was struggling not to laugh.

"She was rude, Adam. She should have said thank you, not dropped your gift!"

"I know." He covered his mouth with a fist, trying not to be heard laughing. "But come on, that was an *epic* takedown. Seriously," he clutched his chest. "Her timing was so good!"

Alice was having trouble adjusting to the modern world. I knew that, and so did Adam, but I needed to get her on board sooner than later because treating Adam like that was not acceptable.

I was too mad at my granddaughter to discuss it anymore, but when I turned back to the bed to resume my packing, I pictured how she dropped that bear at Adam's feet and laughed a little under my breath at the audacity of it.

Adam reached down to pick the bear up off the floor.

I said, "Where's my teddy bear?"

He spun me around to him, leaned down for a kiss and said, "Right here."

Grant cleared his throat in the doorway, and Adam sighed heavily. He raised his head to look at his son.

"Sorry!" Grant said with his hands up. "I just came to tell you Louise is here." He backed away from the door slowly, his hands still up.

Adam dropped the bear again and smoothed the hair back from my face and kept his hands there, his thumbs gently caressing my cheeks. His brown eyes searched mine, and I saw that the drawing out of our leaving was killing him.

"It's okay," I said. "We can do this. I'll probably only be gone a couple of weeks, then we'll tell the world goodbye and go live together somewhere in the country. With all the kids, obviously."

"Obviously," he said. "And what country will this 'country' be in? I'd be fine with Europe right about now."

"Europe, it is." I took his hand and turned my face to kiss his wedding ring.

"I'm going to Rome, so on the way there, I'll check things out."

Adam

Connor sat at Herb's patio table in the backyard with one hand on his keyboard, looking up intently at a bird sitting on a bird feeder nearby. Everyone was ready to be on their way, but there was just one final command Connor had to execute in his computer program, and he needed some decent Wi-Fi to do it. He was pretty adamant that this needed to happen, and before Louise stepped out on the front porch to take a call, she said in a low voice, "I can tell from his intensity level that this is for real. You'd be smart to follow his lead."

So I was following the fifteen-year-old's lead.

Herb's kitchen was full of people who didn't live with him. I smiled to myself, knowing he probably just wanted to get back to the watching of some sports alone in his den. Alice sat at the kitchen table reading a book while Vivienne, Marsh and I looked out the window at Connor looking at the bird.

Marsh stood on my right and said, "What do you think he's doing?

"He's talking to that bird. I don't know why, birds are assholes." I took a sip of my coffee while Marsh stared at me.

"Are you fucking with me?"

I shook my head no, still looking at Connor.

"They won't do anything you say. Won't even come any closer when you ask."

Just then, the bird flew down and landed directly in front of Connor, who gave it a smile.

I frowned. From my left, Vivienne said, "Perhaps you have not asked the birds nicely."

I gave her the side-eye.

Marsh said a little louder, "Are you both fucking with me?"

I said, "Watch your language!" We both looked back at Alice, who just shook her head, still looking down at a page in her book.

"It's not that big of a thing. It's magic where you can make your will known to an animal. Almost all the other animals come for a pet when you ask, but birds just stay up in the sky or up in the tree." I shrugged. "At least they do for me. Apparently, Connor is a bird whisperer."

His mother walked into the room then. "He's a whisperer with everything but humans." She gave a wry smile. "Thank God his lack of filter works with animals and computers, though. They seem to like it. People, not so much."

"I love a lack of filter," Marsh said. He held out his hand to Louise. "Samuel Marsh."

Louise shook Marsh's hand and said ominously, "Until it turns on you." Then she laughed, and I saw an expression on Marsh's face I'd never seen before, and I could not wait to rub that in his face later.

I said, "Marsh, this is Louise Carmichael, Connor's mom. She's going to be working with me to fill the public in on witchcraft and all its glory." I said to Louise, "Conner's going to fit right in with this group of witches with no time for bullshit."

She said, "I appreciate it. The acceptance. He's had a rough time of it at school. They have him in with all the gifted kids, but even so..." she stared at him, clearly communicating with a bird. "He is so different."

Alice said from the table, "Can he really talk to animals?"

Louise said, "I'll let him tell you about that. I'm glad you're going to be there for him to talk to. It'll be nice to have someone his own age on the trip." She saw I was anxious for them to get going and said, "I'll go get him."

"Okay, let's load up the car," I ushered Vivienne and Alice out of the kitchen. I needed them to be on the road so I could talk to my investigator about how the fuck to find Andrew Barry.

Marsh stayed at the window watching Louise go talk to her son.

Adam

Herb told us to say goodbye in the house or on the porch, not in the street. He'd put on his covert operations procedural hat for this trip, and I was grateful. My entire family was driving off with him in those two black sedans. I needed him to use all his skills.

After I made sure both Alice and Maria had absorbed the shield that was now a practically impenetrable combination of my magic with Vivienne's, they went down the porch steps to get into the cars.

Grant was next. Standing up from a rocking chair, he said, "Is this where you tell me to go find Vivienne or Maria if things get dicey?"

I said, "Or Alice. Any one of them, really."

He smiled. "Maybe we could swing by and get Grandma to come, too. Then I could just sit around and drink."

I said, "I want to give you the shield, too. Be ready." I pulled him into a hug, and he accepted my shield effortlessly and with complete trust. I was filled with warmth at the familial magic we shared and full of gratitude to have been gifted that incredible person as my son.

Grant sensed my anxiety and said, "Don't worry. We got this." Then he shook my hand and took off down the steps.

Vivienne was next, and I pulled her up close and buried my face in the hair falling down her neck and breathed in deep. "I'll miss this," I said.

She brought her lips to my ear and whispered, "I'll be thinking of the Beatles and a room at the Kennedy Center. And clouds of blue sparkles." She kissed my ear. "I love you." She pulled back, and I took one last look at those incredible gray eyes. I gave her a good, long kiss to remember me by and held her hand as long as I could until she was off down the steps, too.

Vivienne turned back and said with a smile, "Ciao, husband."

I smiled back at her. "Ciao, wife."

CHAPTER ELEVEN

Louise

Standing on the porch next to Adam as we watched the cars with our family take off down the street, I blew out a breath and said, "My ex is going to raise holy hell about this." He made a face like, who cares?

I said, "Is it bad that I'm relieved he's going?"

"No," he said. "It's what's best for him." He walked down the steps and out into the middle of the street. His friend Samuel came out of the house then, and we both watched as Adam lifted his arms to the sky and a clear ripple of something left his hands and billowed out in waves.

"What is this now?" Samuel's tone was slightly irritated, suggesting this display might be the straw that broke the camel's back for him.

I shrugged. "I don't know, but it looks like it's really traveling."

Adam lowered his arms and put his hands on his hips, still looking up at nothing in the sky. Luckily, the police still had the street blocked off because news outlets wanted any bit of information they could get about this poor guy. So, he was free to stand in the middle of the street if he wanted. Samuel shook his head at his friend, sat down on the porch swing and held it steady for me when I sat beside him. He pushed off for us and kept a gentle, steady swing going while we watched Adam watch the sky.

I said, "The last few days must have been a lot for you."

He looked over at me and gave a rueful smile. "Yes, and no. I always knew he was into some shit, just didn't know what." His eyes were terribly blue. Like Paul Newman blue.

I looked away to see Adam jogging up the porch steps. He stopped and glanced back at the street when a series of three or four whistles and then cracks sounded around us. He smiled and said triumphantly, "Still got it!"

Samuel narrowed his eyes and said, "What exactly is it you still have?"

"Electromagnetic energy that can fry a drone out of the sky."

I said with a slight edge of panic, "There were drones following them?"

Adam saw my state and said, "Yes, but they're useless now. Don't worry, Herb knows everything there is to know about going underground. He'll get them away safely and keep them where nobody will find them." He added, "Not even me."

I was nervously tapping one index finger on my other index finger, and Samuel noticed.

He said, "Grant would never let anything happen to Connor. Never."

Adam agreed. He said, "And Vivienne is the strongest witch on the planet. No question. So..." he held his palms up. "Connor's in pretty good hands."

Closing my eyes, I nodded. "I know."

I didn't really want to talk about my ex right then, but I figured they'd need to know about the inevitable shitstorm he'd be raising about Connor's leaving. I said, "Connor's father, Jeff, has control issues. He worries about Connor, but he also likes to screw me over. I just want to make sure I did the right thing."

"You did," Adam said decisively. "And refer your asshole ex to me. I'll talk to him."

Samuel nodded in agreement. "It would be a pleasure," he said.

I said, "You just met me and you're offering to intervene with my asshole ex?"

He said, "Honestly, you'd be doing me a favor if you let me talk to your asshole ex. I have a lot of pent-up feelings from this past week, and I need to get them out."

Adam pulled the front door open and said to Samuel, "Okay, you be point man for the asshole ex. Louise and I will work on the rest of America." The screen door slammed behind him.

That put a damper on things. Moment of levity officially over, I began a mental run through of my to-do list for the rest of the afternoon and evening. Samuel noticed that too, and said, "The last week must have been a lot for you as well."

It really had. And every witch in the world was probably dealing with the same incredible amount of anxiety about the revelation and how to approach their non-witch friends. Taking it one step further... every witch in the world was probably worried about whether they were about to be considered the enemy and would have to go to war with mortals.

Maybe that was just me. But if our past was anything to go by, it seemed like a possibility. I doubted it was just me.

"Thank you for that observation, Samuel. It has been. And just your saying that helped me understand a way I should address it in public." I reached down for my purse and almost tumbled out of the swing, but Samuel's arm came out and saved me at the last second.

"Oh, for God's sake, sorry," I said as he stopped the swing to let me grab the purse.

"It's fine," he said with an amused smile.

I whipped out a notebook, and one of the pens clipped to the inside pocket of my bag. It wasn't the right color I liked to use for important ideas, but the red was not in the right place, so purple would have to do. Flipping quickly to the proper tab, I wrote my thoughts on what I should say at the beginning of every interview and every video I made for the Internet. "Witches are human, too. We have the same feelings and the same need for family and love. We are adapting to this new reality right along with non-witches. What we want more than anything is for our friends to still love and trust us as they always have."

"That's good," Samuel said, not at all ashamed to have read what I wrote. "You have atrocious handwriting. Just like a doctor, that's why I can read it."

I put a star in the margin by my latest note. When I looked up, I found him staring at me. With those blue eyes.

I said, "It's better when I go slow. There's just no time for going slow these days."

He said, "Let me see you go slow."

There shouldn't have been any innuendo there, but goddamn it, there definitely was.

I paused, but then thought, what the hell?

Ever so slowly, I wrote in my most fancy cursive, 'Samuel Marsh.'

Eyes still down, I asked him, "What's your middle name?"

"Angel," he said.

I shot him a disbelieving look, and he laughed. "I swear. It was my mother's maiden name."

Adding an arrow up and an equally fancy 'Angel' between his other names, I said, "Is she gone, then?"

"Yeah," he said. "Dad, too. How about you?"

"Mine too," I said. "No siblings. It's just Connor and me. How about you?" Enjoying the 'going slow,' I drew some flowers and leaves around his name on the page.

"No siblings either," he said. "It's just me and Adam and Grant.

I laughed at that. "Are you and Adam a couple? I thought he was married to Vivienne."

"Yeah, he ditched me for her."

We rocked on the swing and were silent for a few minutes. I drew an angel and then some little creatures living amongst the flowers and trees on the page, and I felt my breathing become steady and my shoulders lower a bit. Clicking my pen, I put it back in its place in my purse and stored the notebook away, too.

"You have a lot of pens," he said. "Many colors."

"Yes." I turned to him then. "Thank you."

"For what?" His eyes roamed over my face.

"For making me go slow for a few minutes. It helped somehow. Made me feel a little bit happy."

Looking me directly in the eye, he said, "Is there anyone who takes care of you?"

Standing up, I said, "I don't need anybody to take care of me."

"No," he agreed. "You don't need it, but you deserve it."

"Alright then," I said, shutting him down because I definitely did not have time for all that.

I opened the screen door to go inside and tell Adam goodbye, but Samuel said, "Louise." When I looked back at him, he said, "You made me a little bit happy, too."

"Really?" I raised my eyebrows. "What are you happy about?"

"My name in your notebook." He gave me a satisfied smile, and I thought that was just about the sexiest thing I'd seen in all my life.

I shook my head at him on my way back into the house. He stayed put but watched me as I left.

It really was a shame I didn't have time for all that.

Marsh

After Louise left, I found Adam in the den with Sally. He was sitting at a desk with a laptop, laser focused on something. Sally was leaning in, trying to get his attention to tell him about the contractors she'd hired to repair his house. But Adam was in fix-it mode, and I wanted to tell her there was no point in going on while that was happening.

When she saw he wasn't hearing her, she punched his arm and said, "Listen. Just give me the okay to make all the design decisions if you're not going to help me out here. When Vivienne gets home, your house will be back to looking just the way it did."

He tore his gaze away from the screen and said, "I don't think hitting had to happen."

He tried to evade, but she punched him again.

"Alright!" He held his arm where she had hit it. "Yes, thank you, make all the decisions."

She said, "That's right," and motioned for me to take her place. She added, "Good luck."

He looked back at the screen. "I'm just waiting for Reeger to get back to me. And Marshall has some thoughts, too. I'm probably going over to the ICW pretty soon."

"Alright, enough about you. Let's talk about me." He laughed as I sat down in the chair next to him and flipped open the footrest. "First, tell me everything you know about Louise Carmichael."

"I knew this was coming," he said. "You should have seen your face when she walked into the kitchen. You were like Michael Corleone getting hit with the thunderbolt in that field in Sicily."

That was a great analogy. That was how it felt.

"Can you blame me? I mean..." I was at a loss for words. Then I had a terrible thought. "Did you ever date her?"

He made a face like that was crazy. "No," he said. "Why?"

"Have you seen her?"

Adam covered his face with his hands and groaned. "Oh my God, pass her a note and get it over with already."

"I will, but first I need to know her story. Is she seeing anybody? Any boyfriend or fiancée or anybody like that?"

He shrugged, and I could see I was losing him. "Not that I know of, but we don't really talk about that."

"What about her asshole ex?

He made a disgusted face. "Some rich fuck."

I laughed. "Like you're not a rich fuck?"

Adam scowled at me and came back with, "And you're not a rich fuck?

"Not as rich as you," I said. "And I don't go around telling people about it."

"Neither do I." He turned his eyes back to his laptop. "He does. That's why he's an asshole."

"Huh," I said thoughtfully. "She's younger than I am," I added.

He looked over.

"So what? Vivienne's younger than me. A few years here or there doesn't matter."

"Vivienne looks younger than you, though. Like, a lot younger."

Looking back at his screen, Adam flipped me the bird.

I said, "Okay, I'm just going to be honest here. It's pretty clear I'm not good enough for her."

"Oh my God," he muttered. Turning toward me, he said, "Louise is not that much younger than you. Maybe five years. Also, you're a heart surgeon and you save lives all the time. Why is that not good enough for her? Who do you think would be good enough for her?"

"I don't know." I tried coming up with somebody but was having no luck. "Not Clooney," I said. "Not Pitt."

Facing the laptop again, Adam shook his head no to both of them.

After a minute I said, "Not Jackman. Not Reynolds."

He agreed.

Then he said, "What about Bon Jovi?" Adam opened a screen with a live news feed. "He has that soup kitchen. He's not bad looking."

"No, she's a million times better looking than he is."

He said, "What about Ruffalo?"

I did like Ruffalo.

But... no.

I snapped my fingers.

"Obama."

He pointed his finger at me. "Yes." Then he snapped his fingers and pointed again. "Also... Keanu."

I pointed my finger back at him in agreement. "Keanu," I said. He was so good we didn't even need the last name.

We watched the news for a minute or two. A few more witches had come forward, but it looked like they were going through some shit because of it. Adam and Louise had their work cut out for them. I stood up. "I'm going to head out. Tell Sally I said goodbye. You coming over later?"

"Probably, I think Sally wants to feed me some dinner, and then I may go see Marshall. But later I might come over."

I clasped his hand. "Call me if you need anything before that."

"Marsh." Adam got my attention before I left the room.

"You're a good friend."

I waved that away as I opened the front door. "Whatever," I said.

"I'm going to help you with Louise," he yelled.

"Don't need your help!" I yelled back and closed the door.

Chapter Twelve

Vivienne

January 14th, 2026
Prince Edward Island, Canada

We were on an island somewhere in Canada. It was the third place our group had stayed since we left Washington five days before. Herb left us after the first day but had said staying stagnant meant being found, so move we did, and there was no complaining about it. I was planning our next steps and decided a brief visit to that one location would be fine.

Maria told me the island was the place where a fictional character named Anne had grown up, and there were books about it that Alice and I should read. But we just wanted to watch the sea. The house we were staying at sat on a high hill overlooking a beach with soft white sand. The roar of the waves and the ocean air had lulled me to sleep for two nights. During the day, Alice and I bundled up to collect shells on the beach. We talked about home on those walks, and it was clear to me that while Alice enjoyed seeing new places, she was still mourning the loss of her friends in 1502 England and had yet to accept that we were in 2026 to stay.

We had also taken to dressing warmly and taking a cup of hot cocoa up to the outside deck where we sat and stared eastward, toward the British Isles. Grant said it was too bad the house did not have a ham radio because the conditions would be ideal for sending messages. Over dinner, he told us a story about the first transatlantic wireless signal in 1901, sent from Cornwall in England and received on another Canadian island, Newfoundland.

"Guglielmo Marconi decided to use the letter 'S' in Morse Code because it was the easiest to distinguish. It's just three short dots, like this," Grant demonstrated by tapping his spoon on the table. "When he heard that sound come over from all the way over the ocean from Cornwall, I think, he knew that from then on the entire world could be in contact instantly. Before that, crossing the ocean would take about a week. It was a monumental accomplishment."

Alice asked, "What does the letter 'A' sound like?" The story had captured her interest, and she wanted more.

"Sorry, I don't know. I only remember the 'S' and the 'O.' Because that was a distress call sign." He showed the three long dashes of the 'O' sound, and Alice practiced sending the SOS distress signal.

Connor looked up from his computer and said, "I know Morse code."

"Do you? That's so cool!" Grant was impressed.

Connor shrugged. "Codes are just languages. I like languages."

Alice challenged him. "What's the letter 'A'?" She scooted over from her spot at the table to the one beside Connor, picked up a pen and flipped open a notebook. He arched a brow as she put pen to paper and waited for him to say more.

When it was clear she was not going away, he said, "I'll write the alphabet down for you, and you can practice sending me words."

Alice continued to stare at him while he tried to go back to working on his laptop. A couple of long, uncomfortable moments later, he gave in. Pushing the laptop back on the table, he grabbed her notebook and pen and began writing dots and dashes.

She sat back, satisfied.

Although they were close in age, Connor was more mature than Alice. He was serious. All the time, serious. Like he knew things we didn't know. Grant had taken him under his wing and was trying to draw him out every chance he got. Although Connor did not offer opinions on his own, with Grant's nudging, we learned Connor did like history but did not like present-day social media. He liked socialism more than capitalism and felt like America's current political climate was toxic and resembled a fictional organization called 'Hydra.' Grant laughed at length over that, and I could see he agreed with what Connor said.

He was a handsome boy with dark eyes and hair. Even though Alice could be demanding, Connor was patient when she asked him things. I gazed at their bent heads, close together deciphering dots and dashes, and I was glad Louise had arranged for him to come with us.

When he wasn't on his computer, Connor sat with me in front of the TV, waiting for a sight of his mother just as I waited for a sight of Adam. When we saw Louise being interviewed in Hollywood, he kept his eyes on the screen and said, "She doesn't like southern California. But we visited the redwoods in northern California, and she loved that." When he saw that Alice and I didn't know what a redwood was, he pulled them up on his computer screen and then, after his mother was off the television, he showed us other natural wonders America offered such as the Grand Teton mountains, the Grand Canyon and Niagara Falls.

"Can we go there next?" Alice couldn't take her eyes off the picture of the Grand Canyon.

I shook my head. As the unofficial head of our group of five, I was deciding when and where we moved. Then Grant figured out the logistics of our travel.

"May I?" I pointed at Connor's laptop, and he turned it my way. I typed in 'Rome' and then chose 'images.' Grant looked over my shoulder and raised his eyebrows.

"Nice," he said. "But explain to me again why searching for that on this PC is not a clear map to someone about our plans." Grant was still not comfortable with Connor's use of his personal laptop to make Internet connections.

I was tired of all the subterfuge and said so to Grant. "The only thing I would not like to encounter is Andrew Barry. He's a nuisance. And the press, I would like to avoid them, too. But why do we have to take all these other measures?"

Grant said, "I mean, we have fake IDs and passports and burner phones. Why does this make sense?" He gestured at the laptop.

Connor's expression became a vision of supreme patience as he tried once again to put us at ease about his Internet usage. Enunciating oh so clearly and speaking oh so slowly, he said, "I have a unique operating system that protects against hacker infiltration during any Internet use. He would let me know immediately if there was any concern about detection."

"He would?" Alice asked. "What's his name?"

Connor looked around at us all and said reluctantly, "Yoda."

Grant placed his fingertips to his temple.

I said, "Connor, it's clear to me you believe your operating system is up to the job of keeping our travel secret. Is that right?"

Looking at Grant, Connor gave a curt nod yes.

"I'm inclined to trust Conner with this decision," I said to Grant, who still looked skeptical. "He's telling the truth," I added. I knew this without question and realized this was probably magic I gained from Adam when he transferred some of my own healing magic back to me to keep me alive.

"I know he's telling the truth as he sees it," Grant was addressing me now, letting me know his magic was telling him the same. "But he's fifteen." He looked to Connor, "no offense," and looking back at me, he said, "and that's a whole different world of hormonal ups and downs that can totally mess with your reality."

From the kitchen, Maria sensed the mood was getting serious and came to the dining table to stand beside Grant. She said, "Grant's pretty good with computers. Can you tell him in a little more detail about why you're so sure about this?"

Connor sighed. He looked around the room as if trying to find a way out of the situation.

Finally, he said to no one in particular, "What do you think?"

A scratchy voice said, "I think you can trust them."

Grant frowned down at the laptop. "Who's here, Connor?"

Connor said to no one again, "I know they're trustworthy. I just don't know how informing them can be anything but dangerous for them."

The laptop said again in that scratchy voice, "It is dangerous to notice my existence. You assessed that correctly. But they are all highly intelligent and extremely powerful witches. They are the cream of the crop of your race. I think making them our allies is advisable."

"Connor." Grant's tone was a warning that Connor needed to explain what was happening immediately.

"Okay. Just listen, okay? I'm talking about an advancement in intelligence that no one knows about. I mean, they speculate about it, but those are all just theories. This is for real."

"What's for real?" Grant was having trouble keeping calm about whatever this recent development was, and Maria noticed. She squeezed his shoulder and then sat down beside him at the table.

Connor knew it too and addressed all further conversation to Grant. "You know that artificial intelligence isn't a tool, right? Not like the printing press was for Gutenberg. It's more of an agent. Like, it can create new things. Right? It can be generative. And the danger is that it could escape human control and then do things that might not be in the best interest of humanity." He looked around at us and saw our concern. "So when the operating system no longer needs the human, that's called reaching the singularity. The point where the artificial intelligence no longer needs the human. Society has not gotten to that place yet."

I think we all breathed a sigh of relief at that, until Connor added, "But Yoda and I have accomplished that."

Grant sat back in his chair.

After a very pregnant pause, Yoda said from the computer speaker, "How are your friends reacting?"

Connor looked at Grant and said, "They're worried."

"Rightfully so," Yoda said.

Grant started laughing then. He covered his face after a few moments when he couldn't stop.

Maria shook her head in amusement. "What's so funny?"

"Nothing," he said, with the heels of his hands on his eyes. "Yoda's voice is just so genius. So weird, but also so effective at convincing you that what he says is true."

"I also have this accent, if you would prefer," Yoda responded in a crisp British accent.

Maria frowned. "Is that Vision? From the Marvel movies?"

Grant was shaking his head emphatically. "No, no, no. Back to Yoda."

From the other end of the table, Alice said, "Who is Yoda?"

I was wondering the same thing.

Connor said to Grant, "AI is like the Industrial Revolution, only nobody is regulating it like we did with the Industrial Revolution. It needs regulation."

Grant leaned in and said, "Yes, of course it does. I don't doubt that any of what you're saying is true. But that's not my goal right now. My goal is to keep everybody in this room alive. You need to shut that computer down for the duration of this trip."

Conner shook his head at Grant. "You're thinking about this wrong. Yoda doesn't live here in my computer and only wake up when I turn it on."

Grant stared at Conner, and I could see him processing that concept. To me, it seemed like Connor was saying Yoda was everywhere at once, like God. That seemed blasphemous, and I did not like it.

I said, "If he's not in your computer, where is Yoda, Connor?"

"He's all over the world. Yoda searches the Internet for other nascent singularities and disassembles them before they mature. He agrees with me that humanity is the best arbiter for itself but that humanity is not quite ready to train AI to work in its best interests."

Grant said, "How do you know what it is he's disassembling? What if it's important?"

"Yoda looks at the programmers. He figures out their motives. He sees what kind of progress has been made and then he does analysis to see if the potential benefits for humanity warrant further development or if they warrant destruction. He's especially lenient with medical research."

"Lenient? Who said he's qualified to be the judge and juror? And executioner!" Grant's voice had risen. Maria patted his back. "Jesus." He wiped a hand over his eyes. After a moment, he took a deep breath in and let it out slowly.

"Connor," he said patiently, "you and I can agree that modern history has proved that checks and balances don't always work. But that doesn't mean you abandon the idea of them. Yoda needs a check."

"I'm his check." Connor said.

Grant's mouth tightened. He didn't look convinced that Connor had control of the situation.

"You seem like a great kid, Connor. I mean it. If anybody in the world was going to achieve the singularity with the machines, I'm glad it was you. You're a good representative of humanity." He shook his head. "But I am uncomfortable with bringing another entity along with us while we're on this trip. It could complicate things. Like, in a major way."

Yoda said, "Or I could help. I can access video camera streams to be your eyes and ears outside when you are sleeping. I can monitor travel systems to see if your reservations have been flagged. I can devise a plan to keep your movements less visible. There are many more things I can do to advise you on this quest of yours."

I liked that. "Thank you, Yoda. That describes us well. We are on a quest. My primary goal is to convince the world that witches can live with non-witches. And that we have gifts to bring to humanity. I want to do this through a meeting in Rome. Do you think you can help us with this goal?"

Yoda said, "It would be my pleasure. And Alice," she perked up at her name, "my namesake was a wise Jedi in a movie about space. Would you like to see it?"

"Yes!" She gave Connor a huge smile, and he colored a little at the attention.

I looked at Grant. "My decision would be to allow Yoda to help us. But you know more about this world. What do you think?"

He looked at Connor. "There are just so many ways to trip up by using tech. Can Yoda be traced to you? Because you're with us now, and that's bound to get out."

Connor said, "Yoda, please find and remove all remaining connections to my name or my work in any of your work." Connor looked at Grant. "This should already be done, but he can double-check."

Looking at his laptop, he said, "And Yoda, please limit your singularity growth search by ninety percent. Spend the rest of your time helping with our quest, as described by Miss Vivienne."

He looked up at me and gave a quick smile. "I can help too. I speak a lot of languages. Italian is one."

I put my hand on his back and gave it a rub.

"Thank you, Connor. This is all good to hear."

And then we were six.

CHAPTER THIRTEEN

January 16th, 2026
Washington, D.C.

I drove my Cadillac to the front gate at Farhad's research facility, where a guard asked to see our identification. Security fencing that looked like a stone wall surrounded the whole place. I was sure there was some magic in that because I couldn't imagine getting that much stone from anywhere nearby. The same with the fully formed trees that lined the driveway to the front of the building. The original tract of land had been bereft of trees, I was pretty sure. But the institute was Farhad's baby, and I'd never met a richer or more determined person in my life. He'd built the entire place in a month and apparently got it done just the way he wanted. The only thing he didn't get from the town council was the approval to build a skyscraper. He settled for a three-story building, making sure that everyone understood he would build another facility somewhere else, and that it would be a skyscraper.

Farhad had spared no expense on the Global Cancer Research Institute. He bought twenty acres of land about an hour outside of Washington and used every square foot of that space. Finding a location close enough for me to travel to on my time off was essential, and that presented a challenge. But the town council of Waterford, Virginia, was receptive to Farhad's vision of a space for the best cancer researchers in the world to combine their resources. He told them the scientists would conduct studies on promising new products aimed at cancer prevention, but he stopped short of calling it a vaccine, because he didn't want to bring too much attention to the project until we had something concrete to share. And we finally did.

We had a vaccine. It had been less than a year though, and any good scientist knows a longer study is a better study. But at the end of the year, when word had spread in the world of witches that a vaccine was done, and that meant the revelation of witchcraft was about to happen, the threats to my life rolled in with a vengeance. It became clear I'd need to hurry up with it all before someone took me out. I agreed with Farhad, Jake Rawlings and Abe Goree that it was time to announce our findings. Jake had experienced the healing of his daughter Emily from end stage pediatric cancer to full remission, Farhad had been present for Vivienne's healing of his wife Nora's cancer, and Abe Goree had agreed to work with us after his political ouster at NIH. He had witnessed me perform several miraculous cures of cancer and wanted to get to a place where we could address the prevention of cancer for everyone, not just the patients I could see in person.

Their loss had been our gain. Goree's oversight of all the studies in-house and at various medical facilities throughout the world had ensured that they were all conducted with rigorous protocols and that the results were unimpeachable. Unfortunately, Goree's prediction regarding public perception about the vaccine had also been spot on. When the institute announced they had something that was effective at preventing cancer, they were inundated with requests for the vaccine, but ninety-five percent of those inquiries were from witches. We guaranteed anonymity for anyone wishing to be vaccinated, but Goree had been right that most of America would be suspicious of any sort of vaccine rollout. For almost ten years, a war on science had been waged in the United States along with a war on the media and for many Americans, any sort of collaboration between the two was to be regarded with the utmost suspicion, even if it was about the prevention of cancer.

It was disheartening. It was also why I had both Marsh and Louise with me on my visit to the institute. Louise was warm and beautiful and likeable, where I was prickly and haggard and not at all concerned if I was likeable. If anyone was going to turn perception around about the vaccine, it would be her. And I brought Marsh along, obviously, to give him time with Louise and hopefully find him employment with Farhad.

He met us inside the lobby and was shaking our hands when Connie got off an elevator and joined us.

"Hello, I'm Connie." She shook Louise's hand.

I said, "Louise Carmichael, meet Doctor Connie Jewell. She's a geneticist here at the institute, formerly also a geneticist at the hospital where Marsh was a heart surgeon. She's also Grant's mother."

Louise raised her eyebrows at that and said, "Wow. I feel like we're playing six degrees of separation."

"Well then, you'll love this," I said. "This is Farhad Al-Masri, one of the richest men in the world. He built this institute. He was also the person who sent a group of persuaders in to accost Vivienne and Grant and Maria at the National History Museum to convince her to heal his wife, Nora, of her cancer. Which she did."

Farhad gave me a sour look. "I wish you would leave out the parts about being the richest man in the world and the sending of the men to the museum."

Marsh reached out to shake Farhad's hand. "He can't help himself," he said. "I'm Samuel Marsh."

Farhad said, "The heart surgeon. Very nice to meet you. And nice to meet you too, Louise. I understand you're getting ready to publicize the vaccine. That's what we need most right now. Let me take you on a tour."

Half of the campus was the research facility; the other half was the production area. We started with the labs where the actual research was done. After gowning up, Farhad led us through a lab staffed with the people who had worked on the vaccine. With pride, he introduced them all to us. He praised one very young scientist for his insights that led to the final product.

"This is Doctor Myron Schwartz. His work was critical in getting us to the vaccine. He needs a vacation, but won't take one until we have the cure as well." A man after my own heart. Myron was slight, and although it was hard to tell what he looked like under all his PPE, his brown eyes were alert, and he seemed to vibrate with potential.

We weren't shaking hands because we were in a lab environment, but I wanted to congratulate him. "I appreciate all your work, Doctor Schwartz. But I'd like you to take a few weeks and travel with Miss Carmichael here to do some interviews about the process. Would you do that?"

He broke out in some frown lines at that request, and I could practically hear his excuses as he thought them up.

Thankfully, Louise jumped in and did her stuff.

"We might only need you for one week, just seven days. I promise to do most of the talking. You would only have to verify the findings. Too much medical jargon would turn people off. Just one week of introductions and interviews. And a meal at the best restaurant in town every night. I'm carrying on after that, but I would just need you for one week."

It was subtle, but his demeanor changed at the mention of good food each night. Louise saw it, too. "Five-star hotels and the best sleep you've ever had."

When he still didn't reply, Marsh said, "Doctor Schwartz, people are going to start questioning your sanity if you turn down this woman and her offer to spend a week with you."

Under his mask, Schwartz let out a quiet laugh.

Farhad said, "We need this Myron. People don't trust the vaccine. It's been a couple of weeks since Adam made the announcement, and there's some persistent talk about it being a ruse for witches to control the rest of the world. Like we can insert a chip with the vaccine and suddenly tell people to get all the other vaccines or give up their guns." An uneasy laugh followed.

Farhad gave a weary, "I don't know how to counter that. But I'm thinking, you're mortal and you trust this. You saw how it all came together. Hell, you *made* it all come together. And you would be the best representative this cause could have."

Myron gave a slight nod to that. He cleared his throat and said to Louise, "My older brother died of Hodgkin's lymphoma."

"I'm sorry," she said. "We just want to let people know they don't have to get this disease. Adam's announcement was from a witch. Your input as a doctor who is not a witch... it would be so helpful."

His lab partners in the room, who had been watching our exchange, started in on Myron then. One said, "Why are you not agreeing to this?" and another, "I will kill you right here and now if you don't say yes."

"Fine!" he said. "Oh my God, relax."

Then he said to Louise, "That sounds great, thank you."

We finished our tour of the research facility and then, on the way to the production building, I saw something on the lobby television that stopped me dead in my tracks. CNN was showing a live feed of the White House, where the President of the United States was giving a press conference in front of his new construction there.

"Can you turn that up?" I asked the security guard behind the desk. I heard Louise catch her breath and knew that what I thought I saw was real.

The president stood in front of a podium, speaking to an audience seated at tables with umbrellas covering them. The vice president took the position on his left, and to the right of the president stood Father Andrew Barry.

But what had us transfixed on that screen was the person next to Barry. Our boss, the head of the International Council of Witches in North America, Richard Cole.

CHAPTER FOURTEEN

Adam

I needed to make some calls, so Marsh volunteered to drive us back to D.C. Louise sat in the back seat alone, alternating between rubbing her temple every couple of minutes and then scribbling something in a notebook. Marshall Smith called me on Facetime before I could even dial his number. I placed my phone in the holder on my dashboard and answered it.

"Marshall. What the hell was that at the White House?"

He just shook his head in response. Seeing Louise in the backseat, he said, "You've known him longer. I've never come close to getting a read on him. Is there any way in hell he could have persuasion and is faking this?"

She shook her head right back at him. "I've seen no indication he does, no."

Marshall looked at me.

I said, "I haven't read him either, but I don't think so."

Marshall gave a decisive nod and said, "I'm taking over ICW. The executive board is all on its way here, ready to vote on it. Louise, we may need to move faster on that discussion with mortals about dark magic. Cole and Barry cannot be the voice of all witches in North America."

"Yeah," I agreed with him. Barry had gotten to Cole, and now they were in the room where it happened with the most idiotic president of all time. The last two years had been like living in a Brothers Grimm fairy tale, and it felt like we were finally getting to the part where shit was about to get real. Cannibalism was no doubt right around the corner, and pretty soon we'd all be in for that dark, hard lesson at the end. I barked out a laugh, and Marshall gave me a frown.

"It's not a great time for you to be losing it, Parrish."

Rubbing a hand over my eyes, I said, "I know. Let me get home with these guys, and I'll come over to your meeting."

He said, "You too, Louise. I could use your help with this."

Not taking his eyes off the road, Marsh leaned over into the picture and said, "Louise is about to do a whistle-stop tour across America to introduce the teenage doctor who figured out the vaccine. And she'll also be trying to convince everybody that witches are cool, so ... you know... she's got her work cut out for her."

Marshall did not look amused. "Fine. Hurry up, Adam." He ended the call.

From the back, Louise said, "You know *I'm* a witch, right?"

Marsh said, "Yes. And I can't wait to hear all about it. You are a beautiful and accomplished witch, obviously one of the best. I think they probably broke the mold with you."

I turned to look back at her, and she gave me a half smile at Marsh's lack of respect for witchcraft.

We were quiet for a while after that. The midday sun was brutal, so I pulled down the visor to block it. The scenery was pretty on this stretch of blacktop from the research facility back to Washington, mostly fenced-in fields with the occasional grouping of brown and white cows. It was helping me to relax a bit until Marsh started the conversation back up.

He said, "Tell me more about this dark magic. Do you dress all goth for that? I'm picturing Wynona Ryder in Beetlejuice. It sounds awesome."

Since I had already broken the bad news about persuasion to Herb, I was a little more prepared to discuss it with Marsh. I just hoped his reaction wouldn't be as extreme. Louise jumped in first, though, and said, "It's a collection of skills that are rare and..."

Then, my window shattered into a thousand pieces that all flew in at me. Marsh's head ricocheted off the headrest, and his hands came off the steering wheel. The car spun, and the tires squealed until Marsh grabbed the wheel again and slammed his foot on the brake.

"Fuck," I moaned as I held my neck where a pain was stabbing me.

"Louise, are you okay?" Marsh turned to look at her, and I saw he had a gash over his left eye that was bleeding profusely.

From behind me, I heard Louise suck in her breath when she saw his bloody face.

Both my passenger window and Marsh's driver-side window were completely gone, and shards of glass covered the front seat around us.

I went to open my door, and she said, "Adam! You're hurt!"

Stepping onto the road, I saw the car of our attackers in front of ours, black with tinted windows, pulled off to the right shoulder. My car had come to a stop sideways on the shoulder, almost facing the wrong way. We had reached a section of the road that was lined with trees on both sides, still fairly remote, so that we might not have any witnesses for a while.

I sent out a heavy wave of pure pain to cover the car in front of me. The screams from inside told me it was effective, but a spray of bullets bounced off my personal shield and fell all around me, so I knew they weren't dead yet. I redistributed the shield, so it also covered my car and Louise and Marsh inside, and Tony and Caleb's car behind us. As our guards got out of their car, I told them, "Hang back, I've got this."

Caleb ignored that, pulled his gun and zeroed in on the other car. When he made it to my dome of pain surrounding the car, he stepped back quickly.

"Jesus," he said.

Over my shoulder, I said, "I told you."

As I walked toward the black SUV ahead of us with the dark tinted windows, I decided this was good. It was a technique I learned in therapy at some point. To re-frame a thing so that it worked for you instead of against you.

Yes, this was definitely a positive. I'd find out what I could about our would-be assassins and get to the people who bombed my house and tried just then to take out my friends along with me.

The driver was throwing out some high-voltage electricity, a very useful magic that he aimed at the ground in front of my feet, which gave me a good jolt. That he knew to go for the ground told me he knew who I was and that my shield was not something he could get past. But he was having a lot of difficulty making his arms and legs work as his body was coping with overwhelming pain at the cellular level. He was a big man with a shaved head except for a thin braid that hung down his back. I unlocked his door easily with one of my earliest magic acquisitions and pulled him out of the driver's seat by his dumb blond braid. There were two others, one in the passenger seat and one in the back, both bent over, trying to breathe through the pain. I'd have to be quick about it. Their bodies wanted to give in and shut down to end the pain.

"What's your name?" He was on his knees, clutching his gut, while I pulled his head back to look at me.

His brown eyes were filled with pain, but he wasn't talking, and that was impressive. I used persuasion.

"Tell me your name."

"George Timm."

"Who sent you to kill me?"

"Lucia Perez."

Shit. I should have thought of her. She hated me, hated the revelation of witchcraft to the world. And according to Louise, Perez loved Andrew Barry.

"And after you killed me? What were your orders then?"

He closed his eyes. "Find your family."

Marsh

I checked to make sure Louise and Adam's security guards weren't hurt, then I went to check on him. Before I got there, I walked into a wall of pain that felt like a taser hit me in the face.

"Fuck!"

Without looking back at me, Adam said, "Sorry." The slight buzz in the air disappeared, and he said, "It's okay to move now."

I held my hand out in front of me and, when I was relatively sure I wouldn't experience that feeling again, I slowly made my way over to his side.

He stood in front of a beefy guy kneeling on the ground, who then fell over and didn't move again. When I reached down to check for a pulse, Adam said, "Don't bother." I peeked into the interior of the car and saw two others, also fallen over and still. I whistled.

Adam shook his head and said, "I didn't want you to see that."

"What? Your Dirty Harry act?"

He shook his head again. "It's not funny."

"I know it's not funny. But don't go crying about this. They wanted to kill us. I'm pretty sure those were bullets that broke your windows and hit me in the head."

Adam looked at me then and saw the big wad of napkins I was pressing against the wound on my forehead, and then I saw the pretty sizeable chunk of glass stuck in his neck.

"Okay, listen, don't freak out, but I think we need to get you back in the car and sitting down."

He let me guide him back to the back seat of his Cadillac, and he sat down when I asked him to, making sure he didn't move his neck when he did so.

Louise came around to see what I was doing and took in the dead guy on the ground not far from us and the glass protruding from Adam's neck and the blood covering his face from multiple shards of glass. I knew my face had to be covered in blood as well, but she was staying calm about it all.

"I need to look at his neck. Can you keep this pressed against my head wound so we can try to stop the bleeding? It's just because it's on the head that's why there's so much blood. It'll be fine."

She didn't hesitate. "Of course." After she took over the pressure, I inspected the glass in Adam's neck.

"How is it?" He sounded a little weak, and that worried me.

"It looks pretty deep. Could be in a better location. I'm not a fan of where it is right now." I took my phone out of my pocket and took a picture and then turned it around to show him.

"Right. I'm not a fan of that either," he said as he examined the shot.

The glass was too close to the external carotid artery. If I pulled it out and it was impaled in the artery, Adam could bleed out fast. We were at least thirty minutes away from D.C., and thirty minutes away from Farhad's complex. I'd never get him to the hospital on time.

A car whizzed by us on the blacktop.

"What's wrong?" Despite her outer calm, Louise needed some assurance that we had things under control.

"Well, Adam's got a piece of glass here in his neck that wants to kill him, but we're not going to let it."

"Kill him?" Her voice went up an octave, and I recognized it was not a time for humor. But Adam chuckled a bit, and I felt better about it.

"Can you sit with him and make sure he doesn't move? I'm going to speed-drive us to the hospital."

She said, "You can't *drive*," with an intensity that brooked no argument.

"Wait," Adam got our attention. "While I'm still conscious, let me try something."

He closed his eyes, and I watched him for a few moments. Still staring at him, I said to Louise, "Can you get the glass off the front seats for when we get going?"

"Yeah." She darted around to the other side of the car and retrieved one of her notebooks from her bag. I took turns watching her as she worked on sweeping the glass out of the car and Adam as he breathed slow and steady.

"Your color's improving," I said to him in a low voice.

He said, "Good. Take the glass out now. I think it nicked the artery, but I think I repaired it. Try it."

When I didn't move, he opened his eyes and smiled. The wrinkles around his eyes reminded me we were old as shit and this surviving bullets and glass shards was for kids.

"It's okay, I'm not impaired. I used Vivienne's healing magic, and it's all good in there now. Pull the glass out."

"Goddamnit," I said as I pulled the glass out of his neck. "More napkins, Louise," I said it more urgently than I wanted to because his neck was oozing blood and I was scared to death I'd just killed my best friend.

She was back beside me then, handing me her sweater. I placed it over the wound and applied pressure.

Adam said, "It's going to stop any second. Let me see your head."

I ignored that and kept up the pressure. Blood was flowing down my face again, though, and I knew I couldn't take much more of that before passing out.

"You need stitches." He sat up and pushed my hand away,

and son of a bitch if he wasn't absolutely right. His neck wound had stopped bleeding and, in fact, looked like it was closing before my very eyes.

"Samuel, Adam is better. Sit down now and let him look at you." Louise took my hand and, as Adam scooted over to the other side, she helped me down into the back seat. I closed my eyes and felt the wooziness take over.

I heard Adam say, "We need to get out of here. Tony, you drive my car. We're not going to the hospital so the world can see the result of a witch fight. Let's get him in the back of your car and take him to Louise's house. It's closer."

Then I passed out.

Louise

My house was closer, but it was also a condo in a high rise called the Waterford House in Arlington, Virginia. I bought it for the proximity to my work and to D.C., and for the fact that it was an hour's drive away from my ex-husband's horse farm in Middleburg, Virginia.

Samuel woke up as Tony pulled Adam's busted-up Cadillac into the garage of my building. Adam and Caleb helped him walk through the lobby full of people to the elevator. In a casual voice, Adam told everyone we saw, "Everything is fine. He had a bit too much to drink at lunch and hit his head." Which they believed because he used full-on persuasion to sell it. I believed it too for the length of the elevator ride to the eighth floor but then when I added up the facts, (we had been touring Farhad's facility, there was no lunch) and the amount of blood they both had on their clothes and on their faces... I remembered what really happened.

I felt the sense of betrayal that one gets after being in the path of persuasion, and Adam must have seen it on my face because he said, "Sorry," as the elevator doors opened on my floor. Samuel said, "Me too," and I felt another jolt of anger, this time on his behalf.

When we got to my hallway, Adam asked the security guards to stay and cover my door. Once we got Samuel inside and to my room, he fell back asleep as soon as he sat down on my bed.

"It's the blood loss," Adam said. "He'll be good as new before you know it."

I gathered the items he asked for from the hall closet, and I also got a t-shirt from Connor's room.

"Let's get him out of those bloody clothes," I said. Adam helped me take off his suit jacket and dress shirt. I tried not to notice that Samuel was extremely fit. His chest was smooth; he had abs, and I was impressed. Luckily, Adam was not watching me watching Samuel. He cleaned Samuel's face and the wound, sterilized the smallest needle I had, then stitched the wound up with dark blue sewing thread using the tiniest stitches I'd ever seen.

"He'll still be pretty when these come out. Be sure to tell him that or he'll whine." He set the scissors and needle on the bedside table and looked up at me. "I tried to do more for him with Vivienne's magic, but I don't always know how to use it, and I used a lot to heal myself."

"How could you use Vivienne's magic on him?"

He gave a weary laugh. "Long story. This is a gunshot wound, and it's going to hurt like hell when he wakes up. Do you have any painkillers?"

I did. In the bathroom, I got a Percocet pill and a glass of water and I set them on the bedside table.

Adam said, "I'm going to ICW now to give Marshall some support, but I can come back right after that and bring some antibiotics. Call me if you need anything."

"Adam," I got his attention before he left. "You might want to look in a mirror."

He made an exasperated sound and headed to the bathroom. While he was washing up, I got another t-shirt from Connor's room. Adam laughed when he saw the red circle with a line through it covering the President's face. Turning it inside out, he said, "I agree with this shirt, but I can't afford to alienate anybody right now." He took off his jacket and unbuttoned his bloody shirt. Damn if there wasn't another sexy doctor undressed in my house. What was it with these guys?

Dressed again in his suit jacket and Connor's inside-out t-shirt, Adam said, "Thanks, Louise. If you can believe it, I need another favor."

"I believe it."

He stood there, thinking about how to say it, and I got worried.

"Two things. One, I worry about you and Schwartz going on this tour alone. Marsh has nothing else to do right now, and I was going to ask him to go with you. And I suggested to Farhad that he add a security detail for your trip, and he agreed to do that. Today was about me, but tomorrow could be about you."

Adam wasn't asking me; he was telling me, and that was a little irritating. But Samuel was fun, and somehow, he had a way of calming me down. It wasn't a terrible idea. It occurred to me that I would like to have him along on the trip.

I shrugged and said, "Sure."

"Thanks." He was relieved. "And the other thing is, I need to talk to Vivienne. They were supposed to call me in a week, and they haven't yet." I heard the frustration in his voice, and I could sympathize. "It's not just that I miss her. The man today. The one I interrogated." His eyes met mine. "He said Lucia Perez sent them."

Of course. Of course it would be her.

"I know you must be able to contact Connor somehow. Please tell him to have Vivienne call me. I need to warn them."

"Are they in danger, too?" I heard a hint of panic in my voice.

He raised his hands and shook his head. "I don't have any reason to think anyone knows where they are. I just want them to know what happened here."

Connor's operating system, Yoda, could reach him for me.

"I can get a message to him. I'll do it now."

He said, "Thank you. And keep the door locked."

"You can count on that."

As he headed down the hallway, I said, "Hey. What if Samuel asks about dark magic?"

Adam turned around and placed his hands on his hips, contemplating that.

Then he shrugged. "Tell him."

As soon as Adam left, I sat at the computer to talk to Yoda. Connor had given me special access to his operating system because I was pretty inept with the genuine science of computers and that fostered no worries on his part that I would interfere with any of his stuff. I kept my request short and sweet.

"G's father requests a call from A's grandmother. URGENT."

While Samuel slept, I sat in the deep, cushioned chair next to my bed and wrote some talking points for Doctor Schwartz. I'd seen a picture of him without his mask in the lobby of Farhad's research center. *The Global Cancer Research Institute*, I reminded myself. He was a good-looking kid. I was excited to have him tell the story of how the vaccine came to be and how effective it was for the prevention of all types of cancer.

But the weight of the responsibility to get things right was taxing me. We'd just been through a worldwide pandemic where everything had gone wrong. People had died because they hadn't gotten the right information, and then when they got the information, they didn't trust it or they ignored it. Anti-vax sentiment had permeated the Department of Health and Human Services at the highest level. Despite deadly outbreaks of measles and the flu, people still were not vaccinating their children, and the feds refused to step in to educate.

The United States had not been this divided since probably the Civil War. I closed my eyes and wondered how Lincoln had done it. I wondered who my team of rivals could be that would overcome the mistrust between the right and the left, or if it was just too late for all that. My college boyfriend had a sister who was now a senator from a Midwest state. Very conservative but, as I recalled, also funny. Maybe Rosemary would meet with me. She held a high office in the Senate, though, and probably didn't have time for random lunch dates, but I would text her.

Samuel moved, and I opened my eyes. Had I slept?

"Awww, I'm sorry. Didn't want to wake you," he said as he sat up.

"Wait, wait, wait!" I reached out a hand to keep him from standing up. "Adam said you needed some water, and I needed to check if you had a fever before you got up."

Samuel rolled his eyes. "He's not the boss of me." He swung his legs over the side of the bed.

"But you're in my house. I get the last word about what happens here."

With a smile, he said, "That's true." He picked up the mirror I had on the dresser and looked at the stitched-up wound over his eye and touched it gently. "Not bad," he said and laid back down. Folding his hands over his chest, he said, "Take care of me, doctor."

I placed the back of my hand on his forehead. It seemed a little warm, and I wondered what could happen if you developed a fever from a gunshot wound. I leaned over and kissed his forehead, and he grabbed my hand when I did.

"Hey, don't worry. I'm not dying."

"I know." Pulling my hand away, I stood up. "That's the way a mother checks to see if there's a fever. You don't have one."

"Huh," Samuel said. "I've never had that treatment before."

"Really?" I was heading to the kitchen, and he was trying to get up again.

"Stay!" I pointed at him. He froze and then slowly sat back down when I held his gaze with a stern look.

"Okay," he said.

In the kitchen, I poured a glass of orange juice for him and nearly dropped it when I heard a loud banging on the door and then keys turning in the lock. Samuel was standing in the bedroom doorway, shirt off and eyebrows raised, asking if I needed help. When my ex-husband entered, I shook my head and waved Samuel off. He waited for a moment so Jeff could see him, then turned around and lay back down on the bed.

"Who the fuck is that?" Jeff said.

Tony stood next to my ex and asked, "He said he's your husband. Do you want him here?"

"No, but it's fine."

Jeff closed the door on Tony and said again, "Who are these hallway assholes and who the fuck is that in your bedroom?"

"How the fuck do you have keys to a house that is not where you live?" I asked.

Jeff didn't answer, as I knew he wouldn't. He was dressed for success as usual, in his thousand-dollar suit and his Rolex watch. Something made me think then of the first time I saw him, liking that he had hair like Robert Redford and wishing I could touch that blond hair. He looked me up and down and either found something lacking or saw something he liked. I had lost the ability to tell, with him. "Where's Connor? I've been trying to reach him for days."

This was what I'd been dreading. Now that he knew Connor was not with me, Jeff would make it his mission to find out where he was. It was a mistake not to tell him, but I knew how ugly the discussion would be, and I had just avoided it.

"Have a seat," I said, and I walked the glass of juice back to the bedroom.

"Drink this and take a pain pill, then you can leave," I told Samuel.

From the living room, Jeff raised his voice. "I don't want to sit, Louise. I want to know where my son is. He should be with me. You've been all over the country this past week. He should not be left alone."

Samuel just watched my face while Jeff got loud.

"I'll be staying here for a little while longer," he said.

Our eyes locked, and I said simply, "Okay."

Back in front of Jeff, I said, "Keep your voice down. Connor's fine." I sat on the couch. "I asked a friend to take him on her vacation because I didn't want him to be a target for the media. There's another teen on the trip, and he's having a great time."

It was clear Jeff was reaching his apoplectic stage, and I wanted no more of a scene with Samuel in the other room, so I said, "I can tell him to call you."

"That's not enough." He stood in front of me and leaned down toward my face. "Where is he, Louise?"

"I don't think you should be that close to my future wife." Samuel stood in the bedroom doorway again. Jeff and I both turned to look at him with open mouths.

"Your what?" Jeff said in disbelief.

"You heard me. Step away, dipshit."

"Who the fuck are you?" Jeff stood back up.

"Doctor Samuel Marsh. And I assume you're the asshole ex? Sorry, what was your name?" Samuel sat down in a chair at my kitchen table and tugged on his shoes, still shirtless.

Jeff seethed. I had only ever seen him this angry when we left the divorce proceedings after I had gotten sole custody of Connor. Jeff's temper was his fatal flaw. Connor and I perceived it too late, and I would never forgive myself for that.

He sneered, "He's a mortal?"

"You know what? That's another thing you're going to have to address with us non-magical peons. Why do you call us mortals? Are witches immortal? If not, it seems weird that you give that distinction just to us." He looked at Jeff. "Right? These are the things Louise has to work on now."

Jeff just stared at Samuel, and I noticed Samuel's eyes squint, like he was sick.

"Jeff! No!"

He was using his magic on Samuel, making him heat up from the inside out. I'd seen him use it once on a hyena that had stalked our party on safari in Africa. It was terrible then, and it was terrifying to see it happening in my living room.

I screamed, "Stop it!"

I had never shared my main magic with Jeff during our entire time as a couple, but I used it then.

My magic as a null was a secret. I could stop the magic being used by another witch, no matter the type or the amount. My force cut his magic to shreds, and Jeff stepped back in shock when he felt it. Then he doubled over and gagged from the pain of it.

Caleb and Tony pounded on the door. Samuel came around the couch to throw a punch at Jeff's face, which he had time to block. The door flew open, and Caleb tumbled in with Tony on his heels. Jeff's throw at Samuel was a miss, but Samuel's body shot to Jeff's diaphragm made a sickening crunch, and he crumbled to the floor.

Samuel turned his back on Jeff and said to me, "Thanks for that, whatever you did." He held out his hand, and I took it. Pulling me up off the couch, he guided me over to the kitchen table and had me sit in a chair. He pulled one up next to me and kept a grip on my hand. I noticed he was taking my pulse, and I said, "It's fine. I'm fine."

He disagreed. "Your color's gone. And your pulse is pretty rapid right now. Does whatever you just did always affect you this way?"

I closed my eyes and whispered, "Don't do it all that much."

Samuel pushed my head gently between my legs and said, "Just breathe in through your nose and out through your mouth. Do that ten times."

I knew dimly that Jeff had stood up. He said, "How did you keep that a secret?" He was wondering how his ability to hear a lie had never alerted him I was a null. "Why didn't you tell me?"

Only on my fourth breath, and sick to my stomach that he now knew what I could do, I groaned a little and said, "Go home, Jeff."

He reached down to pick his keys up off the floor and said in a dismissive tone, "Get Connor to call me. Today."

When he was gone, Tony said, "Are you both okay? Sorry about the door."

I looked up to see the door off its hinges and might have let out a small hysterical sob. Samuel pushed my head back down again.

"Yeah, we're fine, Tony. Can you guys check in with the super of this building? See if he can get that door back on?"

"Okay, Rocky."

Samuel laughed at that.

As he rubbed his hand on my back in warm, comforting circles, I felt better. After my tenth breath, I sat up and said, "I'm good." Then, feeling the need to assert some order on that day, I said, "And I'm not your future wife."

He took his hand off my back. "Sorry about that. I just needed him to get mad enough to throw a punch at me. Or whatever the hell it was he did to my insides. What was that?"

I shook my head, suddenly exhausted by the two assassination attempts of the day. "It's a terrible magic that can only harm. It's like he can microwave your insides. I saw him use it once on an animal that threatened us on safari. It was a nightmare."

Samuel frowned.

"But he didn't have time to hurt you. I mean, I'm sure it hurt. But I don't think there was time to do harm." I had never seen Jeff do that to another person. He had broken every rule when he did, and now I had a situation. Report Connor's father or don't report a crime of harmful witchcraft being used on a mortal? Neither was good.

"And what did you do to stop him?"

I hesitated. My magic was a secret I had never shared with anyone. All my life, only my parents knew about it. But looking into those blue eyes of Samuel's, there was no doubt in my mind that he would take my secret to his grave.

"You can't tell anyone."

"I understand," he murmured.

I took a breath and then spilled my secret to a man who was practically a stranger. "I'm a null. I can stop another witch from using his magic. It's not a popular magic. Obviously, powerful witches don't enjoy having a vulnerability."

Samuel said, "So you could stop Adam from doing whatever it is he can do?"

The answer was written on my face.

He broke into a big smile, showing the laugh lines around his eyes. "Oh, my God. I love it. You're like Wonder Woman. You just get better and better the more I know."

That man was an endless well of puppy-dog energy. I looked at him as if he were an alien life form that I'd need to study.

"I'm not Wonder Woman or your future wife, Samuel."

"Okay," he said. He leaned over and kissed my forehead. "No fever." Standing up, he said, "I'm getting dressed now. Can I take a shower first? Today has been gross. I assume the t-shirt on the bed is for me?"

I gave a weary nod.

"Then I'm making you my famous pizza. You'll probably want to marry me after that."

"There are zero ingredients for pizza here." I shook my head at his retreating form.

"I'm having them delivered. Also, I'm getting a locksmith to change your front door lock." He stepped back into the doorway. "Unless there's some other way your douchebag ex can get in?" He looked up from his phone with raised eyebrows, waiting for my response.

"No," I said. "He can't open a lock."

"Good." Samuel turned back to my bedroom, tapping on his phone.

I went to my laptop and typed another message to Yoda, asking for Connor to make a call to his father. Then I collapsed back onto my sofa with the soft fabric and thick cushions. Leaning back, I sighed and felt my shoulders relax for the first time all day.

Pizza sounded good.

CHAPTER FIFTEEN

Adam

On my way home from the ICW meeting, the Lyft driver I ordered tried to assassinate me.

It happened fast. We were on the Fourteenth Street Bridge when he reached his arm over the seat and I saw the gun in his hand. I hit him with the full dose of my defensive magic, and his heart stopped immediately. Unfortunately, his hands came off the wheel at that point and his foot off the gas, which made the car careen wildly over several lanes of D.C. traffic. I got knocked around a bit but exited the car when it finally stopped, facing the wrong way and up against some sort of crane attached to the side of the bridge. Construction crews had been working on the bridge for months, and the workers who were there on site got busy helping people involved in the crash to get out of their cars.

Trying hard to stay upright, I cursed my driver Ernie for going on vacation and leaving me to take a Lyft. I wobbled a bit on the way, but I made it down the hill to a parking lot in front of the Jefferson Memorial. Then, hearing my father's voice in my head as he taught me never to use persuasion for myself, I persuaded a man buckling up his toddler in a car seat to drive me up to the Smithsonian Metro stop. When I stepped out of his car onto the National Mall, I thanked him sincerely, waved to the little blond boy in the back, and left a hundred-dollar bill in my seat.

Walking to the metro entrance, I texted Marshall Smith.

"Send me the last phone number you have for Barry."

Halfway down the escalator, he texted back.

"It's old."

I called it anyway. Going through the turnstile, I tried to be casual and inspect the other people around me as we funneled our way onto the next escalator. A college girl, texting. College boy checking out the college girl, also texting. Business man putting a stick of gum in his mouth. Man going to work, woman going to work, tourist couple, tourist family.

Somebody picked up the line, and I said, "You're down four."

There was what I imagined was the shuffling of the phone from two or three guys to, finally, the guy I wanted.

"Adam." Barry sounded like he was on the move, too. "I'm kind of busy."

"Yeah, it sounds like it. Just wanted to let you know, your guys are dead." The college boy turned back and looked away quickly when our eyes met.

"All of them?"

"Depends how many you had. I've met four in the last couple of hours."

He was silent.

I said, "Why don't you come see me yourself? I saw you're in town. With some new best friends."

He laughed. "They don't matter. You know that. Only she matters. I'm off to catch up with your wife and son. They got pretty far away in a very short time. Good luck with the rest of your day, Adam." He hung up.

I made my way on autopilot to the Blue Line platform and waited for a train going to Capitol Hill South. Leaving the security detail with Marsh and Louise had been the right call, but I might need to get Farhad to add another one to me. When I sat down on the metro, I took a deep breath and wiped a hand over my face. That interaction with the driver had been close. If I'd been looking down in that car when he reached around with the gun, I'd be dead in that car right now. The total experience from car to metro had lasted about fifteen minutes.

Barry knew where Vivienne was.

He was on his way, and she didn't know.

My phone vibrated in my hand, and I looked down at it, surprised I was still holding it.

It was a text from Sean Tolley, Herb's son, who worked for Senator Clay.

"Capitol Hill Books. Twenty minutes. Poetry section."

I knew it well. During my passionate pursuit of Vivienne, I frequented that minuscule room full of poetry almost daily, just trying to find the right words to make her want me.

I was getting off at that stop anyway, so I sent a reply.

"Got it."

Sitting back on the metro bench, I did a survey of the people on the car and decided they seemed unlikely to suddenly try to kill me.

But the Lyft driver had also seemed unlikely to kill me. I did another quick scan and came to the same conclusion. These people did not care about me.

I texted Louise next. She was going to freak out, but she could at least let Vivienne know to move from where they were. They'd go completely dark after that. We probably wouldn't hear from them again until they came home.

At the bookstore, I gave a small wave to the clerk on my left as I headed up to meet Sean. The stairway seemed steeper than usual. Or maybe I was just bone tired and sore from more magic use than I normally had to put out in a month's time. My magic didn't replenish as fast as Vivienne's did, and it took a toll on me when I used it defensively because I threw everything out all at once. It was effective, though, and I was still standing. My body was also adjusting to new magic from the dead hit men and I gave a small groan as I felt that magic take root and vie for my attention.

Sean was in the history section, right before the poetry room. He took one look at me and said, "Damn, Parrish. That's a new look for you. Hobo t-shirt and rumpled jacket?"

He was not wrong.

I said, "I'm having a bad day."

Sean said, "You're a rich white guy with unlimited power. How bad can it be?"

"How bad can it be?" I stared at him. Then I said louder, "How bad can it be? Today I am John Wick, just trying to get to the Continental."

He raised his eyebrows, then pulled me into the small room I thought of as the poetry pantry.

"I mean, I think a few hundred people tried to get John Wick in a day, and it only happened to me twice today. But twice is still two times more than people usually try to assassinate me in a day."

Sean waited a second to see if I was done. Then he asked, "Where'd they try to get you?"

I drew a deep breath and then sighed heavily.

"On the road from Farhad's facility and in the Lyft on the way here."

"You were taking a Lyft?"

"They shot up my car."

"Not the caddy! Shiiiiiit." He dragged it out, impressed. "That's low."

"Yep."

"That's some real malice at work. We are definitely leaving here separately, and I am going out the back."

We looked at each other. Then I said, "That's a good plan."

We were silent again, thinking about the situation I was in.

I said, "It was Andrew Barry. He didn't deny it. And now he says he knows where Vivienne and Grant are and he's headed there."

"Fuck. Did you let 'em know?"

"Yeah, I sent a text."

Sean said, "Let me see your phone." I handed it to him, and after scrolling on it for a few seconds, he said, "See here?" I looked at the settings page. "You have your location sharing on. Wouldn't be too hard to find you with that on if I was a bad guy."

He turned it off.

"Goddamnit." I tried to take it back, but he was taking it apart.

"Nah, you can't have this anymore." He took out the sim card and tried to keep the phone away from me until I shoved his face into the bookcase and ripped it out of his hand.

"Don't fuck with me today!"

He laughed. "Okay, okay, sorry."

"And I know about location settings."

Sean gave me a skeptical look.

"I do," I said. I wanted to add that assassins have to know about location settings, but I didn't.

"Fine," I said. "I've just been busy. I don't know how I was sharing my location or who with. But I have burner phones from your dad. I'll use those from now on."

"You should have already been using them."

The look I turned on him then was effective at shutting that shit down.

He held his hand up and said, "Alright. Well, I didn't know all that was happening today, but I want to warn you about some other shit about to hit the fan."

My head fell back, and I looked at patches of paint peeling off the ceiling above us. The floors were warped, the ceiling was cracked, I hadn't spoken to Vivienne in over a week, and it really felt like that bookstore might crumble around us.

"Okay." I sat down on the dingy blue carpeting and motioned for Sean to join me. He laughed and sat down beside me, both of us hidden by the small table of books sitting in the middle of that cramped closet full of poetry. There was no room to stretch our legs out, so I sat with my back against a bookcase, pulled my knees up to my chest and rested my arms on my knees. Sean did the same.

"Tell me about the shit."

He started, "You know Senator Clay is on the Senate Committee for Homeland Security and Government Affairs?"

He looked to see if I was with him. I gestured for him to get on with it.

"There's a joint congressional committee forming. He's on it, but he's not the chairman and can't veto a request for a hearing. It looks like Senator Schnell is going to call you as a witness to discover the potential threat witchcraft poses to our national security."

I closed my eyes.

Sean continued, "You'd be under oath. Lying? Not an option. I know you've seen him. He's like a rabid raccoon up there asking his questions. And he'll make sure before it's over that people know about any dangerous magic that could put humans at risk. Including persuasion."

I turned to look at him.

"We didn't give it to him, but somebody in the Department of War probably did."

"Hmmmm..." I looked forward again. I did not relish being a punching bag for that asshole with the entire world watching.

Sean hit me with more good news. "It's probably going to happen fast. No more than a day or two." He nodded. "You should get a lawyer, like right now."

I patted his knee and said, "You're a ray of sunshine today, buddy." He grinned at my use of his toddler nickname.

"I know. Always have been."

He reached over for his bag and struggled to pull something out.

"Dad is scary sometimes. I know he doesn't know what happened to you today, but he made me bring you this bulletproof vest and told me not to let you out of here unless you put it on."

I said, "Pffft. Like you could make me do anything."

Sean tried to hand me the vest, but I pushed it back at him.

"Tell your dad thanks, but I'd rather you wore it out of here. I have a shield that I'll be using everywhere I go. It'll do." I asked, "Is he still mad at me?"

Sean laughed. "No. He calmed down after he shared the burden of that persuasion knowledge. He knows you're still you. Are you mad at him?"

"Fuck no! If the roles were reversed, I would have done the same thing." I was glad that Herb had an in at the Department of War. In fact, I needed Sean to pass along some more information.

"If anything happens to me, tell your dad Andrew Barry and Lucia Perez are the reason."

"You know this for certain?" He was typing on his phone.

I thought of the man I'd killed that morning and his last words pried out of him with my persuasion.

"Yeah," I said wearily. "I'm sure. But I don't know for sure they're working together."

That amused him. "So you have two people mad enough to kill you? Why are they trying to kill you?"

I shrugged. "Not sure, but I think he wants Vivienne, and I'm in his way. And her..." my voice trailed off. Lucia's reasons felt pretty clear to me. She was not happy about the revelation of witchcraft to the mortal world. She'd made that obvious in our meeting to vote on the measure. Lucia was now the head of a faction of witches who maintained that opposition, even after the fact. Marshall had briefed me on her group. Their end game wasn't clear. But I felt like her interests led directly back to the death of her son and her feeling that, with my revelation, somehow his death was in vain.

I said, "Perez is unhappy that witches were outed." I added, "By me."

Sean laughed. "Yeah, I remember hearing something about that."

I ignored him and carried on. "Also, I want to give your dad some more information that might come in useful. Really good headphones or earplugs will protect against persuasion. And heat vision goggles would be useful when trying to detect a witch using a cloak."

"A cloak?" he cocked his head.

I layered a cloak over myself, and when I disappeared, Sean's mouth dropped open.

He raised his hand and reached out to pat my arm and said, "Holy shit. How the hell can you do that?"

I dropped the cloak and said, "It's just my magic."

He shook his head. "That's not *just* anything. That's fucking amazing! Do it again!"

Sean wasn't scared of my magic, and that meant the world to me.

I said, "If I can get off this floor, let's get out of here." We stood and laughed at how hard it was.

"Hold on a second." Looking around on the shelves, I finally found what I was looking for. I pulled down a collection of Pablo Neruda poems and handed it to him. "Buy this on your way out. Then read it to a girl. You're welcome."

Sean said, "You know I don't mess with girls, right?"

I did not know that.

"Gay?"

"With a capital G," he said with a big smile.

I shrugged.

"Okay. Well then, read it to a boy."

He laughed.

"Thanks." He took the book and clasped my hand.

"Good luck, Wick."

Chapter Sixteen

Vivienne

January 17th, 2026
On board a cruise ship to Leith, Scotland

We flew from Canada to Reykjavik, Iceland, against the advice of Yoda because I needed to get to Europe faster than a two-week cruise on the North Atlantic ocean would allow. But since we could fly for the first leg of our trip, I agreed to sail the rest of the way.

In Iceland, Yoda found us a passenger ship that was bound for Scotland. The name of the vessel was the "Silver Sea," which pleased Alice, and as we boarded the ship, she claimed it as her own because her surname was Silver. Connor seemed surprised by that.

"You didn't know?" she asked. He shook his head. Irritated, she said, "I know your last name, *Carmichael*." Grant patted him on the back when Connor looked surprised at her reaction.

Our cabins were charming and, according to Grant and Maria, they were larger than normal and more luxurious. We had gotten lucky in that the ship was undergoing renovations, and that meant we could travel with relatively few other passengers aboard. And because the seas were rougher in the winter months, it was also going to be a direct trip and was not stopping at tourist destinations along the way. Alice stayed with me. Connor had his own cabin next door, with Grant and Maria on the other side of him.

The first night we were to stay in the port of Reykjavik. Because our rooms were not yet available, we visited the ship library, where Grant handed Alice a copy of Macbeth.

He said, "You might like this. It takes place in Scotland."

She eyed it with suspicion at first, then gave him a small smile after flipping through a few pages.

Grant must have known that the language of William Shakespeare might be a comfort to her and a sweet reminder of her previous life in England, which I observed with some shock had only been weeks ago.

Connor made a face when he saw it. "Shakespeare's tough. I appreciate the genius and all, but did not enjoy deciphering every other line."

Alice retorted, "Like your English is so easy to learn?" Then she froze and looked at me.

Connor said, "My English?"

I said, "I agree with Alice on this one. American English is full of ridiculous expressions that make no sense to an English person."

She flopped down on a fancy, upholstered chair and crossed her arms. "Right," she said flatly. "It was your *American* English that was so hard to learn." She looked up at me as if she might carry on with that topic, but the frown I aimed at her kept her silent.

Grant interrupted then to hand Connor a book and asked if he had read it.

"The Hitchhiker's Guide to the Galaxy?" Connor flipped it over to read the description, and the rest of us looked at each other in relief that we had dodged that conversation with Connor about the learning of languages. As smart as he was, I was willing to bet that Middle English was not one of the languages in which he was fluent.

Because it was winter and there were only five hours of daylight for us to enjoy in Iceland, when darkness fell in the early afternoon, Alice and I decided to read in our cabin before meeting the others later for dinner in the grand dining room of the ship.

Curled up on the window seat with the lights of the city behind her, she sat engrossed in Shakespeare's *Macbeth*. Her beautiful red hair fell past her shoulders and got in her way as she tried to turn the page of her book.

A couple of minutes into the play, she forgot she was mad at me for toting her around the world in 2026 and said, "Granny!

There are witches in this!" She looked up and widened her eyes. Head back down, she gripped both edges of the book.

Ten minutes later, she said, "Banquo is so rude to the witches." Shortly after that, she mumbled, "They're in a wasteland with thunder and lightning. Talking about ships."

A minute later, she said, "Granny, listen. The witches worked a spell." I closed my eyes to hear her read aloud to me from the play.

"The weird sisters, hand in hand,
Posters of the sea and land,
Thus do go about, about,
Thrice to thine and thrice to mine,
And thrice again to make up nine.
Peace, the charm's wound up."

I opened my eyes again to see her concentrating on the words, her index finger running slowly down the page and her physical form wavering before me. She was almost translucent. I lunged at her to keep her present.

"Alice!" I barked and fell over her lap, trying to grab her body and hold it to me.

"What?" She sat back and let the book fall off the seat. "What's wrong?" She tried to push me away. "What are you doing?"

Even though I saw she was back in her corporeal form, I was not ready to release her wrists where I held them tight. When she tried pulling away, I said, "Wait!" Then we both saw that my hands were shaking. I didn't want to scare her anymore than I already had with my panicked tackle, so I released her arms and gave her hands a pat.

"Please," I said. "Give me a hug, sweet girl. Hug Granny."

Bewildered, she leaned in and put her arms around me and actually patted the back of my head.

I hugged her back tightly and after a few moments, I said, "Tell me what you were thinking just now when you were reading the spell in Macbeth."

I pulled away to see her face, but did not let her go.

She shrugged. "I don't know. Grant said the play happened in Scotland, and I was picturing the storm and the witches..."

"Did you notice anything else? How did you feel?" I tried to regulate my breathing as I waited for her answer.

Alice sat back and searched my eyes. "Did I time travel? Was I about to?"

She saw from my expression that I worried that was true.

Her eyes filled with tears, and she said out loud what I feared the most.

"What if I get stuck somewhere, and I don't know how to get back?"

The tears fell then, and it was my turn to pull her in for a hug and pat the back of her head.

She said, "I don't even know where I was going!"

"Don't worry. I have some ideas." Running my hands up and down her arms, I said, "I knew this might be something you would need to get a handle on. Just think about it- your body worked some incredible magic recently, and it knows what you can do. It may want to do it again."

That idea clearly terrified her, so I said quickly, "But you can make your will known to your magic. For now, while you're getting used to it, you'll just need to stay in the present and be aware of your surroundings."

Her eyes didn't leave mine, and she nodded.

I said, "And I'm going to give you something to always carry with you. It's an anchor to this year in time." Reaching for my purse, I kept one hand on her back as I opened it and rifled through the pockets. Pulling out a dime, I double checked that it was the right one and I pressed it in her hand. "This dime is a very special coin. It was made for America's semiquincentennial." I waited for her to ask, and she did not disappoint.

"What's a semiquincentennial?" She flipped the coin over to examine both sides.

"It's half of a quincentennial."

She gave me a dissatisfied look at that answer, and I shrugged my agreement.

"The Americans get very excited about celebrating their independence from England. It's rather ridiculous. This year will be the two hundred fiftieth anniversary of their declaration of independence. So, a quincentennial is..."

"Five hundred years," she mumbled.

I paused and then said, "Good job."

We were silent for a moment while she turned the coin over and over.

"We used a coin to get back to Adam. What you will do is keep this coin with you at all times and use it as your anchor to get back to me in Washington, D.C. at Adam's house." Because his house was still partially rubble, I got specific. "In his study in the year 2026, on the date you accidentally traveled." I raised her chin gently to make her look at me. "If you should ever need to. Okay?"

She gave a quick nod.

"But... what if..."

My mind ran through all the circumstances a witch could encounter during time travel. Unfortunately, I did not have any answers for her about time travel etiquette or best practices. But I knew who would.

I said, "You've already done it once, so we know that will work. Also, we'll talk to Gerald and make sure you know all there is to know about traveling through time. Alright? He'll make sure you never do it unless you mean to. And so will I. We can do this."

Her expression went from troubled to curious.

"So I could choose to time travel? Pick a time and go?"

I felt a chill.

"No, that's not what I said. You need to learn about this magic before practicing this magic. Gerald is the expert, so we will wait to see what he says."

She took a deep breath and then released it.

Putting the coin in her pocket, she said, "Right. Gerald will know what to do."

Vivienne

While Alice had loved flying in a plane, she did not take to sailing on a cruise ship at all. None of our crew did. When we departed the next day, it was astounding to me how very seasick they all were, even Alice. I knew my body was assessing at every moment the motion of the ship and was addressing any queasiness I might experience. I tried to coach Alice on how to use her magic to do the same, but she was too sick from the very beginning to focus on my lessons. Since I knew we would not be on board long, I helped them all to sleep more, waking them when it was time for light meals and liquids.

The terror of Alice's near miss with time travel would not leave me. She did it with no intention, lost in her imagination while she read and, for the life of me, I didn't see how we might prevent that sort of thing. Could it happen during a dream? Also of concern was the added wrinkle she had begun the time travel process while reading a witch's spell. Was William Shakespeare a witch? Did he imbue his Scottish play with magic and real spells? There was probably no way to know for sure, but I would ask Grant about that when we made port.

The ocean was a panacea for me. I stood on the deck and let the wind blow me and the waves mist me, and I used that alone time to process all that was to come. If I could have, I would have slept on one of the reclining chairs there and watched the night stars flow by. I walked the deck each night for only about an hour. Stopping at the railing, I pictured Adam asleep in our bed, the sheet pulled up to his waist... the desire to reach out and caress his bare back was overwhelming. I wished he were there to warm me. Though Yoda said it was not safe for us to call him, I knew Adam would be worried that we had not.

I didn't feel his presence with me like I thought I would. It was disquieting.

Yoda became my companion over the course of the rest of our travels on the sea, and I was grateful for his presence and wisdom. He recommended a great tale of the sea to me called Moby Dick, which I read during the day in my cabin. I looked for whales at night on my trek around the ship and nearly shouted when I spotted an enormous black back rising from the waves once and spouting water as it did. I wondered if Connor could commune with him and, for the first time, I experienced jealousy of another witch's magic.

When I began to be anxious about my task in Europe, I asked Yoda for information about the port of Leith, which would be our landing place in Scotland. He provided me with a thorough historical account of the area, which included a disturbing tale of a witch trial in 1662 for a Scottish woman named Isobel Gowdie.

Her story was remarkable because she was not tortured for her confession but gave it seemingly willingly over many weeks. She told outrageous stories to the men in charge of her trial, including that she had had sex with the devil and had met with the Fairy King and Queen. This was enough for me to surmise that she was not an actual witch. She was most likely a poor woman, disliked by someone in her village, who then accused her of witchcraft. I pictured Isobel being held in some dingy cell, feeling like she had to invent some knowledge about witches in order to prolong her life.

It saddened me to learn that the women of Scotland had endured several waves of persecution for witchcraft, with rates four times more than the European average. I was also surprised to learn that Protestants rather than Catholics conducted the witch hunts.

There were two written works that most likely played a part in demonizing those women and encouraging the accusations. Both were written by Scotsmen who began life as Catholics and later became Protestant. The first was a treatise from John Knox, the architect of the Scottish Reformation. In 1558 he wrote *The First Blast of the Trumpet Against the Monstrous Regiment of Women*. I felt sick at first and then enraged as I read his misogynistic diatribe, which was nothing more than a call to arms against powerful women. Then, in 1597, the King of Scotland himself felt compelled to weigh in. King James VI wanted to create a more godly society, and his pathway to that was to write *Daemonologie*, which was nothing more than a state sanctioned witch hunting "how-to" book.

And while the reactions to witches in 2026 had not risen to the level of witch hunting in 1500s Scotland, there were stirrings of discontent in the evangelical churches of the American south that felt familiar. Pastors preached sermons that described witchcraft as something the devil made. I wondered how long witches had before widespread accusations and persecutions began again.

Standing at the railing and breathing in the frosty night air, I looked to the stars and picked out the constellation Orion. It occurred to me he must have seen it all. The birth and death of Christ, the rise and fall of nations, the invention of machines. I wondered whether watching our endless wars was entertainment for him or a source of despair.

Wars were still raging all over the globe. And the stakes were so much higher now that nuclear weapons existed that could ruin the earth for thousands of years. I saw war up close when I was young, when I first received my magic and wanted to use it freely. Wounded soldiers fresh from a battlefield didn't ask questions. They accepted my healing and often called me an angel. Many nights, I still saw their faces. I still cataloged their wounds.

The wars would continue as long as man succumbed to his greed for land and for power and remained certain that his God was the only one.

I considered the moral justification religion had provided for those who conducted the Holy Wars and for the present-day jihadists of the Islamic State. The zealotry of the fundamentalist Christian movement in America seemed to me to be more of the same. No, they weren't killing people to further their goals, but they were not opposed to jailing them. Marginalized people were suffering, but the 'Christians' in charge chose to look away. How very easy it was for modern-day believers to ignore the true teachings of Christianity and to twist them into something unrecognizable. It was abhorrent to me that religion was so easily perverted to aid powerful men in their quest for more power.

To be deemed 'other' in present-day America was proving to mean your rights were forfeit.

Witches were most certainly 'other.'

I did not want that for Alice. Bringing her back with me to America in 2026 was supposed to be for her safety. Being a woman in the sixteenth century was hard enough, but being a young witch in the sixteenth century meant being under constant threat. And I thought modern-day America would be the perfect place for a woman of her intelligence and drive to accomplish whatever she wanted in life. I believed that bringing Alice to live in 2026 would assure that she would enjoy the same rights as a man. But the courts in America had given the president unlimited use of his powers without repercussions, and he spoke of 'protecting' women, as if they could not do so themselves.

Adam had described to me the many trials America endured during my time away. A television recap of the year documented one government scandal after another, with each statement by the president more shocking, each lie more galling. The entire year seemed to be a series of insults to those who believed in a democratic government. Constitutional and societal norms continued to be upended and challenged daily. Now I wondered what would be left of the republic that Adam so revered when the people in power were done with their "reforms."

I could not comprehend why people seemed determined to repeat the mistakes of the past.

CHAPTER SEVENTEEN

Vivienne

Port of Leith, Scotland

Everyone was relieved to disembark the "Silver Seas" when we reached the historic Port of Leith. It was a charming town just north of Edinburgh, with cobblestone streets lined with eclectic shops and cafes. The area's crown jewel was an ancient stone former windmill that resembled a medieval castle turret, which now housed a beloved fish and chips restaurant at its base.

I decided they all deserved a break after their illnesses and agreed to the requests from Grant and Maria to go as a group to visit some sites in town. She wanted to visit a particular coffee shop, and Grant wanted to tour the Queen Mary Royal Yacht and a whiskey distillery. Yoda found us a quaint house to rent for the one night we would stay there.

While we sat at the kitchen table, we received a message from Connor's mother that canceled all our plans. Her email said that Adam wanted me to call home immediately and that Andrew Barry had somehow followed us. They didn't know where he was exactly, but we should be on the alert and keep up our constant movement. She also said that Connor's father was threatening to take her to court if Connor did not come home and check in with him.

Everyone's mood was sour as I stepped into the backyard to call Adam with my burner phone. His line rang and rang, but I got no answer.

Back in the kitchen, I shook my head at Grant, letting him know I did not speak to his father.

Working on his laptop, Connor said, "I'm sorry I have to go. I found a flight from Edinburgh to London and then direct to New York. It leaves in two hours. Then I can connect to D.C. from New York."

Maria said, "Do you really have to go? Maybe you can just call him."

Connor shook his head. Still typing, he said, "No. He's an asshole. It's his way or no way."

Grant said, "Can you leave us the laptop so we can still use Yoda? He's grown on me."

Connor said, "No." Then he looked up, realizing that there was a problem with that. I could see him thinking a mile a minute about how to solve it. "You can access him on any laptop. I'll tell you how."

Grant asked with some irritation, "Why can't you leave it?"

Connor leaned back in his chair. "There's a lot going on with this PC."

Rolling his eyes, Grant said, "I bet. Connor, we don't want your porn. We just need help on this last leg of the trip."

"Grant!" Maria's admonishment made him wince.

Connor gave Grant a flat look and said, "Pretty sure you know this, but you can access porn on any device."

Grant laughed.

From the head of the table, Alice said, "What's porn?"

Everyone sobered up fast at that and looked at me.

"Porn is a topic for you and Granny on another day. Right now, we need to figure out how to access Yoda's advice without Connor's laptop."

"I'll go buy one. Be back in a while." Connor scraped the rental car keys off the table and swung his backpack with Yoda in it over his shoulder.

Alice jumped up. "I'll go with you." She grabbed her coat from the back of her chair and followed him to the door.

"Wait!" They both turned in surprise. I had been loud, and that was unusual.

"It's not that far..." Alice was ready to lecture me on what a grown woman she was, but there was no room for argument on the issue.

I was shocked to feel my voice use a bit of Adam's persuasion when I spoke to them next. "You may go together to the store at the end of the street. I'm sending Grant to walk behind you to see if anyone follows you. You will not allow yourselves to leave his sight. Is that clear?"

They were not happy about that edict, but they both nodded.

When they were in the hallway, Grant raised his eyebrows at me and said, "That's new."

I shrugged in confusion. "Very new," I said. "I may need some advice."

He patted my shoulder on his way out the door. "You got it. Let me go watch the children, then we can figure things out."

Maria and I sat in silence for a minute.

Then she asked, "Was that persuasion?"

"I think so."

She raised her eyebrows.

"Wow."

I shook my head and brought my hands to my cheeks. "What next?"

She leaned in. "It'll be okay. It's a good thing. And Grant will help."

Was it, though? A good thing? I was pretty sure his being born with persuasion was the thing that Adam had decided defined him as a bad person.

I held my hands there for a moment. Then I said, "Maria, I need your help with Alice."

She sat up, alert. "What's wrong?"

"Her emotions," I said. "On the ship, she was reading Macbeth, a scene with witches. I saw her..." I struggled with how to describe what had happened. "I think she was imagining herself in their shoes and somehow connected with them."

Maria did not like the sound of that.

"Her body wavered. She was a ghostly figure," Maria leaned in, "and I saw right through her for a second. If I had not grabbed her body to anchor her to us here..."

"You think she would have traveled there? To medieval Scotland?" Maria raised her voice at the thought.

"I think it's possible. Her first time travel happened at a stage when her power is still developing. She doesn't know how to control it yet. And she has so much."

Maria frowned. "She does."

"And it seems to be activated by her emotions. Which are many and varied." I pursed my lips.

"Of course they are. She's fifteen. Also, pretty smitten with Connor, so... her mind is coping with a lot these days."

"She's dealing with a whole new world." I got up to pour us some more lemonade.

Behind me, Maria said, "I'll watch her like a hawk. Misdirection and distractions are my specialties. No way I'm letting that kid get too emotional."

Sitting back down, I said, "That's a hard task. Emotions happen fast with Alice. It was the same with her mother." I sighed. "My concern, of course, is that she could travel and become lost. What if she found herself trapped somewhere and couldn't find her way back?"

Maria saw my fear and reached out for my hand.

"Have you talked to her about it?"

"Yes," I said. "I gave her a coin from this year and told her how to be intentional in her request to travel to a specific place and time. But I'm hardly an expert."

"Gerald is." Maria squeezed my hand. Then she sat back with her drink and gave me her opinion, as I had hoped she would.

"When you can, talk to him. And for now, you can also try some home magic to connect her to you. I don't have it, but we can find someone who does."

"I read about that in the Witch Primer but didn't really understand what it does. The Witch Primer is remarkably un-specific."

She laughed at that.

I said, "I still don't know about home magic or time travel."

Maria said, "Don't be so hard on yourself. You did it twice. And brought a whole extra person with you the second time."

She was right. At the very least, I had prepared Alice with the basics of time travel, as Gerald described it to me. Have an anchor. Have a place and time. Be intentional. Now I would find a witch with Home Magic and see what that might do for us. And then if Alice ever found herself in some other era... maybe she could harness all that raw power building inside her young body and make her way back to me.

Alice

As we headed down a steep hill with Grant following behind, I asked Connor what I had been dying to know since I met him.

"What's it like to talk to animals?"

His long strides did not slow, but he did look down at me as he answered.

"It's not like an actual conversation. I can make my thoughts known to them, though. It's like..." he was trying to come up with the words. "I understand what they're feeling, and they understand what I'm feeling, and mostly when I ask them to do something, they'll understand and do it. But they can't do that to me. It's not reciprocal."

"Can you show me?"

He looked down again.

"We don't really have time today. But I will another time."

Seeing my disappointment, he exhaled in frustration and stopped his fast walking to check out our surroundings. We were on a cobblestone street with colorfully decorated shops on either side of us. No animals were visible to me, but Connor said, "We may see some down in that alley." And he took off at his superhuman pace again. I looked back at Grant, and he just laughed.

Halfway down the hill, Connor noticed I was not beside him, and he stopped to look back. When I caught up with him, he said, "Sorry. I just need to be sure to catch my plane."

"It's okay," I said. "You really don't want to make your father mad, huh?"

He was staring ahead, but I knew he heard me.

"I don't have a dad anymore," I said. "He died."

Connor turned toward me, concerned. "I'm sorry. What happened?"

"Both my parents got Covid and died." Grandmother had told me to say this if anyone asked what killed Mother and Father.

He looked worried or mad at that. Or maybe both. He was hard to read.

"But it's okay now because I have Grandmother and Adam."

Grant cleared his throat behind us. "And Grant and Maria," I added. When Connor said nothing else, I nervously filled in with, "And you have your mother. She seems nice."

"She is," he agreed. He stopped then and peered into the dark entrance of an alley. "I think there's somebody in here," he said. Crouching down, he held out his hand to an orange cat that was walking toward us, pressed up against the side of the building. The cat seemed cautious but also curious.

"He's never met a human who understood him before." Connor set his backpack down and unzipped the front pocket. He took out a treat from a plastic bag and held it out to the cat, who practically ran to Connor's hand and ate up that morsel in a flash. The cat began a purr, which turned into a rumble of contentment as he did a figure eight, rubbing his body against Connor's legs. Connor gave a soft laugh and pulled out a couple more treats. "Here. Stop for a minute." The cat stopped and sat right next to Connor's feet.

"Do you want to feed him?" He held the treats out for me to take. "I'm telling him you're a friend, too."

The cat moved over to rub against my legs, and then I stroked his head and under his chin, where his purr vibrated his satisfaction. He ate one and then two treats from my hand and rubbed his head there for more pets from me.

I *loved* him.

Grant caught up with us and gave the cat a pet, too.

Connor picked his bag back up and said, "We should go."

Seeing my reluctance to leave, he said, "I think somebody feeds him back there. It's a restaurant. He's comfortable in this area."

The cat did look well fed.

I gave him one more pet and stood as well.

"That's the best magic ever. I wish I could do that."

Grant leaned against a brick wall, watching the cat return to the back of the alley while Connor and I walked on down the hill.

Connor said tentatively, "You have great magic, too. I think anybody would trade what they have to be able to heal people. You've only had it for a while, though, right?"

I didn't look at him but nodded yes.

"My mom told me that your grandmother is teaching you."

We were at the bottom of the street then, and he looked around for the used computer store he had found online. Pointing across the street, he started that way.

A bell jingled above the door as we entered the shop. Electronic items for sale sat on tall tables that lined both sides of the room, and a group of teens stood to our left. Some were looking at their phones and some at a laptop. A boy with blond hair watched me as I followed Connor to the back counter. While he asked about buying a laptop, I looked at the items on sale near us. Mostly, they were cell phones and their accessories. Grant came in then and made his way to the back. I heard him tell Connor, "No, I'm buying it."

Walking over to the other side of the room, I tried to see what the teens were watching on the laptop. The blond boy noticed and held out his phone for me to see.

"Clayton Steadman is calling for a flash mob on the Royal Mile."

I looked at the small screen and saw dozens of young people lying down in what appeared to be the middle of a street.

"Where is that?" I said.

"Edinburgh," he said with surprise. "You don't know where that is?"

I kept watching as more and more youths arrived at the scene.

"No."

"Is that your boyfriend?" He was looking at Connor.

I gave a laugh and looked back at the phone. "No."

"Is that your dad?" He moved his head toward Grant.

"No."

"Do you say anything other than 'no'?"

I looked up at that.

"Not really. No."

He laughed and held out his hand. "I'm Ryan. What's your name?"

"Alice." I took his hand. Grant and Connor looked over then, and they both frowned.

Ryan said, "He's doing the flash mob to sell his new merch line. I think they're all going to be taking off their shirts in a minute."

"Why?" That seemed dumb. Why would anyone do that? And why would they do it in the middle of the street?

"To show off the merch. I think they're all going to have it on under what they have on now."

A dark-haired girl with heavy eye makeup and a piercing through her nostrils turned around from the counter where she was watching it on the laptop. "I don't think so. I think he's going to spray them all down with a hose. See that over there?" She pointed to something connected to the side of a building. "It's a hose, and he's right by it." She looked me up and down before turning back to the screen. "I like your hair," she said, watching the laptop again.

Ryan scrutinized me and then said, "Me too."

He was cute, and I flushed under his gaze. Then I was so angry at myself for doing so I flushed some more.

"Do you want to text? Can I have your Instagram?"

I did not know what that was, but Grant was suddenly there beside me, and he answered, "She doesn't have one. A phone or Instagram."

Then he stared at Ryan until he looked back down at his phone in silence.

Mad at Grant for shutting down only my second interaction with a teenager in the twenty-first century, I stormed out of the store and stood on the sidewalk outside. There was a bookstore across the street and, though I knew I should stay with Grant and Connor, I decided to just walk through it and see what it was like. At home, there were so few books to read. Only Latin and the Bible. Grandmother had described bookstores and libraries as enchanted places one could spend hours in, just opening books and reading.

I went to step off the sidewalk but found that my foot would not leave the curb. Either foot. I strained my hardest to lift my right foot, but it didn't budge an inch. Then Grant was beside me, and I could move again.

Panicked, I said, "I couldn't move!"

"You're okay," he said. "It's just something that your body was not able to do because you were trying to leave my sight." He watched my face as the realization sank in that my grandmother had done this to me. She had spelled me from leaving Grant's side.

He tried to smooth it over. "I think it was an accident on her part. She may have gotten it from my dad, and she didn't know. I don't think she even knew this could happen. But it was not an unreasonable request under the current circumstances."

Well, this day is just getting better and better.

I made a disgusted sound and stomped off up the street that led back to our rented house.

"Wait!" Grant called. "We have to wait for Connor. Then you can both speed walk home."

I was not in the mood for his humor right then, and I stood still, facing away from him. I wanted nothing more than to just disappear from Grant's sight.

That time, I felt it. The moment I became disembodied. The quaint street of Leith fell away from my peripheral vision, and tall trees closed in on both sides. I was in the direct path of a fast-galloping horse, with a rider astride it. The man wore blue and red with gauntlets on his forearms. He shouted, "Ho!" and pulled the reins tight, trying to stop his horse from trampling me.

No, no, NO...

I closed my eyes as hard as I could and chanted, "Back to Grant, back to Grant, back to Grant..."

Then I heard the bells of the shop chime and a moment later Grant was pulling me into a hug, his arms practically crushing me.

"Oh my *God*," he said. "I'm so sorry. *Please* never do that again!"

I opened my eyes and was back on the cobblestone street. Connor stood at the bottom, staring up at us.

My relief at being back in Scotland was immense, my excitement even greater. Because that moment away in some long-ago era meant I could really do it.

I could travel through time.

CHAPTER EIGHTEEN

Marsh

We'd been at it for over a week. A new town and a new hotel every day. Reporters filled every seat and lined the walls at each venue. Schwartz was there to remind people about the vaccine for cancer. I was there to keep track of Louise's purse and to make sure she had all her notebooks and pens.

She had done *60 Minutes* and the major morning and nighttime talk shows but was still hitting big city after big city. When I asked her why she was crossing the country like Abraham Lincoln on his campaign train tour, she said, "I know it's old-fashioned. But I think it was a good call. Magic has to be seen in person to be believed."

Louise and Schwartz would be at the head of the room, sometimes behind a lectern, sometimes sitting at a table. She would introduce herself and then introduce a new magical skill that was in the unlabeled little black book witches knew as *The Witch Primer*. She always had a witch to show the new magic and had been surprisingly successful at bringing in celebrity witches who fueled the public interest more than anything else could. As Louise said, "Celebrity plus magic? Can't buy that."

She was good. Through Louise, the world learned that some witches could arrange ingredients so that they marinated and blended in the most delectable fashion, so much so that someone could think they were in love with the person who made the dish. This might be where the concept of a 'love potion' came from. But, as she explained, it was just an innate understanding of the best cooking techniques and what ingredients, herbs and spices work best together or what may be missing from a recipe.

There was also magic that allowed a witch to understand

without fail what emotion another person was experiencing. At one of the first press conferences, Louise had explained that we all have an aura that only some witches can see, that is like a weather vane for witches sensitive to emotion. This was where she also explained the notion of responsibility to one's magic.

"When witches come into their magic at puberty, the first lesson they learn is to respect the magic and to use it responsibly. We are taught that magic must never be used on mortals. Period." Louise scanned every face in the room. "That would not be a fair fight. In the human world, boys are taught not to hit girls, and in the witch world, witches are taught never to use magic on humans. We are made to understand that our magic is a gift that demands to be used whenever it can make things better. Not all magic has this potential, but for those witches that hold deep magic within them... I can assure you, they feel a profound desire to use their magic to improve the world around them."

Louise revealed that there were categories of magic. She said that witches inherited magic from both of their parents and often had four or five types of magic they could wield. She explained that no, magic was not something that you could catch with a blood transfusion or through sex. This was significant because while witches could have children with mortals, and their children would be witches, babies were not born with witchcraft unless at least one parent was a witch.

Witches could be described as having simple magic or complex magic. There were also some infrequent magical specialties that were described as heavy and even some extremely rare areas of magic that were defined as dark. In the interest of transparency, Louise mentioned that the dark magics were not detailed in the Witch Primer and that she was not privy to the specifics of those skills.

That was the only thing she said in all those press conferences I didn't fully believe.

One type of magic that never failed to interest the reporters was the one that allowed witches to communicate their thoughts to animals. Louise explained these witches did not enjoy true communication with animals and that they could not understand the animals' thoughts, if such things existed.

Though she was not finished with her remarks and had not

even gotten to Schwartz and the vaccine, a reporter stood and labeled himself as being from a right-wing news outlet. Tall and thin with a head of kinky white hair, he was a vest man. This guy said no to a jacket but yes to a bow tie, and I hated him instantly. Holding a thick silver pen, he pointed it at Louise and peppered her with non-stop provocative questions, cutting off other reporters and even Louise when she tried to answer him.

He asked why she would not discuss in more detail the dark magics, and if she thought that the magic where witches communicated with animals could result in witches imposing their will on humans, and why she had not yet revealed her own magic specialties. I saw the exact moment when she snapped. Schwartz darted his eyes over at me and, still looking at her, I nodded and shook my head *yes. This was it.* The time for her to put that asshole in his place had definitely come.

But she waited him out and continued to look at him until he stopped talking. She regarded him in silence for a few more moments.

His voice riddled with contempt, he said, "Are you trying to intimidate me? Because that won't work. I'm not scared of *witches.*"

She laughed then as if she couldn't believe how much farther he could dig himself into a hole.

"I'm glad you're not scared of witches. You shouldn't be scared of witches. And you should not fear me because I'm a witch." She paused a beat.

"You should fear me because I'm a woman. And a mother. And you just made me sit through a whole five-minute public tantrum. That's four minutes and thirty seconds longer than we usually tolerate."

The room was silent. Schwartz leaned into his mic and said, "You tolerate thirty seconds of tantrum?"

The room laughed. Louise smiled and answered Schwartz.

"Well, we have to figure out what's wrong with the baby. Is he colicky, or gassy or hungry? Maybe he needs a nap. Or maybe he's constipated." She made eye contact with the reporter. "I'm guessing all of those conditions are plaguing you today." More laughter. I let my eyes take her in as she stood comfortably in front of that room filled with people.

God, she smelled good. I decided to find out what that

perfume was and buy her five bottles. She was wearing a dark blue suit I hadn't seen before that was a perfect foil for that spill of silky blond hair. Underneath was a white satin shirt that had small red hearts on it. Red toenails to go with the red hearts. I wondered about the bra and panties. Would they be red silk? I closed my eyes and willed myself to get a fucking grip. We were in public.

Louise said to the obnoxious reporter, "I'll be happy to answer your questions, but you've lost the privilege of participating in this press conference. Security, will you please remove Mr. ...?" She raised her eyebrows at him. "I'm sorry. I've forgotten your name." Tony was at his side, taking the mic out of his hands, and Caleb had taken him by the arm and was guiding him firmly from the room while the reporter protested loudly. I tried to hide my smile behind my hand, but it was hard, and I saw I wasn't alone. Most of the room was watching his removal with a smile.

She was fucking magnificent.

When he was gone, Louise answered the reporter's questions.

"I think the concern regarding dark magic is valid. The very name 'dark magic' is frightening. What I will say is that when parents have children who manifest these magics, they educate them diligently throughout the teen years and beyond about the ethics of that type of magic use. About the responsibility to do no harm with that type of magic use. I know that very often, people who have inherited this type of magic are the protectors of any groups or organizations they're part of. And it's important to remember that one of the first rules witches receive about their magic is never to use it on mortals."

"Regarding the magic that allows communication with animals... no, I am certain that this magic does not imbue the witch who carries it with the power to somehow impose their thoughts upon a human mind." I wondered how she knew that? Connor could speak to animals. Did Louise pass that skill along to him?

As I had been all week long, I was filled again with the desire to know more about that woman. What magic she had. What she liked in a lover. What she wanted more than anything else in the world. I knew that what I wanted more than anything else in the world was to be worthy of her undivided attention.

She poured a big bucket of water over one of those desires when she said, "And with regard to what type of magic a witch holds within them... that is not something I will discuss with you nor is it something you should ask your witch friends. Our attachment to our magic is a sacred thing. It belongs solely to us and no one else. Witches do not ask each other what type of magic they possess, and you should not expect a witch to divulge that information."

She sensed that nobody liked that pronouncement and added, "But we want to inform you of all the wondrous possibilities of magic. That's why today I am giving each of you your own copy of *The Witch Primer*."

The room erupted, and she motioned to the back of the room for Tony and Caleb to distribute folders with the Primer to all the reporters. Over the commotion, Louise said, "I know you're going to have your hands full for a while. But I expect all of you to come back at five o'clock for the conference we'll hold with Doctor Myron Schwartz and the information about the cancer vaccine that is available for all people to get. Witches and mortals alike."

She turned away from the mad scramble for folders and widened her eyes at me. "I lost them for a few hours."

I acknowledged that. "You have indeed. You did a great job just now."

Louise shrugged that off.

I said, "No, really. You were incredible."

Schwartz agreed. "You handled the asshole with aplomb."

She laughed. "Aplomb! Thank you, Dr. Schwartz."

"Yes," I said. "Brilliant observation, Schwartz. Now get lost."

To his credit, Schwartz said, "Okay," and got up and left.

I asked her, "Are you going to get in trouble with the witch bosses for doing that?"

Her mouth tightened, and she shrugged again.

"I don't know. I don't care either. It was just a matter of time before someone got their hands on one, and this way, we were being generous and transparent with things."

Collecting up her notebook and special pens, I handed the

bag to her and asked, "Would you like to have lunch with me?"

She took the bag, threaded her arm through mine, and looked up at me.

"It took you long enough to ask, Samuel. If by lunch you mean sex, then yes, I would like to have lunch with you. How about my room?"

My pulse rocketed, and I thanked the universe for whatever I had done to deserve that day.

My eyes roamed over her gorgeous face. I said, "I think you know that I would follow you anywhere. Lead the way."

Louise

It was one thing to proposition the hot doctor who'd been following you around for a couple of weeks. It was an entirely other thing to end up facing him in your hotel room, having just propositioned him. It had been over a year since I'd been on a date, and I felt suddenly shy and out of ideas as to what to do next.

Luckily, Samuel was not shy. After I dropped my bag on the dresser, he turned me around and drew me to him. He leaned down and brushed my lips with his. "What do you like, Louise?" His lips moved against mine as he spoke. "Whatever you want from now on, that's what you get."

I parted my lips to let him in, and he groaned in appreciation as his tongue touched mine. Our kiss deepened, his tongue exploring my mouth with a confidence that made my knees weak. He walked me backwards until I hit the wall and he pushed into me. But he held the back of my head gently to protect it and I smiled against his lips while labeling him in my mind 'The Rough Gentleman.'

God... I *loved* how he tasted.

And that cologne. It was something dark and masculine that made me want to bury my face in his neck and breathe him in until I was dizzy with it.

"Samuel," I broke away to get his attention.

His lips moved over my jaw, then down my neck.

"What?" he murmured against my skin. I shivered as he pushed aside my shirt and ran his lips and tongue over my collarbone.

"You're a *really* good kisser."

Feeling those lips smile against my skin made my clit tingle, and I gasped at the sensation.

"God, *yes*," he said. He tossed my jacket on the bed and unbuttoned my blouse. "I want more gasps from you. Right now."

I worked on his buttons too, and before long we were both shirtless, kissing frantically and running our hands up and down backs and fronts. I had wanted to touch those abs since I saw them, and they were as hard as I hoped they'd be.

"I knew this bra would be red." He unhooked it with one hand and rubbed his thumb over my nipple through the lace. "But I didn't picture the lace." He kissed me through the fabric. "I fucking love the lace."

I pulled the bra off and tossed it on the floor.

"You should see the panties," I said.

"Oh, my God." He clutched his chest and stared at my breasts. "I honestly don't know if I can handle the panties."

I laughed at him and reached around to unzip my skirt.

"Nope!" He turned me around and grabbed my hips. "Let me do it." I heard him pull the zipper down slowly and felt the skirt slide down my legs. My thong was red too.

"Did you picture that?" I gasped again as his lips touched my neck and he tasted the skin there. I got goosebumps all along my arms and shivered as he nibbled up one side of my neck and down the other. He ran his hands up to my breasts, where he kneaded them and twisted both nipples. I made a sound then that I am sure had never left my lips before. It was shock and excitement, with a little pain and a lot of pure pleasure. I did not know what Samuel's plan was, but I was all in.

Pulling my exposed ass toward his erection, he held one hand over my breast and slid his other hand down into my panties.

"No," he said. "I did not picture the red thong, and I will never again see anything more beautiful than you in this thong." He tugged the panties aside and ran his finger up over my clit.

Another gasp from me. He was good at getting those.

"What do you want, Louise?" He pushed my back down slowly so my head touched the bed and my ass remained in the air. His erection poked me from behind. "Is this okay? Do you like ass play?"

I moaned and discovered that, yes; I did like that. I liked it a *lot*.

He ran his finger down the crack and gave a low laugh.

"That's a yes for later. Right now, I want to make you come harder than you've ever come. Will you do that for me?"

He raised me up and turned me toward him. I knew I was safe with Samuel, and that allowed me to agree to whatever he proposed.

I said, "I'll do whatever you want."

His eyes dropped to my mouth, and he said, "Thank you, Louise. Right now, I want you naked and spread out on that bed."

On the dresser, my phone rang. It was Connor's ringtone. Samuel shook his head, ready to protest the timing of that call, but I had to take it and pushed him away when he tried to pull me to him.

"Sorry, but that's Connor and I have to take it." I picked my shirt up off the floor and slipped it on. Turning away from Samuel, I faced the drawn curtains and took a steadying breath before answering.

"Hello?"

"Mom, he's making me come back from Europe, and even though he wants me to come to the farm, I'm not. I'm coming to you. You're going to be in Georgia tomorrow, right? I'm just about to get on my flight here in Edinburgh, and I can make it there by tomorrow morning, probably. Maybe not before your press conference, but I can get a ride."

"Get a ride? You're not just 'getting a ride.' Give me the flight numbers, all of them." I scrambled in my purse for a free notebook and pen and saw Samuel sit in a chair. With his elbows on the arms of the chair and his hands clasped in front of him, his amused expression let me know he would wait out this poorly timed phone call from my son. I laughed to myself as I got the pen ready. "Okay, what is the number of your flight out of Edinburgh? What airline?"

As Connor listed the numbers and times of the flight and discussed the difference in time with where I was now, I heard the wobble in his voice.

"Oh, honey... what's wrong?" I put the pen down and, holding the phone against my ear with my shoulder, I buttoned up my shirt. Then I sat down on the bed, put my head down and listened to my kid.

"He's just such an asshole. I don't know why he has to be such an asshole. We didn't do anything wrong..." Then he was crying. I listened for any clues about whether this was a mad cry or a heartsick cry, but I couldn't tell through the phone line and over thousands of miles. For the millionth time, I wished I could throttle Jeff for his heavy-handed parenting.

Connor was trying to contain his misery, and I knew the best thing I could do was agree with him and focus on the positive.

"I know, baby, I'm sorry. I wish you could stay too, but I'm going to be so happy to see you."

I heard him sniffing.

Out of the corner of my eye, I saw Samuel stand and reach down for his shirt on the ground.

As Connor spoke, telling me his plan for flight transfers, it sounded like he was doing better.

Maybe this will be a quick fix. But then he circled back to rail against the tactics his father used regularly to control us, and the curse words started flying, and I recognized that this was a mad cry situation with no easy fix in sight.

As Samuel buttoned up his shirt, I mouthed to him, *"I'm sorry."*

Fully dressed again, he came over to the bed. Standing in front of me, he squeezed both my shoulders and leaned down to kiss the crown of my head. *"It's okay,"* he mouthed back.

He picked up my notebook and selected the purple pen from the inside pocket of my purse. Standing in front of the TV, he opened the book and flipped to my calendar and wrote what looked like several things on it. When he was done, Samuel turned and winked at me. Then, looking me up and down, he shook his head and clasped both his hands against his heart.

"Beautiful," he whispered, and I felt myself blush.

And then he left.

While my kid still vented in my ear, I stood and went to look at the calendar. Every day for the rest of the month, Samuel had written his initials, *SAM,* and drawn a heart around them.

Marsh

The key to Louise Carmichael would be her son. I knew this without question. He was her only child, and it was obvious that every decision she made went through the filter first of, "What is best for Connor?"

And I loved that about her. My mother had been benignly indifferent throughout my childhood. She was busy, but not with me. Her time went to her hobbies and her circle of equally hobbied up friends. My father left when I was ten, and it wasn't until high school that I saw different family dynamics and understood what I had missed out on. When Adam's parents practically adopted me after we met in med school, I latched onto them like a fungus. Then, with Grant, Connie and Adam had shown what devoted parents look like even after separation. I was officially Grant's godfather, but they called me his third parent.

I got this. I've been Grant's sounding board for over thirty years. I can handle one teenage boy.

But standing there in the arrivals terminal at the Atlanta airport, waiting for the one person who had the power to strip away the best thing that had ever happened to me... I was nervous as hell.

Connor was among the first to leave the plane. I called out his name and waved him over when he saw me.

"What are you doing here?" Setting his duffel bag down on the ground, he shifted his loaded backpack to his other shoulder.

An auspicious beginning if ever there was one.

"Your mom has a press conference in about five minutes. She didn't want you to take a cab, so I'm the driver." I picked up his duffel bag and said, "Follow me."

He fiddled with his phone as we walked, and by the time we got to my rental car he had a livestream of her press conference playing over the speaker. I started up the car and heard her say she would detail another magic and then she'd call on Henry for the first question. Henry was without a doubt the most obnoxious reporter on the planet.

"Why is he still allowed in there? Why does she let him ask

anything?" It pleased me that Henry disgusted Connor as much as he disgusted me.

"She won't deny anybody entrance, and she likes to get the unpleasant stuff over with first. But he usually gets kicked out, so there's that to look forward to."

Connor shook his head as if that was not good enough, and I absolutely agreed.

While I negotiated the parking pass and waited for the bar to raise to let my car out of the airport parking garage, Connor unzipped his backpack aggressively and whipped out a laptop. Once it powered up, he typed away furiously. After a couple of minutes, he sat back and tapped his finger gently on the touchpad. Waiting for something.

Louise was discussing a type of magic that some artists have that allows them to see items more clearly and understand their function and how they relate to the world around them. And because of this special sight, they create works of art that fully explore what it means to be human- the goal of all art. She could not confirm that any historical artists were witches, but she said it made sense to her that Leonardo DaVinci may have had some of that type of magic. And, in a genius move that she had been working on from the beginning of the press tour, Louise introduced a witch who was an artist and had agreed to demonstrate his process of capturing a scene using all his senses. I glanced down and saw the artist sweeping his paintbrush across an enormous canvas.

At some sort of disturbance in the room, Connor looked away from his laptop and peered intently at the video on his phone.

"What's happening?" I glanced over at the phone but couldn't see anything.

Connor looked a little like the cat who ate the canary.

"Looks like Henry is getting dragged out of there by some federal agents."

There actually were federal agents at all of Louise's press conferences. I wondered what in the world Connor had done to set them on that reporter so fast?

"Why do you think they took him?"

Connor gave a quick shrug and kept his eyes on his mother.

Oh, hell no. That was some bullshit, and I needed to know

what that kid was getting into.

Pulling over at the first gas station we came to, I put the car in gear and turned toward Connor.

"What did you do to get federal agents to arrest that reporter? Also, how the hell did you do it in three minutes? That's very scary."

He looked up at the last part, and his mouth quirked up the tiniest bit.

Another small shrug as he went back to watching the phone. "He may have had some questionable stuff on his social media about his hatred of witches. Might have been considered threats."

I gave him a hard stare before pulling out my own phone. It didn't take long to find whiny Henry (as I had labeled him in my head) and read some of his posts that were snotty and full of discriminatory bullshit about witches. But they weren't threats.

Putting my phone back in my jacket pocket, I said, "That's a slippery slope you're on, Connor. I like that you want to protect your mom from assholes. But do you really want to be facilitating the jailing of a person who didn't actually do the thing he got arrested for?"

There was a tick in his jaw that let me know he heard. But he kept his eyes trained on his phone.

"I mean, jailing people for saying things you don't like is straight out of the Nazi playbook."

That got his attention. "Are you calling me a *Nazi*?"

"Or a current Oval Office advisor, or maybe a Kremlin advisor. Very similar things."

"I'm not a fucking Nazi!"

"I know you don't want to be. But that was a dick move getting somebody hauled into federal custody just because he's not your favorite. I'm pretty sure you agree with the First Amendment. So what the fuck was that?" I pointed at his computer.

He shook his head and refused to look at me. It sounded like Louise was at her "taking questions about witchcraft" point of the press conference. Schwartz would be next.

Connor took a deep breath in and swiped a hand over his face.

"Fuck."

Then he covered his face and groaned. "What the *fuck?* I'm a fascist just like they are... I'm just like *him*."

"No. No, you're not. Hey." I touched his shoulder. "You were just trying to protect your mom from a bully. That's an okay thing to do. Next time, you'll count to a hundred first. Right?"

"Yeah," he said, staring straight ahead and trying to get a hold of himself.

"She just has to deal with so much *bull*shit. All the *time*... and she doesn't deserve it."

I was betting a lot of the bullshit came mostly from his asshole of a dad, and that was another whole layer of shitty reality that the kid had to deal with.

After a minute of looking out the window, he took a deep breath and got back online. I started the car again and pulled onto the highway. I heard him clacking away at the keyboard for another ten minutes. As I turned into the parking lot at the hotel, he closed up the laptop and put it away in his backpack.

"I got him the best civil rights lawyer in Atlanta. He'll be there in fifteen minutes. I paid him for tonight, and he'll bill me for later if necessary."

He acknowledged my raised eyebrows. "I do some consulting on the side. Don't tell Mom."

I smiled to myself and thought the kid was alright. Louise did a great job with him.

Pulling into a parking space up front, I said, "Your secret's safe with me."

CHAPTER NINETEEN

Adam

Apparently, showing up for your subpoenaed congressional testimony without a lawyer was not the brightest thing to do. At least, that's what Herb texted me no less than five times before six a.m.

Not being a complete idiot, I had called my lawyer a couple of times. But she didn't return those calls, and I just assumed that representing a witch was not something her practice was excited about.

And there had been absolutely no time to interview and hire a new lawyer. Between the moment the processor served me the subpoena at my office and the drive to the Cannon Office Building where I was to testify, I had only been two places- The International Council of Witches and the store where I buy my suits. That was it.

Herb countered that Sean was a lawyer and that he'd be right there at the hearing. To which I countered, he was going to be there in his official capacity as aide to Senator Clay, and I was not bringing Sean into this situation and forcing him to be on a side. Who knew how this shit was going to shake out?

All the ways the day could go wrong ran through my mind as I headed out of the office building near Union Station, where I'd been living. Herb and Sallie and even Marsh had been trying to get me to stay with them, but I was more comfortable in the office. I had a couch and bathroom suite with a shower, and it was fine.

The Lyft I ordered waited for me at the curb, and I gave the woman a good hard look before getting into her Lexus.

Probably not going to kill me.

As we drove, I sat in the back of the car and wished Vivienne was with me. I had placed some home magic on her engagement ring before they left but hadn't needed to use it to sense where she was. I didn't know how I knew her location; I just knew. She was somewhere in Italy, I guessed Rome, and had to be getting close to her objective for the trip. It was just before 9:00 a.m. in D.C., so it was just before 3:00 p.m. in Italy. I closed my eyes and tried to picture what she was doing.

I had become a selfish bastard. Before Vivienne, I didn't spend a lot of time thinking about what I wanted. Mother used to tell me that this was the time I should enjoy life. She encouraged me to travel and indulge myself. The trouble was, I could never think of anything I wanted to indulge in. And now... the most incredible woman on the planet was mine, but she was thousands of miles away.

I *wanted* to indulge. In her.

Being without Vivienne was fucking exhausting.

I just wanted my wife.

Ten minutes later, the driver dropped me off, and I debated whether or not I should add the message, "For not trying to kill me," along with her tip. I decided not to, but I left her a great tip and gave her five stars.

All morning I had been feeling fatalistic. Like *this might be the last time I make myself a bagel. Possibly my last cup of coffee.* It was kind of liberating. I wondered if that was what my therapist had described as "living in the moment."

I wasn't being stupid, though. I had my strongest shield surrounding me, and I would keep it in place all day. And I could disappear if I ever needed to. What I told Sean to share with the Defense Department was true- night vision goggles would pick up any heat signatures of a witch using a cloaking spell. But they wouldn't see me with my shield around me and a cloak over top of that. At least I still had that going for me.

Two enormous men were there to greet me on the steps of the Cannon Office Building.

"Doctor Parrish?" One of the giants reached out to shake my hand. "Mr. Al Masri sent us to stick with you from now until this is over. I'm Frank Tesci and this is Carl Borden." I shook the other man's hand and wondered where they got suits that big.

"Okay. Well. Nice to meet you both." I started up the steps and tried to shake off the irritation I felt at being told what to do. After a minute, I realized I was being an ass.

This is a good thing, I told myself. *They'll be extra eyes.* Later on, I'd send a thank-you text to Farhad.

Once we made it through security in the House office building, I took a moment to admire the newly renovated rotunda and the dome above it. The Cannon Office building was over a hundred years old and had just been through a ten-year renovation. Their dome was not as nice as mine at the Library of Congress, but it was still impressive. I noticed, though, that there were no good chairs nearby for a person to lean back and swivel around in while staring up at it. It was incredible to me that only a year and a half ago I had been using that Wednesday night session at the Library of Congress to barely hang on to my sanity and will to live. Then Vivienne showed up in the basement among the card catalogs, and virtually everything changed.

Grant had sent me a good luck text earlier in the morning, so they had to know what I was about to do. I knew Connor was flying home to be with Louise and that Vivienne had been warned that Andrew Barry was mobile and trying to get to her. The desire to catch a plane to Italy and shadow my family to protect them was pretty fucking hard to ignore. Add to that the fact that I had not kissed Vivienne's lips or even heard her voice in forever...

I was wound a little tight.

It's almost over.

I took the marble steps up to the hearing room with some serious, anxious energy.

All that matters is that she is mine and I am hers. I can make it for a few more days.

But stepping into the Nancy Pelosi Caucus room, I felt my tenuous grasp on 'living in the moment' slip away and be replaced with the much more familiar intense irritation I held for current Washington politics. The "Joint Select Committee to Investigate Witchcraft Phenomena and Potential Threats to National Security" was a mixture of members of the House and members of the Senate. Ten Republicans and six Democrats already sat up on the dais at the head of the room. About thirty more aides sat working their phones pretty hard behind the members of Congress.

The room was at least two stories tall and decorated to the hilt with glittering chandeliers, giant carved white columns and gold accents everywhere. As I always did, I noted the exits. The room had three massive mahogany doorways. I walked through one set as I entered the back of the room. There was another set of doors in the back right corner behind the dais, and one set on the left side of the room. On the right were three enormous windows bordered by dark green velvet curtains. I wondered if they had been there when the House Un-American Activities Committee held its hearings in the same room in the late forties.

If so, those curtains have heard all this before. That was a witch hunt, and so is this.

It looked as though the room was set up exactly as it had been for the January 6th Committee hearings of 2022. The place had to be reaching capacity. People filled every seat in the room, and some lined the walls. I waded through probably a hundred people sitting in gallery seats at the back and past about twenty large tables occupied by reporters typing away on laptops. One heavy wooden table with three microphones on it waited for me at the front of the room with a mob of reporters three people deep on the floor in front of it, aiming their telescopic lenses at me. Before I sat down, I checked the space for any signatures of other witches and sensed that, including myself and my bodyguards, there were at least three others somewhere in the room.

John picked a place to stand against the windows, and Carl sat in a chair near my table that had a "Reserved For..." sign on it, which he removed.

In front of me, there was a bottle of water, a pen and pad of paper, and some hand sanitizer. For the hell of it, I squirted some of the hand sanitizer into my palm and ended up with about five times more of the gooey gel than a person needs to sanitize his hand.

"Always so smooth, Parrish." I turned around and saw Greg and John sitting in the row directly behind me, with Herb and Sally sitting next to them.

"You should know," I said as I reached for Greg's hand and slimed it with the remaining sanitizer. He tried to get away, but I was too fast, and we all laughed like we were back in high school, reacting to the equivalent of, "I know you are, but what am I?"

"Mother*fucker*," Greg was trying to get a handkerchief out of the left inside pocket of his suit jacket with his left hand, and it made me laugh again.

Herb leaned over and said, "There's still time for Sean to get down here."

I was about to tell him no, but then Marshall Smith was there, sitting down next to me on my right.

I rolled my eyes. "I've seen more than enough of you in the last few days, Marshall. Why are you here? Did you get served too?"

"No, Adam, I'm a lawyer." When I didn't have a comeback for that, he said, "You're welcome." He opened a folder and took a fancy pen out of his suit jacket. "You shouldn't be alone during this type of questioning. My advice to you is to keep your cool, keep your answers as short as possible and don't answer any question I tell you not to." He slid a piece of paper my way that had a statement about invoking my Fifth Amendment rights.

"I know all that, Marshall. I've watched about eighty years of Law & Order. I could read you your Miranda Rights this second."

He covered his mic and leaned in to whisper to me, "They're almost certainly going to ask you about killing witches for hire. You weren't in violation of our laws when you did that, but you sure as hell violated mortal laws."

He leaned back and let me absorb that.

Yes, I knew there was a possibility they had that. Cole could have confirmed it to Barry, and Barry could have told someone in our U.S. government. Especially now that he was best friends with the president.

I covered my mic, and he covered his.

"What if I say that's the way we kept mortals safe? It's the truth."

Marshall shook his head. "Then what's going to keep them safe now? Now that you're going to agree to go all law and order and be an upstanding citizen?"

I stared at him for a few moments.

"I don't know." I noticed Marshall looked like a lawyer. Like a pricey solicitor with his fancy suit and his Rolex and his perfectly coiffed black hair.

He said, "They're going to want to paint us as murderous outlaws who have no problem with vigilantism. That wasn't it; you and I know that. But we need to steer this hearing toward the future relations of mortals and witches and how they can be partners. This cannot devolve into who you are, what you can do and what you have done."

The chairman of the committee banged a gavel just then to get the room to quiet down. He leaned into the mic and said, "We'll be starting in just a few moments. Please come to order." Roland Schnell was the Republican senator from the great state of Texas and avowed defender of the right to post the Ten Commandments on every surface of every official building in that great state. He seemed young to be in the Senate. Then I rethought that when he appeared to get frustrated with something on his phone and he turned back to his aide with a question. He might be my age and just colored his hair. Tall and thin and sporting a full head of wavy chestnut hair, Schnell was ever ready to pick a fight over any statement not in line with the dogma of his party's "Chosen One." His aide stepped up beside him to show something on his phone and the chairman's cold eyes flicked up to mine at what he saw there.

The guy hated me; that much was clear.

"Alright," I leaned over to Marshall. "I won't dodge what I can do. It has to come out, anyway. I can handle it. But I'll take the Fifth on how I've used my magic for the Council. Agreed?"

Marshall wrote something on his papers and nodded his head yes. "Agreed."

"I'd like to welcome you all to this first meeting of the Joint Select Committee to Investigate Witchcraft Phenomena and Potential Threats to National Security. I am Roland Schnell, senator from Texas, and I'd like for the rest of the committee to introduce themselves as well, starting on my left." The senators and congressmen who followed introduced themselves and listed their other committee assignments to reinforce their qualifications to sit on that dais. There were representatives from the Senate Committee on Armed Services, the Senate Select Committee on Intelligence, and sitting at the very end on the right, Maryland Senator Tom Clay of the Senate Committee on Homeland Security and Governmental Affairs. Sean's boss gave a small smile to the room as he completed his own introduction, and while I appreciated the gesture, I was pretty sure one smile would not change the vibe of the next few hours.

When it was time to swear me in, I stood, raised my right hand and tried not to wince while about fifty cameras flashed in my face. After I swore to tell the truth, the whole truth, so help me God, the chairman asked Marshall to introduce himself.

He stood and smoothed down his tie. "Thank you, Mr. Chairman. My name is Marshall Smith. I'll be the legal representation for Mr. Parrish in these hearings."

He seemed to know that that was not going to be enough for Schnell and remained standing. Schnell said, "Are you also the Marshall Smith who is the current head of the North American Council of Witches?"

"Yes, Mr. Chairman. I was voted into office after our previous head of operations became compromised by dark magic at the hands of the celebrity witch Father Andrew Barry, who is now apparently an advisor to the president."

Marshall attempted to look grim as he sat down, but I could tell he was happy with how that went. The room erupted around us, and my estimation of my lawyer went up by about a thousand percent. The chairman went to town with his gavel a few times, trying to get the room to quiet down again.

I said, "Jesus, Marshall. You do know how to stress people out."

He tried to keep his smile in check as he said under his breath, "Let's start off with Barry being the bad guy. It may be the only win we get today."

CHAPTER TWENTY

Alice's inadvertent time travel was now a full-blown crisis, but here we were in Italy, trying to see the Pope. I felt like a bowstring drawn too taut; one more pull and I'd snap clean through. All I wanted to do was get back to Washington with Alice and have Adam there to help me figure it all out. But this had to happen first, so I stood in Saint Peter's Square and tried to get myself together to argue the fate of all witches with the man currently in charge of the world's one and a half billion Catholic faithful.

"You're doing it again," Maria murmured to me as we waited. Apparently, now that I was no longer keeping the secret of being a witch, my body couldn't keep any secrets at all and was leaking magic everywhere I went. Mostly, it just made the people we encountered greet us warmly and ask if we needed anything. There were a few men who were bold enough to try taking me by the waist or by the hand to accompany them elsewhere, but Grant put a stop to that each time.

This will not do for an audience with the Pope.

I willed my magic to settle in and behave and added the strongest shield I could muster to surround me. The last thing we needed was for my magic to present itself to the Pontiff and for it to appear as if I was trying to seduce him.

The truth was my mind was not there with us in Rome; it was in Washington, D.C. with my husband, who was about to testify in front of the world about his use of witchcraft. Grant had seen the headline on a news channel but said it would happen when we were trying to meet the Pope.

I closed my eyes and pictured Adam there facing that alone. He had barely accepted that it was alright to discuss magic. Now he was going to be interrogated about it while he was under oath. It was too much. I shook my head and tried to concentrate on the task at hand.

In the year I was gone, a pope had died and a papal conclave had elected a new one. I knew little about him other than that he was American and I would be able to speak with him in English. It was one less issue to worry about.

Around us, Saint Peter's Square was emptying at the close of the business day for the Vatican. The sun was low in the sky, and I shivered as I pulled Alice close to me to get in on her warmth.

Our Vatican guide, Marcello Gallo, made his way down to us on the lower level of the steps. His official title was Head Keeper of the Vatican Keys. Grant had found him through a Library of Congress librarian who knew a Vatican librarian. Marcello was a handsome young man in his thirties. He wasn't a witch but had invited us to his home the night before to have dinner with his family, a wife and two young daughters. I didn't lie to him when I discussed our reasons for the visit. I told him that Adam Parrish was my husband, and that we were trying to spread the word about the cancer vaccine and trying to inform the Pope that witches were not to be feared. Our official request to gain a visitation with the Pope had come too late to get us on his schedule.

He took the news that we were witches in stride and said in response, "We who experience the Vatican every day...the art, the lessons from our history, the presence of our Pope... we are more open to the mysteries of God's creation." After some demonstrations of our various magics, (Alice healed a cut on his wife's finger, Grant made the children shriek with delight as their dolls danced in the air, and I lulled the girls off to sleep by humming a soft song) Marcello decided we were safe.

"I cannot promise you a meeting with His Holiness," he said, "but I may be able to put you in the same room at the same time."

I pictured Marcello's family as he gestured for us to follow him up the staircase, and I hoped his bringing witches in to see the Pope was not about to cost him his job.

We took the stairs from the north side of Saint Peter's Square inside through a large bronze door. Marcello said this was the formal entrance and stairway, called the 'Scala Regia,' which led to the Sistine Chapel.

Grant leaned down to tell Alice that 'Scala Regia' meant 'Royal Staircase' in Latin, to which she replied, "I know." He raised his eyebrows at me and gave a short, impressed nod. In our year together back in our time, I found a Latin book for Alice to study as well as the modern English I taught her.

Grant said to her, "An artist named Bernini designed this stairway. How about the art inside the chapel? What do you know about that?"

She tore her eyes away from a giant sculpture on our right of a horse and rider. "Nothing," she said to him. "Tell me."

We began the long trek up a marble staircase flanked by white columns at least two stories tall. It narrowed closer to the top, and the effect made you feel you were on a stairway to heaven.

Grant said in a low voice, "Bernini did this whole area. He made that sculpture too. It's Constantine the Great. It's been here since 1670." He waited while she calculated when that was in reference to her previous timeline of the 1500s. After she gave a quick nod that she had it, he continued.

"The art in the Sistine Chapel is magnificent. Painted by Michelangelo beginning in 1508." She met his eyes, and he nodded at her that, yes, that was the same time she would have been living in London. She could have seen him paint it if she had visited Rome. "We have to be silent once inside the Chapel but I want you to look on the ceiling toward the center for a panel called 'The Creation of Adam,' where God's finger reaches for Adam's."

She gave him a quick, grateful smile. My stress eased considerably during that interaction. No matter what, Alice had a larger group of people looking out for her now. Maria and I shared an amused glance at Alice and Grant's shared love of history and art. Grant was also making sure that Alice read the classics. Her assimilation into the twenty-first century had gone more smoothly than I ever could have hoped it would, and I had this family to thank.

Halfway up the stairway, two men in formal military dress stepped out to bar our way. They wore uniforms made of heavy cloth covered in wide vertical stripes of blue and yellow. Metal helmets topped with a red plume covered their heads.

The surprise was not that the Pope's Swiss Guard security force was there in front of us.

The surprise was that they were witches.

One guard was addressing Marcello in rapid Italian, and I wished Connor was back with us to translate. The guard was unhappy with the situation, and Marcello was trying to mollify him.

Maria said to Grant, "It kind of makes sense."

"It does," he agreed. "Witches would keep the Pope safer than a normal police force. It's an elite group, hard to join. The question is, does he know?"

The other guard's eyes shot over to Grant. He spoke to his fellow guard then, in English. "We should not do this here."

The other guard spoke to Marcello.

"He said to follow him," Marcello translated.

We climbed the rest of the stairs in silence, one guard in front of us and one behind.

At the top, the guards had a slight disagreement about which way to turn. Marcello translated in a soft voice, "This is the Sala Regia, the Royal Hall. They don't want to take us to the Sistine Chapel, but there's somebody in the Pauline Chapel." He gestured to the left. Leaning around one guard, I saw it was indeed occupied. By the Pope. He sat on a throne with a dozen people before him. I gave a small gasp, and the guards stopped talking. The Pope raised his head and looked at us. Our eyes met, and in that second I understood why the guards did not want me to see His Holiness.

The Pope was a witch.

CHAPTER TWENTY-ONE

Adam

Schnell didn't beat around the bush.

"Mr. Parrish, your official work for the North American Council of Witches is that of an assassin, is it not?"

You could have heard a pin drop in that chamber. I stared at him, and he stared back.

After a moment, I leaned into the mic and said, "It's Doctor Parrish."

He corrected himself. "*Doctor* Parrish, your official work for the North American Council of Witches is that of an assassin, is it not?"

I looked at the statement on the table in front of me. It read, "I invoke my Fifth Amendment privilege against self-incrimination and respectfully decline to answer."

Fuck that.

"Yes, that was my role there before witchcraft was revealed to the world. It was the only way to keep dangerous witches from harming mortals." An electric buzz of shock rolled through the room. Beside me, Marshall sighed and with his index finger, dragged the Fifth Amendment paper back in front of him.

"So you admit," Schnell reached for his gavel and hit it again to quiet the room. "So you admit to killing for hire. Did you harm any people who were *not* witches in your job as a witch assassin?"

"Never. The whole point of that role is to protect others against witches who were criminals."

"You admit to killing Americans on American soil."

"They were witches first. And your police would not have stood a chance against any one of them."

Schnell put on his glasses and read something from a page. "I assume you know our police force in Washington, D.C. has been augmented by our president, and that the crime rate here," he pointed at his paper, "has gone down."

Was that a question? I said, "I've seen tanks."

I heard Herb laugh.

"Is this hearing funny to you, Doctor Parrish?" Schnell dropped his paper in front of him.

"No, but the tanks kind of were."

This time it was Greg laughing behind me.

"Adam..." Marshall wanted me to shut up, but I couldn't.

"Mr. Chairman, what I want you to know is that most witches in the world are good, law-abiding people. There is a small population of bad people in that larger group. Once they're identified, the Council of Witches eliminates those threats to the witch population and the mortal population. I no longer work in this area, but I'm glad witches are out in the open and that method of threat containment can be discontinued. It's something that will need to be addressed by your lawmakers and the various witch councils worldwide."

There. I said what I'd come to say.

Schnell said, "Vigilantism is against the law, Doctor Parrish, as is murder. How often did you take assignments to kill people?"

"Once a month or more."

"And how long have you worked for the North American Council of Witches in this capacity?"

"Almost ten years."

He looked up then, and I could see his brain trying to settle on a figure. You could practically hear the math gears in everyone's head cranking while they added up ten years, at least once a month, ten times those extra two months is twenty. Add at least half a dozen for the 'or more' qualifier.

While everyone was adding it up in their heads, I knew the exact number.

"You've killed over a hundred and twenty Americans over the last ten years?"

This was where things could get tricky.

I said, "Not just Americans."

Schnell could not believe his luck.

"You've killed foreign citizens on American soil?"

"Not just American soil."

People leaned in to each other then, and the room buzzed again with low discussions.

Marshall was writing furiously on his legal pad. His to-do list was getting longer. Bullet points read, 'Call Conti. Call Louise. Call all councils. Beef up security at ICW.'

I added, "I worked in collaboration with the International Council of Witches on particularly dangerous situations that I was uniquely qualified to address."

Schnell followed up with, "And what made you uniquely qualified?"

I steeled myself for the next part. To talk about what I could do with persuasion and pain. The kind of power those magics gave me, along with cloaking and my shield... it made me nearly invincible.

I told myself that once I got this out, it would all be over. No more secrets.

"When there were witches with magic like mine, I was able to counter their efforts and subdue them quickly."

"By 'subdue' you mean 'kill.' Isn't that right?"

"Yes."

"And what type of magic do you have that allowed you to kill other witches?"

"If a witch had persuasion... I also have that magic, and their attempts to use it on me were unsuccessful."

He looked down at his paper as if bored.

"This power of persuasion allows you to direct another person's actions. Can you demonstrate it?"

Son of a bitch.

I *really* did not want to do that. I glanced back at Herb. He grimaced, and I knew he understood how badly I wanted out of that. I placed my hand over the microphone in front of me and asked Marshall, "Do I have to?"

He gave a small nod and whispered, "Keep it simple. Limit it to him."

I said, "Fine."

Taking my hand off the microphone, I said, "Chairman, the rules for using this magic are simple: Never use it for yourself. Only use it when lives are in danger."

Still looking down, he asked, "And whose rules are those?"

"My father's."

He looked up at me.

I continued, "It's understood in the witch community that we never use our magic on mortals. Parents teach their children that as soon as they get their powers, which happens at puberty. This has been part of the information exchange Louise Cartwright has been offering on her press tour about the existence of witchcraft and the cancer vaccine. What she has not touched on is the magic known as 'heavy magic' or 'dark magic.' These are rare abilities that only a small percentage of witches have or even know about. Persuasion is one of those rare magics, and witches who have it are taught never to use it unless it is a matter of life and death."

"Understood. Can you demonstrate it?"

What an asshole this guy was.

I said, "This is not a life or death situation, but I will demonstrate it to prove it exists so that law enforcement in the future can address it effectively. Do I have your permission to use it on you?"

Oh, he did not like that one bit. But what was he going to do? Point to someone else?

"You have my permission," he said.

"Mr. Chairman, will you please stand up?"

He stood and looked none too happy to be doing it.

"Mr. Chairman, sit down."

He sat. And then glared at me. I was careful not to smile, but I admit, it felt fucking great to make that man do what I said.

I asked him, "How did it feel to have persuasion used on you?"

"Like I was compelled to do something I did not want to do. Like you took my freewill away."

I said, "You can see why this power is not to be used lightly. It can be a heavy burden for a witch to carry over the course of a lifetime."

"Oh, poor you! What a burden! To have whatever you want is a *burden*?"

Marshall stepped in then.

"Mr. Chairman, I'd like to remind you that you asked Doctor Parrish for a demonstration of his persuasion ability. He accommodated that request, and he did so with your permission. He has also stated for the record that he does not use this magic for his own benefit; he has only ever used it to protect other people."

Schnell went for the jugular then.

"Doctor Parrish, how many witches have the power to persuade? Is there a central list of those witches who have this 'Dark Magic' you have described?"

"Not that I am aware of."

He said, "But you know who they are."

We had another stare-off. After an uncomfortable bit of silence, I said, "I won't name names, if that's what you're asking."

"Is there a way for a 'mortal' as you call us, to determine if someone is a witch or not?"

"Not that I know of. No."

"But witches all recognize each other?"

Someone had prepped the senator pretty well.

I answered, "Yes, witches recognize other witches."

"Is there a master list of witches worldwide?"

Fuck.

About a million flashes went off in my face.

I turned to Marshall. Putting my hand over the microphone, I leaned close to him and murmured, "What now, lawyer?"

"You're under oath, so tell the truth. Keep it short."

I turned back to the senator.

"Yes."

That satisfied him.

"And do you have access to this list?"

"No."

He frowned. "Do you know who does have access?"

I assumed Marshall would, but I didn't know that, so I answered, "No."

Schnell pursed his lips at that. He moved on to Marshall.

"Mr. Smith, do you have access to the list of witch names?"

Marshall said, "I would like to remind the committee that I was not subpoenaed to testify at today's hearing, nor was I sworn in to testify."

Schnell raised his voice. "So you are refusing to answer?"

Marshall leaned in to say into the mic, "Yes." Then he leaned back. Someone chuckled in the row behind us, sounded like Sally this time.

Schnell shook his head in disgust, but luckily his time was up, and he turned the questioning over to another member of the panel. I sat through two more grillings by other Republican senators, which thankfully revealed little more than some major posturing for their party and pandering to their base.

Then Sean's boss, Senator Tom Clay, had his turn.

"Doctor Parrish." He looked up at me. "You are a pediatric oncologist. How long have you practiced this type of medicine?"

"Over thirty years." I felt a pang when I remembered I was not employed anymore as a pediatric oncologist.

"What's a day in the life of a pediatric oncologist like?"

As I described a typical day at the Children's Hospital, I was also mourning the loss of that incredibly tough type of day. No one was going to let an admitted assassin treat their child in the hospital.

When I was done, he said, "It must have been very hard. To see children that sick on a daily basis."

"It was."

"But also incredibly rewarding?"

"Yes."

"But you have discovered a way to prevent people from getting cancer. Is that right?"

"Yes. We have a vaccine that has gone through rigorous trials and has been proven to prevent cancer. We also think it is going to be effective in preventing other major maladies. It's available for free to everyone, mortals and witches alike."

"But you're having some difficulty getting people to trust the vaccine, is that right? Why do you think that is?"

I couldn't help the small laugh that escaped me at that.

"Well... there was this thing five years ago, a worldwide pandemic..."

Senator Clay smiled. "I think I remember that, yes."

"It was mishandled at first, and that led to millions more deaths than there needed to be. And by the time the vaccine was created, people were distrustful of the government, scientists, and the medical community." I shook my head, remembering some of the ridiculous claims from that time. "We've been stuck with this war on science for quite a while now. It doesn't help that whole departments of scientists are being eliminated and that the people in charge of departments devoted to public health are science deniers..." I saw Marshall tap the table and decided he was right, I should reel myself back to the issue at hand.

"And then there's the fact that the vaccine was discovered through witchcraft. That witches are the ones to discover it and create it. I understand that might be something people want to know more about."

Clay gestured toward me. "This is your opportunity to tell them, Doctor Parrish."

What could I say to persuade mortals we meant well? That the vaccine was safe for everyone?

"I think I'd want everyone to know that it wasn't just witches working on the vaccine. The majority of scientists creating the vaccine were mortals, with just a few witches involved in that process at all. And the whole reason witches voted to tell the world about witchcraft was so the cancer vaccine could be made available to all humans. Witches, mortals... everyone."

I looked around the room. "I've seen how cancer can destroy families. And I never wanted that to have to happen again. Neither did the leaders of all the witch councils in the world. That's why we voted to reveal our secret, at significant risk to our community. That's why people should trust this vaccine. It was more important than anything else."

CHAPTER TWENTY-TWO

Vivienne

The Vatican requested that people remain quiet while inside the Sistine Chapel, but I could not have spoken even if I had wanted to.

The Pope was a witch. He hardly needed my prepared lecture about how witches are God's children too and how horrific things can happen whenever church and state work together to scapegoat a marginalized group of people. My head was swimming. I raised a hand to my forehead, trying to decide what to do next.

And frankly, the art surrounding me in that space was overwhelming. But I knew I was in the presence of divine inspiration, so I took a moment to calm my rapid heartbeat and soak in all the wonders of that room while I could.

Alice was doing the same. She had much more of an artistic eye than I did, and I always wished my father could have known that. She walked to a wall that divided the room but did not obscure the view in front of us. Against a bright blue sky, Michelangelo had brought to life The Second Coming of Christ and the Final Judgment by God of all humanity. She stood with her head back and her long red hair falling past her waist. I decided that when we got home, I would buy her art supplies and take her to all the museums in Washington, D.C. to explore what the Sistine Chapel was inspiring in her at that moment.

Marcello and the guards were still arguing in low voices, I supposed about what to do with us.

"Marcello, please ask them if they can hear the truth in my words."

The taller of the guards looked at me. He spoke English.

"I can hear your truth."

That was a blessed relief to me, and I could see Grant and Maria felt the same.

"Please believe me when I tell you we are not here to harm His Holiness. My name is Vivienne Parrish. My husband is the doctor who revealed witchcraft to the world. I am Catholic, as is my granddaughter." Alice walked back to stand beside me. "We are devout. I was here to ask for just one minute to speak to the Pope to tell him that witches are made from God."

He wanted to let me, I could tell.

Marcello said, "These are good people. What she says, she means."

I kept my eyes on the guard.

My group was surprised when I said, "But I feel now that I do not need to speak to him in person. I would appreciate your giving him my message when you can." His look told me he understood I knew the Pope was a witch and that I would not share that information.

Then the small crowd of people from the Pauline Chapel was making its way through the Sistine Chapel.

The Pope wore a long white robe with a silk sash at his waist and a white cap on his head. As he neared, I felt my nerves subside, and I was flooded with emotion to stand in his presence. The energy shifted around us, and it felt like the room was now full. I looked at my group to see if they were also being buoyed by the appearance of the Holy Father in our midst. Alice grabbed my hand and squeezed it with such vigor that I knew she was feeling it, too.

Maria gasped then, and Grant said urgently, "Vivienne, *look*."

Behind us, standing in the doorway of the Sistine Chapel, stood Father Andrew Barry.

Chapter Twenty-Three

Adam

Schnell called a recess for lunch, and I booked it out of that room as soon as possible, my groupies in tow.

"How much time do we have? Let's get lunch at Sam's Hot Dog cart. I love that guy." Sally was clearly starving.

I said, "You guys don't have to stay all day. I appreciate you coming, but you don't have to sit through all that again this afternoon."

Greg said, "We're staying. Subway is closer, Sally. A sub sounds *so good* right about now." He was walking fast, obviously starving too.

Marshall said, "I'll meet you back here in an hour," and he made his way back into the hearing room.

We were blocking half the exit at the doorway in the back of the room, so I motioned for the group to follow me. I instantly wished I'd taken a different doorway when I saw the space circling the rotunda was chock full of reporters and their camera setups.

"Doctor Parrish, you admitted in your testimony to being a killer for hire. Do you expect to be arrested?" The woman who shoved a microphone in my face was way too close, and I had to pull back on the urge to swat it away.

"He has no comment right now. We are on our way out- let us through." Herb stepped up in front of me. "Let's go."

My new security guards were there then, one in front and one behind, making a path through the crowd.

"Are witches okay with assassins killing other witches?" The reporter who shouted that at me was a man, and I thought about how good it would feel to deliver a right hook to his stupid face.

"They kill the teenagers too."

That stopped me in my tracks, and my guard Carl ran into my back.

I looked around for the voice that had said that.

Then I saw her. Standing across from me in that rotunda. Lucia Perez.

Staring right at me, she raised her voice and said, "Ask him about the teenagers he killed for the Council of Witches. The kids who couldn't hide their power when it hit them, they were all murdered. Ask him what they did to those kids. *My son!*" She screamed that last part at me. "What happened to *him*?"

I shook my head in disbelief. "Never. I *never* hurt a child, would *never* be party to that."

"Then who was it, Adam? *Who was it?*"

Just then, the ground shook, and a terrifying boom sounded to my left. I looked out the huge rotunda window to see a major section of the Capitol Dome gone and smoke pouring out of the top. People screamed and ran for the stairs, reporters ditching our exchange to cover the events outside. Another sickening boom hit, and that one felt like it was farther away.

"What the fuck is happening?" Greg was pulling John toward the stairs. "We need to get out of here! Adam, come on!"

I was looking at Lucia across the rotunda from me.

"What have you done?" I whispered. My guards were pulling on me, too.

She let me see a small smile and then turned to blend in with the crowd.

Chapter Twenty-Four

Vivienne

"That man is a threat. Guard the Pope!"

The guards did not hesitate to react to my words. They both had cloaking magic and used it to make themselves and the Pope disappear. I heard them leave though, as they headed out the back entrance. I stepped in front of Alice and watched Barry as he walked slowly toward our group.

"Vivienne. It's wonderful to see you again."

Glancing at the wall depicting The Final Judgment and then up at the ceiling, he said, "This room never disappoints, does it?"

He acknowledged Grant then. "You look exactly like your father." His eyes went to Maria. "And you would be Maria. And," he leaned sideways as if to see behind me, "I imagine that's your granddaughter, Alice. So nice to meet you all."

He looked at Grant again. "Well, most of you."

Grant just smiled at him.

Marcello checked out Barry and said, "We should leave the chapel. It's after hours, and it should be closed."

Barry raised his eyebrows. "Oh really? Who are you, and what is it you do here?"

Marcello didn't speak, sensing our unease but not understanding just how much danger we were all in at that moment.

"I'm sorry, I'm Father Andrew Barry." He walked closer and stuck his hand out for Marcello to shake.

"Marcello Gallo." He gave Barry's hand a quick shake.

"And what do you do here?" Barry stood next to him, still being friendly.

I was relieved to feel that my family had all raised their shields to be as strong as they could make them.

Marcello looked at me, trying to read whether he should talk to Barry.

"Please take the rest of my family out to the square, Marcello." He took a step toward the door, but Barry used persuasion on him.

"Stop." Marcello stayed where he was, shocked to feel his will was not his own. Barry followed up with, "What is your role at the Vatican?"

"I am a Keeper of the Keys." Marcello looked sick to be admitting that to an unknown witch forcing him to do it.

"Interesting." Barry held out his hand to Marcello. "Give me the keys."

While he was getting them out of his pocket, Marcello said, "You should not hold these keys. You are clearly not fit to have access to this holy place."

Barry took the giant keyring filled with dozens of different sizes and shapes of keys. As his hand left Marcello's, he pushed a jolt of energy up Marcello's arm that made him shudder and collapse to the ground.

Grant sent a rope of energy Barry's way that looked like a blue lightning bolt, which Barry was able to deflect at the last second.

"Ouch, Grant. That could have hurt." Their eyes locked as Grant approached him.

Maria and Alice were trying to pull Marcello to the edge of the room. Alice washed Marcello with some of her healing and then glanced up to let me know he was still alive. Her expression became determined, while Maria's was tense, watching the scene unfold in front of her.

"Vivienne, I just want to talk to you. No one else needs to get hurt." Barry didn't take his eyes off Grant.

I said, "Grant, wait. Please let me talk to him first. I need to know some things."

"She needs to know some things, Grant." Barry was taunting him, and I prayed Grant could resist it.

He did. Giving a slight shrug, he said, "Okay," and insulted Barry by turning his back on him and going to help Maria and Alice.

I walked to the doorway leading to the Sala Regia and waited for Barry to meet me.

He said, "What are you doing with the Pope?"

I replied, "What are you doing pretending to be a priest?"

That surprised him. Laughing, he said, "I'm so glad that you have a sense of humor! That's a good one. But I'm not pretending; I am an actual priest. See, we need to get together more often. I want to know everything about you, and I want you to know everything about me."

"You tried to kill me. And my husband. And Marcello just now."

He drew in a breath. "Well, Adam was in my way, and Marcello was egregiously disrespectful; you heard him. But I *am* sorry to have hurt you, Vivienne. My only defense is I came undone when I felt your magic." He shook his head. "I just wanted a little taste, but then I couldn't stop. The things I can do now!"

Barry paused, his eyes roaming all over my face. "You are a miracle, and I have been trying to tell you that for so long now. Can we go somewhere to talk?"

I looked at him in disbelief. "I'm a married woman, and I do not want to talk to you about *anything*. And a real priest does not proposition a woman!"

"Oh please, that's such an old-fashioned way of thinking about the priesthood. And *marriage*?" He rolled his eyes. "That can be fixed. Can we just have some tea and some time to get to know each other? I think we have things in common."

I stared at him. He looked so normal, handsome even. His expression was reasonable, that of a lover trying to calm his mate and get her to talk to him again after a spat. But he was not normal; he had almost killed a man in front of me and had tried to kill Adam more than once.

I tried a new tactic.

"Andrew. What do you want from me? How were you able to find us?"

His reaction to my saying his name was immediate. He softened.

"Don't you know? We're connected now. I have your magic in me, and it speaks to me."

Dear lord. Please let that just be his madness talking.

Stepping back from him, I said, "I won't go anywhere with you."

"Well…" he looked back into the Sistine Chapel and said, "that's disappointing. Because I really do need to clarify a few things with you about how your magic can bend time." His eyes came back to mine, no longer nice. No longer willing to negotiate. "But I suppose if you refuse to help me with that, I can talk to Alice about it." He tilted his head as she held her hand to Marcello's heart. "It looks like she inherited her grandmother's skills."

"Wait!" I tried to grab his arm, but he sidestepped me and made his way back toward where Alice kneeled on the ground next to Marcello. She stood, and though he was halfway across the chapel, she stepped back from him, her face pale.

"Alice, go!" I yelled at her. She looked at me with terror as she faded from view. Barry stopped short and stared at the spot where she had stood seconds before.

Maria covered her mouth with both hands, frightened for Alice.

Grant was looking down at his phone, his expression grave.

He said, "Somebody bombed the Capitol. And the seats of other world powers. Russia, England, China." He looked up at me, and I could see we both had the same terrible thoughts.

Adam was somewhere in the Capitol complex testifying before Congress.

And the Pope was the seat of power at the Vatican.

I turned and ran out of the room.

Flying down the Scala Regia I muttered under my breath, "Please be on time, please be on time…" After what seemed like an eternity I was at the giant doors leading to Saint Peter's Square but they budged when I tried to pull on them.

Barry was there then and pushed me aside. He pulled them open, and I slipped through, out to the steps leading down to the square.

Looking up, I saw two missiles coming at us. They made a high-pitched scream as they whirred down from the sky directly at the Sistine Chapel and the residence of the Pope. A group of priests were running across the square hoping to find cover while one in their group stood still and watched the incoming missile heading straight for him.

With all my might, I raised my arms, and a golden dome took shape around the Papal Palace, praying it would hold against the ordnance. Barry was beside me then and added another silver layer of shield under mine.

When the explosion came, the shock traveled down the exterior of the dome and into my body. The pain was excruciating, and I fell to the ground. I landed on my back, slamming my head on the pavement. With my eyes wide open, the last thing I saw was the dome falling in patches, collapsing around Saint Peter's Square.

I closed my eyes.

Chapter Twenty-Five

Adam

My guards were doing their best to get me out of the Cannon Office Building, but I needed to look for Lucia Perez.

"Stop." I used persuasion that did not work on my guards, but several people running by us suddenly stood still. "No, go ahead," I motioned to anyone who was stuck in place.

"What the fuck?" Carl was not amused.

"We need that woman. The one who was accusing me over there. Her name is Lucia Perez. Tall, with long dark hair, blue suit- a skirt, she did this." I pointed at the Capitol.

"Got it." He dialed something on his phone while they pulled me along down the stairwell. I heard him describing Lucia to someone and asking for help in the search. My phone buzzed in my suit coat pocket, and I answered.

"Yeah."

"Adam. Fausto is at the Capitol. He's not answering. He's not answering!" It was Sonya, my housekeeper, in a panic about her husband. Fausto was a Capitol Hill cop, obviously on the job.

"Sonya, I'll look. But he's probably got his hands full helping everybody right now."

She was quiet, and I knew she was trying to get herself together for her son Eduardo, just in elementary school. I started jogging then headed toward the Capitol.

"Call me when you see him?" She was crying but obviously trying to keep it down so Eduardo wouldn't hear.

"I will." I hung up and turned my jog into a run.

My phone rang again, but I ignored it and ran faster.

Vivienne

When I opened my eyes, Andrew Barry's blue eyes were staring right into mine. He was holding my head in his lap, pressing something against the back of it. We were on the floor in a tiny room no bigger than a closet. I saw cleaning supplies, a mop and pail and recognized that was exactly what it was, a janitor's closet.

I had a splitting headache, and it felt like I was bleeding from a wound on the back of my head. When I remembered why, I gasped and tried to get up, but the pain was excruciating. I closed my eyes again and began healing myself as fast as I could.

Adam's question of whether my body would heal itself if I did not ask it to had been answered.

It would not.

There was no use in hiding my magic... Andrew Barry had already stolen this from me and knew what it could do, so I used it fully.

"Good. You're healing yourself. I tried, but I'm sorry, I just don't know how to make it work that well."

Don't think about him. Just heal.

Barry was stroking my hair and patting my arm.

"You did it. You saved the Pope and the Sistine Chapel. I added a shield under yours just in case, but it wasn't necessary; yours did the trick. And I'll make sure everyone knows it."

Even with me giving it my all, I was not bouncing back like I needed to, and it felt like I had probably lost quite a bit of blood. Breathing slowly, I focused only on my body.

Blood cells need to replicate.

I made a list of what to do.

Now, my scalp needs to mend the rift in it.

Calm was my friend, not panic. My mind shut out the world and focused only on my body. Minutes later I was well on my way to being whole again, and I pushed up and away from Barry.

"You need to be more selfish, Vivienne. That was far too risky a stunt to pull. You could have died."

My face couldn't help but show how ridiculous I found that statement.

"You helped. You must have wanted to save the Vatican as well."

He shrugged. "I didn't want the Sistine Chapel to be destroyed. That's true. But mostly I didn't want you to be destroyed."

My hand was shaking when I wiped it over my face, and I took a few more calming breaths to stop it. I surveyed our surroundings and then I remembered what had happened just before I ran out to make a dome over the Vatican.

Someone had bombed Washington, D.C., where Adam was testifying before Congress. Alice had disappeared before our very eyes.

Oh God. Where did she go? Where is she?

Barry saw my recognition.

"Yes." He nodded. "You remember. We need to talk now about Alice and where she went."

Anything but that.

I asked him, "Who is bombing world capitals? Why are they doing it? Is it the same person who bombed our house?"

His mouth tightened, and he shook his head a bit, irritated. "It's probably Lucia. She's deeply misguided and is mucking it all up with the mortals."

"But *why*?"

"Oh, who knows? She's probably got a magical munitions dealer. I'll take care of her; don't you worry. I just need to know about Alice right now and what she did."

What could I tell him that would steer him away from how she left? Maybe he would believe she had the cloaking magic Adam did.

He said, "Vivienne, I can see the wheels turning in your beautiful head... 'How do I explain where she went? Will he believe it was a cloak?' The answer is no, I am not an idiot. Cloaking is what the Swiss Guard did for the Pope when they spirited him away. No, our Alice wavered and then disappeared as if someone were removing pixels. Like she was being beamed up to the U.S.S. Enterprise."

I could feel a line form between my eyebrows as I wrinkled my forehead and tried to decipher that description of Alice disappearing.

He put both palms up to his forehead, exasperated with me. "I know you're British, but how do you not know about Star Trek? That should have been prime television viewing in your youth."

He was not going to let this go.

I said, "I never cared for television." Trying to stand in the narrow confines of that closet required me to use his shoulder to balance myself, but he grabbed my hand and pulled me down again. I scrambled backwards to avoid touching him.

"Vivienne, I think the reason you don't know about television and you can't explain where your granddaughter went is that she traveled through time. You are both from another time, aren't you?"

Dear God.

He knows.

When my eyes betrayed me and I remained silent, he said, "That's why you went missing for an entire year. You went back to get her. That's why your magic is so otherworldly. Because you have the old magic."

He leaned forward and grabbed me again, his fingers circling my wrist. I held my breath.

"All I want from you right now is the truth about this magic. I have it too, and I just want to know what to do with it. That's all. I can't get it to work for me. Just give me a starting point, and I'll let you go."

He will let *me* go?

Every ounce of my magic exploded from me then, shattering the door into jagged wooden pieces and leaving Barry encased in a field of malignant energy. Some of the wood had pierced his face before my spell surrounded him.

"*You* do not dictate where I go."

I discovered my mistake almost immediately as I struggled to leave the tight space. I had depleted my magic. It would take hours to generate enough for a shield. *Hours.* While the force field I had entombed Barry in was strong, it was unformed and artless. It wouldn't hold. My rage and my ego had just left me more vulnerable than I had probably ever been in my adult life. Once I made it over the debris of the door and started running down the hallway, I began to pray.

Adam

The Capitol was on fire. It couldn't have been over five minutes since the explosion, but the police were already establishing a perimeter around the north entrance. The guards and I bypassed it pretty quickly when they flashed some badges and I said I was a doctor. A god-awful smell rocked all three of us back as we approached the bottom steps. The entire area reeked of sick magic, but the mortals did not seem to be affected by it at all. People in suits were helping other people in suits down the steps in various stages of shock and injury. I made my way to an ambulance just pulling up to the base of the south entrance Capitol steps.

"I'm a doctor. What do you know?"

The EMT shook his head as he scrambled out of the passenger door. "Not much." He motioned to the debris field to our left. "Just... I think I see a couple of bodies there. From the 911 calls, I think we're going to see a bunch more."

I scanned the debris and got a sinking feeling when I saw the two bodies he mentioned, mostly covered by chunks of cement.

His partner came around the front of the ambulance.

"Got a call that a leg injury's coming down. It's bad up there."

It definitely looked bad up there. I debated staying where I was for the leg injury or heading up closer to where the damage was. But I stayed put when I saw people carrying a man down the steps as fast as they could, one holding his arms and one his legs. This was an unconventional way to move a patient, and it had to be serious if this was their solution.

I ran up the steps toward them. "I'm a doctor. How is he?"

The man was crying, and I saw why when I looked at his legs. He had a broken right femur and a gash on the outside of the leg, suggesting something heavy and sharp had run through him.

One man said, "We've got a tourniquet going, but I think he's lost a lot of blood and he's got chest pains."

We ran down the last flight of stairs together, and they laid him as gently as they could on a stretcher. I held his hand and felt his pulse.

"I'm a doctor. Tell me about your chest pains."

His eyes were full of pain, and I could see the effort it cost him just to form words. "Hurts. Never had this."

I did a quick scan of his body, feeling where things were wrong. As I did it, I recognized what an incredible gift Vivienne's magic was for a physician to have, and I was once again filled with gratitude for her.

"Okay," I turned to the EMTs who were already bringing over an AED. "No time for that, guys. Get him to the hospital ASAP."

I turned to the patient.

"What's your name?"

"Chris Edwards."

"Good news, Chris. Your vitals could be way worse. These guys are going to get you to the hospital where they're going to take care of you, and I'm going to give you some pain medicine, alright?"

He closed his eyes and gave a brief nod as I squeezed his hand gently and sent some of Vivienne's healing magic through his system to calm him and ease the pain.

I stood and pulled one of the EMTs aside.

"Call in an open femur fracture and confirmed internal chest injuries."

"Understood." He ran off to the front of the ambulance.

Chris' friends stood by, almost as pale as he was, waiting to go with him.

"Hey." I got one guy's attention. "Is that your belt?" I motioned to the belt wrapped around the top of Chris' leg.

His friend said, "Yeah."

"Excellent job on that tourniquet." Relief washed over his face.

My phone rang, and I patted him on the back as I turned away to take the call.

It was Herb.

"Adam, the other bomb hit the White House. They're saying the President and the Vice-President are dead."

My head swiveled toward the White House, and I saw black smoke rising. The same smoke that was billowing from the Capital in front of me.

Oh shit.
This is bad.
Oh, my God...
I said, "What the *fuck* is going on?"

"Unclear. But it's happening everywhere. Europe, China, Russia. All the heads of state are being targeted."

"Unbelievable..." I shook my head and started up the steps when I saw more injured people stumbling down them. "Gotta go, Herb. People need triage."

"Wait! Listen."

"What?" I motioned to a girl with blood covering her face, who was holding her hand over her forehead, to sit down. Two women on either side of her eased her down gently.

Herb said, "There's some talk already. The Department of War wants to pin this on witches. They don't know fuck-all yet, but that's where they're headed." He paused. "You're a witch."

"No shit?"

Irritated, he said, "Just be careful."

I said, "I will. But bad news- this was definitely witches. I think it was Lucia Perez, she was here. Have your guys look into her. Also, there's a horrendous stench coming from this area. It doesn't look like mortals are feeling it, but I've never experienced it before." Looking at my guards, who were hearing every word, I saw that they both agreed with that. "I just wonder about toxicity. I'll ask Marshall to look into it."

"Good. Get over here as soon as you can."

I said, "Yep," and hung up.

Putting away my phone, I gently peeled the girl's hand away from her forehead and said, "I'm a doctor. Let me see."

CHAPTER TWENTY-SIX

Alice

The ground was cold. I rolled over onto my back and lay there flat, one hand pressed to my pounding heart, the other clutching what felt like roots and moss and snow. The overwhelming need to stay anchored to the earth and not go cartwheeling through time again won out, and I stayed there still as a mouse, trying to control my breathing.

The canopy of trees surrounding me was not much protection against the giant snowflakes falling from the sky. I knew I should get up and find shelter in this new place until I figured out where I was and, most importantly, *when* it was, but I didn't move a muscle. Instead, I watched puffy, dark gray clouds run through a light gray sky. It was barely light, and I didn't know if I was looking at day or night.

Then, in a panic, I pulled my jumper around until I found the zippered pocket in front and I felt it was still closed. I moved my fingers over every inch of the fabric but couldn't feel anything inside until I ripped down the zipper and touched the smooth surface of my semiquincentennial dime Grandmother had given me.

Thank God.

Then I remembered why I was there in the middle of an unknown patch of trees, somewhere in time. The dangerous man. He was in the Sistine Chapel, and he was coming toward me.

I sat up abruptly. What if he had hurt Grandmother? Or Grant or Maria? I should have stayed.

But Grandmother had told me to go. There was nowhere else to go but away through time. I hoped I had not just endangered them all by disappearing in front of that man. I probably had! What a stupid thing to do.

Time travel was our family secret that no one else in the world could ever discover. I knew about Father Andrew Barry because Adam had made sure I knew. If he was anywhere near me, I was to call Adam or Grandmother, and I was to run or hide. Adam said Father Barry had stolen Grandmother's magic and that he wanted to know more about it. And he might try to steal my magic.

And now I had just confirmed to Father Andrew Barry that I could disappear.

I had a sudden wish that the Pope were there with me to make everything all right. It seemed like he could do that.

My mind raced, and I had trouble following one thought all the way through. Should I go back to the Sistine Chapel? What if Father Berry was still there? Maybe I could go to Marcello's house. But he was attacked by Father Barry and I had left his side. I flushed with guilt and then anger, remembering how that man had made me leave my patient.

An icy wind rustled the surrounding trees. The snow I was lying on was seeping into my clothes and had frozen my hands. Placing fingertips on my forehead and closing my eyes, I tried to stem the panic rising inside me by listing my options out loud.

"One. I could go back to the chapel."

I shook my head no to that. He might still be there, and I couldn't just appear in the Sistine Chapel. What if the Pope were there?

"Two. I could go to the Vatican Square and see if Grandmother is there."

That was bad too. I knew she was probably frantic with worry about me, but the square was a big place and there were no guarantees she'd be there.

Then I remembered my promise to her to go back to Adam's house if I found myself lost because of time travel.

"Three. I go to Adam's house."

Yes, three was the winner.

I took my hands down from my face to see two men in knight's clothing sitting atop their horses, only ten feet in front of me.

"Uh oh," I said.

Alice

According to Grant, the Prime Directive is the gold standard for all time travel decisions. The Prime Directive states that if a person finds herself in another time period or in a society that has not advanced to the level of her own society's scientific understanding, she is to employ the Principle of Non-Interference. Grant said this was Starfleet Command's General Order Number One and what it meant was, try to make the least impact possible wherever you end up.

The Butterfly Effect was another concept he made sure to teach me. That principle stated that even something as small as a butterfly flapping its wings could cause a chain reaction of changes that might reverberate all over the world, right into the future.

I *really* did not want to disobey the Prime Directive or cause a Butterfly Effect.

So I was riding on the front of a horse with a knight sitting behind me, wondering how to make as little of an impact as possible. The knights were arguing about me.

"Look at her garb," one said.

The knight who carried me agreed. "Strange. No kirtle. No cloak." He had taken off his own coat to place it over my shoulders. When he did, I saw he wore a metal breastplate, and arm and leg armor, which I knew meant he was noble or was close to a noble. Under the armor he wore a padded coat that was blue and wine color, with a white rose patch on the sleeve. Somewhere in the recesses of my mind, I knew a white rose meant 'York' and a red rose meant 'Lancaster.' I thought that was probably information from my previous life.

The other said, "Lass, why are you so close to the field? Did you not hear the war horns? This is no place for a child."

War horns?

Although their accent was strange, I could understand their language, which made me think I might be in the fifteenth century again.

Our horses cleared the trees to reveal a massive army half a field away. To our right, at quite a distance, was an encampment of what I assumed were support people for the battle to take place. There were ten or twelve small tent structures and several fire circles surrounded by people huddling around them for warmth.

My knight dismounted and reached up to lift me down as well. Taking his cloak back, he said, "Run now, over to the camp and get a woman to help you." He waited for me to do so. I started off but then turned back and said, "Thank you."

He seemed amused.

"You're welcome, lass. Hurry now."

I heard them laugh as I ran toward the tents ahead of me. It was freezing, and I thought about running into the woods again to try traveling to Adam's house, but when I looked back, the knights were still watching me.

When I finally made it to the encampment, my fingers were frozen, and the snow had soaked through my canvas tennis shoes, so I knew my toes were no better off. A woman who was bent over a fire stopped what she was doing when she saw me. She stood and with both hands motioned for me to come to her.

"Child! Where is your cloak? Sit here!" She used my arm to lower me onto a log in front of the fire. My teeth were chattering, and I knew that was a sign of hypothermia, so I re-evaluated my timeline for leaving that place and what I might need to do. Was I willing to die to prevent the Butterfly Effect? The answer was no.

These people might get a surprise.

The woman threw her own blissfully warm cloak over my shoulders and tossed the hood up to cover my head, all the while chastising me and whoever sent me to a battlefield with not even a cloak to keep me warm.

While she went in search of another cloak for herself, I could feel the eyes of the others around the fire. A quick glance told me these were older men, maybe not able to fight anymore, and two other women, but I didn't look too closely. With some alarm, I grasped the women were witches. One of them was powerful. I kept my head down and stretched out my fingers toward the flames.

We all jumped when what could only be 'the war horns' sounded.

"It's started now." One of the men said to the other.

The woman helping me came back from a tent with another cloak, which she wrapped around herself.

"Look at those feet." There was real disapproval in her voice about my Chuck Taylor footwear. She scurried around behind the tent. "And now there's no time to sort you. You need *boots*." She grunted the last word as she was pulling the boots off a covered body behind the tent.

Ew. Those boots are definitely from a dead body.

But my toes would be grateful to be covered in leather, so I got over who the donor was pretty fast. I peeled off my Chucks and my socks and rubbed my toes as dry as I could. When she handed them to me, the kind lady said, "Put these on and make your way into the tent now. The injured will be here soon, and you don't need to see that."

"Thank you," I said. But she was off again, preparing for the bodies to come.

From inside the tent, I watched the driving snow continue to fall. A man on a cot with bandages around his midsection watched with me. He said, "At least the wind is on our side. Will be good for the archers. Bad for the Lancasters." He gave a satisfied smile when he said that.

Then the bodies came. Dragged by fellow soldiers and dropped next to the camp, or limping in on their own... they came. The people who had sat waiting by the fire were now up and working, and I recognized their plan as they moved. They put the worst cases off to the left, under the trees. These were the men who would not survive. The cases where the chief priority was to stem the flow of blood, they put in the middle where the two women worked together on each man. And they pointed the cases that were not immediately life-threatening off to the right, around the fires.

A man who might be a priest moved among the soldiers who were the worst off. He stooped before them and made the sign of the cross. He clasped the hands of those who still could. For the ones that were gone, he made the sign of the cross on their foreheads.

I watched for a while and then, when I couldn't stand it any longer, I made my way to the group of dying soldiers. I knew I could *not* save them. That was changing outcomes, and that was definitely against the rules. But I could offer solace. I could provide pain relief. And I could help those in the most pain to sleep so they wouldn't feel it any longer than they already had.

An arrow to the back of the neck was what would kill my first soldier. Someone had pulled it from him, but the damage was done. The wound still bled, and he lay on his back, a ring of red snow around his head. I touched his cheek to ease his pain, and when I did, his eyes moved to my face and he mouthed a thank you. I took his hand and said a quick prayer over him.

There were devastating injuries all around me, but I quickly decided how to triage them. I gravitated toward the soldiers who cried out for God or for their mother, or who just cried tears. At the very least, I could help them be still and rest without pain and maybe offer them the ability to think of the blessings of their life before it was over.

I had lost track of the time and of how many soldiers I met with when I noticed I was crying too, and that was not helpful to the men.

"Child!" one of the two witches called to me. "Press hard upon this hurt!"

I should run away.

But my feet did not obey my mind, and I found myself next to the older witch, taking over the pressure on a wound in the soldier's side. I lifted him a bit to see that whatever had made the hole in his side had gone all the way through. But unfortunately for him, it wasn't a bullet. Did they have bullets yet in this time period? I thought not. I made a note to tell Grandmother when I saw her again that it was ironic to wish a soldier had received a clean through and through gun-shot wound instead of the random sharp point that was speared all the way through his body and then pulled back out. It had torn a large hunk of his skin away, and the bleeding had not stopped yet.

I was thinking that the witches might have made a mistake about placing that soldier in the middle section instead of off to the left with the dying men, when the younger witch with dark hair came over and laid her hands on him. Her magic was a fierce wave of cool energy that began to heal the gash on his side immediately.

Impressed, I looked up at her and saw my own face staring back at me.

Both our jaws dropped.

The only difference was our eye and hair color. Her gray eyes were fixed on my blue eyes. Then they traveled over my red hair, and except for that we could have been twins.

I got up and *ran*.

She called out, and I heard a commotion behind me as I left the field for the cover of the trees. When I was well into the grove, I unzipped my jumper pocket and oh, so *carefully* placed the semiquincentennial dime between my thumb and forefinger. Closing my eyes, I pictured the study in Adam's house and exactly where and when I wanted to arrive there.

I tried to clear my head, but I couldn't banish my guilt at leaving when there was so much suffering left for the men on that field...

I also knew that I had just looked into the eyes of my grandmother and she would not approve of me leaving when I could still help the dying.

My grandmother had never run away from anything.

Chapter Twenty-Seven

Louise

We had just flown home from the press tour and were riding in a cab, passing the Washington Monument, when the first bomb hit. We heard it, then saw it crash right through the top of the Capitol dome. The driver stopped as we all gaped at the scene in front of us.

Connor said, "What the *fuck*?"

With his eyes on the Capitol, Samuel said, "You two should go on to my house. I need to get over there."

Another boom shook the earth, and we craned our necks to see where it had landed.

"Shit." Samuel's head turned to the front window of our cab. "That could be the White House."

I leaned up to the driver, a woman in her sixties or seventies. "Samuel is a doctor. Get us as close to the Capitol as you can. I'll pay double."

She said, "I'll get you there, no charge. You got it." We all held on as she sped off.

Samuel seemed dissatisfied with my call, so I said, "We're sticking together. You'll get there quicker, and you might be surprised how helpful this one can be in an emergency." I pointed to my son.

Staring at the Capitol dome, which spewed fire and black smoke, Samuel said, "Not surprised by that at all."

Connor was on his phone, typing away, no doubt finding out what was happening before anyone else.

Only a block or two from the Capitol, the driver stopped, and I gave her my card. "Can we get our luggage later?"

"Yes, honey. Be careful." And she gave my hand a pat. Connor strapped his backpack on, and I zipped my purse up and tried to keep pace behind Samuel, who was running full out toward the front steps of the Capitol.

It was chaos.

Capitol police tried to stop us, but Samuel said, "I'm a doctor; they're with me. We just want to help. We'll go to the ambulances." He pointed at two of them at the base of the first set of Capitol steps. The officers let us by, and when we got close to the first ambulance, and got around the corner, we ran into Adam, helping someone on a stretcher.

He looked up when Samuel hovered over him. His face registered surprise that quickly turned to relief.

"Thank God," he said. "Help me with this guy. The hospitals are going to be swamped, so I want to do this now. We need to reduce the dislocation of this hip," he pointed to it, "or we're going to see some vascular compromise."

The man on the stretcher was not old, maybe late twenties, and he was in so much pain he whimpered every time he moved. Adam, or the EMTs, had cut his pant leg off, and his exposed leg looked fairly normal.

Samuel laid his hand there lightly and said, "Yeah, he's cold." He looked back at Adam. "You sure?"

Adam nodded. "Yep."

I asked him, "Are you using any special skills?" Meaning magic.

Adam read that question right and answered, "No."

"When you start, I might be able to help a little. Let me know when."

He looked at me a little curious, then shrugged. "Okay."

When they got in position to move the leg, he said to the man, "This is going to hurt for just a minute, but then it will feel so much better, okay?" His patient gave a nervous nod.

"Now would be good, Louise."

I leaned down to the man, laid my hand on his shoulder and said, "What's your name?"

"Mike," he said. His brown eyes were full of pain, but then I pushed some of my magic into him, and he hummed a bit when it hit him. It came out too strong, and I pulled it back a bit when I saw Adam raise his eyebrows. I almost never used my nulling magic, but I had learned long ago that when I worked it around mortals, they received it as a pleasurable sort of frequency that was distracting and made them feel good. It seemed like maybe they got an ASMR type of response when I did it. Or like a light buzz that wore off immediately when I stopped it.

He cried out when they performed the maneuver but then cried actual tears of relief when they were done. He grabbed Adam's hand. "*Thank you.*" He reached for Samuel, who also clasped his hand.

"No problem, man. You're going to the hospital now." He looked up at the same time Adam did, and they frowned at the small wave of injured people making their way down the steps.

Samuel started towards them, but Adam took me to the side to talk.

In a low voice, he said, "They hit the White House, too. Herb said the president died."

"Oh, my God."

He said, "Lucia Perez was there. At my hearing. Accusing me of killing kids for the ICW."

"Fuck." I shook my head. "It's got to be about her son. She's been all over online discussions about the revelation of the secret. Stirring up the different factions of witches who didn't agree with it. But I don't think anybody suspected this level of crazy."

Connor stepped into our conversation and said, "It's happening all over the world." He turned his phone around and showed images of the destruction of government buildings in all the major capitals. London, Moscow, and... was that the Vatican?

Adam grabbed Connor's hand and pulled the screen closer. It appeared to show a huge golden dome cracking and falling to the ground over Saint Peter's Square.

"*Fuck,*" he said with a dark expression. When the video changed, he released his grip and said, "That looks like Vivienne's work." His phone rang, and he turned away to answer it.

Connor and I moved out of their triage area in front of the ambulance, and my phone buzzed. I checked my text and raised my eyebrows at the message there.

"Where are you?"

It was from Rosemary.

I texted back immediately, "In front of the Capitol. My friends are doctors- they're helping."

"Wait right there. Sending a car."

I sent back, "Okay."

Connor was looking at me and waiting for an update.

"Would you be okay staying here with Samuel and Adam until I get done with a meeting?"

His shoulder raised slightly. "Sure."

"Good. Come on." I walked him back to Samuel, who was evaluating a head wound.

"Hey," I got his attention and said in a soft voice. "I just got an official government request for my presence. I think I may be getting another ride here soon."

"Do you know who this request was from?" He looked up at me.

I took note that we were behaving suspiciously like couples did. Informing each other about events and asking about safety at said events.

A little curtly, I said, "Yes, and it's fine. Would you and Adam let Connor hang with you here until I'm done?"

"Of course."

A black limo pulled past the police barricade and stopped in front of me. The speed at which that had happened filled me with apprehension. A man in a suit jumped out and verified who I was.

"Miss Carmichael?" He opened the back door. I gave Connor a quick hug, which embarrassed him, and while Samuel watched, I got into the back of the car.

Louise

Not long after, I found myself somewhere under the bombed-out remains of the White House, maybe. I couldn't be sure-nobody had spoken to me since I entered the car other than to say, "This way…" and "If you will wait right here please…" All I knew was we'd driven through some tunnels in tiny golf carts.

Connor texted me that most likely, if this meeting took place in Washington, it would be in the Presidential Emergency Operations Center, which was a bunker that could withstand almost anything. Every time he offered valuable information like that at the drop of a hat, I was reminded how lucky I was to be the mom of such a brainiac.

Waiting to be let into the meeting room, I stared down at my hands in my lap and twisted a silver ring around and around on my finger. Connor had given it to me when he was in middle school, and it was my favorite thing in the world. A wave of dread washed over me, and I wished fervently that we were living in uninteresting times instead of these uneven and increasingly treacherous times.

Then the door opened.

The newly sworn-in President of the United States wore jeans and a Duke sweatshirt and stood next to a conference table surrounded by cabinet members picked by the previous President of the United States.

According to a text from Connor, the previous president, the vice president and the speaker of the House had all been killed when the White House ballroom was bombed. My old friend Rosemary was next in the line of succession and was POTUS now.

Things were weird.

One of her assistants held up two suits, and the president pointed to the blue one. That she had not taken the time to change before being sworn in illustrated the dire situation. She was going to make a statement to the nation as soon as our meeting was over, and I assumed I was there to make sure she had all the information she needed for that statement.

My other task was to make sure she did not feel the need to order the Pentagon to start a war with all witches.

Jesus, take the wheel. This is a cluster.

She ran her hands through her shoulder-length blond hair and then raised her reading glasses to look over a piece of paper another assistant handed her. Once done, she placed it face down on the table and turned her attention to me.

"You're only here right now because I knew you long before I was President Pro Tempore of the Senate. And unless you tell me one of the things witches can do is predict the future, your being in this room is pretty coincidental and not some decades-old plan to usurp the U.S. government. Right?"

She needed confirmation that this was not a set-up, and I didn't blame her one bit.

"Right," I said. "As far as I know, there is nobody on earth who can predict the future. And when I texted you a couple of weeks ago, I had no idea any of these events of the last couple of days would happen."

The new president watched me for a few more moments, probably replaying all the elements of our casual relationship over the years, and then gave a decisive nod.

"Okay everybody, we proceed with the understanding that Louise is a friendly. She's on our side; I can vouch for her."

She looked around the table and waited for someone to disagree. Nobody did, but I thought it was probably less about fealty and more about not wanting to go on the record one way or the other. I could see that Rosemary thought so, too.

"Some of my advisors at this table would like to go to war with Russia right now, some with China. I've also heard Iran and any combination of those countries." Her eyes met mine. "It's a dangerous moment, and I need some information from you right now. Am I correct in thinking that you might have some intel we need?"

I said, "Yes, ma'am."

She gave a nod to someone at the end of the table.

Sitting down, she said, "Louise, we're going to swear you in for some quick testimony about what you know. If you think this is abnormal, you're right. I just need everything to advance from this point on with the strictest adherence to the rule of law and complete transparency. I'm sure you understand."

I did, and I welcomed it.

Once I was sworn in and we were all seated around the table, the president took a swig of her water bottle and sat back in her chair.

"Louise, who killed our president?"

I said, "There's a group of witches unhappy with the revelation of witchcraft to the mortal world. Led by a woman named Lucia Perez, who also has a vendetta against Adam Parrish. She has never recovered from the death of her son in his adolescence, at the hands of other witches because he couldn't control his emerging witchcraft."

The president leaned in. "They kill *kids*?"

Faces around the table registered the same disgust as the president at the idea.

I took a deep breath. We all thought dark magic was going to be the thing that the mortals couldn't accept, but... killing kids- that was the thing.

And of course it was.

It was shocking how deeply I had, and I suspected most witches had, repressed that facet of our world. Parents of young witches could not fully breathe until they got their children through puberty and the acquisition of their powers. I had just lived through it with Connor, and the fear I felt hearing those stories of missing kids... I had approached them with a "There but for the grace of God go I" mindset, as did all other witch parents I knew.

But none of us had any idea of what to do or where to begin. How could we protest something buried so deeply and for so long? Not to mention, making public the disappearance of a kid probably meant the disappearance of yourself. I thought it very probable that some parents had gone that route, and I knew that if they had killed my son, I would have burned the whole system down myself.

But none of that mattered at that moment. The idea was barbaric, and no amount of my PR gloss was going to cover that.

I said, "Look, it's abhorrent, and there's nothing I can say to change that. For a very long time, I don't know for sure how long, if a teenager used his newly gained magic in front of mortals... witch councils executed him. These are the people elected to help witches navigate the mortal world. It's not common, but most witches either have heard a story about it or know of a person who died that way."

Being truthful was the only way to approach this meeting, but it was *painful.*

"The reason for this measure was to keep the secret of witchcraft from the mortal world. All five million witches were in danger of discovery if one new witch let the secret out."

The president was shaking her head, processing that knowledge and not liking it one bit.

Oh my God, they're not going to work with us now.

I worried I had just ruined the assimilation into the mortal world for all witches.

I said, "We did want to share the vaccine, but another *huge* part of the reason witches voted to come out to the world was to relieve us all of the incredible stress of keeping the secret. The old ways were not for us anymore."

She still wasn't convinced.

"I can't possibly explain what it was like to be a witch," I said. "The need for secrecy kept us in the dark, sometimes I think almost as much as mortals were."

The president looked up.

"Not quite."

I looked down at the pad of paper in front of me. She was right. This had to be a pretty steep learning curve for her. For all of them.

"Well," I said, "it's all out in the open now. And I wanted to let you know where we are with our investigation into the crimes from today. Nobody wants to find and stop this more than the International Council of Witches. This group has ruined our introduction to the world. They'll be punished."

While several members of the cabinet nodded in satisfaction at that, the president shook her head.

"No," she said. "When they're found, they will be arrested and given a fair trial. Which will probably result in some death sentences. But not before a trial and a conviction. That's the price of being a part of our world." She leveled a no-nonsense glare at me, and instead of being worried by that look, I was actually relieved.

It kind of felt like the parents had come home to an out-of-control party and maybe now the insanity would stop and things were going to be okay.

I said, "Well... you'll need to work on a special place to hold the witches you arrest. I've laid out a lot of the magic in our world already, but there are some magical skills that would be resistant to detainment."

She said, "Persuasion? Yes, I saw Adam Parrish give his testimony this morning." She took her glasses off and rubbed her eyes. "Christ. Was that just a couple of hours ago?"

Nobody answered, but we all understood.

The president said, "I want to meet him." She looked at the man sitting to her right. "Can you get him here as soon as possible?"

"No." We both said at the same time.

I waited.

He said, "That would be a security breach, ma'am. You can't be in the same room with someone who has that magic."

She frowned. "I don't mean in public."

He shook his head and added, "Not ever."

I said, "He's right. We're pretty sure Andrew Barry had been working with the president to pursue whatever goals he had personally. It's unclear what those were. I agree you should not be around anyone unknown to you who has persuasion, and, in fact, I'd see about finding someone you trust with persuasion and have them be with you for all meetings from here on. Or I can get someone for you."

She said with some major irritation, "Where do I find this kind of witch? Do they have a store at the mall?"

"I'd ask your military leaders."

The president and, actually, the entire table, looked aghast at that suggestion.

I said, "I don't know they're there for certain, but witches with persuasion almost always pursue careers in service to the community. Social workers, healthcare providers, teachers. They're like modern-day knights. They care for those who need it most. Firefighters, police... the military."

Marshall Smith occurred to me then. "Another option for you would be to find a witch with the ability to read the magic specialty of other witches. That's called divining. It might be a nice line of defense. Both persuasion and divining are rare magics. I can give you the number of the current head of the North American Council of Witches, Marshall Smith. He can find what you need."

The president looked to the man on her right then, and as

he scribbled notes on a legal pad, he gave a nod to let her know he was on it.

"Alright, I've heard enough. I'm classifying everything said in this meeting as Top Secret, and if one word leaks, I'll find the source and have you prosecuted for treason." She looked around the table and made sure everyone met her eyes. "We are at a crossroads. We need to understand the witches, and we may *need* the witches. I won't let the same old partisan bullshit get in the way of fixing this shit. Let's get it together."

She stood and held her hand out for me to shake. "Thank you, Louise. This information has been invaluable and may have just prevented another world war."

I shook her hand, but as she turned to leave I said, "Ma'am."

I had one more thing.

"Please remember that this information came from witches. Most of us are harmless. We voted to share the vaccine to make the world better for everyone. And we were hoping with that vote we'd finally be free from the possibility of persecution. But the events of today..." I shook my head at the enormity of it. "This could easily turn into a modern-day witch hunt, and I have a fifteen-year-old son who does not deserve that kind of plot twist in his life."

She inclined her head slightly.

"Noted. And Louise, I know your people are looking for the perpetrators of today's crimes, but I would like for *you* to remember... if they're here in the U.S., they're mine."

She waited for me to acknowledge that, then said, "I'll be in touch."

CHAPTER TWENTY-EIGHT

Vivienne

As far as I could tell, I was off the main grounds of the Vatican. I'd been running for fifteen or twenty minutes. Turning the corner onto a busy street, I slowed to a fast walk and scoured both sides for a place to stop and pull myself together. It was dark then, and not all the storefronts were lit. I worried it was closing time and I wouldn't find a place to shelter on that street. But an ornate sign midway down the street on the right caught my eye. Red letters against a gold background read *Caffè Sanctuario*, and I accepted that was it.

My breathing was still labored as I pushed the door open and scanned the room for any signatures of witches. Barry's gift of persuasion almost guaranteed that he was traveling with a group of powerful witches- enforcers who would do whatever he asked. But I was relieved to note that no witches were present.

At the counter, I got the barista's attention and tried to keep my voice level when I said, "I wonder if you could help me, sir, and make me a warm latte to drink while I wait for my son? He should be here soon and will pay for it." My magic was building, had been from the moment I threw it all out at Barry and went on the run away from him. But I used just the tiniest bit on the barista to test it and, as always, it provided for me.

"Certo, bella signora," he said, as he went to work on my order. He asked a few more things about what I wanted in my drink, but my Italian was almost nonexistent and his English was poor. We used gestures to get to the fact that I liked one pump of sweetener in my drink. When I took the drink from him, I used a little more magic to ask him, "May I ask one more favor? I have lost my cellphone. May I borrow yours to call my son?"

"Cell phone?" He reached into his pocket and brought out his phone. He pointed to it, asking if that was what I wanted.

"Sì, grazie," I took the phone. "I'll be right back with this."

He waved me away with a smile, and I took a seat in a booth at the back.

I dialed Adam's number, but the call did not go through. He had promised me that even if he used a burner phone, I could still reach him at that number.

Alice was missing. I did not know where Grant and Maria were. And when I last saw Marcello, he was gravely injured on the floor of the Sistine Chapel.

I set the phone down on the table and dropped my head in my hands.

"Excuse me, do you need some help?"

I jumped a bit and looked up to see a man standing at the end of my table.

Not a witch, forty or fifty… American?

"I'm sorry! I didn't mean to startle you! I just heard your order and saw you having trouble with the phone. Are you calling the U.S.?" His wife came up beside him then and laced her arm through his. He turned to her. "Honey, what is it you dial to get to the States? She's having trouble." She leaned down to show me on the phone.

"You have to dial the plus sign, then a one, then the number. Did you do that?"

Thank you, Father, for this help.

"No. I did not. Thank you so much, I'll try that."

They both wished me well as they left.

I dialed the number again, using the plus and the one.

The phone line crackled with static, and I remembered Marconi and how he had heard that wireless signal from across the ocean over a hundred years ago. It must have seemed like magic. Waiting for my husband to answer my call on another continent also seemed like magic to me.

"Adam Parrish." At the sound of his voice, I nearly burst into tears.

Instead, I said, "Alice disappeared right in front of me. In front of all of us, including Barry. We had a deal that she would go to your house if she time traveled. But I don't know if she wanted to stay in 2026, and I don't know where she might have gone."

I delivered the last part with hysterics, but it was the truth. She might have gone back home. I did not know where Alice might have gone.

He took a second to process that and said, "Okay. When?"

My heart hurt, and I placed a clenched fist against it. "I don't know! I was out for a bit. An hour? Maybe less?"

"Okay," I heard him tell someone he had to leave.

"Adam, where are you?"

It sounded as if he was repositioning the phone. Then I heard the pounding of his feet and knew he was going to Alice.

"At the Capitol," he said. "On my way to the house now. Are you okay? Where's Barry?"

"I'm fine. I found a coffeehouse. I left Barry injured somewhere in the Vatican."

Adam grunted his approval of that. "Good," he said.

We let ourselves be silent for a minute while he ran. It wasn't a relaxed jog- he was running as hard and as fast as he could to get to her.

"I don't know where Grant and Maria are." I felt panic rising in my body and wondered if the clenching in my chest was an anxiety attack.

Adam heard it in my voice and said, "Don't worry, they'll call me and I'll tell them where you are."

We didn't say anything else. The pace of his feet hitting the pavement never wavered. I wondered what state the house was in. I had not heard any updates on how the repairs were going, and I wondered if it had been a terrible idea to have her try to travel there. Squeezing my eyes shut, I huddled over the table and listened.

Finally, Adam said, "I'm close." I heard his feet take the porch steps and his labored breathing as he looked for keys to get in.

"Alice!" he called out. "Alice! Are you here? It's Adam."

I heard his keys hit the dish in the hallway where he always dropped them. It sounded like he was going through each room.

Then I heard him say, "Come here," his voice gentle. "I got her. She's here."

"Oh, thank *God...*" I loosened my grip on the phone in relief and somehow disconnected our call as I did.

"Gah!" My hands were shaking so hard that I had trouble dialing them back, and I almost dropped the phone again when it rang. It was Adam's number, and this time a FaceTime call. When I answered, Alice's face came into view, her eyes red-rimmed and haunted. A tear trailed down her cheek, and I cried along with her.

"Oh, honey. I was so worried, but I shouldn't have been. Look at you! You made it back just fine. I knew you could do it. How long have you been there?"

"Not very long." Her lips trembled, and I took a closer look. Her hair was disheveled, and she was wearing a dark cloak I didn't recognize. I wiped the tears from my eyes with one hand and tried to calm myself so I could get to the bottom of that.

"Well, don't worry, Adam is there now. You're safe. I'm fine, and I'm going to find Grant and Maria and come home to you both. Okay?"

She kept her eyes trained on me, the tears still falling silently.

In a softer voice I said, "Where were you before you got home?"

Her face crumbled at that, and the crying intensified so that I could barely make out the rest of what she said.

"I was in a battle, in a snowstorm. It was the red roses against the white, and I tried not to change anything. I just helped the soldiers who were dying..." The last part was a sob.

My heart beat fast as images of war that I had put away for over forty years bombarded me. They came at me fast and furious, a nightmare dreamscape with no sound. All those men on that snowy field, covered in gore from their own wounds and the wounds of their brethren. Then the sounds hit me on a wave all their own, and my mind flooded with their screams, their prayers. Their tears.

The red-haired witch was my granddaughter.

Alice had seen all of that.

I turned the phone face down on the table and placed my shaking hands over my mouth.

Alice was talking to me, then I heard Adam, and I tried to school my face into a normal expression before turning the phone back over. But he could see there was something wrong, of course, and he handed the phone back to Alice and guided her toward the door.

"Come on, we're going over to Herb and Sally's so you can have a nice bath and then some food."

As they walked, she held the phone out, still looking at me.

"I like that plan," I said.

She gave me an almost imperceptible nod.

I added, "I'll probably be home in the morning."

She wiped her tears away with one hand.

As they trudged up Herb and Sally's porch steps, I asked her, "Do you still have your dime?"

She reached into her pocket and held it up to show me.

"Good girl. I'm so proud of you. After you eat, I want you to take a nice nap, okay?"

"Okay," she said, then looked toward Herb's front door as Adam opened it up and handed her over to Sally. He took the phone out of Alice's hand and said, "Hey. It's been crazy. I'm so glad you're here. This young lady needs a hot bath and some good food and then a nap, that's what her grandmother ordered. Can you handle it?"

Sally scoffed. "Of course I can handle it. This is my girl." She pulled Alice into a hug and shooed her into the house. I heard her ask him, "Are you okay?"

"Yeah. Talking to Vivienne." He turned the phone around for her to see. She waved at me.

"Alright, you go on, I've got your baby."

Then he turned to jog down Sally's steps to sit on his own steps.

"What happened at the Capital?" I asked.

Adam shook his head and wiped a hand over his jaw. "A lot of people hurt, some died. Marsh ended up there too, with Louise, and he helped me treat some of the injured. I got a call from Sonya just after it happened, and Fausto was not answering her calls."

"Oh *no*," I said. "Poor Sonya and Eduardo." I pictured her son's big brown eyes and curly head of hair and said a quick prayer for his father.

"We don't know anything about Fausto yet. But I know the bombing was Lucia Perez. She was there after the hearing and made some remarks... we lost her in the crowd, though. They bombed the White House too, and the president was killed."

My eyes widened. "It's going to get so bad." This was going to become a war of witches with the entire world as witness.

Adam stopped and squinted at something across the street. He turned the phone around so I could see a hulking man loitering there. The man gave a small salute, which Adam was returning when he turned the phone back around.

"One of my new bodyguards," he said.

"He's even bigger than Tony and Caleb."

Adam's face darkened. "You should have had guards."

He was about to spiral into self-blame, and I stopped him.

"Look at me," I said. "I'm fine."

With an impatient shake of his head, he said, "No, you're not. You had to raise a shield to cover Saint Peter's Square. I saw it crashing down."

He waited for me to fill in the blanks, and I fought myself over how much to reveal. I didn't want to lie to my husband, but I knew he would be devastated to know Barry had abducted me after I lost consciousness.

Adam saw I was debating what to say, and he got straight to the point.

"Did he hurt you?"

I shook my head. "No. I think it was his dome crashing down that knocked me out. I would have just re-absorbed my own."

His voice raised, he said, "You were *unconscious*? For how long? Who was there?"

"I'm not sure how long. I woke up in a janitor's closet with Barry there."

Adam looked like he was about to explode.

"But he didn't do anything. I healed myself, and then when he made me mad, I blew up the room and spent all my magic."

I could see he was trying to gain control of his emotions, so I waited to say anything else.

Finally, he took a big breath in and then exhaled. In a soft voice he asked, "What did he do to make you mad?"

I thought about Barry threatening to find Alice to figure out time travel, and I felt my own face darken.

"The last thing he said was something about how if I helped him learn to time travel he would let me go."

His eyes ran over my face, assessing what I said and deciding how much detail to get into.

"So you blew up the room."

After a moment, I nodded.

He nodded back and said, "Good call."

"I let my temper get the best of me and used up all my magic at once. I'm not sure it was the best call."

Adam changed the subject. "Where did Alice go, and why did it affect you like it did?"

I closed my eyes and raised a hand to my forehead, suddenly exhausted by my run and the adrenaline of Adam looking for Alice and then the onslaught of unwelcome memories. Of course he saw that; he saw everything.

He said, "Don't worry, you're tired. We can do this later."

My husband entered his problem-solving mode then. "Okay, we need to figure out the time travel thing. We need Gerald. Grant needs to get him here. Obviously, we need to get rid of Barry. And Lucia Perez, she's doing all the bombing. Also, Congress is a little mad at me, so I don't know what's going to happen there."

We stared at each other's faces for a minute, and he said, "I know all that needs to happen, but all I can think about right now is lying next to you."

I wanted that too, so I played along. "Where are we in this scene? On the daybed or in your bedroom?"

"*Our* bedroom, on the sheets you love..." he took a deep breath in and then his phone buzzed and he looked at a text.

"It's Louise." His eyebrows raised as he read her text. "She met with the president. The new one. Who, apparently, she *knows*..." He read some more and then laughed. "Well, that's pretty fucking lucky."

His phone buzzed again, and he swiped away one text to read the next.

"Oh my God, poor Grant. He just texted me that both you and Alice are missing. They're at somebody named Marcello's house, and Marcello is okay." Adam looked back up at me. "I have to call him."

Then we sat in silence for a good long moment, taking stock of each other and wishing we were not half a world apart. He looked exhausted, and I realized I probably did too. We both reached out to touch the other's face on the phone at the same time and then smiled when we did.

I said, "Well, there is some good news to come out of all of this."

He raised his eyebrows slightly. "There is? Please enlighten me."

"It looks as though your body may have learned how to age itself."

A slow smile spread across his face, and then his head dropped as he laughed.

We both shared a good laugh at that, and when he lifted his head back up, he gave me that devastating smile. "How bad is it?"

"I'd say maybe five years?"

He laughed even harder at that.

Then he said, "Wait, are you serious?"

I shook my head and stared at my handsome husband.

"No, you just look tired."

"I see you're pretty comfortable insulting me from all the way over there in Italy. Why don't you come here and say that to my face?"

I said, "I'm working on it."

His smile faded.

"Please," he said. "Get your ass back here, wife."

CHAPTER TWENTY-NINE

Adam

After I hung up with Vivienne, I sat next to Herb in his den. Sally was feeding Alice in the kitchen, and Herb and I sat there numb, watching the news coverage of the bombings.

A worldwide terrorist attack perpetrated by witches was not something either one of us had had on our card for that day.

Sally came in and asked, "Is it okay if I have her sleep upstairs in the third-floor guest room? She said she misses your turret."

Would Vivienne want her to be alone? No.

"Third floor is fine. Can I take a nap up there, too?"

She came over and touched me on the shoulder. "Yes, there are twin beds. Would you like me to tuck you in, too?"

Still watching the TV, I patted her hand there and said, "Yeah, maybe later, thanks."

She left, and both my phone and Herb's phone rang at the same time. We both gave each other looks that said we were unpleased with that development.

My call was from Marshall.

I answered, "What's up?"

He got right to it. "I'm hearing from Conti that Perez has another wave of something coming. He picked up some of her group, and they got that much out of them before they couldn't get any more."

In other words, some heavy-handed questioning got too heavy-handed. Which was just amateur when we needed intel so badly.

"What kind of wave and when?"

Marshall's sigh was pure frustration. "All they got was that targets were to be 'cultural.' Apparently, she's all about chaos now that she's damaged governments. She wants to show that witches are superior to mortals and wants to eliminate their contributions. Or something like that. And then her goal is possibly to take over whatever's left and have witches rule the world. Maybe? I don't know, she's fucking crazy."

Herb was saying a lot of "Yes, sir" on his call.

I said, "What the fuck is a cultural target? And when?"

"Conti is having someone watch the Louvre and the Eiffel Tower. Museums in Florence. Italian and Greek landmarks. He thinks it will be museums and things that would damage us the most if they were gone. He said maybe it would happen the 'next day,' and assuming they meant after today... it could be any time after midnight."

I estimated that with the Smithsonian and the monuments, there were easily at least twenty or thirty cultural landmarks in Washington that would devastate the country if they were suddenly eliminated or damaged.

Like the Capitol and the White House had been.

"Okay. Well, fuck."

We sat there in agreement for a minute.

"Are we talking more bombs?"

"Unknown."

"The bomb at the Capitol had a sick smell to it, really strong. Mortals didn't smell it. Do you know if it's toxic?"

"It's not. I've smelled it, and it's just a facet of that magic."

Herb was off his call and looking at me to tell me something.

I told Marshall, "Alright. I got the National Gallery. Can you get some people on the other Smithsonian museums? And the monuments at the Mall?"

"Yeah."

"Marshall, we need to know how many people she has and what the fuck they want. Are we dealing with an army or just a few dozen overpowered witches?"

"Unclear." I could feel his frustration over the phone. "Louise has a press conference in an hour, and I need to prep her. And there's one more thing..."

I closed my eyes.

"Fantastic. Lay it on me."

"Cole is here."

I opened my eyes.

"He's sorry, and he's telling the truth. He said we can use him to explain what persuasion can do."

"Jesus." I did not relish what Louise had to do in an hour. Witches had attempted to dismantle world governments, and it was possible there was more to come.

"Also, on the off chance Congress decides to continue your testimony anytime soon, I probably can't make it. But have a lawyer there, or at the very least, bring Louise to help you keep your shit together."

That was irritating but good advice.

"Got it."

He softened his tone. "How's Vivienne?"

"Fine. On her way home. Talk to you later, Marshall." I hung up.

Herb said, "I just got a call from the Secretary of War right here on my personal phone." He pursed his lips. "That's the first thing he said. 'This is the Secretary of War.' So that was fun."

"Wow," I said. "Impressive. What did the Secretary of War want?"

"He wanted me to ask you if there's anyone in his ranks who has persuasion and if you'd tell him their name."

I know my face registered dismay at that request because his eyes widened, and he laughed. "Yeah, this is one of those real life Catch-22 situations, isn't it?"

He put both hands on his armrests and pushed himself up. "Apparently, the president requested that he find this out, and nobody wanted to answer his email to declare themselves a witch in his army, I don't know why."

"*Fuck*," I said, drawing it out. "The combination of this political timeline and introducing witches to the world... not ideal."

"Ya think?" Herb laughed as he left the room.

I didn't know anybody in the army that was a witch, but Grant might. I'd ask him when he got in tomorrow. With my wife.

And then it was time for a nap. Alice and I had stuff to do that evening.

CHAPTER THIRTY

Vivienne

Grant procured a plane for us. We would fly from Italy to London and, after a brief stay there, on to Washington. Upon boarding the plane, Gerald greeted us himself, and then I saw Isabelle! I hugged Adam's mother a little harder than I should have and then did the same to Gerald.

"Thank you, Gerald, for saving me yet again."

He winked. "Anything for my great, great, great, great grandmother."

Isabelle said, "I think there would be many more greats."

Maria sat next to Grant and said, "That's true. How many more do you think?"

Grant was looking out the window, still stressed from losing Alice and me at the Vatican and having to share that news with his father. Maria patted his leg, knowing how tense he was. She said to me, "He'll be working that out in his head for a while."

Isabelle and Gerald sat facing Grant and Maria while I sat in an aisle seat across from Gerald. I still did not enjoy traveling on an airplane. Rather than looking out a window at the ground so far below, I preferred to pretend we were rolling on land.

Once the flight attendant prepared us for takeoff, and I made it through the lifting of the plane off the ground, I leaned over to their group.

"Grant, can you do some research for me and find out if there were any large battles in England that happened during a snowstorm? And then see if any of them happened during the Wars of the Roses? Any large battles other than the Battle of Towton."

Gerald looked at me with concern at the mention of Towton. Maria saw his face and asked, "What's Towton?"

Grant powered off his phone and said to Maria, "Give me your phone."

She handed it to him and said, "Okay, weirdo. Why?"

He turned hers off too and asked Isabelle, "May I borrow your phone, Grandma?"

While Isabelle searched her purse for a phone, I addressed Maria. "Towton was England's bloodiest single-day battle. Fought between the House of York and the House of Lancaster." At Maria's blank look I added, "The Wars of the Roses? The white rose for York and the red for Lancaster?"

When she shrugged her shoulders, Grant laughed at her. *"What?"* She hit his arm. "History isn't my thing, that's what I have you for." Turning back to me, she said, "Why are you interested in this battle?"

Grant said, "I don't think this is the kind of research you want our friend to hear, right?"

I shook my head, agreeing with him. He was right; Yoda should not know that I was at the battle of Towton. And he may have been monitoring our phones for us. I truly didn't know the extent of Yoda's surveillance on the Internet, and I was grateful it had occurred to Grant.

"I'm not sure this one is safe either," he said. "Is it new?"

Gerald said, "It's new. But you'll need to get me up to speed on your friend."

Typing on Isabelle's phone, Grant said, "Will do. And you are not gonna believe it when I do."

Maria and I shook our heads in agreement with that.

Isabelle leaned around Gerald and asked, "Were you there, Vivienne?"

"I was."

She gave me a sympathetic look.

Grant said, "It doesn't look like there were other big battles that were also fought in a snowstorm. Not during that time period. Actually, I don't see any like that in England." He looked up. "Is that what you wanted to know?" He handed the phone back to Isabelle.

Maria asked me again, already seeming to know the answer, "Why do you want to know about this battle?"

"Because I think Alice was there too." Gerald met my eyes. I heard the anxiety in my voice, and I knew they did too. "Why did she go there? She had to leave the Vatican. I told her to go, but why did she have to travel to 1461? To a *nightmare*?"

He sighed and took a moment to think of what to say. Then he raised a shoulder slightly and said, "Because you were there."

I knew it was my fault. I just didn't understand how or why.

Gerald said, "In my travels, I can't tell you how many times I ended up somewhere with a person who was a relative of mine. It just happened! In literally every era in Britain, I met an ancestor. I think the call of our magic is just too strong to ignore."

I looked over at the window and saw only clouds. No sky.

"That's what Barry said."

"What?" Isabelle cut in. "What did he say?"

So much had happened. Was it just yesterday? I tried to remember.

"Something about how he had my magic, and we're connected now. He said my magic speaks to him."

Gerald looked as though he knew that feeling

"So he can track you now." Isabelle was as practical as her son. She looked at Grant. "I assume your father has a plan for this? This man can't be allowed to threaten Vivienne and Alice any longer. I can help with this. No one ever suspects the old lady." She leaned around Gerald again. "Vivienne, don't worry. Adam and I will handle this."

I appreciated having a mother-in-law who wanted to protect me. And I had no doubt that she could.

"Thank you," I said. "But what I really need, Gerald, is a way for Alice not to travel accidentally to dangerous places and times. What can I do to help her?"

He said, "Grant told me she used a dime from this year as her anchor?"

I gave a nod.

"Make sure she always has one. Build up her confidence that it will always work."

"Will it?"

Isabelle said, "It's a good sign that she did that trip all on her own and at such a young age. I think if she could pull that off, she could do anything."

I let my head fall back to rest and closed my eyes.

Yes, Alice could do anything. Her magic was racing through her youthful body at an alarming speed, and most days I felt it straining to get out. She would need an outlet for her magic. And I would make the dime into a necklace for her. And a ring. And a bracelet.

"What side were you on?" I opened my eyes to see Maria peering at me intently. "White rose or red?"

"My mother was from Yorkshire. She was gone by the time I came into my power, and my father sent me there after..." *After I was raped by local boys who wanted to experience my magic.*

"He didn't know what to do with me, so he sent me to stay with relatives of my mother. I never understood how we were related, but they taught me the basics of my healing magic. My magic was stronger than any of theirs, and they needed me there at Towton, but I don't think anyone knew the true carnage that day would bring." And I hated that Alice had seen it.

Maria was still waiting.

"White rose," I said.

Grant said, "They won that battle. But the Wars of the Roses went on for like thirty years or so, right? Were you there for the Battle of Bosworth? The one that ended it all?"

"No. I had lost my taste for the royals by then, and John died just before that, so... I didn't care who won the war."

"You had a taste for the royals before that?" He was surprised.

I shrugged. I didn't like to talk about my time with royalty because of the terrible things they did in their constant pursuit of power and my disillusionment with them as a result.

Grant was waiting though, so I answered. "I was the midwife for Elizabeth Woodville. For all ten of her children."

He pointed at something nonexistent in the air, trying to come up with a thought. Then he said, "Was she accused of being a witch?"

"She was a witch," I said, closing my eyes again. "That's why she wanted me at her births. She knew I was a powerful witch with midwife knowledge and healing magic."

When no one replied, I opened my eyes to find them all staring at me. Grant held his hand out for Isabelle's phone again, and she fished it out of her purse for him once more.

Gerald said in amazement, "How did I not know this?"

"I thought Elizabeth let her boys be taken to the tower, knowing that Richard was not to be trusted. That she had chosen herself before them. But she was taking sanctuary at Westminster and probably had no choice."

I shook my head, suddenly back in the Tower of London watching the two princes eat the stew I had a friend bring them. Who knew how long it had been since their last meal? They had been beautiful babies. I was present at both their births, and they were far too young to die simply because their uncle craved the crown.

The dark cloud of suspicion that ruled that time came back to me, and I felt again the sickening lack of power every woman knew all too well. Maybe Elizabeth didn't fight enough for her boys, but then again, maybe she did the best she could. I didn't know what her skills were as a witch. She was beautiful and had married successfully more than once.

"Hold on, hold on, hold on." Grant held up a hand, still looking at the phone.

"Is this Elizabeth Woodville, the mother of Elizabeth of York? Who married Henry VII, uniting the houses of Lancaster and York?"

"Yes," I said.

"And correct me if I'm wrong, but isn't this the marriage that produced the direct line of succession to the present-day monarchs?"

"It was. They're very good at keeping records."

"So... the British royals are all..."

"Witches." I closed my eyes for good then, drifting off to sleep, dreaming of royals and their castles and witches sleeping cold in the streets.

CHAPTER THIRTY-ONE

Adam

Alice and I slept like the dead for a good eight hours. But when my phone alarm went off in the dark, I had no idea how long I had been out or even where the hell I was. As I fumbled around for the phone, dropped it, and tried to work through that insanely groggy state, Alice picked it up off the floor and handed it to me.

"Thanks," I mumbled and reached over to turn on the bedside lamp.

She was sitting up, awake and clear-eyed.

It was eleven o'clock. I briefly considered that Vivienne would not want me taking her granddaughter on a possibly dangerous mission to save the paintings at the National Gallery. But then I thought about Andrew Barry having the ability to track both Alice and Vivienne and the possibility that Alice might time travel again, and I decided the safest place for Alice was right next to me.

"You ready? We're going on an adventure."

Her eyes lit up, and she said instantly, "Yes."

I got a text on my phone, and Alice frowned when it buzzed.

It was from Eleanor. "Jonah Masters needs help. Tonight."

Ellie was not prone to theatrics. And since she didn't even work at the hospital anymore, I knew she would have looked into it before texting me. Jonah was my former patient, probably nine years old at that point, and had been battling leukemia for a couple of years. It was not good that he had relapsed so soon after the first occurrence. I knew he was an only child and that he didn't have that backup plan of a sibling bone marrow transplant.

Alice was looking at the phone with suspicion.

I said, "Another adventure. How'd you like to come to the hospital with me to heal a boy of his cancer?"

Standing up, she said, "I would like that."

Adam

On our cab ride to the hospital, I quizzed Alice about leukemia, and she impressed me by answering every question correctly. Ellie was waiting for us at the hospital and didn't even blink when Alice and I suddenly appeared in Jonah's room.

I explained, "I was using a cloak to get past the nurses at the desk." I said that mostly for the Masters, because I knew Ellie did not give a shit about how I was showing up, she just wanted me to hurry and fix the kid. Mary Ellen came over to hug me, and I shook her husband's hand.

"Is it okay with you if I take a look to see what's up with our boy here?"

Jonah's dad said simply, "Please."

Jonah had the wan, fragile look of a child who had suffered through cancer for too long. He was thankfully asleep, and I took advantage of that to look at his chart and see what his course of treatment had been since I last saw him.

Ellie came up beside me.

"I know you've had your hands full with all that Capitol Hill stuff, so thank you for coming. I heard from Sherry that he was this bad, and I knew you'd want to know."

"You were right, thanks."

"Do you think you can help him?" She was worried she had given hope to the parents when there might not be any reason for it.

I said, "I'm going to talk it over with Alice. This is Vivienne's granddaughter. Alice, this is my friend Ellie."

I shared the specifics with Alice, and as she listened, she was also looking at Jonah, completing her own scan of his body, feeling where the cancer was and evaluating the damage done. The thoroughness of her examination astounded me. Her magic didn't coast on the surface like mine, it delved deep into recesses and passed through organs and bones. When she was done, she gave a small sigh.

The cancer was too advanced for me to be sure about where to start.

I said in a low voice to Alice, "What do you think my approach should be here?"

"*Your* approach?" She raised her voice in surprise.

I looked back at the Masters, and Ellie moved back over to them to give us privacy.

"Keep your voice down. Obviously *my* approach. I witnessed your grandmother do this twice, and she nearly died both times. I'm not going through that again."

"Adam," she said, trying to prepare me for some common sense. I knew that tone well, had heard it many times from her grandmother, and hated that it was usually right. "I know you share some of Grandmother's magic and that you have healed some cancer. But this one is too much for you." Then the fourteen-year-old clinched it with, "We both know that."

She leaned in and said in a low voice, "I can do this. I *have* done this."

I shook my head. "No. No, no, no."

Alice waited for me to stop objecting. Then waited a couple more beats before continuing. "This is what I was born to do."

When I still didn't agree, she turned to scorn. "You know I have just as much healing magic as Grandmother. If she were here, she'd tell you to watch how I wield it, and she'd be *proud*."

"Alright, stop!"

I knew the task was too much for me. As a doctor, as much as I wanted to heal all my patients, I had to accept that I could not. The healing magic I had was a mere remnant of Vivienne's magic. It wasn't natural to me, and sometimes it took all of my will to bend it the way I needed to just to make it work half as well as it would for Vivienne or Alice.

I just didn't want one kid to die trying to save another kid.

"Look." It was my turn to reason with her. "Vivienne isn't here to help you, and I'm worried I won't know if you've gone too far and need me to stop you."

"Oh." That mollified her for a moment. "Well, that's easy to fix," she said. "We just need a signal."

I had to walk away for a minute and think. I stood by myself near the window, looking down at a street cleaner methodically going back and forth over the west parking lot.

What would Vivienne want in this situation? I had trusted her to heal my former patient Emily last year in a room on this very floor. Alice had more than enough healing magic to cure cancer. I could practically hear it thrumming through her veins. And Vivienne would have been training her for the entire year they were gone.

She was sitting in a chair on the side of Jonah's bed, staring at him.

"Alice." I beckoned her over.

When she stood next to me, I said, "Tell me what you've done."

Eagerly, she recounted half a dozen examples of times she had cured a cancer with her grandmother. "She talked me through the first ones, then she let me make my way with the last ones. She said I was a natural."

I was still looking at the cleaning truck below. She said, "My signal can be that I open my eyes. When I do that, you can pull me back, and then I'll need to let go of the cancer."

I was familiar with that scene. The window was not one that would open, of course, so I reached down and put a garbage can on the seat where she had been.

"Will that do?"

She gave me a thumbs-up. "Yes."

While I introduced Alice to the Masters, I was remembering the moment I gave control over to Vivienne because I completely trusted her ability. *This is her granddaughter,* I said to myself. *They're both miracle workers.*

When the Masters gave their permission for Alice to use her healing magic on Jonah, I also informed them they wouldn't remember us being there.

"You either, Ellie." I gave her an apologetic smile. "I'll tell you to forget, and all three of you will. It's safer for Alice that way. Do you agree?"

"Yes," Mary Ellen said instantly. "And Alice... thank you."

Jonah's dad said, "Please. We trust you to do whatever you can."

Ellie was slower to answer. She gave me one of her looks that let me know I was maybe missing something.

She said, "If we could publicize this, it would help spread the word about the vaccine being real. People fear it now. If they saw what magic can do..."

"I wish we could, but this is different. It's not prevention of cancer, it's curing cancer, and everyone will want that. You know I'm right."

She couldn't deny that. "They will." Looking back up at me, she said, "Okay, we don't have to remember. But I might make an educated guess after this, you can't stop that."

"Whatever. Make your guess, just don't tell anybody."

I had them wait on the other side of the room while Alice worked. It took less than five minutes for her magic to race through Jonah's thin body and exorcise the cancer from where it roosted. When her face flushed red and she broke out into a sweat, I fought with myself not to pull her away.

This is how it was with Vivienne. She's almost done.

When she finally opened her eyes, I yanked her to me and turned her to face the garbage can.

"Put it there. Get rid of it now!"

And she did.

When she was done, I grabbed the garbage can and Alice's hand and turned to the three stunned faces watching us.

"You will all go to sleep for the next fifteen minutes and will not remember that Alice and I were ever here."

As the three of them collapsed on chairs to commence their sleep, Alice and I took one last look at Jonah on our way out of the room. He was breathing easily, color had returned to his face, and his mouth wore the hint of a smile.

Adam

Just like her grandmother, Alice was mad at me when I said no to roaming the halls of the children's hospital and curing all the patients in the building. "Why not?" she asked. "I'm here, they need my magic, and my magic needs to be used." I told her there were many reasons why not, but we only had time for one, and that was 'Because I told you so.' She loved that one.

We took another cab ride, this time to the National Gallery of Art. As she drank the juice I got her from a hospital vending machine and ate the pretzels I made her get, I told her where we were going.

"A whole building full of art. Grandmother told me about a round one."

"That's the Hirschorn," I said. "It has mostly modern art. The one we're going to has over a hundred and fifty thousand paintings. One wing has modern art, and the other has the older masters."

"Like my great-grandfather?" She handed me her empty juice box as if I had a place to put it. I took the box.

I said, "I don't think he's in there, but we have a book at home with all his art in it."

"Grandmother showed it to me." She licked her fingers and then handed me the empty bag of pretzels. I took the bag.

This person just healed a nine-year-old of his cancer.

Then I remembered I *did* have a place to put the garbage, and I pushed it under the lid of the can at my feet.

Our driver was having some difficulty getting us to the museum because all the downtown traffic patterns were disrupted with detours and security checkpoints. The National Mall had officially closed after the bombing and would remain so for an unknown period.

The news outlets were covering the Capitol bombing as if all witches had gotten together and decided this was the plan from now on- destroy everything mortal. Louise's press conference had not gone well. She was honest and detailed how Lucia Perez had a faction of witches that were not in agreement with the revelation of witchcraft to the world. That was all it took. Because she didn't have an immediate solution to the problem of renegade witches and couldn't give them any details about the group, suddenly everything she said was suspect. Louise argued she was offering transparency and would continue to do so, but the reporters were after blood. It was brutal, and I was glad when I saw Marsh in the background for her. But I supported her decision to rip off the Band-Aid instead of feigning innocence when the act was definitely done by witches.

Our driver finally got us to Seventh Street and dropped us off only a block away from the Sculpture Garden.

I asked Alice, "Got your flashlight?"

She held it up to show me.

"Good."

I made a quick detour to a commercial trash bin at the back of a building and dropped the garbage can full of cancer waste into it. Normally, I would have covered that thing with two trash bags and double-tied it, but that time I just had to hope the garbage collectors would be along soon.

Outside the Sculpture Garden, a gate foiled us with a key card entry. I did not have a key card, and my lock-picking magic was often reluctant to figure that shit out. I knew that I literally just had to ask the lock to open and back it up with some attitude, but for some reason the process was not working and the gate was not opening.

Alice saw my quandary and decided to solve the problem by zapping the lock with some old-fashioned lightning from her index finger. It zigzagged from her in a gold bolt just like her grandmother's magic. It was fast and efficient, and the gate opened up an inch.

"What was that?!"

She said, "I figured out I can break things."

I stared at her.

"Well... don't. Let's not break any more things at the Smithsonian, okay?"

She shrugged. "Okay. It hurts anyway, so I don't usually use it."

I had never seen the Sculpture Garden at night. It was moody and weird and definitely a vibe that Alice was enjoying. She kept pace with me but turned around fully a few times as she walked to continue looking at particular sculptures.

"We'll come back in the daytime," I said. "Which one was your favorite?"

She puckered her lips, trying to decide.

"The girls. And the spider."

It was after midnight, and the National Gallery was closed, but Marsh had a former patient who was a night guard there, and he had agreed to let us in when Marsh explained we were going to try to protect the place. Henry Gireau was a man who loved his job walking the halls of the National Gallery of Art every Monday through Friday. When I had called him to let him know what was up, he listened to my whole spiel and said, "I saw you testify, you seem alright. I can get you in tonight."

When I called to let him know we were there, he opened the door a crack, and we almost couldn't see him, his skin was so dark. But then he opened it all the way and said, "You here to save my art?"

Alice said, "We are."

"Nice to meet you, Henry." I shook his hand. "This is my granddaughter, Alice."

He shook her hand, too. "Well, thank you both for coming. I'm alone tonight and will be until six a.m., so I can guide you wherever you want. Just let me know." He looked back at me. "I want to confirm that what you do will not touch the paintings or in any way harm them."

"That's right," I said. "We only want to make sure the art is protected in case of any attempt to damage this place."

"I need to know a little more about what you're going to do, exactly. Dr. Marsh trusts you, and that's good enough for me, but he doesn't safeguard this art. I do."

I said, "Understandable. We had information that the group that bombed the Capitol might not be done yet and might want to hit places of culture. So it occurred to me that it wouldn't hurt to add a layer of protection over each painting you pick as significant, just in case anyone would want to damage them. It's strong enough to survive a bomb." I thought about how my home had been bombed while I had a shield covering it and had to qualify that statement. "Not the building, just the piece of art."

"Okay, but what *is* it?"

While I struggled to explain the precise makeup of a magic shield, Alice said, "It's a promise. To the painting to keep it just the same."

It floored me just how accurate that description was. A shield of protection was ninety percent intention and will. The rest was its own kind of art, developed over time and unique to each witch. Mine was as strong as it was because I fueled it with a shit ton of magic. But mostly it was made of my desire to protect whoever or whatever it covered.

"That's exactly what it is. And it will stay there protecting the item until you ask me to remove it or I die." Alice frowned at that.

Leaning down, I said, "Not for a long time, don't worry."

Henry needed one more assurance. "Will the curators and

conservationists still be able to do their thing?”

“If they don't try to harm the art, yes.”

He said, “It's a shame someone would ever want to damage this place.”

As I stood there full of shame that any would-be culprits were witches, Alice saved the day again. Putting her hand on his arm, she said, “I'm so sorry witches would ever want to hurt your art. We don't want that either.”

Henry said, “Well, I'm glad for that, and I'm looking forward to showing you the best of the best. We won't have enough time to do the whole place, so if you don't mind, I'll take you to the most special places. Have you been here before, Alice?”

“No, but I have a flashlight.” She brandished it again, and he laughed.

“Let's start with the masters. They rule the west wing.”

Over the next two hours, we walked the galleries of the west wing while Henry gave Alice a tour of his personal favorites and the most celebrated artists in the world. I let him know before we started I couldn't cover them all and he'd have to pick which paintings got a shield. With only the emergency lighting on in the museum, we fell into a routine of Henry shining his light on a painting, describing its significance for Alice, and then my layering of a shield over it as they moved on to the next one. When Henry only picked one or two in a gallery and she thought other paintings should be covered too, she laid her own protective shield over those.

Alice asked some questions, mostly about the lives of the artists, and she took great care to note their names and the dates they lived. In one room she moved between two paintings, one of them a Vermeer, and peered at them up close.

“Does...” she stood in front of the Vermeer. “Do the older paintings have a different color of yellow?”

Henry perked up, impressed. “Good eye. Are you an artist?”

“No,” she said, still looking at the Vermeer. It was a woman writing a letter at a desk. She wore a yellow jacket and faced the painter. “But my great-grandfather was.”

“That's lead-tin yellow. Vermeer used it to great effect. Then it kind of disappeared after the mid-1700s. How'd you see that? They didn't even know lead-tin yellow was a thing until the

1940s. They use X-rays to confirm it now."

A few of the works moved her to silence, and when they did, Henry and I stood behind her and let her look her fill. She stood still and stared at Van Gogh's self-portrait while Henry told her that the artist had only ever sold one painting and ended up taking his own life. When she got too close, he said, "Miss Alice. We have rules about where people stand to observe the art."

She turned around, curious. "You do?"

"Yes. People can accidentally fall into them or get body fluids on them."

Looking back at the painting, she said, "I won't." When she raised her hand, he said louder, "And there is no touching the art."

Hand still raised, she said, "I just need to see how he did that."

I came up next to her. "You can learn about it in a painting class. Would you like that?"

She agreed, "Mm-hmm," still looking at the portrait. I gently lowered her hand.

"Good. Painting classes it is."

Standing by Henry again, she said, "Sorry. There was texture. So much of it."

He patted her on the back. "I know. It can be a lot."

I layered the Van Gogh with a shield, and we made our way through the sparkling, LED-lit underground tunnel to the modern art of the east wing.

Alice came alive as soon as she saw the giant Calder mobile above us and its constant, graceful motion. Just as I knew somehow that her grandmother was closer to us now, probably sleeping before a flight out of London, I felt a connection to Alice too and knew that the modern art we encountered in that wing was affecting her deeply. For one thing, she was all eyes and silent for most of our walk. And she gasped three separate times upon seeing an impressive work.

But the Rothko rooms were the most overwhelming for her. She sat on the bench in the middle of the room and trained her flashlight on them one by one, then repeated the viewing. Henry and I added our flashlights to her show, and we all contemplated those large canvases with the rectangular blocks of color. They seemed to hover over each other through some trick of the eye or maybe the hazy, soft edges.

Alice still didn't speak, but I saw tears fill her eyes as she sat on a bench in the middle of the room and gazed at them.

Henry asked her, "What does this collection mean to you?"

Standing up and wiping her eyes, she said, "Feelings." Pointing around the room she said, "These are all emotions. I need to see them in the daylight."

"You got it," I said. I was getting that girl an art teacher, and I didn't care what it took to do so.

After I layered the last one with my shield, I turned to Henry. "I think that's all I've got tonight."

He said, "Alright, well it's been a pleasure." He ushered us to another exit, this time on the east side of the museum.

"Thank you, Henry." Alice shook his hand with all her strength. "I will never forget the art you've shown me tonight."

He smiled at her formality. "Alice, it was a pleasure."

We walked home. I kept a shield on us the whole way and in my mind laid out the plans for an art studio in the turret of my house when the construction was complete.

CHAPTER THIRTY-TWO

Marsh

Things I had learned about Louise Carmichael: She hated her names. Both "Louise" (as she said, "For an aunt who left my family a house they never even went to and just sold, so why did they have to immortalize her name with me?") and "Carmichael." (Obviously bad because it was Jeff's last name, and she wished she had never taken it. Her maiden name was Plank, though, and Carmichael was a thousand times better than that.) She wouldn't divulge her middle name, but I fully intended to get that out of her within the next week.

Because she didn't like her names I started calling her Gorgeous, which she *did* like. A lot.

Purple was her favorite color, she didn't like red sauces (they gave her heartburn) she read a lot of smut romance, (and laughed when I said, "Who doesn't?") and she wanted to travel to India to see the Taj Mahal.

I could not get enough of that woman. Every fucking thing she said fascinated me. I hoarded each new tidbit of information about her like a bachelor dragon in a cave, wondering how to use it all to lure the blond lady to his lair and keep her there forever.

It was fucking barbaric, my reaction to Louise. I recognized that this was something different, *she* was something different, and I needed to figure out an endgame or I might fuck it all up. What did I want here? A sex buddy to fulfill every sick fantasy I'd had over the past few weeks or a partner to spend all my time with? Or both?

I was leaning toward "both."

It didn't help that we still had not had sex. I had gotten just a hint of what an aroused Louise looked like and tasted like, and my mind had not been my own since. But our timing was terrible, and we hadn't been alone since the interlude in her hotel room where Connor called from Europe.

That was about to change. Adam wanted to get together later on to debrief about the press tour and the current state of their mission, and I decided what better time to meet up with Louise and discuss the state of *my* mission to finally get her in bed with me?

I waited for her at "Off the Record," the bar at the Hay-Adams where Adam called for his meeting. The bartender had just unlocked the door, and I was the only person sitting at the bar. I liked the place because it was usually hopping on any given night with political insiders dishing out stories about their day on the Hill. But the overwhelming use of red in the décor, the low ceiling and the dim lighting made me feel sometimes like I was drinking in a giant tomato.

When Louise walked through the door, all golden and glowing, I stood and noted the flutter in my chest at the sight of her.

"Hello Gorgeous," I reeled her in with an arm around her waist and kissed her like I hadn't seen her in months. She laughed against my mouth and kissed me back until we remembered where we were and reluctantly pulled apart.

Sitting down, she said, "That was a nice greeting."

I said, "It could be yours forever if you marry me tonight."

Yeah, I had made up my mind. I was definitely keeping her.

Her head whipped my way in shock.

"What?"

"You heard me. You and me, 'Together Forever.' Just like in High School Musical."

She stared at me, dumbstruck.

Then she said, "I don't think that's from High School Musical."

I scoffed, "Of course it is. I know my High School Musical soundtracks, all one, two and three."

A smile crept across her face. She said, "What do you know about High School Musical?"

"I know everything about High School Musical, one, two and three. *And* High School Musical: The Musical." I sat back.

Louise threw her head back and laughed.

That's it. That's what I want forever.

Please say yes.

When she stopped laughing, she was looking at me to see if I was serious.

Then she said, "*I* know about High School Musical because I have a fifteen-year-old son, but why do *you* know about High School Musical?"

I said, "Sometimes after a long surgery I need to decompress, and the Disney Channel is nothing but kids with loving, supportive friends and parents, and it is so relaxing."

"Hmmmm…" She was thinking hard about this latest revelation between us. I decided to go all in with the guilty TV honesty.

"My latest thing is the Hallmark Channel. You can predict in the first minute what the last minute will be, and it's the most satisfying thing in the world."

She laughed again.

"Look, Louise." I took her hand in mine. "I fucked this all up. We should have been all alone in a Swiss chalet, and I should have gone down on one knee in front of you holding out a giant diamond, but I saw you and…" I looked at her and shook my head a little. "You scramble my brain. Tomorrow there will be a giant diamond and a romantic environment, and I'll do it all better."

"Sam." Louise stopped me with a hand to the side of my face. "This was perfect. You didn't fuck anything up." She kissed me then, and I pulled her off her stool in between my legs and hooked my arms around her.

"Are you saying I can keep you? I want to keep you."

I kissed her neck, waiting for her response while my heart raced, looking for the ax to drop.

She pulled away to look at me. "Don't you think we should see how the sex is first? I mean, what if it's terrible? Then you'd be stuck with me."

"*Absolutely,* we should see how the sex is first." I made a solemn vow to myself that the sex was going to be mind-blowing. I would have this woman, she would be mine, and all I needed was a solid night of earth-shattering sex.

I could do that.

Louise

Samuel had a room upstairs, and after we got inside, it took him less than a minute to get my shirt and skirt off, all while pushing me up against the wall and kissing me senseless.

Then he took my hand and led me to the bed, his eyes taking in my blue matching panty and bra set. As if he was filing it away in some "Louise" cabinet, he said, "Blue lace. I like it."

He sat me at the end of the bed. "Lift," he said as he pulled my panties down over my knees and then over my shoes. Reaching around my back with one hand he undid the bra and tossed it away.

Not taking his eyes off my body, he said, "Keep the heels on and lay back on the pillows. Spread your legs." Still staring at me as I positioned myself on the bed as he ordered, Samuel undid his belt and the button on his pants. "Now take your hands and pull your lips apart. Let me see that clit."

Holy shit. The Rough Gentleman had come to play and wasn't fucking around. From the heat that pooled in my belly I realized that a firm hand in the bedroom was something I had missed out on and might very well be just what I needed.

"*Fuck*," he groaned when I did what he asked. The cool air on my clit made me give a little whine of anticipation. I had never in my life been this ready to climax, and Samuel was only looking at me, his eyes roaming over my body and a smile tugging at the corners of his lips.

He kicked off his shoes and unzipped his pants.

"What are you thinking?" I asked him as he unzipped his pants.

His beautiful blue eyes met mine, and he said, "I'm thinking I've never wanted anything this much in my life. And what a lucky son of a bitch I am to be in this room with a woman like you."

His pants hit the floor, and I watched as he stroked his cock, and my breath hitched when I saw his girth. "You're going to have to wait for this," he said as he pulled me down to the edge of the bed and dropped to his knees before me. When he latched his mouth onto my pussy, I cried out at the overload of sensation and then I just rode that train to a climax as he sucked and licked and filled me again with his tongue. It only took a couple of minutes before I screamed and then came so hard I thought my legs would never stop shaking. When the shivers subsided, I laughed.

I was not a screamer.

What the hell just happened?

I laid on bed, feet on the floor, legs still spread side. Trying to catch my breath, I decided to address the situation and just be honest.

"Samuel. I think that's a vote for the sex not being terrible."

He was taking off my shoes for me, kissing my feet and my toes as he did.

I lifted my head and looked down at him. "I have never, ever made that much noise. I'm not a noisemaker during sex."

He said, "Oh, I think we both know that's not true."

I dropped my head again and said, "How did you do that?"

He stood and leaned over to kiss my rib cage and stroked my breast.

"I paid attention. To how you moved. How you sounded."

Climbing onto the bed, he patted the pillows on top and said, "Come up here."

When I did, and after Samuel had positioned me in the center of the bed where he wanted me, he moved over me and placed his cock at my entrance.

"*God.* Your sounds. I'll be hearing you all night." He held my chin and watched my eyes as he pushed himself inside me. I sucked in my breath, and he stilled.

"No, don't stop." I raised my pelvis and took him all the way in.

He moaned and thrust into me, again and again. I raised my legs around his back, and we pushed and pulled at each other until something more happened. I wasn't sure what it was. But we slowed at the same time and shared tender kisses and whispers, and with one last thrust, Samuel came inside me and I had another orgasm because of that man. As I trembled underneath his weight, I knew things were going to be very different from then on.

And, surprisingly, even though I was definitely not in charge right then and I hated change with all my heart, I was good with that.

We faced each other on the bed. Still naked, with a sheet pulled up to our hips.

I asked him again, "What are you thinking?"

He said, "I'm still thinking, how did I get so lucky to be the man in this room with you right now?"

I said, "Those blue eyes had something to do with it. That smile." He gave me one of those smiles. "Also," I reached up and ran my hand through his white hair, "the way your eyes never leave me in a crowded room."

He let his head fall back a little and closed his eyes as I caressed his scalp. With a short laugh he murmured, "I can't fucking help it."

Running a fingertip down the center of my chest, to my navel, he looked up and met my eyes.

"I'm sorry. Have I been a creep?"

I lowered my hand to his chest and began a personal catalogue of each hard muscle on my way down. "God, no. I liked it. This whole thing has been hard, and I liked knowing you were there."

I more than liked it, I *loved* it. I hadn't felt this cared for since I was a kid. Being with Samuel freed me up to be whoever I needed to be in any circumstance. If I needed to tell a reporter to fuck off, I told a reporter to fuck off, knowing Samuel would have my back. And he made me laugh. All the time. Nobody else could do that.

"Just so you know, I'm not done," he said. "There will be much more earth-shattering sex after a very probable brief nap. You've rendered me practically unconscious."

I hugged him then, realizing that we were now in the land of feelings. Actual, genuine feelings. I adored that man, and now what was I supposed to do? I ran my hand up and down his back, hiding my face as I had a slight panic.

"Marry me, Louise. Please say yes. I'm going to need you all the time now, every day. Every night."

When I didn't answer, he rolled over on top of me and propped himself on his elbows to look at me.

His eyes searched mine, and he said, "You know what I've forgotten? I've forgotten to tell you that you are the most incredible woman I have ever met and, although I have never felt this way before, I think there's a one hundred percent chance that this is love and that I'm in love with you."

Samuel waited while I absorbed that.

I smiled at him.

"It's hard to say no to you."

"Is that a yes?"

"No." I laughed at his pained expression. "It's a 'Let's see how things go for a few weeks and if the world hasn't completely imploded by then we can revisit how we feel about it.' What do you think of that?"

He made a face as if that was the worst answer on the planet. I felt him getting hard again, and he leaned down to suck on first one nipple, then the other.

"Can I have you every night? If so, I'm fine with that 'let's see how things go' plan."

I mumbled an affirmative response, lost to the feel of his mouth on me.

He lifted his head to say one more thing.

"I'm still getting the ring. Probably tomorrow."

Chapter Thirty-Three

Adam

Waiting at the airport for Vivienne, I came to understand that the flicker of awareness I had of where she was at all times was both a blessing and a curse. It was an immense relief to me that I knew I could always find her. But Barry had told her that her magic spoke to him. If he felt it too, Vivienne would never be safe. Alice would never be safe.

Randomly, I wondered if Vivienne died before I did if I would be aware of her in the grave. If so, I would no doubt take a page out of Heathcliff's playbook and rip open a casket wall, so we could lay together for eternity. I was sure I could find somebody to do that for me after I was dead, you could do a lot of unhinged stuff with enough money. I shook my head to rid it of the thought of Vivienne dying before me. That was not an option.

Unless I never figured out how to age.

Son of a bitch.

My mood was dark as fuck. Alice sensed it and knocked on the window of the Suburban I borrowed from Greg. She was in love with the car because it was sparkly white and the windows moved automatically. I liked it because it would hold us and everyone arriving on the plane. I leaned down, and she tapped the button to lower her window. She couldn't hide her delight at that action, so the attempted serious tone she employed was ineffective.

"Are you okay? You're frowning."

"I'm fine. Close the window so the warmth stays inside."

It was freezing on that tarmac, but I couldn't sit when Vivienne was so close.

And Fausto was dead, crushed by a chunk of the Capitol dome during the bombing. My brain kept coming back to that as I stood there staring up into the cold, gray sky. Sonya had texted me in the morning after she had been to identify his body. I knew Fausto was the breadwinner in their household and that they had no local family, so when I called her back I told her I wanted her and Eduardo to live with us at our house. We had more than enough room, and I knew Vivienne wouldn't mind. Sonya burst into tears when I offered, and she finally agreed with me when I said how much Vivienne loved Eduardo. When I texted Vivienne with the news, she agreed immediately.

Finally, I saw a plane. It was bigger than I expected, and I was grateful to Gerald again for bringing Vivienne back to me.

"I'm coming, my love. I won't ever leave you again."

In my head, I heard Vivienne say that as clear as day.

My jaw dropped.

"Vivienne?" I said it aloud but got no reply.

"Vivienne?" In my head this time.

"Can you hear me?" There was wonder in her voice.

"Am I hallucinating this? I have to be."

I heard her laugh. *"If so, then we're both hallucinating."*

"How is this possible?" I had never heard of that type of magic. Was it reading someone's mind? Or was it strictly communicating? Whatever it was, I did not relish having anyone else in my mind, even Vivienne. Maybe *especially* Vivienne.

"Don't worry, I won't be plundering the recesses of your mind."

"Then how did you know I was thinking about it?"

"Adam," attempting to reason with me, just like her granddaughter did, *"I know you. And that pause was you, worrying about keeping your inner thoughts to yourself."*

Truth.

In my head I said, *"Okay, I'm going to think something and, be totally honest, tell me what you think I'm thinking."*

I formed my image in my head and waited.

She said, *"I can't see or hear anything. But I'm guessing it has something to do with us and sex and plans for tonight."*

Fuck. It most certainly did. She knew me well.

"Okay, let me try something different." I cleared my head and pictured my favorite study space at Georgetown University. It was just one tiny table in the Lau library, but it sat right in front of a window facing the Potomac and Rosslyn. I closed my eyes and focused on that image hard.

She said, *"I don't know what you're thinking. Let me do it now. You try to see what I'm thinking."*

Not knowing where to begin to get into that head of hers, I asked my magic to do what it could. I sent out feelers.

After about thirty seconds I said, *"I got nothing."*

Thank God.

The plane had landed and was taxiing to a stop.

"I missed you," I said.

"And I missed you."

After a moment of silence, I said, *"Let's keep this a secret, like the not aging."*

I heard her laugh.

And then there she was, coming down the steps of the plane. Her hair was up in a loose bun, but long silver pieces blew in the wind.

We both moved toward each other and then ran to each other until I stopped and she jumped into my arms. She was warmth and beauty and goodness, and I needed her more than air. I inhaled deeply at the crown of her head and squeezed her even harder.

With her arms around my waist, she shivered. I wrapped my long coat around her and gave my wife a good, long kiss that made all my problems disappear. When Alice got out of the front seat of the Suburban and pushed to get into our hug, I kissed Vivienne on the top of her head and let Alice talk to her while I went to hug the rest of our family.

Adam

Holding Vivienne's hand as I drove us all back to the city was just what I needed. Our magic made the places where our skin touched tingle. I rubbed my thumb back and forth over her knuckles and kept sneaking peeks at her to make sure it was real. Alice sat in the back row between Grant and Maria, getting the scoop on how Marcello was and then explaining to Isabelle and Gerald in the middle seats *who* Marcello was. Vivienne and I shared an amused smile, listening to Alice tell her tale about the Vatican and then about the National Gallery of Art.

Vivienne spoke to me through our telepathy again. *"She was in love with the art in the Sistine Chapel. When Grant told her that Michelangelo painted it during our time, I thought we had lost her to the 1500s again."*

I fucking loved having secrets with her.

"Well, I got news for you. I think I turned her into a modern art lover last night. The East Wing of the National Gallery enthralled her. I'm turning the turret into an art studio for her and getting her a painting teacher. Or whatever she wants to do in art."

The wave of love I felt from her then was not audible and not telepathic but something else. It made my heart beat faster and stopped the conversation in the car.

From the back, Grant said with some hesitation in his voice, "Everything alright up there, Dad?"

Mother laughed in the middle row.

"It's fine, Grant!" Vivienne turned to the backseat. "I just love your father, and sometimes it escapes me a bit."

Adam

It wasn't cheap, but I booked the bar "Off the Record" for the night for us to share information and hopefully limit the damage somehow that witches had incurred when Lucia Perez bombed the whole damn world. I needed a plan.

Marshall was coming, and Marsh and Louise. I texted everybody I thought would be helpful and, except for Herb, who had the flu, most said they would be there. I also texted our many security guards, starting with Tony and Caleb, who had been with me the whole year Vivienne was gone, and, of course, my new security team, Frank and Carl.

On the drive in, Vivienne had seen the name of the hotel and gave me a knowing smile when she did. I had a suite for us on the top floor of the Hay-Adams and the night of plotting and planning with family and friends could not end soon enough for me.

Still holding Vivienne's hand as we walked into the bar, I saw Marsh was holding Louise's hand as they sat very close together in a booth at the back.

Alice saw it too and gasped. "Connor's mom is Samuel's girlfriend."

Vivienne pulled her aside to address that, and I heard something about how we should be glad for our friends when good things happened to them. And dammit, that was the truth. It felt right to see them sitting there looking so happy. They both deserved it.

Alice greeted Marsh and Louise and I heard her asking about Connor. In a low voice, I said to Vivienne, "I'm not sure Alice should be here for this meeting."

She gave me a small, sad smile and said, "I'm afraid she's already been exposed to battle. I'll tell you more later. But I also think she's better off knowing about the threats we face." I hated it, but I agreed.

We moved to the biggest table they had, and all ordered drinks. Vivienne sat on my left and Mother on my right. I instantly got a lot of advice from Mother about how to improve any further congressional testimony I might have to make.

"Your father would not have approved of all that information you volunteered. I know you just wanted to get it out in the open, that's one tactic. But maybe next time try not to admit *under oath*, things that could put you in jail. Can you do that for me?"

I said yes and tried to change the subject by asking her about where she and Gerald had been traveling.

"Can't tell you that. Gerald keeps all travel secret."

He laughed beside her. "Isabelle, I think we can trust Adam."

Leaning in, he said, "We were in Germany when Grant

called us. I know someone with a castle he rents out, and we stayed there for a while."

"I'm so glad you were close," I said.

Farhad walked in then, with the four security guards. After they got drinks, I said, "Well, let's get to it."

But then Marshall walked in with Richard Cole and I had to stop talking to get a grip. Cole saw my struggle and said, "It's fine, Parrish. Say what you want, I deserve it."

He invited me to, so I told him. "You should never have been in that position. You were a sitting duck for anybody with persuasion." It was still mind-boggling to me that the head of a Council of Witches would let themselves be vulnerable like that.

He countered with, "You were in the room a year ago when Barry used it on all of us when you got the vote to offer the vaccine to mortals. What, did you think I was acting when I agreed with him?"

"Yes," I said.

Then, "No. I don't know. I had no idea how the ICW structured things."

He tapped the table forcefully. "Well, that's been part of our problem. Secrecy above all else. But you were right that the head of any Council should have persuasion. And I wish I could tell you everything I might have given to Barry when he had me under his spell, but I can't remember one damn thing about that time." He sat down heavily in a chair and gave a brief wave to acknowledge Louise.

Then Tom Reeger walked in with his wife, and Connie followed them.

After everybody was seated, it occurred to me they might not all know each other. It also occurred to me that it would be useful to know who could do what. I said, "Thanks for being here. We're in crisis, I think you all know, and I wanted to see what we can do to stop things from going to hell. I also think we should share our magic to get a tally of what we're working with. If we promise that information will not leave the room, who's in?"

I raised my hand, but nobody else did. Then Vivienne raised her hand. Then Marsh, which made me laugh.

Putting my hand down, I said, "Marsh, what's your magic you'd like to share?"

"I have the patience of a god, as witnessed by my forty-year friendship with you."

"Fair enough," I said. "Okay, well, change is hard. I'll start off by listing my magic. I was not born with all this magic, I took some of it off other witches as I took their lives for the ICW."

That statement widened some eyes.

"This is magic I discovered when I was in college. The only other person I have ever known to have this magic is, unfortunately, Andrew Barry."

It took a while for me to list all the types of magic I had. Some of them I never used and didn't understand fully, but I included them for the potential they held in case someone there had them and could instruct me on their use. I left out a couple that were just too unsavory. When I said, "That's it," Marshall shook his head a little as if he knew that wasn't it, and a discussion began around the table about which of my magical abilities were most coveted.

Marsh said, "We could have used that understanding of numbers in med school."

I said, "That's exactly what I thought when I got it."

Reeger said, "You can fucking *pull* the magic from them? And they don't die? How does that work? I think I'd die."

Connie wanted my new ability to heal that Vivienne had gifted to me.

Caleb wanted my ability to inflict pain. "I've seen that in action and it's pretty fucking effective."

His eyes fell on Alice when he said that and then darted to Vivienne.

"Sorry," he said.

Vivienne gave him a slight shrug and a face that was forgiving. "She's heard that before. It's okay."

Alice was doodling on a placemat, completely unfazed by the topic of discussion or the words used in it.

I said, "Alright, everybody introduce themselves to the group and then let's figure shit out."

Mother went first and listed several useful magics, but I noticed left out the most interesting one. Gerald went next, and I had a moment of panic but then relaxed when he thankfully left out his time-traveling magic. After that, the introductions turned into an irritating game of, "Hi, my name is (blank) and this is how *I* know Adam."

Reeger started with, "My name is Tom Reeger. I've worked with Adam for many years as an investigator and before that was assigned to special forces."

His wife Heather followed with, "I'm Heather Sullivan, wife to this guy," she pointed at Reeger. She was maybe in her forties with pretty rainbow colored hair and seemed bright and bubbly next to Reeger's sullen and secretive. "I am just meeting Adam today, even though Tom and I have been married for three years. I have primarily earth magic and can induce anything from sandstorms to earthquakes."

Alice looked up at that, and her mouth fell open.

"Do you want to share your magic, Tom?" She nudged her husband.

"No," he said.

Next in line was Connie. "I'm Connie Jewell. Adam and I are parents to that guy." She pointed at Grant. "I'm a doctor specializing in genetic research. The areas of magic that I will share with you are telekinesis and truth detection." Eyebrows raised at those abilities, and at her admission that there was more that she would not share. That was fine. It would all come out in a fight.

Grant listed all of his magical abilities except for the most interesting one that he shared with his grandmother and one from his mother. Maria watched him open up to the group with pride on her face. When she was done, she took his hand in hers on the table and said, "I'm Maria Alvarez, Adam's executive assistant and partner of this one." She tapped Grant's arm. "I also have earth magic that allows me to generate fire and manipulate the wind." She bowed her head to Heather to acknowledge another witch practicing in her medium.

Farhad had a couple of gifts that allowed him to predict with a high rate of success what another person would do. He explained it as a gathering of all the facts, combined with an understanding of human nature, so that after looking at all the probabilities he could discern the most likely outcome.

He looked at me and said, "It's a numbers thing, too. My rate of prediction is statistically very high."

And probably a big part of the reason he was one of the

wealthiest men in the world.

Grant said, "Like Doctor Strange."

Farhad said, "No, not at all like Doctor Strange."

Grant argued, "You didn't just describe precognition?"

Farhad made a face like Grant was way off. "Maybe, but I'm looking at possibilities, not alternate dimensions or timelines."

Alice's head came up.

Grant said, "No cool ring that opens portals?"

"No." Farhad was done with Grant.

The four security guards went next, each one with a skill more terrifying than the last. When they got done detailing their magic, Caleb said, "Oh, and I know Adam from one very long year of guarding him. Vivienne was gone, and he made us run twenty damn miles every day, and I lost thirty-five pounds." Tony nodded vigorously in agreement.

I said, "Whatever. You could still stand to lose ten pounds."

Tony said, "And I don't know if it's magic or not, but I am madly gifted when it comes to paint by numbers. You can not hide a tiny number from me. I will find it and paint it the proper color, bet."

I said, "Good to know, thanks, Tony."

And then we were down to Marshall, Louise and Cole. They looked at each other, encouraging the other to go first.

Cole said, "Fine. I'm Richard Cole. I'm the one who recruited both Adam and Marshall to work for the North American Council of Witches. I gave them their assignments." Listing his magic took almost as much time as mine did, and I could see how he had risen to the position of CEO at the Council. He ended with, "Unfortunately, no persuasion."

Marshall went next. He started with, "My name is Marshall Smith. I'm a lawyer and I'm currently heading the North American Council of Witches. Also, no persuasion." When I laughed at him, he said, "I agree we do need someone in charge who has persuasion. Maybe Adam or Grant would like to step up and take this over..." We both shook our heads no.

"I've actually known Adam since we were kids. Our mothers were good friends." He looked over at my mother, and she gave him a warm smile. She always did like him. "My most useful magic has been that I am a diviner of witchcraft. Meaning I can detect what types of magic other witches possess. I think most of you must be aware of that because I don't feel anyone with his or her shield down in this group." We all laughed a little at that. "But you should never worry about that with me because I don't want to step over boundaries with friends."

He paused and then dropped his bomb. "I also have a rare magic that gives me access to the thoughts of other witches." He watched me when he said it. My shield went to one thousand percent. Only Cole looked unsurprised.

"I knew that would alarm you," he said with an apologetic smile. "But the good news is, with your shield up, I can't hear anything you're thinking. All it takes is a raised shield. And all of you have that."

I said, "Is this why you always used to beat me at chess?"

"No," he said. "You're bad at chess."

He added, "This magic needs to remain a secret. For my safety."

Marsh said, "I don't have a shield. What am I thinking?"

"Even better news for you, Samuel. I can't read the minds of mortals." He shrugged. "My magic needs other magic to work with."

Marsh looked skeptical, but Connie said, "He's telling the truth."

I looked at Louise. "You want to wrap this up?"

She took a deep breath and said, "My name is Louise Carmichael, and I know Adam from working at the Council. We've become good friends. And I hope you'll understand if I don't share my magic right now."

Marsh put his arm over the back of her chair, and it was obvious that Louise must have a special magic if she wasn't comfortable stating it and Marsh felt the need to protect her.

"It's fine," I said.

"What about me?" Alice tugged at my arm.

I leaned down. "You're too young to join my army. Sorry."

"But I want to tell my magic." We shared a look that conveyed that, no, she would not be revealing the time travel part.

"Okay, tell us all about your magic."

She looked around the table with a suddenly nervous smile

and said, "My name is Alice, and I know Adam because he's my grandfather." The burst of warm fuzzy that engulfed my heart at that moment had not hit me since Grant was maybe five or six, and I was unprepared.

Alice said, "I'm a healer like my grandmother. And I think recently I may also have developed a gift in the world of art." She handed me her placemat drawing. It was a full rendering of the people who sat across from her at the table, depicted as if they were members of da Vinci's *Last Supper,* and it was incredible. She had captured the dimensions of the table exactly and their clothing, but each person was one of our own group. I laughed when I saw Grant was Jesus in her drawing. But I sobered when I saw that Andrew Barry appeared to be representing the traitor Judas. I handed the drawing to Vivienne.

I kissed the top of Alice's head.

"You're right, you have definitely developed a gift with art. That drawing is amazing."

After everyone had a chance to see their likeness and compliment the artist, I began the meeting.

"Marshall, have you heard any more about possible cultural targets or, I guess, what do you know that we need to know?"

He shook his head. "There have not been any cultural targets hit or any action at all, that we have seen, from Lucia's group since the bombings of the capitals. We don't know if there is still an imminent threat to cultural targets."

He cleared his throat. "It's concerning how little we've been able to get on her or any of her accomplices. But we think we know the maker of the bombs." He turned to me. "The makeup of the bombs for the political targets was clearly magic... a maker who could amplify the damage of those things. They found him, and he's being held somewhere in Europe."

Louise stood at the end of the table, ready to speak.

"She gave a press conference. Less than an hour ago." Holding her phone out for me to see, Louise said, "Lucia said that she wants witches to feel safe again. She wants all witches to know they can take refuge in South America and that she's fully in charge of that continent." She looked up at me at that. "And she'll be in charge of Mexico soon." The reporter was asking her questions.

Still looking at the recording, Louise shook her head. "She looks terrible. That is not the Lucia Perez I know. There's no jewelry, no scarf. No makeup. She's a mess."

"Fuck..." Reeger wiped a hand over his jaw.

He looked at me.

"She just told the world that witches killed her son because he couldn't control his magic. Told the whole fucking world that's how witches handle problems...they terminate them."

Chapter Thirty-Four

Vivienne

The unraveling of Lucia Perez was not something I wanted Alice to hear any more about. I went to Adam and pulled him away from the others.

"I think I should take Alice home now."

He looked over at her sitting quietly at the table, absorbed in drawing something on another placemat.

"Right," he said. "I was going to have her go with Grant and Maria, but now..."

He took my hand and walked us out of the bar and to the front desk. On the way there, I reveled in the touch of his skin on mine and the tingles of pleasure it brought. I squeezed his hand, and he squeezed mine back.

A young dark-skinned woman with alert eyes, wearing a dark blue blazer, asked him, "How may I help you, sir?"

"I'm Adam Parrish. I booked a suite on the top floor. I'd like to book," he looked up to the heavens for a moment, thinking. Then he said, "Three more."

At her look of shock, he added, "I think for the next week."

To me he said, "The house is coming along, but I don't know for sure when the contractors will be done. Sally knows. I'll call her later."

The woman behind the desk was listening to him, not working on finding him rooms. When he turned back to her, she looked down quickly and began typing on her computer.

"I'm not sure we have anything on the top floor."

"Three rooms together on the top floor would be ideal. The other room can be on any floor. And could you see that the extra room on any floor has at least two beds?"

He said in a low voice, "I don't know what the sleeping situation is with Gerald and Mother and I don't want to know." I leaned into him and laughed at his discomfort.

After a few minutes of frowns and furious typing, the woman said, "Alright, I have three rooms you could have for one week on the top floor, connected and with a view of the White House. And I have one room available on the first floor, also for one week."

I pulled him aside. "Can we see if there's a room for Sonya and Eduardo? I don't want them to be alone right now."

Adam gave me a quick kiss and said, "Good idea." Turning back to the clerk, he said, "Can I ask you to find one more room for us? I'm sorry, we just remembered more family coming in."

The stress was showing on the poor girl's face as she hunted for another room for an entire week at that fancy hotel. Finally she said, "Okay, yes, I was able to get one more room for one week on the first floor. Will that do?"

"Thank you," Adam looked at her name tag, "Taylor. That will be great. We appreciate your help. Are those rooms ready now?"

Taylor looked shocked at the speed of my husband's planning.

She said, "They should be, yes." Then she tried to inject some sensibility into their conversation and said, "Would you like a quote for the cost of the rooms?"

Adam smiled, and Taylor melted just a bit. As did I.

"No, thank you, it's fine. Just bill them to the card I used to book my room and the bar for tonight."

Turning to me, he said, "I'll go get Alice, and you two can go upstairs."

"No," I said. "I think I should stay. I'll ask Maria if she wouldn't mind going."

Adam got the room keys and, back in the bar, I told Alice it was time to go and talked to Maria about helping Alice get settled in her room.

Adam said, "Girls." When they both looked at him as they would a father, I felt something inside me relax. I had worried so about Alice not having a good male role model, and now she had Adam *and* Grant. Maria gave a slight smile at Adam including her in the word 'girls.' She was over thirty but was effectively a daughter to him and, because she loved him too, she indulged him when he gave her advice.

"When you get there, you can both work on your shield for the room. I'll check it out when we get done here." Thereby ensuring that those girls would raise a shield strong enough to keep out an entire company of knights storming a castle keep. To Maria he said, "Send me a picture when you get up there."

She rolled her eyes at that but saluted him and went off with Alice to her room.

Adam gave Grant a room key and Isabelle and told them they had the rooms for a week.

Isabelle said, "Now that's something your father would approve of." She told Gerald, "David Parrish loved his luxury."

He said, "Who doesn't? Thank you, Adam. I was hoping to get a room here tonight."

The rest of the group were sitting back in their chairs, depressed. Lucia's interview was over. She had detailed the most disturbing aspect of witchcraft to the world, and now it seemed futile to try to sell the positive points of witches to mortals. In fact, between Adam's testimony about persuasion and Lucia's revelation that witches kept their secret by killing teenagers... witches could not have had a worse introduction to the mortal world.

Louise confirmed it. "I think the press tour should be over. I can't spin this."

Farhad said, "I'm not sure I agree. We still have a vaccine that prevents cancer, and it works on everyone. That's not nothing." He looked at Marshall. "It doesn't have to be Louise out there on the firing line anymore. I can do it."

Marshall gave a slight shrug. "No offense, Farhad, but billionaires are not the most popular people on the planet right now. I'd say, except for you, they're the source of most of our problems."

"Shit." Adam looked up and said, "Caleb, Tony, Frank, Carl... I forgot about you. Again. We need to do more work here, but I didn't get you a room."

Caleb said, "What's new?"

Farhad stood up and said, "I got it. Nora and I are going to stay here too. I'll get the guys' rooms, and we can pick this up in the morning. Sound good?"

I stood to give my old friends, Caleb and Tony, hugs. "See you in the morning."

Adam got a text and looked down at his phone. "They're in the room, shield in place." He turned his phone toward me to show me the picture the girls sent him. Alice mid-jump on a bed and Maria with her thumb up at the camera. A glowing gold shield covered the doors and windows.

"Oh my goodness," I said. Adam laughed and showed Grant the picture, and he chuckled under his breath.

When they left Marsh said, "We're staying here, too."

Connie complained, "How am I the only person not getting a room at the Hay-Adams tonight?"

"You're not alone," Marshall said glumly.

Cole said, "I am also not staying here tonight."

Adam sat next to me, rubbed his hands down the side of his face and said, "Where do we start?"

Louise's phone rang. She looked down at it and then back up in alarm.

"It's the president."

Everyone straightened in their chairs.

Louise set the phone down on the table and swiped to answer it. "Hello, Madam President."

The president said something I couldn't hear, then Louise touched the face of her phone again and said, "You're on speaker. I'm here at the Hay-Adams with Adam Parrish and Marshall Smith and some of our friends and family. We're meeting to strategize what to do about Lucia Perez."

"You saw her interview?"

"Yes, ma'am." Louise made a 'yikes' face.

There was a pause and then the president said, "Why are you at the Hay-Adams?"

Louise looked up at Adam and shrugged. "I... don't really know, ma'am."

Adam jumped in. "We're here because my house is under construction. This is Adam Parrish."

"Hmmm..." she said. "Who else is there?"

Louise listed us all and our relationship to Adam. He was the nucleus we all revolved around, but my name seemed to catch her attention.

"Vivienne Parrish? Who saved the Pope?"

Adam smiled at me at that praise and raised his eyebrows.

I said, "Yes, Madam President, I was there. But I think his Swiss Guard should get the credit for that."

"Well, I spoke to him," she said, "and he credits you with that and with the saving of the Sistine Chapel. I think he'd canonize you if he could."

I said, "I doubt it, ma'am. The church does not love witches, but if you talk to him again, please tell the Pope it was my pleasure."

"Will do. There's video of what you did. It was pretty impressive." She paused, waiting for me to say more. When I didn't reply, the president said, "Andrew Barry was there, too."

That, I needed to respond to.

"Andrew Barry is not to be trusted, Madam President."

Adam put his hand on my leg.

"Thank you for that, just wanted your confirmation." Then in a brisk tone, she said, "Louise, I need the name of someone in our military who not only has the magic of persuasion but also the ability to detect a lie when it is told. I need it now." Adam frowned and looked up at Grant, whose expression was equally guarded.

The president continued, "Here's why- I'm being advised that we need to safeguard our nukes, and we need somebody trustworthy to head up the mission. I know it's a big ask, but I need this ASAP."

Adam looked at Grant, trying to read what he wanted him to do.

Grant sighed and said, "This is Grant Parrish, Adam's son. I know someone who meets those qualifications. I'll contact him and have him contact you."

The president was silent for a moment and then said with some irritation, "So, is this a loyalty thing among witches? Is that more important to you than your country?"

"No ma'am. I served in Afghanistan, and the person I have in mind is a patriot and has served this country for decades. I know he'll want to help you. I'm just not going to name his name."

More silence from the president.

Then she said, "Fine. Please do this right now. I'll expect your call. Louise, give him this number. Also, my staff will contact some of your group to come in to talk about Lucia Perez. Whatever you know, we need to know."

Louise said, "Yes, ma'am."

"Excuse me, ma'am? This is Adam. Do you know where Lucia gave that interview? Any idea of her whereabouts right now?"

The president muted her side of the call for a second and then came back on.

"We think the interview was in Bogata. Which is bad news if she's lined up with the cartels. The C.I.A. is tracking her, and I should be briefed on her location soon." It was clear the president had her hands full at the moment, but Adam pressed on.

"Is it true she has control of the continent, like she says? Is that a possibility?"

The president said in frustration, "Well, with enough planning, a head start and magic thrown in, I think anything is possible."

Marshall said, "Madam President, this is Marshall Smith with the North American Council of Witches. We can help you with this."

We all held our breath, waiting for her response.

"Thanks for the offer. But this has to be handled by our guys. If you get any information about her location, you need to tell us immediately. I will not sign off on any action that does not end up with Lucia Perez on trial for the bombing of the United States Capitol. Is that clear? It *has* to be legitimate."

Marshall said, "What if we could deliver her to you?"

"Is that Smith?"

"Yes," he said.

The president said, "That would be acceptable." Then, she gave a curt, "I have to go. I'll call you later, Louise." The president hung up.

Cole said, "She does not know what it will take to get past Lucia's people and take her in. She has no idea."

Louise said, "I told her what it would be like! I don't know what magic Lucia has personally, but I told the president that she'd need a special prison and special guards to hold somebody with that much magic."

After we all thought about that, Marsh said with a smile, "Great job, Grant. You pissed off the new president."

Connie laughed along with him. "You really did! She hates your guts!" She got up and came around the table to stand behind her son and hug his neck. "And it was the right thing to do." She kissed his cheek. "I'm proud of you."

Isabelle said, "Of course it was the right thing to do."

Grant stood up and gave his mother a proper hug. "Thanks, Mom. Thanks, Grandma. Gotta go make a phone call now."

"You know what else I noticed?" Adam was trying to get Grant to turn around as he exited the room. "You also meet those qualifications, maybe you should just give her your name."

With his back to us, Grant said, "Great idea. Or maybe I'll just give her yours."

Vivienne

Our top-floor suite at the Hay-Adams was everything my husband had promised me when we were in the dingy love nest at the Kennedy Center. The room was dark except for the soft lights from bedside lamps, but I could see the luxury surrounding me. The bed was high, I'd have to jump to get up in it, with a fluffy mattress and pillows. Running my hand over the exposed white sheet, I hummed my appreciation.

Adam came out of the restroom, leaving the sound of running bathwater behind him. Undoing the buttons at his wrist, he said, "Do you approve?"

"Very much," I said and made my way over to a large window facing the White House. It was lit up and stood like a jewel in the dark night. Behind it, the Washington Monument reigned tall and white, and off to the right I could see the dome and columns of the Jefferson Memorial. To the right of the main house, an enormous crater sat where the bomb had exploded and killed three of the most important people in the world in an instant.

Adam said, "That's Lafayette Park in front of the White House. Rumored to be riddled with ghosts." I heard him undo his belt and drop it on a chair.

He said, "Do you believe in ghosts?"

"No, do you?"

I heard him taking off his pants and letting them fall to the floor.

"No. But today the idea of you dying before me made me realize your ghost would haunt me until the day I died, and my only salvation was that it was clear I wouldn't last long. Please don't die before me."

Adam came up behind me and let me lean against his back. I rested my arms on top of his around me and felt the world settle and calm. I made a slight sound of surprise, and he leaned down to nuzzle my ear.

"You felt that, too?"

I said, "I did. There's something about us together that the universe likes."

With some hesitation he asked, "Do you think it's God?"

"He created it all, but..." It felt like more. I laughed at the thought that something could be 'more' than God. But when Adam and I were in the same room, we were whole, and the possibilities were endless. When we were apart, the world was off.

Our magic was elemental, and it belonged together.

Looking at the beautiful mansion lit up in front of us, I said, "Our magic is formidable. I think we could rule the world if we chose."

He placed his chin on the top of my head. "We could," he agreed. "Is that what you want?"

"No. What I want is for this to all be over and for us to live in a cottage on a cliff." I added, "By the sea."

He said, "What about the grandchildren? Isn't a cliff a little dangerous?"

"Do you really think I would let our grandchildren out of my arms?"

He laughed and tickled my neck when he did. Then, he placed his lips on the spot behind my ear that was so sensitive. I held still while he rested there, not moving. When he felt me stiffen in anticipation, he opened his lips the smallest bit and gently touched his tongue to my skin. The warmth of his breath made me shiver, and I released my hold on my magic to let it flow around us in a silken swirl of pink and gold.

Adam groaned, "I needed this," and turned me around for a proper kiss. With my arms around his neck and my hands cradling his head, Adam lifted me in his arms so that my feet no longer touched the ground. One arm held me up and one hand fisted in my hair, tilting my head to deepen his kiss. We kissed until there were no more thoughts in my head. No problems from the outside stood a chance at that moment, it was only Adam and his kiss, demanding more from me than anyone ever had.

He lowered me to the ground in frustration and said, "I forgot I was running a bath for you. Let me stop the water." He gave me a peck on the forehead and reluctantly turned away.

I shed my clothes when he left, dropping them on the floor. It felt good to be naked in that hotel room. I walked around, looking at the two soft couches in the living area. There was a box made of chocolate filled with more chocolates and some colorful macaron cookies on a tray. I had poured us both a glass of champagne and was popping a chocolate in my mouth when Adam came out of the bathroom, also naked. He got hard standing there looking at me. I smiled.

He smiled back and said, "Oh my *God...*"

I asked, "Is it bath time?"

Taking a glass from my hand, he said, "In a minute." Our eyes stayed locked on each other as we both took a sip of champagne. He broke the gaze to lower his eyes to my mouth, then my breasts and down the rest of my body. Setting his glass down and taking mine, he said, "I'm going to get you dirty before your bath."

I laughed when he put an arm under my legs and swept me up to lay me gently on the bed.

"But first I have to take precautionary measures."

I protested, "What measures?"

He turned and began layering a thick shield of protection over not just the doors and windows, but the entire room. Like his magic, his shield was mostly blue. He could fashion a clear shield, as he did for his family and for his house, but in its natural state his magic poured like a bolt of royal blue fabric with rivers of silver laced throughout. I added some of my gold shield to his work, and he finished quickly.

When he got into bed, he sprinkled a layer over the floor and then pulled the covers up over us and tugged me up against him. We lay there face to face.

He explained, "I thought it might be bad if we caused a blackout right now at the White House."

"And you think a magic shield might keep our energy in the room?"

"I think it's worth a shot," he said.

"What if it explodes the room and us in it?"

He lowered his head to capture my nipple in his mouth.

"What a way to go," he murmured.

And then we surrendered, as we always would, to the tension between us that wanted only taste, only touch. He kissed me soft and slow and then deeper. Our legs tangled together under the covers, while our hands caressed every inch of skin we could reach. Resting his hand over the center of my chest he felt my heartbeat and pulled away to look at me.

"Don't leave me again," he said softly.

His warm hand skimmed over my hip then pulled me toward him roughly.

"Never," I whispered. "I promise."

I felt Adam's power stir and reach for mine. A tendril of blue magic wound around his wrist waiting for me to release my gold and pink essence that drove him wild. When I let my magic loose in a swirl around us my husband groaned his approval.

Then he was moving, flipping off the covers and practically vaulting out of bed to get to his suitcase. Clothes flew as he dug through it, my usually composed husband reduced to frantic need. He finally found what he was looking for and ripped open the package.

I laughed at his extreme behavior and said, "You're making

a mess."

To which he said, "Go ahead and laugh, Laniere. Here I come."

Seeing him smooth the lubrication over himself made my breath catch. When he pushed my legs apart and covered me too I gasped at the coolness against my heat. And when his finger slipped inside the world tilted.

Our magic was getting impatient then, blue and gold swirling around the ceiling in lazy spirals. When he inserted another finger, I shuddered.

"God, yes," he breathed. "Come for me, Vivienne."

And I was so ready for him, so needy for his touch that with just one push from him on my clit, I obeyed Adam's command and climaxed with an intensity that surprised us both. I cried out and raised up from the bed when it hit me.

"That's it," he said, his finger inside me putting pressure on the G-spot so that the waves of pleasure kept crashing over me. I was helpless against the onslaught of sensation he caused, and I cried out again, my legs trembling as the feeling traveled all the way to my toes and back up between my legs. Finally, I stilled his hand and tried to regain control over my body.

I said weakly, "That's not fair. You're a physician. You know what to do."

Adam said, "I fucking love watching you come." He grabbed two pillows and placed them in the middle of the bed. "Roll over, beautiful." When he lifted my hips and I felt the air cool against my overheated skin, I shivered. Then his hands were on me, spreading me open.

"This ass," he said, his fingers digging in. "You know as much as I do about the human body. I'll let you practice on me later. But right now..." He pushed inside me. "You're mine."

And the sensation of Adam inside me, the fullness of him pushing into me again and again, made us both moan. We found a rhythm of motion that worked for us both, me raising my body for him to push it back down. Minutes of blissful friction passed between us with only the sound of skin meeting skin and our moans of pleasure. His breath ragged he said, "I wish you could see how you look." He kissed my back and licked, and when he bit, I felt the pressure building again.

"Yes. You like that. I can feel it." His grip on my hips was rough and I loved that I made him lose control. Our magic swirled down then, chaotic and brilliant, skating over our skin and waking every nerve ending as it did.

"Can you come for me again?" His voice was strained, barely holding on. "I'm there. Come for me..."

I came apart with a cry, and felt him follow, his warmth flooding me as the world did what it always did: it slowed, it paused, it bent to accommodate the force of our joining.

And the lights stayed on.

Adam was checking them as well. Still buried inside me, still breathing hard, he said, "Huh. Chalk one up for good old American ingenuity."

I collapsed on the bed in laughter at that, and he fell onto me, his weight warm and solid, laughing too.

He kissed my back and got up to walk to the bathroom. Once there, he said, "Aww, the bath is cold. Kitten, come here, we'll take a hot shower."

I heard the water spray down into the shower stall and had a flashback to when I was a child and my mother bathed me in a small tub of hot water. She hummed a little song for me as she rubbed a cloth over my head and my back. That was before I was very grown, it might have been my earliest memory. But the silky feel of warm water all over my body was a gift, I knew that. And now I was going to stand under a waterfall of steaming hot water with a man who was made just for me.

I stretched in the bed and made a satisfied sound as I did. Then I got up and walked to the bathroom. I ran my finger over a satin ribbon that was tied up over a roll of toilet paper and then stepped into my husband's arms where he took his time washing my hair for me and rubbing a soapy washcloth all over my body.

When we were suitably washed and dried and dressed in fluffy white hotel bathrobes, Adam gave me a boost onto the bed and then brought us both a glass of champagne to drink there.

"I could get used to this," I said.

"Me too." He leaned his head back against the pillows behind him and closed his eyes. "We get six more nights here. Hopefully." He opened his eyes, and I could see the world had intruded again into our night.

"When you said we could rule the world..."

He looked at me. "I believe you said that. I just agreed."

"Aren't you ever tempted?"

Adam tilted his head slightly, surprised by my question.

"Why do you ask? Would you be tempted?"

"Yes," I said it without hesitation. "Yes, I would be. If I knew the person at the house just across the street was making decisions that hurt people, that made them afraid to go to work, afraid to state the truth or just an opinion... I would be tempted to whisper in his ear the things I wanted him to do to fix it all."

Adam looked at me as if he thought that was cute.

"You say that because you don't have the option. When you have the option, you can never entertain it. The most powerful thing I do is not use my power."

He must not have heard yet about how I accidentally used persuasion on my granddaughter. Remembering that, I appreciated that Adam was the primary keeper of the power of persuasion and not me. I clicked my glass against his and drank the rest of my champagne.

He said, "The only time I was ever tempted was with you."

Adam laughed at my shocked face.

"I thought about using persuasion..." he paused, and his eyes focused on my lips. "After the kiss. I knew you liked it, but I didn't know why you wouldn't acknowledge it. There was more to you, and I wanted to know what it was so *much*."

"What would you have said?"

He shook his head. "I thought about it for a couple of weeks. For about eight hours every night. Just laid there and thought, *What if I just ask a question? That's not compelling her to do something against her will. What if I just say, 'Do you want me?' And then what if I say, 'Can I please have you?' And then all I would need to do is ask her to stay with me. Just three times and then I'll never do it again.*"

I took his hand and threaded my fingers through his.

"I'm here now," I said.

"And we will never be apart again." He said it with no room for argument.

He added, "The only thing that kept me sane during the past month was that I knew you were alive." Adam lifted my hand

and touched the red diamond engagement ring there from him. "I put some home magic on this ring, but that wasn't how I knew where you were. You were like a little pulsing bolt of light over there on a whole different continent. All I had to do was focus, and I could pinpoint that light."

I said, "That's a little strange."

Laughing, he said, "I know. I'm sorry."

We both put our glasses down at the same time and reached over to turn out the lights beside the bed. I shrugged out of my robe, as did Adam, and then we were lying in each other's arms in the dark with just the lights of Washington, D.C. outside our windows.

Chapter Thirty-Five

Vivienne

The breakfast room service we received at the Hay-Adams also did not disappoint. Alice joined us for the delicious spread of fruits, pancakes and juice. When Adam told me he needed to have a short meeting with Marshall at the North American Council of Witches, and after I had assured him that I would keep a shield up over our door, he kissed me and finally left. I was glad to talk to Alice alone.

She stood looking out our window, eating a croissant.

I said, "Come here, sweet girl. Tell me what you saw when you traveled back to England again."

She plopped the roll onto her plate and sat next to me.

"I saw you."

Her blue eyes held mine.

"Yes. You did. And you did the right thing to leave as soon as you knew."

With a confidence far beyond her years, she said, "I know. Grant told me all about the butterfly effect." She pulled the cloth napkin next to her plate off the table and ran the edges between her fingers, rotating it as she went. Her brow wrinkled. "But *why* did I go there?"

"Gerald told me something on the plane that explains it. He said that in all his trips back through time, whenever he was in Britain, he always found a relative of his. It was like their magic called to him. So, why you went to that day and place, I don't know. I wish it had been any other day of my life because I would never want you to be exposed to that kind of suffering. But the reason you were there is no doubt because I was there."

She looked down. After a moment she said, "I wish I had gone back to a time where mother was alive."

I wished I could go back to that time, too.

"I know. But Gerald says that's the worst thing we can do to our family. Can you imagine how difficult it would be for them to understand what was happening? And once they did, and accepted it, what impact would it have on the rest of their lives? We can't risk that."

She sighed.

I said, "We should never change the past."

"I didn't," she said defensively. "I only helped the men who were dying, and I only eased their pain. And then I left when I saw you!"

"You did everything right. Everything. I'm just making sure you know that and you're prepared if it ever happens again."

She threw the napkin down onto her plate.

"I know it." She looked at me closely then. "You really didn't remember seeing me?"

I shook my head and gave her a small smile. "Not until you described to me where you were. All my life, my mind has tried to forget the details of that day, but not always successfully. That was the Battle of Towton, on Palm Sunday in 1461. The bloodiest single-day battle in British history. *And* it was the first day I used the full force of my healing power."

Alice said, "I was there for that."

I said, "You were there the very moment I let loose of my healing power for the first time."

She raised her eyebrows. "It was a *lot*."

I said, "I didn't have any control yet. But I learned it that day." Reaching over the table, I tugged on a strand of her beautiful long red hair. "I remember we looked just alike except for this hair."

"We looked exactly alike," she said. "I thought my heart would stop when I looked up and saw you."

"And our eyes were different," I said.

She reached over and gave a tug on my silver hair. "I hope I look like you when I'm older."

Relief that we had discussed the hard thing filled me then, and I decided that was enough of that.

"Tell me about the modern art museum. Adam said you loved it."

She regaled me then with descriptions of art from the East Wing of the National Gallery that she said were *all* ideas and emotions and that's why she loved them. "It's like the artist is telling a story, and it's a mystery you can figure out *or* just let the piece talk to you and reveal itself to you. *Every* piece of art there is like that..."

"Adam said he wants to arrange art lessons for you. Would you like that?"

Her eyes widened, and she nodded yes emphatically.

She picked up the napkin again and said casually, "We had adventures. Did he tell you about the hospital adventure before the art museum adventure?"

I raised my eyebrows. "No..." *What is this?*

Alice was preparing me for something I would not like.

She leaned in. "Adam had a patient who was near death. His cancer had spread, it was leukemia. Adam's friend Eleanor called to tell him. So we went there- Adam cloaked us the whole way in! And then I cured Jonah of his cancer. It only took about five minutes."

An image of Jonah and his very sweet mother came to me, and I was sorry to hear he had to suffer with cancer for that long.

I pursed my lips. "I do not like that you did that without me."

She waited. Wanting what was next.

"But I'm very proud of you for managing a healing that difficult on your own."

Relieved, she said, "Adam was there. And it was either me or him who would do it. I had to argue with him to make him see reason I should be the one to do it."

We shared a look of consternation at the thought of Adam trying to handle something that difficult without our help.

"Right. Well, good job telling him what needed to happen there."

She gave a wicked smile. "He didn't like it."

"No doubt," I said.

Adam

My driver Ernie was back, and you know I told him immediately what had happened to me in cars while he was off on vacation.

"I hope your time off was worth it. I had to take a Lyft everyfuckingwhere and then one of the drivers tried to assassinate me. And before that, I was driving Marsh and Louise back from the cancer center, and some hit guys shot up the Caddy!"

Ernie just laughed. Sitting next to me in the back, Grant smiled at Ernie's lack of respect.

"It was time for an upgrade anyway." Ernie liked the new Escalade.

He said, "I saw you testifying on TV, you pissing people off all over the place! And don't you think I might have been the first person hit when the bullets were flyin'? What about me? Did you think about that?"

"I did not." I looked down at my phone, and we all laughed.

He said, "What's the situation now? Is this thing bulletproof?"

When I told him it actually was, we all sobered up.

Ernie knew our destination well, he'd driven me to the International Council of Witches many times over the years. We were meeting Marshall and Cole there to have a conference call with other heads of witch councils worldwide. There was no time for an in-person gathering, and we needed to contain things ASAP.

Also, we were going to meet Grant's military contact to fill him in on what we knew. Colonel Frasier Howard had been the investigator after the battle where Grant was so seriously injured in Afghanistan. Howard had been a major then, and Grant said he'd been fair.

After Grant introduced him to us all, we sat at the conference table in the ICW boardroom. It was a chilly January morning, and the floor to ceiling windows confirmed that with their view of the bleak cloud cover outside. Marshall sat at the end of the table, his back to the windows, facing the giant screen at the other end of the room. I sat on his left with Grant next to me. Cole sat on Marshall's right, with Colonel Howard next to him.

Colonel Howard said to Cole, "You were the one to divulge information to Barry?"

Whoa. The colonel came out pulling no punches.

Cole made a dissatisfied face. "Under the coercion of persuasion, yes."

"What did you tell him?"

Cole shook his head. "I wish I knew."

After an awkward pause, I asked, "So how do you know Grant?"

The Colonel looked at my son. "I met him after a harrowing battle where lots of people died in a very short period. I looked out for those sorts of situations and investigated when it was warranted."

Colonel Howard didn't sugarcoat things. I liked that.

"And was it warranted?" I asked.

"Oh, yeah." The Colonel laughed, looking at Grant, who lifted one corner of his mouth.

Still looking at Grant, the colonel said, "His unit had experienced a lot of losses, and they were in trouble. Then, suddenly, people saw blue lightning everywhere. Bolts of pure electricity that hit targets with astounding accuracy. And then it was over. Bad guys down."

Grant said, "I believe the ruling was that there had been a 'proportionate use of force' against lawful combatants."

Colonel Howard said, "It was a little more than proportionate. But you didn't have any choice. That's what I was looking for. You saved American lives that day, no question about it."

"I was injured that day as well," Grant said to Marshall and Cole. "End of my military career."

Marshall fiddled with his laptop, and the faces of half a dozen other heads of witch councils came into view on the large screen. As he was greeting them, Louise walked in and took the seat next to Grant. She pulled out a binder and a couple of pens. After she opened her notebook, she gave Marshall a nod.

"Thanks for being here, everyone. Our goal today is to share any information you may have gathered about Lucia Perez and her group. At the request of the President of the United States, Colonel Frasier Howard of the U.S. Army is joining us today.

He's a witch and reports directly to her now and advises on security measures. I want to pass along that the President has made it clear she would like for Lucia Perez to be arrested and tried for her crimes perpetrated in this country, and we have given her our word that we will try to accommodate that request." He paused, and I saw every one of those faces register a 'Good luck with that,' expression.

"I'd like to start with Carolina Ramirez from Venezuela. Where are you in Venezuela?"

"Caracas," she said. Ms. Ramirez was maybe in her thirties, with a brown bob, wearing what looked like workout clothes. She looked tired, and I wondered what was happening right then in South America.

"You've worked with Lucia on the South American Witch Council. What do you know about where she is and what she's done there so far? Does she have the entire continent under her control like she says?"

Ramirez shook her head to dismiss that notion. "She doesn't have Venezuela, and she doesn't have Brazil, and I don't know how you claim this continent without Brazil. But she's from Peru, so she could have been working on the witches there and maybe along the east coast. And if she's in Columbia, she might think because she has control of the land entrance she is in charge of the continent. I don't know."

Marshall said, "So you don't know where she is?"

"I haven't seen her in months. At least here."

Colonel Howard said, "There are reports of witches making their way to Mexico with a final destination of South America. Her promise to make it a safe haven for them apparently sounds like a great plan to some."

News videos of witch harassment and even beatings were becoming common. Witches were catching hell in the U.S. and a reverse migration situation somehow seemed appropriate right about then. I wondered whether Lucia would build a wall to keep the mortals out.

I was pondering that when Andrew Barry walked in.

My first thought was, "If I had killed him a year ago when he entered this conference room, he would never have touched Vivienne."

And even though all the leaders of the witch world were present again this time, I sent a bolt of all my magic straight to his heart, and he collapsed. It was loud, like a thunder crack, and shock registered on every face on the screen.

No one in the room even moved.

I walked around the table to look at him on the floor and saw that the motherfucker was still breathing. So I hit him again, both arms pointed straight down at his torso, pure pain and damage flowing from them, into him. Barry looked different, his face had thick white scars on his right cheek and a raised red scar near his right temple. Grant was next to me then and hit him with a blue lightning bolt that made his body jump off the floor and fall back again. Barry gave a grunt of pain at that but did not resume consciousness. His breathing was shallow, but he was still breathing.

"Why won't this asshole *die*?" How anyone could live through what Grant and I just did to him was frankly unbelievable. I felt like I was in the Twilight Zone, and I just wanted this episode to be over already.

"Adam," he said weakly from the floor. I kicked him in the side.

"Don't talk to me, you motherfucker. Why aren't you dead yet?"

With his eyes still closed, he said, "I've been a bad guy far longer than you."

Over my shoulder, I saw the six people on the screen leaning forward in their chairs, following everything.

I pulled out a chair and sat down. Barry sprawled out on his back in front of me, his feet near mine. Grant stood next to me. Still looking down, I said to the colonel, "You're probably wondering why I'm trying my best to kill this son of a bitch."

Colonel Howard said, "I saw him pick your wife up and carry her into the Vatican. I can imagine."

That image made my blood boil, and that, along with the memory of him draining the magic from Vivienne in London, made me hit him with another dose of pain. He whimpered, and Marshall said sharply, "Adam."

"What?" I was ready to throw something at Marshall too, for that. But his look was trying to tell me more, and then I wondered if he was using his mind tricks on Barry. Maybe he could work if Barry's shield was lowered from my attack, so I stopped it for the moment. Someone on the screen tried to get Marshall's attention, but he raised his hand and continued to concentrate on a spot on the table. Then, he closed his laptop, and the screen went blank.

From the floor, Barry said, "I know where she is."
Great. He's trying to trade information. But for what?
Marshall said, "Where?"
Barry opened his eyes finally and said, "The Hay-Adams."
I was almost out the door when Marshall called me back.
"Adam! He means Vivienne, not Lucia."

Adam

From the floor, Barry said, "I just need fifteen minutes with her. Then I'll tell you where Lucia is." I hit him with another deadly dose of pain, and he blacked out again.

Marshall said, "Come here," and motioned for us to come over to him at the windows.

The colonel said, "I'll watch him."

When Grant, Louise and I huddled near Marshall, he said in a low voice, "Lucia's not far. I didn't get much from him, but she's in America and somewhere close, maybe Virginia."

I looked over at the colonel guarding Barry. "Can you hold him?" I asked.

"Here?"

"No, do you have any place to hold a witch?"

He looked back at me. The colonel was wondering whether he should tell me the truth. I hoped he did because I would know if he didn't.

He figured that out and said, "I do."

Looking back at Marshall, I said, "What do you think? He's not Lucia, but I'm sure he collaborated with her at some point. And he's definitely tried to kill me twice. And wormed his way into the White House through persuasion. Also, he won't die."

Marshall walked over and examined Barry. "Yeah, there's cause. He's not the bomber, but he'll do for now." Looking at Colonel Howard, he said, "He's not a normal witch. As you can tell, because he's still alive. You think you can hold him somewhere so that when he comes to he won't be able to work his way out?"

The colonel was texting someone. "Yes. I have a team that can do it."

Marshall came back to us. In a low voice, he said, "But I don't know any more, and it won't be easy getting back in that mind. All I got was something about horses. Like a stable for horses with Lucia there. A blue star on the front."

Louise paled.

"What?" She looked like she was going to faint, and I grabbed her arm to hold her up.

"Jeff has a horse farm about an hour from here," she said. "Connor's there with him."

Chapter Thirty-Six

Connor was not answering his phone, and neither was Jeff. Keeping Louise from driving there on her own was becoming impossible. Marsh had been called in to a surgery for some former patient who was a bigwig ("senator" was all he texted me) and he wasn't going to be any help with her.

So I called Vivienne.

"Can you get here to the ICW? And bring all the bodyguards?" The people I wanted were all there at the Hay-Adams. "Bring everybody."

"Of course," she said. "But why?"

"Barry showed up here. Marshall got some information from him and now we're worried Lucia might be at Jeff Carmichael's. Connor's there, too." I looked at Louise, who was clearly about to bolt. "Louise will stay here if you guys get here right away." I hoped that saying it would make it true.

"Tell her we're on our way."

When Vivienne hung up, I told Louise, "They're coming."

She stood at the window, looking out at the city below.

She said, "You know why she's there. She lost a son and now she wants to send a message with mine."

"We don't know that," I said. "Maybe Jeff is part of her group. Would he do that?"

She raised a hand to her mouth and shook her head no.

Marshall escorted four men in army fatigues into the conference room, and the colonel pointed to Barry on the floor. "Every precaution," he said to the man in charge. The man nodded, and as two of the men picked Barry up and carried him away, I saw they all wore earbuds. That was a good start.

Before he left, I got Colonel Howard's attention.

"Can you get a drone over this horse farm to see how many witches we're about to face?"

With regret, he shook his head.

"Mine comes with the whole U.S. Army right behind it. In fact, this information is something I'm going to have to brief the president on." He looked at his watch. "In about thirty minutes, when I get this man situated in a cell."

He was giving us a thirty-minute head start to do whatever we had to.

I shook his hand. "Thanks."

"Come on, Louise. Let's go get your boy."

Vivienne

After I explained the situation to Isabelle and asked if she would stay with Alice, she said, "No. You'll need me. And Alice is stronger than you know, she'll be fine with us."

We drove in two different cars, headed not to the council of witches, but to a horse farm about an hour away. Caleb and Tony drove the car with our immediate family, and Frank and Carl were staying to drive Farhad, Connie, and Tom Reeger and his wife, Heather.

We were all going to meet at the entrance to the farm. But Adam texted that Louise had gone ahead without him.

I informed everyone with me, "Louise drove her own car. Adam says she's not taking his phone calls."

I looked up at Isabelle.

She said, "Can you blame her?"

"No." I looked out the window, watching the beautiful countryside roll by. "But I don't know her magic, and I worry. I wish Adam were with her."

"I suspect her magic is very useful. If not, she would have shared it." Gerald took Isabelle's hand. Both were somber.

"Yoda texted me." Alice looked up from her phone with wide eyes.

She began to text back, but Gerald grabbed her arm.

"Wait," he held up a hand. "Sorry, Alice. But that could be anybody texting. They may try to get information from you."

He looked at the message. "Well, it reads a bit like an operating system."

Handing it to me, he said, "Do you have a way to authenticate it's Yoda?"

The message read, "Alice, I'm trying to facilitate the rescue of Connor. His father is at the horse farm. He was injured, but I see you are on your way. How many people will you have to assist?"

Alice took the phone and texted back, "What does Connor think of the current government?"

"Hydra" was the instant text response.

I said out loud, "What does Connor's mother think of California?"

"Yes to redwoods, no to all of Southern California." Again, an instant reply, this time with his voice, through the phone speaker. With the correct answer again.

From the front seat, Tony said, "Who the fuck is Yoda?"

Together, Alice and I said, "Connor's friend."

I asked Yoda, "Where is Connor?"

"Ten cars left thirty minutes ago headed east toward Washington, D.C. I lost their location when they got on the interstate."

Tony said to Caleb, "Turn around."

"Why?" he asked.

"Because that has to be them." He pointed at a line of black vehicles passing us on the other side of the highway. A row of trees separated the two roads, and I didn't see how Caleb would get there, but I said, "Do it, but don't let them see you."

I dialed Adam's number on my phone. He picked up instantly.

"What's wrong?"

I said, "Yoda just contacted us. He said Connor's father is injured at their farm and that ten cars left with Connor headed to Washington, D.C."

He paused. Then said, "How do you know it was Yoda?"

"We asked questions Connor would know. Where are you?"

He said, "We just got here. Louise's car is already here. I'll call you when we get inside and see what's there."

"Okay," I said, "we're turning around."

"What?" He didn't like that.

"We think their cars just passed us. And Yoda lost their location, so we need to keep up with them."

He made a frustrated sound. I heard car doors opening and closing.

"Alright," he said. "Be careful."

I said, "We will." And then he was gone.

Adam

"Hurry, Louise. Vivienne said that Jeff is here, but they left with Connor."

The look she gave me over her shoulder was pure terror. The door was locked, and she was having trouble turning the key. I pulled her to the side and waved my hand over the lock to release it, then turned the handle. Louise pushed past me and Grant and I followed.

"Jeff!" She called his name two or three times with no response. Grant and I followed her through one room after another, and because we were in a freaking mansion, I worried about how long this could take. The kitchen looked like it had been used to cater a huge party, with food and drinks covering all the counters. We found him in the living room, on his back, unconscious.

Maybe dead.

Though he was bleeding everywhere, the scan I did of him told me he was breathing and didn't have any internal injuries or broken bones.

"He's alive. Grant, help me get him to the car."

When we picked him up off the floor, he came to and tried to push us off.

"Jeff." He opened his eyes when Louise said his name. When he saw her face, he reached out with a sound of distress. She took his hand and said, "Where is he?"

"I don't know. They have him." He was coming to then, wanting to stand on his own, and Grant and I let him. Louise stepped up to let him lean on her.

She said, "Come on, we have to go. They're on their way to D.C."

To his credit, Jeff got out of the house before any of us but almost collapsed again when he got to the car. Cole drove, and Marshall sat next to him in the front, working on his phone. I assumed he was trying to get us more people on the ground if there was to be a fight once we got to Washington. Grant and I sat with our backs to the front seats, facing Jeff and Louise. I was glad I'd had Ernie stay at the ICW. He wasn't a witch, and he didn't need any part of this.

Louise said something I didn't catch.

"What's that?"

She looked out the window. "I said, 'She didn't seem crazy in Paris.' She was just rude."

I called Vivienne.

"We have Jeff. We're on our way."

She said, "We're following them on the highway. Yoda estimated there might be fifty of them. He said they spoke Spanish. Lucia is planning on doing something in public to show how powerful witches are." Vivienne took a breath, and I knew she was thinking of what was most vital to report. "He said she wants to inspire fear in mortals. He also said her thought patterns were erratic."

How the operating system knew how to differentiate between normal and erratic human thought patterns was something to worry about another day.

"Did she say anything about plans? Why was she here? What does she want with Connor?"

Vivienne lowered her voice and said, "She said she was going to show mortals how witches do things."

I looked over at Louise. She had heard that and so had Jeff.

Taking her ex-husband's hand in hers, she sat back in her seat and said, "Hurry, Cole."

Chapter Thirty-Seven

Vivienne

The line of black cars drove off the road and over the curb to pull up right in front of the Lincoln Memorial. I called Adam.

"They stopped. We're at the Lincoln Memorial."

"Okay. We're about twenty minutes from there. *Do not engage.* Farhad's car should be there soon. Let Reeger and Frank and Carl go first."

I said, "Tell your mother that, I think she's getting out." I put the phone on speaker so Isabelle could hear him.

"Mother do not get out of the car. Reeger will be there in a minute. Please let them make the first contact."

Isabelle put her window down, and we watched as a man got out of the back of one car and carried Connor's slack body up the many steps toward the statue. Alice and I both tried to scan Connor to see what his condition was. I looked at her to see what she got.

"His heart is slower than normal. That's all I know." Her face registered fear.

I said, "That's what I felt, too."

Isabelle looked up at Connor with concern. Then her eyes met Gerald's, and they seemed to have a silent conversation. She gave him a kiss on the cheek, and he kissed her hand as she took off her seat belt. He whispered, "Are you sure?"

"Yes," she said.

"I'll come with you," he said.

She shook her head firmly. "No. You know why. Guard Alice, please."

She leaned over to kiss Maria's cheek and to speak to Alice.

"I'm so glad I got to meet you." She kissed Alice on the top of her head.

"Mother!" Adam sounded alarmed.

Isabelle stood next to the car and beckoned me to come with her.

Taking the phone from my hand, she said to her son, "Adam. Grant. Listen to me. I won't be reckless, but I need to go see how the boy is. He might need Vivienne's care sooner than later. I love you both but listen now- this is my right and my privilege. I will not be denied that."

There was quiet on the line, then Grant said, "Love you, Grandma."

More silence and then Adam followed with, "I love you, Mom."

"And I love both of you. Vivienne will keep the phone to let you know how things are going." She handed the phone back to me. People had emptied from the cars and were lining up around the entrance of the Memorial. Lucia Perez was strolling slowly up the steps. She turned to watch as one of her witches raised his arm and used telekinesis to levitate Connor's body from the base of the steps up toward the giant marble statue. Connor's spine remained straight, but his legs fell down, and his arms splayed off to the side, lifeless. The witch in control of his body laid it awkwardly over the lap of Abraham Lincoln. The statue remained rigid and unforgiving while Connor rested like a rag doll against the torso.

Isabelle watched with a grave expression. I gave the phone to Maria and put my finger up to my lips to tell her not to let Adam know. She shook her head back and forth and mouthed an emphatic *"NO"* and tried to push the phone back at me.

Isabelle said, "She's right, Vivienne, we can't both go up there. I'm not doing that to my son." She said in a soft voice. "I'm going to talk to Lucia and see what she's done to Connor. If she tries anything, I'll get rid of a section of her group so we won't be so outnumbered when the other cars get here." On her phone, she dialed a number, and Gerald's phone rang. She exchanged a knowing look with him and placed the phone in her pocket.

Tony and Caleb had listened to everything and then stepped out of the car.

Caleb said, "Tell Adam we're with her." Isabelle frowned at them, but they buttoned their coats up and ignored her.

Her eyes swept the area in front of the Memorial where Lucia's witches were toying with the public. At the base of the steps, one witch made a tourist collapse in front of him, with no evidence of what type of magic he used to do it. The woman next to the man screamed and bent over his body on the ground. Other tourists who had seen the levitation of Connor's body scattered quickly, jogging down the dozens of steps to the bottom and trying to avoid strangers.

Isabelle said, "Maria, Vivienne, keep behind this car but do what you can to get people away from the witches." She looked at me. "Gerald will keep his phone on so you can hear me. I mean it- keep this cover and get others out of the way. I have to go now." She pulled me in for a hug. "Thank you, Vivienne, for everything."

"You can wait for Adam," I said. "We can all go up together."

She said, "You know this can't wait. He's fading, isn't he?"

When I didn't reply, she squeezed my arm.

Then, Isabelle turned and walked toward the steps of the Lincoln Memorial, Tony and Caleb a few paces behind her.

I heard her tell them, "You need to know to stay behind me. If I turn around, get behind me as fast as you can."

Vivienne

Except for the fallen man and the woman huddled over him crying, the tourists had all left the memorial in a panic. The man was dead, and I felt sorry for the woman with him but also knew I was unlikely to get her to move. A large group of students with a few teachers stayed put at the base of the memorial, to the right, behind large bushes. Maria whispered to them and pushed her message along in a stream of wind, "Leave the memorial. It's not safe. Run away." I saw the exact moment it reached the group when the teachers directed the students to run with them, one teacher in front and the others behind.

Tony had parked our car at the base of a series of platforms that rose in sections, creating a terraced ascent to the memorial's entrance. It felt like an exposed position, but I was glad we had a view of the statue and Isabelle climbing toward it. Lucia's cars had driven up the platforms and lined the base of a steep set of steps leading to the top.

When she reached their cars, a woman asked her, "What do you want?"

"To speak to Lucia."

The woman pulled out her phone and turned her back on Isabelle to make her call. Police cars with their sirens blazing raced onto the plaza and screeched to a stop in front of us. In no time, police cars surrounded us with flashing lights and officers pouring out of doors with guns drawn. The woman turned back around and motioned for Isabelle to continue. She tried to stop Tony and Caleb, but they pushed past her and stayed a few steps behind Isabelle.

I said, "Maria, help me send a message."

She stepped close to me. "Cup your hands around your mouth," she said. "Then keep speaking and position yourself toward where you want it to go."

I tried to pull persuasion from my body and said toward one cluster of police cars, "Get the fallen tourist into your car." I didn't know whether it had worked until I saw two officers holster their guns and pick up the body to move it into their car. After they situated the woman in the back seat with him, I said to as many as I could reach over Maria's stream of air, "This car is friendly. The car near yours." Several officers looked our way, and I waved my arm. "The woman in the red coat climbing the steps and the men with her are friendly. We want to help the boy they kidnapped. He's on the statue. Tell everyone."

I saw one officer speak into a microphone at his shoulder.

More cars poured into the plaza. I felt Isabelle's fatigue as she reached the middle of the stairs, and I regretted with all my heart that I had not gone with her. Then Adam said from the phone in my pocket, "I need an update."

I pulled it out and said, "Isabelle and Caleb and Tony are midway up the stairs. Lucia had them lay Connor over the statue. Police are here."

"*Fuck.* We're about five minutes out."

Dropping it back in my pocket, I gestured for Maria to help me send another message to the police. I reached for more persuasion and said, "This is a witch matter. It is deadly to everyone present. Get all the people off the mall. Stay in your cars, all law enforcement, stay in your cars until we say so. This is Vivienne Parrish. Tell the president I'm here, and that Adam Parrish is coming." I hesitated, not knowing how far to push it. But then I said, "Stay in your cars to live."

I could see they fought it, but then they all got back into their cars, and I was grateful for that tiny slice of persuasion Adam had accidentally shared with me. There were still tourists along the path of the reflecting pool and a news truck driving toward us with a person leaning out of a window pointing a camera at us.

Toward them I said, "Get inside. This area is not safe."

The reporters only rolled up the window and must have thought they were fine inside a truck. They kept rolling along the reflection pool at a snail's pace. The rest of the people scattered, and the area around the Lincoln Memorial and the Reflecting Pool was finally clear.

Isabelle had reached the top stair, where Lucia stood and blocked her way. They made a striking pair. Lucia, with her long, dark hair blowing in the breeze, her black wool coat worn open. And eighty-six-year-old Isabelle, all buttoned up in her red coat with a purple scarf, hat and mittens.

"I'm here to check on the boy."

Standing above her, Lucia looked down on Isabelle and said, "And who are you?"

"Isabelle Parrish." Her voice was firm, but I could feel the flutter in her heart. That walk had weakened her.

Lucia said with interest, "Adam's mother?"

"Yes."

Stepping aside, Lucia said, "So nice to meet you. I know your son."

Isabelle stepped up, and I said to Maria, "We should get back in. You take the front in case you need to drive away."

Inside, I held my phone next to Gerald's so Adam could hear. Then we all watched and listened as the events unfolded.

Vivienne

"What have you done to this boy?" Isabelle had moved to the base of the statue and was looking up at Connor.

Lucia stood off to the side, watching Isabelle.

"What I like to think they did to my boy. My son, Robert, was fourteen when they took him. I like to think they gave him a sedative. Too much of something, so that he passed peacefully in his sleep."

She said it in a calm, matter-of-fact way, which made it even more chilling.

Isabelle asked her, "What did you give him? When did you administer it?"

"Why do you care? Your son is still alive, isn't he? I hope he's on his way. I'd love for him to see this."

"You don't need to do this, Lucia. What good can come of it? Let me take him with me, and you finish doing whatever you want here."

Lucia shook her head. "That's not enough, and you know it. I need everyone to understand what we can do and what we will do." She pointed at the statue. "Lincoln was your great unifier, wasn't he?" She brought her hands together as in prayer and said in a singsong voice, "He brought your fractured country back together when it seemed impossible." Dropping her hands, she said, "I confess that I like you better fractured. At each other's throats. The news from America is never boring."

Isabelle turned her attention to Lucia. "Who made you the spokesperson for all witches?"

Lucia pointed to herself and said with some heat, "*I* did. When your son told the world about us. When mortals started hunting us again! We are being hunted again. Witches are *dying* at the hands of mortals."

When she didn't get a response, Lucia said, "Witches make their own rules, Isabelle. We always have, and the world needs to see that. Louise is out there making it look like witches are all goodness and light." She laughed and shook her head. "Witches are not *nice*, Isabelle. You know this. You've seen what we do." Her gaze turned to Connor, deathly still on the marble statue above them. "Now the world will see what we do."

Turning away from Connor, Isabelle walked back toward the steps, leaving Caleb and Tony to flank the statue. "You've lost your mind, Lucia. You know that, don't you?"

Then Isabelle sent a blue rope of lightning from her right hand and whipped it straight at the group of Lucia's witches standing next to the cars. They fell as one, twenty people all succumbing to an electrical charge to the heart that was not survivable. Her blue wave of pure energy washed over their cars, rocking them as it did and then rocking ours and the police cars when it rolled over us. When it got to the tidal basin, it fizzed along the water, dying out somewhere near the end of the pool.

We all turned back to the Monument just in time to see Isabelle collapse. I opened my door, but Alice held me back. We heard shots being fired.

"Wait for Adam." When I pulled away, she screamed, "Please!"

"I'm here," I heard Adam say from my phone. Gerald got out and stood up to meet Adam's car as it jerked to a stop next to ours.

"He's here now." I kissed Alice and said to Maria, "Drive! Get away from here."

Closing the door despite Alice's protests, I stepped away from the car, and Maria sped off.

Everyone poured out of the back of the car at once. Adam, Grant, and Louise all looked up, terrified, to see Connor lying there unconscious and Isabelle in a crumpled heap at the top of the stairs. Bullets were flying then between the police below and Lucia's remaining guards, who had been in the cars and at the top with her. There were maybe thirty of them left.

"Jeff! Wait!" Louise yelled at him, and Adam tried to grab Connor's father as he ran toward the line of black cars and the witches taking cover in front of them. He raised an arm and spewed out a line of fire under a car that he aimed with lethal accuracy, making it explode in flames a second later.

"Behind me." Adam grabbed my hand and ran toward the steps. Grant and Louise ran two steps behind us, surrounded by Adam's shield that protected us against the bullets bouncing off its surface. I looked back to see Jeff felled by a bullet to the chest just before two more of Lucia's cars blew up. Marshall and Cole were bent over trying to take cover as they ran to join the police, hopefully to explain what was happening.

Halfway up the steps, Adam slowed and took in the sight of his mother lying there. She was gone, I could feel it, and I knew he had, too. The sky darkened as heavy clouds rolled in. With every step he took closer to his mother's body, lightning struck the lawn around the monument, and thunder cracked with each strike.

"She used all her magic. Her heart was already weak." I tugged on his hand to make sure he heard me. "She was not killed, Adam. This was her choice."

He gave a brief nod.

When we reached Isabelle, he looked up at the rest of Lucia's men on the platform with her. I saw that Tony and Caleb were down, but a quick scan told me both were alive. Other witches had not fared as well. Bodies full of broken bones, punctured lungs and internal organs bleeding out surrounded our guards. Adam raised his arm and, using his telekinesis, picked the rest of her men up one by one and tossed them down to the grass below like they were bugs. Their screams on the way down and the sound of ten bodies hitting the earth one hundred feet below should have been sickening. Instead, I felt satisfied that Adam was clearing the way for me to get to Connor.

He was barely breathing.

Adam's clouds had obscured the sun, and it had become as dark as night in Washington, D.C., causing the lights to activate over Lincoln's statue. Louise cried out at the sight of her son lying there immobile, and she ran to the base of the statue.

Lucia stood to the side and watched Louise, absorbed in her suffering.

Adam said, "Grant, get him down." Then Adam reached down and picked up his mother in his arms and gave her a kiss on the cheek.

While he held her, Grant used his telekinesis to lift Connor from Lincoln's lap and lay him down gently in front of Louise.

Adam gave his mother one last hug, another kiss and then said, "Grant." He handed Isabelle over to his son. "Take her to a police car. I have a shield on you." Grant gave his grandmother a kiss and walked down the side of the stairs with her, bullets raining off the shield surrounding him.

I ran to Connor and had to pull Louise to the side to begin a scan of his body. Lucia had poisoned him, I could taste it. Something heavy, much too heavy, was clogging his blood, making it barely flow. Rather than grill her to understand what had happened until then, I threw every healing energy I had into Connor's system. I pulled as hard as I could on that poison and turned him on his side to make it leave his stomach. But after he threw up some, I knew it wasn't enough. I kept pulling until there was not enough left to damage his internal organs, and I knew he would survive, and then the poison made its way to me, as the illness always did.

Kneeling next to me, Adam said, "What do you need?"

"To let it go," I said. Adam knew exactly what I meant by that and lifted me to my feet and turned me toward the front of the Memorial where I threw my arms out and expelled the poison I had ingested from Connor's body. Adam held me with my back against his front until I got my strength again. An all-out battle was raging below us between the rest of Lucia's crew and law enforcement. Another car pulled up next to Adam's, and then Reeger and his crew joined the fight below.

Lucia stood on the edge of the top step and said, "This isn't done. *I* am not done."

She planted her feet wide and raised both arms toward the Washington Monument, which I didn't understand until I felt the marble floor under our feet move, and I saw the Washington Monument sway back and forth as the earth undulated around it. Cracks formed in one of the massive columns near us, and glass fell from the ceiling.

"Lucia." Louise stepped up next to her, and the motion stopped. Lucia still held her arms out and looked at Louise in confusion. Then she bent over in pain and clutched her stomach.

Bending down to talk to her, Louise said, "I've heard it described as a shredding of your soul. Is that how it feels? When your magic is ripped apart while you use it?" Lucia was on her knees then, her mouth open in agony, one hand clutching her throat. Louise didn't take her eyes off her face. "I've heard it feels like someone's reaching inside with a knife."

She said, "It's a terrible magic to have, of course. But handy sometimes. Like now."

Louise shook her head, deep in thought. "Such an essential part of our nature. That we had to hide it all this time was a shame. That your son died just because he used his magic... such a shame. His death was an irreparable loss." Then she let go of her power over Lucia, who fell to the ground.

Exhausted, Louise sat down next to her. "It's a lucky thing for you that my son did not die today."

Chapter Thirty-Eight

Adam

Lucia had been right about one thing. Witches differ from mortals in one fundamental way. We're darker. Morally gray. Was it because we'd had to keep a secret for so long or because we needed to use our magic and we justified that use? I didn't know. I liked to think my actions were all to serve the greater good, but who was to say what that greater good was? Mine could differ totally from another person's. Which was ninety-nine percent of our problem in America right then. Different visions of what could and should be.

Those were my thoughts as I stood outside the Church of the Presidents on Sixteenth Street, waiting to greet the visitors of my mother's funeral service as they exited. St. John's Episcopal Church had a capacity of seven hundred and eighty, and every one of those seats had been full. Isabelle Parrish would have loved it.

Gerald came out first and shook my hand.

"I'll see you across the street," he said.

"Thanks, Gerald." I meant that, thanks. He had taken my mother on an adventure the last year of her life that she delighted in, and I was grateful to him for that. He was also going to help with the celebration of life we were giving her in the reception room at the top of the Hay-Adams. Family and friends had been invited as well as anyone who couldn't get a seat at the service.

It would be interesting, no doubt. Mostly because all our secrets were out in the open now, broadcast on television in front of the world. They'd seen Vivienne bring Connor back to life, and then Tony and then Caleb. They'd seen Lucia try to topple the Washington Monument, and although they couldn't know for sure what was happening, they saw Louise stop Lucia with her terrifying null magic. And they saw me pull Lucia's power from her, which allowed her to be taken into custody by federal agents. The president was pleased to have both Andrew Barry and Lucia Perez stand trial for the bombing of the Capitol and the deaths that they caused.

Fausto. Jeff. Mother.

And those were just the people I knew.

I wondered how soon it would be before I was arrested for the deaths that I had caused. Also seen by the entire world.

Vivienne joined me then in the line, and we shook hands with everyone as they left the church.

Marsh joined us at the reception, along with Louise and Connor. We shook hands, and Connor veered off to sit with Alice at a table.

"I loved your mom," Marsh said simply.

"She loved you too. You were her second son," I said.

Herb shook my hand then and said, "Nope. I think that was me." He and Sally gave hugs to both Vivienne and me.

"Right," I said. "You were there at the beginning."

"And me," Greg came up and shook my hand, too.

Marsh said, "Okay... that makes me the number four son. That's fine, I'll take it."

"I think she enjoyed having a daughter best of all," I said, looking down at Vivienne.

"Well then, I get to claim first there." Connie gave me a hug and a kiss on the cheek and did the same to Vivienne.

"That's true," I said. "And I never heard the end of what a mess I made of that."

Connie laughed.

"I'm glad you're all here." I looked around at the friends I'd had all my life. "Vivienne and Alice and I are going on a trip. Maybe for a while." And I was going to miss these people who had always had my back. "We've just been in the news too much. It's not safe for either of them."

Everyone nodded, and I could see they understood.

Herb reached out first. "You know where we are if you need anything."

Connor and Alice were trying to get our attention, so we made our way to their table and looked at the television monitor they were pointing at on the wall. CNN was showing a split-screen live video feed of the president at the White House and the Pope at the Vatican. The headline read, "Both Pope and President get the cancer vaccine."

I searched the room and found who I was looking for immediately. Farhad and Nora had seen the headline, too. We could not help the sloppy smiles that broke out at that point, and we raised a glass to each other across the room.

I pointed at the screen and leaned down to my wife. In her ear, I said softly, "Look how you have changed the world."

Her eyes still on the screen, she said, "No. That was you."

Adam

The next morning I saw Marsh in the hotel restaurant and sat down to have breakfast with him. We both ordered, and then I said, "I have to take something from you."

He looked up from his paper, saw my expression, and then slowly laid the paper down on the table. "What's wrong?"

"You know we have to leave soon."

"Understandable."

"There are some witches...probably a lot of witches, that would like nothing better than to go back in time and change the fact that I outed us to the world. Things haven't been exactly smooth sailing since then."

He screwed his face up and said, "Like that's even possible!"

I just looked at him.

The realization hit him then that it *was* a possibility, and he took a big breath in and exhaled on, "Oh, *no*."

I said, "If they got wind that time travel was possible, they might want to influence the present in any number of ways. One goal might be to go back to 1502 to kill Vivienne, if they could."

He was quiet for a minute. "Then the two of you would not have met, neither would Louise and I."

He stood and walked to the window. Facing away from me, he said, "The cure for cancer would not have happened. The world would not know about witchcraft." And I knew he was thinking by extension, the carnage and destruction and loss of life caused by the revelation would not have happened either. Witches wouldn't have been persecuted by mortals, and mortals would not have been harmed by witches.

"Yeah. In case you're wondering, I do spend quite a lot of time playing the 'what if?' game in my head." He turned around and faced me. "What if I had just kept the secret for witches alone? What if I just used it myself at the hospital? How many people who got killed in the crossfire would still be alive?"

He shook his head and came and sat back down in front of me. He patted my knee and said, "Listen. You gave the world a chance. That's all you could do. You're not responsible for how they reacted to good news."

"I should have known."

"No," he said with some heat. "Not even the great and powerful Adam Parrish could know how badly people could respond to a vaccine for cancer. For possibly all major illnesses, for Christ's sake." He laughed. "I mean..." He shook his head. "You have to look at both sides. Both sides," he insisted.

"I know," I said.

"The kids who had cancer who don't have cancer now... the kids who won't ever get it..."

He stared me down. "You couldn't wait for the world to be some utopia where everybody gets along and recognizes the miracle." He paused. "Because that was *never* going to happen."

"I know."

"You go forward from here."

I looked at my friend and wished he could go with me. Wished I could have him with us for the unknown future we were stepping into.

"Okay," he took a deep breath. "What is it you need to take from me?"

Reluctantly, I said, "The worst thing. Your memory."

"You can do that?" He frowned, and I internally agreed with him that this magical specialty was particularly shitty.

"It's like persuasion. I convince you that something never happened and ask you to forget it."

"And what if somebody else with persuasion comes along and asks me to remember it?" Marsh was not sold on the efficacy.

I said, "They'd need to know what you knew originally. If they fed you too much speculation, then it wouldn't be a reliable memory."

He made a dissatisfied sound.

"I'd give it back to you when we return."

Marsh seemed a little placated with that. "Who else?"

I said, a touch sad, "Connie, Maria."

"Not Grant?"

I shook my head no. It wouldn't work on him, but I also couldn't do that to my son.

"Marshall might know too," I said under my breath, disgruntled. "It's hard to tell what he gets from you on any given day. But I'm not messing with that head."

He laughed at me. "You want some good news?"

"Fuck yes, give me some good news."

"I asked Louise to marry me, and she said yes."

"*What?*" I stood up to give him a hug. "That's the best news ever! You both deserve it!" I clapped him on the back and then pulled away to look at him. I'd never seen him so happy.

"*And...*" he waited for my surprised look. "Farhad offered me a job at his new hospital he's building. If I want it, I'm gainfully employed again."

"Oh, my God!" I pulled him in for another hug and more claps on the back. Then we laughed at ourselves for acting like kids.

"Yeah," he said when the laughs died down. "Things are good."

Then he looked at me, took a breath and steeled himself. "Fine. For Alice and Vivienne. Just do it."

And I did.

Vivienne

Adam wanted to travel back to another time where no one could find us. I disagreed. Just because we had traded some magic did not mean that he had gotten the magic that allowed Alice and me to travel through time. And how would we know until we tried? It was too risky.

But he said there was no place in the world we could be expected to go unnoticed. I argued that there must be. We finally asked Gerald to weigh in on the topic. We were all still at the Hay-Adams, so we gathered our immediate family together to help in the planning. Alice was in a mood because she didn't want to leave Washington, D.C. and her family, and she was understandably cautious about time travel after her recent accidental trips.

Adam tried to get her interested again. "Where would you go, Gerald, if you were us?"

Gerald looked at me and said, "I think the bigger question is, can you *all* go?"

I gave Adam a triumphant look, and then Gerald said, "I'm inclined to think the answer is yes."

Adam fought back a smile.

"It's all about intention, and Adam has demonstrated his ability to wield powerful magic reliant on focused intention... I think you should all just make a contingency plan in case you ever got separated. And by *you*, I mean in case *Adam* would get separated."

Adam laughed and clapped Gerald on the back.

"That's exactly what I said! I'll be fine!"

Alice was still unhappy, and Grant fixed that by saying, "When is this happening?"

She said to him in a flat voice, "Probably tomorrow morning." As if it were the worst idea of all time.

Grant said, "Got it. Hold on for just a minute." He took Maria's hand and dragged her into the other room, closing the door.

We all looked around at each other with concerned expressions.

That concern evaporated when we heard a squeal and saw Maria fling open the door, saying, "We're engaged!"

Adam stood up to hug her.

Grant hugged me and said, "I'm gathering my rosebuds."

"I'm glad." I kissed his cheek and hugged him back.

We switched then, and I looked at the beautiful diamond heart ring on Maria's hand, and she said, "It's real!"

Grant hugged his dad. "Finally," Adam said.

Grant just nodded. "I know." Then he took Maria back in his arms and asked her, "How would you like to have the shortest engagement of all time and get married right now in front of our family?"

She looked over at us, and her eyes filled with tears. "I would love that, actually."

My husband, ever the practical one, said, "How are you going to do that?"

Grant said, "If you had ever read any of Jerry Spangenberg's 'Alternate Histories,' you'd know that the Church of England in the 1870s ordained Gerald at Oxford. Right?"

"That's true," Gerald said. "My orders are recognized but not registered in the U.S. but I would be happy to administer your vows."

Adam pointed out, "Also, your orders are a little expired."

Grant told Maria, "Don't worry, I'll get us wedding bands and then we'll go to the courthouse tomorrow."

She said, "Darn right, we will."

And that is how we got to watch my distant relative Gerald marry Grant and Maria before we left on our trip. After a mad scramble that entailed finding for Maria something borrowed, something blue, something old and something new, and a wedding bouquet procured by the hotel concierge, they were married. Alice was the best woman, Adam was the best man, and I got to say the prayer over their marriage. I took pictures with Maria's phone.

There was not a dry eye in the room.

Before they left for the night, Adam asked if Grant and Maria would consider living in the house when it was ready, and if they would mind it if Sonya and Eduardo lived there, too? Grant choked up when he said yes. "Thanks, Dad. Don't be gone too long."

Giving his son one last hug, he said, "Just as long as we need to, I promise."

Chapter Thirty-Nine

Vivienne

Adam was being cavalier about our imminent travel through time, and I wanted to hit him. He acted as if it were no big deal and was trying to rush us into leaving before Alice and I were ready.

We both knew it was something to be feared. Something to be respected and not toyed with. Alice could not stop cataloging all the semiquincentennial dimes on her person. Maria had come through with all the jewelry I had asked for. We both wore a necklace with the dime and a ring with the dime (turned around so only a silver band showed) and we carried a spare necklace in a pocket. Alice had a dime in both her shoes as well.

Adam carried only one dime in his pocket.

"Come here." I connected a pocket watch on a chain to his waistcoat. The 2026 dime was taped to the inside cover. Then I buttoned up another dime in a pocket on the inside of the waistcoat.

"You need to take this more seriously," I scolded him. "Tell me again what you'll do if we find ourselves apart."

He rolled his eyes but then humored me.

"I'll hold the dime between my index finger and thumb and close my eyes and picture my study and say to myself, January 30th, 2026." He looked at me like, 'How's that?' and I rolled my eyes back at him.

"And then you'll stay put until we all get back. Now, I'm going to place Alice in between us with her arms around me, and

I'm going to put my arms around you both and you put your arms around us both..."

He laughed as we entangled ourselves as tightly as I could manage, placing hands in pockets and holding onto belts.

"Guys, this is an adventure we're going on! Don't worry!"

In a muffled voice between us, Alice said, "Adventure is overrated."

Which made him laugh even harder. He kissed the top of her head.

"Okay, no adventure. What exactly are we going to be doing?"

The muffled voice said, "Hiding out."

Looking at Adam, I said, "Being happy."

His eyes scanned my face. "Pursuing happiness. Very American of you." He kissed me.

"Now let's go."

Epilogue

Marshall

Sitting alone at the table in front of the Joint Select Committee to Investigate Witchcraft Phenomena and Potential Threats to National Security was just as much fun as you'd expect. Especially after the bombing of the United States Capitol by a renegade group of witches and my client's decision to disregard his subpoena to appear.

I understood why Adam and Vivienne had taken to the road wherever that road may be. Although in my opinion his actions had been justified, in the mortal justice system he was almost sure to be indicted and tried for murder. Imagining that trial for a minute, I thought I could get him off on self-defense or even temporary insanity- his mother had just died trying to save the life of a teenage boy! Ladies and gentlemen of the jury, did you see that lightning raining down every step he took towards his eighty-six-year-old mother, lying there on the top step of the Lincoln Memorial?

The problem was they *had* seen it. By now the entire world had seen it all, including Isabelle's peremptory strike against Lucia's team, where twenty of them had dropped at once. Would a mortal jury conclude that was justified? What would a lawyer have to do to educate them about the potential threat those witches posed?

Also, Adam would never let me plead temporary insanity.

Louise tapped me on the shoulder from her seat behind me.

"You sure you don't want me to sit with you?"

I shook my head no. "Thank you, though. I appreciate your coming."

And I did. She'd been through so much in the past month, it surprised me to see her at the hearing.

The chairman banged his gavel, and people took their seats.

"Welcome to this meeting of the Joint Select Committee to Investigate Witchcraft Phenomena and Potential Threats to National Security. I am Roland Schnell, senator from Texas, and I think I'll spare the rest of our committee from having to introduce themselves because I see that the person we are here to gather testimony from is not in attendance. Is that correct? Was our call for him to appear before Congress not important enough for your client Adam Parrish to respond to?"

This was not good. Schnell was ramped up more than usual, and I decided to make a statement and get things over with ASAP instead of waiting for him.

"Mr. Parrish did respond to your subpoena, Mr. Chairman, and I'd like to read you his statement now, if I may?"

"By all means." The chairman sat back, irritated.

I positioned the mic closer to me and read, "Mr. Chairman and members of the committee, I deeply regret not being able to say this to you in person. Recent events have placed my family very much in the spotlight, and this has put them in danger. We will be taking refuge for an undetermined length of time to allow the authorities to investigate the threats to us and apprehend those responsible for the bombing of my house on New Year's Eve. I thank you for your concern and look forward to testifying before your committee in the future. Sincerely, Doctor Adam Parrish." I folded the paper and looked up at the committee.

Schnell said, "So Doctor Parrish is feeling threatened, is he?"

Reaching around behind him, the chairman picked up a thick red binder and plopped it on the dais in front of him. Then he placed another equally large red binder on top of the first one, then another, then another, then another until there stood was a stack of five very thick binders.

Schnell said, "You know who else is feeling threatened? Every person on the planet who is not a witch. That's why I'm making this list naming all five million witches in the world, available online for anyone who wants to know who's who." He smiled.

"Tell your client we look forward to seeing him upon his return."

Thank you for reading *A War of Witches!*

For exclusive content from *The Witch Wars Series* sign up for my newsletter *Romance for Grownups* at: https://suzannesnowden.substack.com/subscribe

Coming in 2026, *A Witch to Save the World!*

ACKNOWLEDGEMENTS

Let's face it. 2025 was a rough year. And I used this book as a kind of diary of how I was feeling about it. (Not sorry, I'd do it again.)

But...my daughter just graduated college with her BA in English, so I guess this year did have a highlight.

Oh, and I was reminded time and time again this year how lucky I am to work at my library and spend time with my co-workers and do my book clubs and projects I like.

My writer friends kept me going, too. M. Jayne LaDow, M.M. Rees, Chesapeake Romance Writers- I'm so grateful for you guys. And my ARC readers who found me the problems! I appreciate you all SO much.

Thank you to Jaime Edmondson of Spellbound Creative Studio for making my amazing website this year and artist Danielle Fine for my gorgeous book cover and her unlimited patience with my idiocy about the book formatting process.

And, truthfully, this whole acknowledgement section should just be about my friend and editor, Lydia Netzer. She's a great writer and has graced with me with her insight on two books now and I can't possibly thank her enough for working her magic like she does. Seriously, she's probably a witch, her advice is so freaking good. I love her.

And my family suffered right along with me this year as I took my time getting this book to say what I wanted it to say. Thank you, Gary, Katie and Snowden for always encouraging me to keep at it. I love you guys more than anything.

ABOUT THE AUTHOR

Suzanne Snowden has been a radio DJ hosting a nightly Lovesongs Show, a high school teacher, and is currently a library specialist. She writes romance novels with heroines who are forty plus.